# THE CHASE

## BRIAR U

# ELLE KENNEDY

**Bloom** *books*

Sourcebooks and the colophon are registered trademarks of
Sourcebooks. Bloom Books is a trademark of Sourcebooks.

Published by Bloom Books, an imprint of Sourcebooks
P.O. Box 4410, Naperville, Illinois 60567-4410
(630) 961-3900
sourcebooks.com

Originally self-published in 2018 by Elle Kennedy Inc.

Cataloging-in-Publication Data is on file with the Library of Congress.

Printed and bound in the United States of America.
LSC 10 9 8 7 6 5 4 3

# 1
# SUMMER

"Is this a joke?" I gape at the five girls who are holding me in judgment. They have various hair, skin, and eye colors, and yet I can't tell them apart because their expressions are identical. There's a whole lot of *smug* peeking through the phony remorse they're trying to convey, as if they're truly devastated by the news.

Ha. They're enjoying this.

"I'm sorry, Summer, but it's not a joke." Kaya offers a pitying smile. "As the Standards Committee, we take Kappa Beta Nu's reputation very seriously. We received word from Nationals this morning—"

"Oh really? You received word? Did they send a telegram?"

"No, it was an email," she says, completely missing the sarcasm. She flips her glossy hair over one shoulder. "They reminded the committee that every member of this sorority must uphold the behavior standards set by them, otherwise our chapter will lose its good standing with Nationals."

"We *have* to remain in good standing," Bianca pipes up pleading at me with her eyes. Of the five bi-otches in front of me, she seems like the most reasonable.

"Especially after what happened to Daphne Kettleman," adds a girl whose name I can't remember.

Curiosity gets the better of me. "What happened to Daphne Kettleman?"

"Alcohol poisoning." The fourth girl—I think her name's Hailey—lowers her voice to a whisper and quickly glances around, as if there might be a bug or two hidden in the antique furnishings that fill the living room of the Kappa mansion.

"She had to get her stomach pumped," the no-name girl reveals gleefully. Which makes me question whether she's actually thrilled that Daphne Kettleman almost died.

Kaya speaks up in a curt voice. "Enough about Daphne. You shouldn't have even brought her up, Coral—"

Coral! Right. That's her name. And it sounds as stupid now as it did when she introduced herself fifteen minutes ago.

"We don't speak Daphne's name in this house," Kaya explains to me.

Jee-zus. One measly stomach pumping and poor Daphne gets Voldemorted? The Kappa Beta Nu chapter of Briar University is evidently a lot stricter than the Brown chapter.

Case in point—they're kicking me out before I'd even moved in.

"This isn't personal," Kaya continues, giving me another fake consolatory smile. "Our reputation is very important to us, and although you're a legacy—"

"A presidential legacy," I point out. *So ha! In your face, Kaya!* My mom was president of a Kappa chapter during her junior and senior years, and so was my grandmother. Heyward women and Kappa Beta Nu go together like abs and any male Hemsworth.

"A *legacy*," she repeats, "but we don't adhere as strictly to those ancestral bonds the way we used to."

Ancestral bonds? Who says that? Did she time-travel from the olden days?

"As I said, we have rules and policies. And you didn't leave the Brown chapter on the best of terms."

"I didn't get kicked out of Kappa," I argue. "I got kicked out of school in general."

Kaya stares at me in disbelief. "Is this a point of pride for you? Getting expelled from one of the best colleges in the country?"

I answer through clenched teeth. "No, I'm not proud of it. I'm just saying, technically speaking, I'm still a member of this sorority."

"Maybe so, but that doesn't mean you're entitled to live in this house." Kaya crosses her arms over the front of her white mohair sweater.

"I see." I mimic her pose, except I cross my legs too.

Kaya's envious gaze lands on my black suede Prada boots, a gift from my grandmother to celebrate my admission to Briar. I had a good chuckle when I opened the package last night—I'm not sure Nana Celeste understands that I'm only attending Briar because I was expelled from my other school. Actually, I bet she does, and just doesn't care. Nana will find any excuse to get her Prada on. She's my soulmate.

"And you didn't think," I go on, an edge creeping into my voice, "to let me know this until *after* I packed up my stuff, drove all the way down here from Manhattan, and walked through the front door?"

Bianca is the only one who has the decency to look guilty. "We're really sorry, Summer. But like Kaya said, Nationals didn't get in touch until this morning, and then we had to vote, and…" She shrugs weakly. "Sorry," she says again.

"So you voted and decided I'm not allowed to live here."

"Yes," Kaya says.

I glance at the others. "Hailey?"

"Halley," she corrects icily.

Oh, whatever. Like I'm supposed to remember their names? We literally just met. "Halley." I look to the next girl. "Coral." And then the next girl. Crap. I legit don't know this one. "Laura?"

"Tawny," she bites out.

Swing and a miss! "Tawny," I repeat apologetically. "You guys are sure about this?"

I get three nods.

"Cool. Thanks for wasting my time." I stand up, push my hair over one shoulder, and start wrapping my red cashmere scarf around my neck. A bit too vigorously maybe, because it seems to annoy Kaya.

"Stop being so dramatic," she orders in a snarky voice. "And don't act like *we're* to blame for the fact that you burned down your former house. Excuse us if we don't want to live with an *arsonist*."

I struggle to keep my temper in check. "I didn't burn anything down."

"That's not what our Brown sisters said." She tightens her lips. "Anyway, we have a house meeting in ten minutes. It's time for you to go."

"Another meeting? Look at you! A packed schedule today!"

"We're organizing a New Year's Eve charity event tonight to raise money," Kaya says stiffly.

Ah, my bad. "What's the charity?"

"Oh." Bianca looks sheepish. "We're raising money to renovate the basement here in the mansion."

Oh my God. *They're* the charity? "You better get to it, then." With a mocking smile, I flutter my fingers in a careless wave and march out of the room.

In the hall, I feel the first sting of tears.

Fuck these girls. I don't need them or their dumb sorority.

"Summer, wait."

Bianca catches up to me at the front doors. I quickly paste on a smile and blink away the tears that had begun to well up. I won't let them see me cry, and I'm so frigging glad I left all my suitcases in the car and only came in with my oversized purse. How mortifying would it have been to lug my bags back to the car? It would've taken multiple trips too, because I don't travel light.

"Listen," Bianca says, her voice so quiet I strain to hear her. "You should consider yourself lucky."

I raise my eyebrows. "For being homeless? Sure, I feel blessed."

She cracks a smile. "Your last name is Heyward-Di Laurentis. You are not, and will never be, homeless."

I grin sheepishly. Can't argue with that.

"But I'm serious," she whispers. "You don't want to live here." Her almond-shaped eyes dart toward the doorway. "Kaya is like a drill sergeant. It's her first year as Kappa president, and she's on some crazy power trip."

"I've noticed," I say dryly.

"You should've seen what she did to Daphne! She acted like it was the alcohol thing, but really she was just jealous because Daph slept with her ex-boyfriend Chris, so she made Daph's life miserable. One weekend when Daphne was away, Kaya 'accidentally'"—Bianca uses air quotes—"donated every piece of her clothing to these freshmen who were collecting stuff for the annual clothes drive. Daph eventually quit the sorority and moved out."

I'm starting to think that alcohol poisoning was the best thing that could've ever happened to Daphne Kettleman, if it got her out of this hellhole.

"Whatever. I don't care if I live here or not. Like you said, I'll be just fine." I put on the cavalier, nothing-in-life-ever-*ever*-gets-to-me voice that I've perfected over the years.

It's my armor. I pretend that my life is a beautiful Victorian house and hope that nobody peers close enough to see the cracks in my facade.

But no matter how convincing I am in front of Bianca, there's no stopping the massive wave of anxiety that hits me the moment I slide into my car five minutes later. It stilts my breathing and quickens my pulse, making it hard to think clearly.

What am I supposed to do?

Where am I supposed to go?

I inhale deeply. *It's okay. It's fine.* I take another breath. Yes, I'll figure it out. I always do, right? I'm constantly screwing up, and I always find a way to unscrew myself. I just have to buckle down and think—

My phone blares out its ringtone rendition of Sia's "Cheap Thrills." Thank God.

I waste no time answering the call. "Hey," I greet my brother Dean, grateful for the interruption.

"Hey, Boogers. Just checking that you made it to campus in one piece."

"Why wouldn't I?"

"Gosh, who knows. You might've run off to Miami with some hitchhiking wannabe rapper you picked up on the interstate—or what I like to call a recipe for becoming a serial killer's skin-suit. Oh wait! You already fucking did that."

"Oh my God. First of all, Jasper was an aspiring *country singer*, not a rapper. Second, I was with two other girls and we were driving to Daytona Beach, not Miami. Third, he didn't even try to touch me, let alone murder me." I sigh. "Lacey did hook up with him, though, and he gave her herpes."

Incredulous silence meets my ears.

"Dicky?" That's my childhood nickname for Dean. He hates it. "You there?"

"I'm trying to understand how you think your version of the story is in *any way* more palatable than mine." He suddenly curses. "Aw fuck, didn't I hook up with Lacey at your eighteenth birthday party?" A pause. "The herpes trip would've happened *before* that party. Dammit, Summer! I mean, I used protection, but a warning would've been nice!"

"No, you didn't hook up with Lacey. You're thinking of Laney, with an 'N.' I stopped being her friend after that."

"How come?"

"Because she slept with my brother when she was supposed to be hanging out with me at *my* party. That's not cool."

"Truth. Selfish move."

"Yup."

There's a sudden blast of noise on the line—what sounds like wind, car engines, and then a barrage of honking. "Sorry," Dean says. "Just leaving the apartment. My Uber's here."

"Where are you off to?"

"Picking up our dry-cleaning. The place Allie and I go to is in Tribeca, but they're awesome, so worth the trek. Highly recommend."

Dean and his girlfriend Allie live in the West Village in Manhattan. Allie admitted to me that the area is way fancier than she's used to, but for my brother it's actually a step down; our family's penthouse is on the Upper East Side, making up the top three floors of our hotel, the Heyward Plaza. But Dean's new building is near the private school where he teaches, and since Allie has a lead role on a television show that shoots all over Manhattan, the location is convenient for both of them.

It must be so nice for them, having a place to live and all.

"Anyway, are you nice and settled at the Kappa house?"

"Not quite," I confess.

"For fuck's sake, Summer. What did you do?"

My jaw falls open in outrage. Why does my family always assume that *I'm* in the wrong?

"I didn't do anything," I answer stiffly. But then defeat weakens my voice. "They don't think someone like me is good for the sorority's reputation. One of them said I was an arsonist."

"Well," Dean says not so tactfully. "You kind of are."

"Fuck off, Dicky. It was an accident. Arsonists intentionally set fires."

"So you're an accidental arsonist. The Accidental Arsonist. That's a great name for a book."

"Awesome. Go write that." I don't care how snide I sound. I'm feeling snarky, and my nerves are shot. "Anyway, they kicked me out, and now I have to figure out where the heck I'm going to live this semester." My throat catches on a lump that appears out of nowhere, and a choked almost-sob squeezes past it.

"Are you okay?" Dean asks immediately.

"I don't know." I swallow hard. "I... This is ridiculous. I don't know why I'm upset. Those girls are awful and I wouldn't have enjoyed living with them. I mean, it's New Year's Eve, and they're all on campus! They're doing some charity fundraiser thing instead of partying! That's so not my scene."

The tears I've been holding at bay are no longer controllable. Two fat drops slide down my cheeks, and I'm so glad Dean isn't here to witness it. It's bad enough that he can *hear* me crying.

"I'm sorry, Boogers."

"Whatever." I angrily swipe at my wet eyes. "It doesn't matter. I'm not going to cry over a few mean girls and an overcrowded house. I won't let it get to me. Would Selena Gomez let it get to *her*? Absolutely not."

There's a confused beat. "Selena Gomez?"

"Yes." I jut out my chin. "She's a symbol of class and purity, and I try to model myself after her. Personality-wise. Obviously, when it comes to style, I will forever strive to be Coco Chanel, and I will forever fail because nobody can be Coco Chanel."

"Obviously." He pauses. "Which era Selena Gomez are we talking about? Justin Bieber or The Weeknd? Or Bieber part two?"

I frown at my phone. "Are you for real right now?"

"What?"

"A woman isn't defined by her boyfriends. She's defined by her achievements. And her shoes."

My gaze lands on my new boots, courtesy of Nana Celeste. At least I've had smashing success in the shoe department.

The rest of it, not so much.

"I guess I can ask Dad to call the housing people and see if there's availability in any of the dorms." Once again, I feel defeated. "I really don't want to do that, though. He already had to pull strings to get me into Briar."

And I'd rather not live in a dorm if I can help it. Sharing a bathroom with a dozen other girls is my worst nightmare. I had to do it in the Kappa house at Brown, but the private bedroom made the bathroom situation easier to swallow. No way will there be any singles left in the dorms this far into the school year.

I moan softly. "What am I supposed to do?"

I have two older brothers who never, ever pass up an opportunity to tease or embarrass me, but sometimes they display rare moments of compassion. "Don't call Dad yet," Dean says gruffly. "Let me see what I can do first."

My forehead wrinkles. "I'm not sure you can do anything."

"Just hold off on calling him. I've got an idea." The squeal of brakes fills the line. "One sec. Thanks, bro. Five-star ride, for sure." A car door slams. "Summer, you're coming back to the city tonight anyway, right?"

"I wasn't planning on it," I admit, "but I guess I don't have a choice now. I'll have to grab a hotel in Boston until I figure out my living arrangements."

"Not Boston. I meant New York. The semester doesn't start for a few weeks. I figured you'd be staying at the penthouse until then."

"No, I wanted to unpack and settle in and all that crap."

"Well, it ain't happening today, and tonight is New Year's Eve, so you might as well come home and celebrate with me and Allie. A bunch of my old teammates are driving up too."

"Like who?" I ask curiously.

"Garrett's in the city for a game, so he'll be here. And the current Briar brigade is coming. You know some of them—Mike Hollis, Hunter Davenport. Actually, Hunter went to Roselawn Prep, think he was a year behind you. Pierre and Corsen, but I don't think you ever met them. Fitzy—"

My heartbeat stutters.

"I remember Fitzy," I say as casually as I'm capable of—which is not casual at all. Even I can hear the excitement in my voice.

Who can blame me, though? Fitzy is short for Colin Fitzgerald, and he just happens to be THE UNICORN. The tall, sexy, tattooed, hockey-playing unicorn of a man who I might have a teeny-weeny itsy-bitsy crush on.

Okay, fine.

A big motherfucking crush on.

He's so…magical. But he's also out of reach. Dean's hockey friends are usually all over me when they meet me, but not Fitz. I met him last year when I visited Dean at Briar, and the guy barely glanced my way. When I saw him again at a birthday party for Dean's friend Logan, he said about ten words to me—and I'm pretty sure half those words were *hello, how are you*, and *goodbye*.

He's exasperating. Not that I expect every male in my vicinity to fall at my feet, but I *know* he's attracted to me. I've noticed the way his brown eyes smolder when he looks at me. They frigging smolder.

Unless I'm just seeing what I want to see.

My dad has this super-pompous saying: *perception and reality are vastly disparate. The truth is usually found somewhere in between.* Dad used that line in his closing arguments for a murder trial once, and now he busts it out any time it's even remotely applicable to a situation.

If the truth lies somewhere between Colin Fitzgerald's outward aloofness toward me (he hates me), and the heat I see in his eyes (his fiery passion for me), then…I guess split the difference and say he views me as a friend?

I purse my lips.

No. Absolutely not. I refuse to be friend-zoned before I've even made a move.

"It'll be a good time," Dean is saying. "Besides, it's been ages since we were in the same place on New Year's Eve. So get your butt to New York and text when you're here. I'm at the drycleaner's now. Gotta go. Love you."

He hangs up, and I'm smiling so broadly it's hard to imagine I was in tears five minutes ago. Dean might be a pain in the ass most of the time, but he's a good big brother. He's there for me when I need him, and that's all that really matters.

And—praise the Lord!—now I have a party to go to. There's nothing better than a party after a shitty day. I need this badly.

I check the time. It's one p.m.

I quickly do some mental math. The Briar campus is about an hour away from Boston. From there it's a three-and-a-half, four-hour drive to Manhattan. That means I won't arrive in the city until the evening, which won't leave me much time to get ready. If I'm seeing my unicorn tonight, I plan on dolling myself up from my head down to my toes.

That boy isn't going to know what hit him.

# 2
# FITZ

"Dance with me?"

I want to say no.

But I also want to say yes.

I call this the Summer Dilemma—the frustrating, polar reactions this green-eyed, golden-haired goddess sparks in me.

*Fuck yes* and *hell no.*

Get naked with her. Run far, far away from her.

"Thanks, but I don't like to dance." I'm not lying. Dancing's the worst.

Besides, when it comes to Summer Di Laurentis, my flight instinct always wins out.

"You're no fun, Fitzy." She makes a tsking noise, drawing my gaze to her lips. Full, pink, and glossy, with a tiny mole above the left side of her mouth.

It's an extremely hot mouth.

Hell, everything about Summer is hot. She's hands down the best-looking girl in the bar, and every dude in our vicinity is either staring enviously or glowering at me for being with her.

Not that I'm *with* her. We're not together. I'm just standing next to her, with two feet of space between us. Which Summer keeps trying to bridge by leaning closer to me.

In her defense, she practically has to scream in my ear for me to hear her over the electronic dance music blasting through the room. I hate EDM, and I don't like these kinds of bars, the ones with a dance floor and deafening music. Why the subterfuge? Just call your establishment a nightclub, if that's what you want it to be. The owner of Gunner's Pub should've called this place Gunner's Club. Then I could've turned right around when I saw the sign and spared myself the shattered eardrums.

Not for the first time tonight, I curse my friends for dragging me to Brooklyn for New Year's Eve. I'd way rather be at home, drinking a beer or two and watching the ball drop on TV. I'm low-key like that.

"You know, they warned me you were a curmudgeon, but I didn't believe it until now."

"Who's *they*?" I ask suspiciously. "And hey, wait. I'm not a curmudgeon."

"Hmmm, you're right—the term is kind of dated. Let's go with Groucho."

"Let's not."

"No-Fun Police? Is that better?" Her expression is pure innocence. "Seriously, Fitz, what do you have against fun?"

An unwitting smile breaks free. "Got nothing against fun."

"All right. Then what do you have against *me*?" she challenges. "Because every time I try talking to you, you run away."

My smile fades. I shouldn't be surprised that she's calling me out in public. We've had a whopping total of two encounters, but that's plenty of time for me to know she's the type who thrives on drama.

I hate drama.

"Got nothing against you, either." With a shrug, I ease away from the bar, prepared to do what she's just accused me of—run.

A frustrated gleam fills her eyes. They're big and green, the same shade as her older brother Dean's eyes. And Dean's the reason I force myself to stay put. He's a good friend of mine. I can't be a jackass to his sister, both out of respect for him, and for fear of my well-being.

I've been on the ice when Dean's gloves come off. He's got a mean right hook.

"I mean it," I say roughly. "I have nothing against you. We're cool."

"What? I didn't hear the last part," she says over the music.

I dip my mouth toward her ear, and I'm surprised that I barely have to bend my neck. She's taller than the average chick, five-nine or ten, and since I'm six-two and used to towering over women, I find this refreshing.

"I said we're cool," I repeat, but I misjudged the distance between my lips and Summer's ear. The two collide, and I feel a shiver run up her frame.

I shiver too, because my mouth is way too close to hers. She smells like heaven, some fascinating combo of flowers and jasmine and vanilla and—sandalwood, maybe? A man could get high on that fragrance. And don't get me started on her dress. White, strapless, short. So short it barely grazes her lower thighs.

God fucking help me.

I quickly straighten up before I do something stupid, like kiss her. Instead, I take a huge gulp of my beer. Only it goes down the wrong pipe, and I start coughing like it's the eighteenth century and I'm a tuberculosis patient.

Smooth move.

"You okay?"

When the coughing fit subsides, I find those green eyes dancing at me. Her lips are curved in a devilish smile. She knows exactly what got me flustered.

"Fine," I croak, just as three very plastered guys lumber up to the bar and bump into Summer.

She stumbles, and the next thing I know there's a gorgeous, sweet-smelling woman in my arms.

She laughs and grabs my hand. "C'mon, let's get out of this crowd before it leaves bruises."

For some reason, I let her lead me away.

We end up at a high table near the railing that separates the bar's main room from the small, shitty dance floor. A quick look around reveals that most of my friends are drunk off their asses.

Mike Hollis, my roommate, is grinding up on a cute brunette who doesn't seem to mind in the slightest. He's the one who insisted we make the drive to Brooklyn instead of staying in the Boston area. He wanted to spend New Year's with his older brother Brody, who disappeared the moment we got here. I guess the girl is Hollis' consolation prize for getting ditched by his brother.

Our other roommate, Hunter, is dancing with three girls. Yup, three. They're all but licking his face off, and I'm pretty sure one has a hand down his pants. Hunter, of course, is loving it.

What a difference a year makes. Last season he was uneasy about all the female attention, said it made him feel a bit sleazy. Now, it appears he's perfectly cool taking advantage of the perks that come with playing hockey for Briar University. And trust me, there're plenty of perks.

Let's get real—athletes are the most fuckable guys on most college campuses. If you're at a football school, chances are there's a line of jersey chasers begging to blow the quarterback. Basketball school? The groupie pool doubles and triples in size when March Madness comes around. And at Briar, with a hockey team that has a dozen Frozen Four championships under its belt and more nationally televised games than any other college in the country? The hockey players are gods.

Except for me, that is. I play hockey, yes. I'm good at it, definitely. But "god" and "jock" and "superstar" are terms I've never been comfortable with. Deep down, I'm a huge nerd. A nerd masquerading as a god.

"Hunter's got game." Summer is studying Hunter's entourage.

The DJ has switched the beats from electronic garbage to Top 40 hits. Blessedly, he's also turned down the volume, probably in anticipation of the nearing countdown. Thirty more minutes and I can make my escape.

"He does," I agree.

"I'm impressed."

"Yeah?"

"Definitely. Greenwich boys are usually secret prudes."

I wonder how she knows Hunter is from Connecticut. I don't think I've seen them exchange more than a few words tonight. Maybe Dean told her? Or maybe—

Or maybe it doesn't frickin' matter how she knows, because if it *did* matter, then that means the weird prickly sensation in my chest is jealousy. And that, frankly, is unacceptable.

Summer does another visual sweep of the crowd and blanches. "Oh my God. Gross." She cups her hands to create a microphone, shouting, "Keep your tongue in your own mouth, Dicky!"

Laughter sputters out of me. No way Dean could've heard her, but I guess he possesses some sort of sibling radar, because he abruptly pries his lips off his girlfriend's. His head swivels in our direction. When he spots Summer, he gives her the finger.

She blows a kiss in return.

"I'm so glad I'm an only child," I remark.

She grins at me. "Naah, you're missing out. Tormenting my brothers is one of my favorite pastimes."

"I've noticed." She calls Dean "Dicky," a childhood nickname that a nicer person would have stopped using years ago.

On the other hand, Dean's nickname for Summer is "Boogers," so maybe she's right to torture him.

"Dicky deserves to be tormented tonight. I can't believe we're partying in *Brooklyn*," she grumbles. "When he said we were ringing in the New Year in the city, I assumed he meant Manhattan—but then he and Allie dragged me to horrible Brooklyn instead. I feel duped."

I snicker. "What's wrong with Brooklyn? Allie's dad lives around here, doesn't he?"

Summer nods. "They're spending the day with him tomorrow. And to answer your question—what *isn't* wrong with Brooklyn? It used to be cool, before it got overrun by hipsters."

"Hipsters still exist? I thought we were done with that nonsense."

"God, no. And don't let anyone tell you otherwise." She mock shudders. "This whole area is still teeming with them."

She says "*them*" as if they're carriers for a gruesome, incurable disease. She might have a point, though—a thorough examination of the crowd reveals a large amount of vintage attire, painfully skinny jeans on men, retro accessories paired with shiny new tech, and lots and lots of beards.

I rub my own beard, wondering if it places me in the hipster camp. I've been rocking the scruff all winter, mostly because it's good insulation from the bitter weather we've been experiencing. Last week we got hit by one of the worst Nor'easters I've ever seen. I almost froze my balls off.

"They're so…" She searches for the right word. "Douchey."

I have to laugh. "Not all of them."

"Most of them," she says. "Like, see that girl over there? With the braids and the bangs? That's a thousand-dollar Prada cardigan she has on—and she's paired it with a five-dollar tank she probably got at the Salvation Army, and those weird tasseled shoes they sell in Chinatown. She's a total fraud."

I furrow my brow. "How do you know the cardigan cost a grand?"

"Because I have the same one in gray. Besides, I can pick Prada out of any lineup."

I don't doubt that. She was probably deposited into a designer onesie the moment she popped out of her mother's womb. Summer and Dean come from a filthy-rich family. Their parents are successful lawyers who were independently wealthy before they got hitched, so now they're like a mega-rich super-duo who could probably buy a small country without even making a dent in their bank account. I stayed at their Manhattan penthouse a couple times, and it was goddamn unreal. They also have a mansion in Greenwich, a beach house, and a bunch of other properties around the globe.

Me, I can barely make the rent on the townhouse I share with two other dudes. We're still on the hunt for a fourth roommate, though, so my share will go down once we fill that empty room.

I'm not gonna lie—the fact that Summer lives in penthouses and owns clothes that cost thousands of dollars is slightly unsettling.

"Anyway, hipsters suck, Fitzy. No thank you. I'd way rather— oooh! I *love* this song! I had backstage passes to her show at The Garden last June and it was *amazing*."

*The ADHD is strong with this one, my friend.*

I hide a smile as Summer completely drops her death-to-all-hipsters tirade and starts bobbing her head to a Beyoncé song. Her high ponytail swishes wildly.

"Are you sure you don't want to dance?" she pleads.

"Positive."

"You're the worst. I'll be right back."

I blink, and she's no longer beside me. Blink again, and I spot her on the dance floor, arms thrust in the air, ponytail flipping, hips moving to the beat.

I'm not the only one watching her. A sea of covetous eyes ripples in the direction of the beautiful girl in the white dress. Summer either doesn't notice or doesn't care. She dances alone, without an ounce of self-consciousness. She is completely comfortable in her own skin.

"Jesus," Hunter Davenport rasps, coming up to the table. Like most of the men around us, he's staring at Summer with an expression that could only be described as pure hunger.

"Guess she hasn't forgotten any of those old cheerleading moves." Hunter slants another appreciative look in Summer's direction. When he notices my quizzical face, he adds, "She was a cheerleader in high school. Member of the dance team too."

When did he and Summer engage in a conversation long enough for him to learn these tidbits?

The uncomfortable prickling sensation returns, this time traveling up my spine.

It's not jealousy, though.

"Cheerleading and dance, huh?" I ask lightly. "She tell you that?"

"We went to the same prep school," he reveals.

"No shit."

"Yeah. I was a year behind her, but trust me, every hetero guy with a working dick was familiar with Summer Di Laurentis's cheer routines."

I'll bet.

He claps me on the shoulder. "Gonna hit the head and then grab another drink. Want anything?"

"I'm good."

Not sure why, but I'm relieved that Hunter's not around when Summer returns to the table, her cheeks flushed from exertion.

Despite the frigid temperatures outside, she chose not to wear tights or pantyhose, and, as my old man would say, she's got legs for days. Long, smooth, gorgeous legs that would probably look so hot wrapped around my waist. And the white dress sets off her deep, golden tan, giving her a glowing, healthy vibe that's almost hypnotizing.

"So, you're…" I clear my throat. "You're coming to Briar this semester, huh?" I ask, trying to distract myself from her smokin' body.

She gives an enthusiastic nod. "I am!"

"Are you going to miss Providence?" I know she spent her freshman and sophomore years at Brown, plus one semester of junior year, which makes up half her college career. If it were me, I'd hate starting over at a new school.

But Summer shakes her head. "Not really. I wasn't a fan of the town, or the school. I only went there because my parents wanted me to attend an Ivy League and I didn't get into Harvard or Yale, their alma maters." She shrugs. "Did you want to go to Briar?"

"Definitely. I heard phenomenal things about the Fine Arts

program. And, obviously, the hockey program is stellar. They offered me a full ride to play, and I get to study something I'm really into, so…" I offer a shrug in return.

"That's so important. Doing what you love, I mean. A lot of people don't have that opportunity."

Curiosity flickers through me. "What do you love to do?"

Her answering grin is self-deprecating. "I'll let you know when I figure it out."

"Come on, there's got to be something you're passionate about."

"Well, I've *been* passionate about stuff—interior design, psychology, ballet, swimming. The problem is, it never sticks. I lose interest quickly. I haven't found a long-term passion yet, I suppose."

Her candidness surprises me a bit. She seems way more down-to-earth tonight compared to our previous encounters. "I'm thirsty," she announces.

I suppress the urge to roll my eyes, since I'm sure that's code for *go buy me a drink*. Only, it's not. With a naughty smile, she swipes my beer from my hand.

Our fingers brush briefly, and I pretend not to notice the spark of heat that races up my arm. I watch as she wraps her fingers around the Bud Light bottle and takes a long sip.

She's got small hands, delicate fingers. It'd be a challenge to draw them, to capture the intriguing combination of fragility and surety. Her fingernails are short, rounded and have those white French tips or whatever you call 'em, a style that seems way too plain for someone like Summer. I'd expect extra-long talons painted pink or some other pastel.

"You're doing it again." There's accusation in her tone. A bit of aggravation too.

"Doing what?"

"Zoning me out. Curmudgeoning."

"That's not a word."

"Says who?" She takes another sip of beer. My gaze instantly fixes on her lips.

Dammit, I gotta stop this. She's not my type. The first time I met her, everything about her screamed *sorority girl*. The designer clothes, the waves and waves of blonde hair, a face that could stop traffic.

There's no way I'm her type, either. I have no idea why she's spending New Year's Eve talking to a scruffy, tatted-up goon like me.

"Sorry. I'm not very chatty. Don't take it personally, okay?" I steal my bottle back.

"Okay, I won't. But if you don't feel like talking, at least entertain me in other ways." She plants her hands on her hips. "I propose we make out."

# 3
# FITZ

ONCE AGAIN, I CHOKE MID-SIP.

Oh, sweet Jesus. Did she seriously just say that?

I glance over, and she's got one perfect eyebrow arched, awaiting my response. Yup. She said it.

"Uh…you want to, um…" I cough again.

"Oh relax!" Summer laughs. "It was a joke."

I narrow my eyes at her. "A joke," I echo. "So you have zero interest in making out with me?" Hell, why am I challenging her? My dick twitches against my zipper, a warning that I shouldn't be entertaining the idea of kissing Summer.

"I mean, it wouldn't be the end of the world if we did," she says with a wink. "And it's always nice to have someone to kiss at midnight. I was mostly joking, though. I just like making you blush."

"I don't blush," I object, because I'm a dude, and dudes don't go around declaring they're blushers.

Summer hoots. "Yes, you do! You're blushing now."

"Oh really? You can see this supposed blush right through my beard, huh?" I rub my face defiantly.

"Uh-huh." She reaches out and strokes my cheek above the heavy beard growth. "Right. Here."

I gulp. My dick stirs again.

I hate how attracted I am to her.

"Fitzy," she whispers in my ear, and my pulse goes careening. "I think we—"

"Happy fucking New Year!"

Saved by Hollis.

My friend lurches toward us and plants a sloppy peck on Summer's cheek. They'd just met tonight, but she doesn't seem offended by the kiss, only mildly amused.

"You're about twenty minutes too early with that sentiment," she informs him.

"And you don't have a drink in your hand!" He fixes her with a disapproving glare. "Why doesn't she have a drink in her hand? Someone get this beautiful woman a drink!"

"I'm not a big drinker," Summer protests.

"Bullshit." Dean cackles. He's wandered over, his girlfriend Allie Hayes at his side. "You were off your face when you burned down the sorority house."

"You burned down a sorority house?" asks a familiar voice.

Dean spins around. "G!" he crows. "Just under the wire!"

"Yeah, we almost didn't make it," Garrett Graham says as he strides up to the table. "There was a ten-car pileup on the bridge. Sat there for almost an hour before traffic started moving again."

"Han-Han!" Allie says happily, throwing her arms around Hannah Wells. Hannah is Garrett's girl, but she also happens to be Allie's best friend. "I'm so glad you're here!"

"Me too! Happy New Year's Eve."

"Garrett Eve," her boyfriend corrects.

"Dude," Hannah retorts, "give it up. I'm not calling it that."

Summer snorts. "Garrett Eve?"

Dean rolls his eyes at our old team captain. "Pompous ass." He glances at Summer. "His birthday is New Year's Day."

"Garrett Day," G says automatically, before turning to greet me and Hollis and the other guys from the team who made the trek to

Brooklyn. Summer gets a quick hug and a peck on the cheek. "Good to see you, Summertime. You torched a sorority house?"

"Oh my God. No. I didn't torch anything!" She glowers at her brother.

"Bro, everyone's staring at you," Hollis suddenly says, grinning at Garrett.

Hollis is right—several heads have turned in our direction. Most of the people here are too hammered to pay much attention to their surroundings, but some of them have recognized Garrett. He's in the middle of one of the most explosive rookie seasons in Bruins history, so I'm not surprised he's attracting attention even outside of Boston.

"They're probably gonna start heckling me soon," he says glumly. "We lost to the Islanders last night. Final score was five-four."

"Yeah, but *you* scored a hat trick," Hannah counters. "Anyone who heckles a player with a hat trick is a stupid moron."

"Can a moron be anything other than stupid?" Dean asks with a grin.

"Oh, shut it, Di Laurentis. You know what I mean."

When a few more people start looking and pointing at Garrett, Allie teases, "How does it feel to be famous?"

"You tell me," G jokes back.

"Ha. I'm *so* not famous," says the person with a role on an HBO show.

Allie's show is actually based on a book I really enjoyed, and although I'm happy that she's a working actress, I secretly think the book was better.

The book is always better.

"Stop being so modest!" Summer slings an arm around Allie, who's almost a head shorter than her. "Guys. I saw her sign *four* autographs tonight. She's a star."

"Only half the season has aired so far," Allie protests. "We might not even get renewed."

"Of course you will," Dean says, as if it's not even up for debate.

Summer releases Allie and returns to my side, laying a hand on my arm. It's not a possessive grip by any means, but I don't miss the way both Garrett and Hunter zoom in on it. Dean doesn't notice, thank God, because Allie is dragging him away, saying she wants one more dance before the countdown.

Beside me, Hollis examines the room with a surprising degree of intensity for a drunk guy. "I gotta decide whose tongue I want in my mouth at midnight," he announces.

"Classy," Summer says.

He leers wolfishly. "You play your cards right, that tongue could be yours."

Her response is to throw her head back and laugh.

Luckily, Hollis has an ego made of Kevlar. He shrugs and wanders off, which spurs most of the other guys to scatter. Pierre, our resident French-Canadian, and Matt Anderson, a junior defenseman, head for the bar. Only Garrett and Hannah remain. And Hunter, who's got a beer in one hand and his phone in the other. He's taking a video of the crowd for his Snapchat story.

"How about you?" Summer asks Hunter. "I saw you dancing with seven different girls tonight. Which one are you going to kiss?"

"None of them." He lowers the phone, his blue eyes dead serious. "I don't do New Year's kisses. Chicks always try to find meaning in them that isn't there."

Summer rolls her eyes so hard I'm surprised she doesn't pull a muscle. "Right, because all women start planning their weddings after *one* kiss." She glances at a laughing Hannah. "Wanna hit the ladies'? I want to touch up my makeup before the countdown. My lip gloss needs to be *perfect* for when I kiss my future husband at midnight." She directs another eye roll at Hunter.

He winks at her, unfazed. "Better hurry, Blondie. Only sixteen minutes left." He nods at the huge digital clock hanging over the DJ station.

"Be right back." Hannah gives Garrett a kiss and then follows Summer.

"I need a refill," I tell Garrett. I gesture at his empty hands. "And you need a drink."

He nods, and we leave Hunter at the table and make our way to the bar. We stop at the far end of it where it's quieter, near the arched doorway leading to the restrooms.

I order two beers and hand over some cash. When I turn back, I find Garrett eyeing me.

"What?" I say awkwardly.

"What's going on with you and Summer?"

"Nothing." Fuck. Did I answer too fast?

"Liar. You answered way too fast."

Goddammit.

His tone becomes cautious. "When she got handsy back there… you didn't seem to mind."

He's right. I *didn't* mind. The last time I saw Summer, I made a conscious effort to keep my distance. Tonight, I let her touch my arm. I shared a drink with her. Honestly, if I liked to dance, I probably would've let her drag me onto the floor.

"She's… Well, she's into me," I say slowly.

Garrett snorts. "No shit, dude. That chick wants to ride your dick."

"I know." Guilt pricks my throat. I hope I haven't been leading her on tonight. "Don't worry," I assure him. "I won't go there."

He looks startled. "Why would I be worried?" His eyebrows furrow. "Wait. You might be misunderstanding. I'm not warning you away from her. I think this is a *good* thing."

A frown touches my lips. "You do?"

"Of course. I mean, one—you never hook up."

I swallow a laugh. That's not true at all. I get lots of action. I just don't talk about it.

"Two—Summer's cute. She's fun. Easy to talk to." He shrugs. "She could be exactly what you need. You'd have to run it by Dean first, though. He thinks she's a brat, but he's protective of her."

Run it by Dean? As in, ask Dean for permission to bone down with his little sister? Garrett is frickin' crazy if—

My thought process halts.

"You're talking about more than a casual hook-up here," I say.

"Well, yeah. She's Dean's sister. He'd kill you otherwise."

"I'm not dating her, G."

"Why not?" He reaches forward to grab our beers, passing one my way.

I twist off the top and take a deep gulp before answering. "Because she's not my type. We've got nothing in common."

"She likes hockey," he points out. "That's a start."

"And I think it might end there," I say dryly. "I design and review video games. I'm into art. I'm covered in ink and I binge-watch crime shows on Netflix. And she's… I don't even know." I scan my brain. "She's obsessed with shoes, according to Dean. And he insists she has a shopping problem."

"Okay. So she's into fashion. Some people consider that art."

I snicker. "You're reaching."

"And you're judging. She seems like a good girl, Fitz."

"Dude, she got kicked out of Brown for partying too hard. She's a party girl. She's in a sorority."

I'm on a roll now, because my dick is still semi-hard and I'm desperately grasping for reasons to not screw Summer.

"She's…fluff," I finish.

"Fluff."

"Yeah, fluff." I shrug helplessly. "You know, not serious about anything. She's surface level."

Garrett pauses for a long moment, searching my face.

He stares for so long that I fidget with the sleeve of my hoodie, feeling like a specimen under his microscope. I hate that intrusive sensation of eyes boring into me. It's a scar left over from childhood, a need to blend into the background, to be unseen.

I'm two seconds from telling him to cut it out when he starts to laugh. "Oh, I get it. I was wasting my time trying to sell you on her. You were already sold." His gray eyes light up gleefully. "You have a thing for Dean's sister."

"Naah," I say, but it's a halfhearted denial at best.

"Really? 'Cause it sounds like you're trying to convince yourself that she's not right for you." He grins. "Is it working?"

I sigh in defeat. "Kind of? I mean, I've managed to keep my hands off her all night."

That gets me a laugh. "Look, Colin—can I call you Colin?" His jaw drops. "I just fucking realized *I've never called you Colin.*"

Garrett literally shocks himself into silence, until I let out a growl of impatience.

"Sorry," he says. "That just blew my mind. Anyway. Fitzy. On paper, Wellsy and I don't seem like we'd work, right? But we do, don't we?"

He has a point. When I first saw them together, I couldn't make sense of it. Hannah was an artsy music major. Garrett was a smartass jock. They're opposites in so many ways, and yet they really do click as a couple.

But Summer and I… We're not even on the same piece of paper. From what I've seen and what Dean has told me, she's drama-llama at full force, all the time. She craves the spotlight. I shy away from it. It's bad enough that our games are televised every Friday night on the local New England network. And the major games make it to ESPN. Makes me cringe to think of strangers watching me skate and shoot and brawl on some huge screen.

"All I'm saying is, keep an open mind. Don't fight it." He claps me on the shoulder. "Just let it happen."

*Let it happen.*

And, fuck, it absolutely could happen. All I'd have to do is smile in Summer's direction, and she'd be in my arms. She's been sending out interested vibes left and right. But…

I think what it boils down to is that she's out of my league.

I play hockey. I'm fairly intelligent. I'm good-looking, if we go by my success in the chick department.

But at the end of the day, I'm that nerdy kid who would hole up in his bedroom playing video games, trying to pretend his parents weren't fighting like cats and dogs.

In high school I had a brief moment where I tried expanding my horizons. I started hanging with a nihilistic crew who got a charge out of rebelling against any cause. But that came to an abrupt end when they got into a brawl with some kids from a neighboring school, and half the group was arrested for assault. I quickly reverted back to my loner state after that, not just to save my place on the hockey team, but to keep from giving my parents new fighting ammunition. I listened to them scream at each other for two hours about which one was to blame for me running with a "bad crowd." It was easier just being a loner.

Needless to say, I didn't have girls like Summer throwing themselves at me. And I didn't party with my teammates after hockey games, so not even the puck bunnies wasted their energy on me.

In college, I've made more of an effort to be social, but deep down I'm still the guy who wants to remain invisible.

Summer is the most visible person I've ever met.

But Garrett's right. I'm being a judgmental bastard. She might come off as a bit spoiled and superficial at times, but she deserves a chance. Everyone does.

Hannah's already back at the table when Garrett and I return. "Cutting it close!" she scolds, pointing at the big clock. It's two minutes to midnight.

I frown, because Summer's not with her. Dammit. Where is she?

I've decided to take G's advice and stop fighting it. I'm going to give in, kiss the hell out of her when the clock strikes midnight and see where it goes from there.

"One minute to go, boys and girls!" the DJ's voice thunders.

I give the room a visual sweep. Summer's still nowhere to be found.

I want to ask Hannah where she is, but Hannah's got her arms looped around G's neck, and they only have eyes for each other.

"Thirty seconds!" shouts the DJ.

All around me, people are coupling up or gathering with their group of friends. Allie and Dean are already making out. Hollis has reunited with the brunette he was dancing with earlier.

Still no Summer.

"TEN!" everyone yells.

The red numerals on the clock tick down in time with the crowd's screams.

"NINE!"

Each passing second brings another jolt of disappointment.

"EIGHT! SEVEN!"

And then I spot her. Or at least I think it's her. The strobe lights are going off now, zigzagging over the sea of bodies crammed in the bar. Each burst of light helps me form a clearer picture of the girl against the wall.

"SIX! FIVE!"

White dress. Red ballet flats. The ponytail.

"FOUR! THREE!"

It's definitely Summer.

"TWO!"

But she's not alone.

"ONE!"

I wrench my gaze away the moment Hunter's mouth hungrily collides with Summer's perfect lips.

"HAPPY NEW YEAR!"

# 4
# FITZ

I WAKE UP THE NEXT MORNING WITHOUT A HANGOVER. THAT'S what happens when you only drink three beers and are back in your hotel room before one a.m.

On New Year's Eve.

Aren't I the poster boy for good behavior?

My phone informs me of a dozen messages and missed calls. Dragging a hand through my messy hair, I roll onto my back and sift through the notifications.

My parents each texted at precisely 12:00 a.m. I can just imagine them sitting in their respective houses at 11:59, hands hovering over their phones like they're preparing to slap the buzzer on *Family Feud*, each one desperate to be the first to get a message through. They're so frickin' competitive.

**MOM:** Happy New Year, sweetie!! Love you so soooo much! This is going to be the best year ever! YOUR year! Woot woot!

Oh dear God. Mothers are not allowed to say "woot woot." My dad's text isn't much better.

**DAD:** Happy New Year. We got this.

We got this? Got what? Parents trying to sound cool is a whole other level of secondhand embarrassment.

My friends' messages are more entertaining.

**HOLLIS:** Where da fuck r u?? Patty's just getting started
**HOLLIS:** *patty
**HOLLIS:** *parting
**HOLLIS:** Party!!!!!! FUCK THIS PHONE
**GARRETT:** Happy New Year!! Where'd u run off to, Colin??
(Still feel weird calling u that)

My old teammates Logan and Tucker send their New Year messages to our various group chats. Tuck and Sabrina include a picture of their baby, which prompts about a million heart-eye emojis from our friends.

Pierre texts something in French.

My teammates blow up our team thread with well-wishes and random videos, grainy and impossible to hear, of the various parties they attended.

One teammate's name is noticeably missing from the group chat and my phone in general. Shocking. No word from Hunter.

I bet he was too busy to text anyone last night.

Busy, busy, busy.

I ignore the sharp clenching in my chest and force all thoughts of Hunter and his busy, busy night out of my head. I continue scrolling through my phone.

A girl I knew in high school sends a generic note. For some reason, she still has me in her contacts list, so any time a holiday rolls around I get a message from her.

Hollis sends a few more texts that make me chuckle.

**HOLLIS:** Yo. bar's closing. where u at. assuming getting a bj or sumthin?

**HOLLIS:** after patty at Danny's house. new buddy. u'll luv him
**HOLLIS:** OK then
**HOLLIS:** gunna assume u ded
**HOLLIS:** hope ur not ded, tho!!! I <3 u, bro. new year, new us. word.

Oh man. Someone needs to confiscate that dude's phone when he's wasted. Still laughing, I click on the next message in my inbox. It's from Dean.

My humor fades the moment I read it.

**DEAN:** Happy New Year!! Was hoping to talk to u before u took off. I need a huge favor, bro.
**DEAN:** Are u guys still looking for a 4th roommate?

# 5
# SUMMER

**TWO WEEKS LATER**

The assistant dean is putting on a fake British accent.

I've been sitting in his office for about seven minutes now, and I'm convinced of it. I want to grill him about where he grew up, but I don't think Mr. Richmond would appreciate the interruption. He's clearly receiving way too much enjoyment from this lecture.

"...academic probation," he's droning. His voice has a weird, raspy croak to it. Like if a frog could talk, that's how I imagine it would sound.

A nickname forms in my head—Asshole Frog.

"...zero tolerance policy, given the nature of your previous expulsion..."

Or maybe Froghole. That has a better ring to it.

"Summer."

He pronounces my name *Sum-ah*. I try to remember how Gavin used to say it. Gavin is the sexy duke I dated last year when I spent the summer in England. I don't think their accents are comparable, though. Gavin's blood runs blue, so he'd have that upper-crust accent only those in line to the throne have. Granted, there are about forty members of the royal family ahead of him in the line of succession, but that's still a whole other stratosphere above Mr. Richmond.

Briar's assistant dean is no duke. And his first name is Hal, which doesn't sound very British. Unless it's short for something? Hallam? Halbert?

"Ms. Di Laurentis!"

My head snaps up. Froghole's expression is as sharp as his tone. I'd zoned him out, and he knows it.

"I understand that rules of conduct and academic policies aren't the most exciting subject matter, but you, of all people, should be paying attention to this. The remainder of your college career could depend on it."

"I'm sorry," I force myself to say. "I don't mean to be rude or ignore you on purpose. I have, um, attention problems."

He nods, eyes on my file. "ADHD, according to this. Are you on medication for it?"

I bristle. I'm not, but that's none of his frigging business. Right?

I make a mental note to ask my parents, who are both lawyers. But I'm fairly certain a student doesn't have to disclose to the school the medications they're on.

I brush past the question in a way that would make my father proud. "I'm sure your file also mentions my writing issues?"

The distraction works. Froghole glances back at the file, shuffling a few pages. "Difficulties with written expression—yes, that tends to be a symptom of ADHD. Your advisor at Brown recommended alternate assessment methods for you if possible. Extra time on tests, extra tutoring, and oral exams to reduce the amount of writing. Are all written assignments a problem for you, or just longer essays?"

"Most written work is an issue." My cheeks are on fire. It's so frigging embarrassing sitting here talking about how stupid I am.

*You're not stupid, Summer. You just learn differently.*

Mom's voice floats through my head, reciting the same encouraging words I've been hearing my whole life. But although I love my parents dearly, their support doesn't make it any less humiliating that I can't organize my thoughts on paper. Hell, I can barely hold on to those thoughts for five seconds before my mind wanders somewhere else.

Other people have learning disabilities, I know that. But when your parents and two older brothers all got into Harvard Law and you're the fashion major who has trouble writing one measly paragraph, it's a little hard not to feel…less than.

"We'll try to offer the same academic assistance you received at Brown, but not all your professors will be able to accommodate you." Froghole flips to another paper. "Let's take a look at your schedule… I suspect you'll only have to worry about written assignments in History of Fashion, and Fundamentals of Color and Design. The rest of your courses seem to be more hands-on."

I'm unable to hide my relief. Along with the two classes he just named, I'm also taking Textiles, which I'm excited about. Sewing and Tailoring, not as excited for. And an independent study that requires I design a line and debut it at the end-of-semester fashion show. All three are almost entirely practical. I fulfilled most of my degree requirements during my first two years at Brown, the awful ones like Lit and Sociology and Gender Studies. That's probably why I was always on academic probation there. I barely passed any of those.

"But as I mentioned before, there are no strikes here. No second chances. If you cause any trouble, if you can't meet the minimum academic requirements and maintain your GPA, you will be expelled. Are we clear?"

"Crystal," I mutter.

"Brilliant."

Argh. That accent is *fake*. I'm certain of it.

"Hey, Mr. Richmond, if you don't mind me asking, where exactly in the UK are you from? You kinda sound like my friend Marcus, who's from—"

He interrupts with, "Your attention issues are quite concerning, Summer. You never did say if you were on medication...?"

*Oh fuck off.*

We have a stare-off that lasts a couple of seconds. I clench my teeth and ask, "May I go now?"

"One last thing," he says, a snide edge to his voice.

I force myself to stay seated.

"I'm sure you've noticed that your schedule doesn't list the name of your advisor."

I hadn't noticed, actually. But, sure enough, there's a blank space after the academic advisor line.

"That's because I will be looking after you personally."

A rush of anxiety courses through me. What? Is that even legal?

Well, I'm sure it's *legal*. But...why would the assistant dean serve as the advisor for a fashion major?

"It's not a role I would normally take on. However, given the circumstances under which you were admitted to this university—"

"Circumstances?" I cut in, confused.

His dark eyes gleam with...I think that might be spite? "I understand that your father and the dean are longtime friends and golf chums—"

Definitely spite.

"—and I'm quite aware of the numerous donations your family has made to this school. With that said, I'm not a supporter of the I'll-pat-your-back-you-pat-mine mentality. I believe that admission to this college—to any college—should be granted based on a student's merit. So..." He shrugs. "I feel it would be prudent to keep an eye on you academically and ensure you're conducting yourself according to the rules and policies we just went over."

I'm sure my cheeks are redder than tomatoes, and I hope my two-hundred-dollar foundation is doing its job. It is absolutely mortifying knowing my father had to call in a favor with Dean Prescott to get me into Briar after the Brown fiasco. If it were up to me, I'd be done with college for good. But I promised my parents I'd get a degree, and I hate disappointing them.

"We'll meet once a week so I can evaluate your progress and guide you academically."

"Sounds great," I lie. This time I get to my feet without asking permission. "I have to run now, Mr. Richmond. Why don't you email me our meeting times and I'll add those days to my calendar. Thanks so much for all your guidance."

I'm sure he didn't miss the sarcastic note in that last word—*guidance*—but I don't give him a chance to respond. I'm already out the door and waving goodbye to his secretary.

Outside, I inhale the chilled air. Normally I adore the winter, and my new campus looks particularly magical covered with a layer of white frost, but I'm too stressed out to enjoy it right now. I can't believe I'm being forced to have regular contact with Richmond. He was such a jerk.

I take another breath, adjust the strap of my Chanel tote, and start walking toward the parking lot behind the administration building. It's a beautiful brick building, ivy-covered and incredibly old, like pretty much everything else on campus. Briar is one of the oldest and most prestigious universities in the country. It's produced a couple of presidents and a ton of politicians, which is impressive, but only in the last decade have they begun to offer cooler, less academic-based courses. Like this Fashion Design program that's going to give me a Bachelor of Fine Arts.

Despite what *some* people might think, fashion isn't fluff.

*I'm* not fluff.

*So take that, Colin Fitzgerald!*

Bitterness rises in my throat, but I gulp it down because I'm not a bitter person. I have a temper, yes, but my anger usually comes out in a fiery burst and then dissolves almost instantly. I don't stay mad at people for long—who needs that kind of negative energy in their life? And I certainly don't hold grudges.

Yet it's been two weeks since New Year's Eve, and I still can't let it go. The stupid, thoughtless, mean-spirited comments I overheard at the bar refuse to leave my mind.

He called me fluff.

He thinks I'm surface level.

*Forget him. He's not worth the mental anguish.*

Right. So what if Fitz thinks I'm superficial? He's not the first to think that, and he won't be the last. When you're a rich girl from Connecticut, people tend to assume you're a materialistic bitch.

*Says the materialistic bitch with the silver Audi,* an inner voice taunts as I reach my shiny, expensive car.

Ugh. Even my own mind is trying to make me feel bad about myself.

*It was a gift,* I remind my traitorous brain. A high school graduation gift from my parents, which makes the car three years old. That's like a senior citizen in vehicle years. And what was I supposed to do, refuse the present? I'm my dad's baby girl, his little princess. He's going to spoil me whether I like it or not.

But having a nice car doesn't make me surface level.

Having an interest in fashion and being part of a sorority doesn't make me surface level.

*Forget him.*

I click the key fob to unlock the car door. But I don't get into the driver's seat. Something keeps my boots planted to the asphalt.

I believe that something is called: *oh sweet baby Jesus, I don't want to go home and see the guy who thinks I'm fluff.*

It's hard to believe that two weeks ago I was excited about seeing Fitzy.

Now I'm dreading it. My unicorn is no longer a unicorn. He's a judgmental donkey.

I press the *lock* button. Screw it. Maybe I'll grab a coffee from the Coffee Hut first. I'm not ready to see him yet.

*Coward.*

I quickly unlock the car. I'm not a coward. I'm Summer Heyward-Di Laurentis and I don't give a flying hoot what Colin Fitzgerald thinks about me.

I lock the car.

Because clearly I *do* care what he thinks.

I unlock the car.

Because I shouldn't care.

Lock.

Unlock.

Lock.

Unlock.

"Okay! This looks like fun!" exclaims a highly amused voice. "Let me guess—your ex's car?"

I jump in surprise. I was so focused on the stupid key fob that I didn't even notice the girl approach me. "What? No. It's mine."

A pair of dark eyebrows furrow at me. "Really? What's with the maniacal clicking, then?"

I'm equally confused. "Why would it be my ex's car? What did you think I was doing to it?"

"Draining the key battery so he wouldn't be able to unlock it later. I figured you stole his keys and were looking for a way to screw him."

"Are you kidding? That sounds like the most exhausting payback scheme ever. I'd have to stand out here for hours to drain this thing. If I wanted revenge, I'd just slash a tire or two. Fast and effective."

"Tire slashing? That's insane and I love it." She nods in approval, causing her thick chestnut-brown hair to fall over one shoulder. "Anyway. Enjoy whatever the hell it is you're doing, crazy girl. Later."

The brunette starts to walk off.

"Hey," I call after her. "You need a ride somewhere?"

Awesome. I'm offering rides to complete strangers now? The level of dread Fitzy has instilled in me is off the charts.

She turns with a laugh. "Thanks, but I'm going to Hastings," she says, referring to the nearest town. It's a short drive from campus and also happens to be my destination.

"I'm going there too," I blurt out. It's a sign—I'm not supposed to go home yet. The universe wants me to give this chick a ride first.

She slowly walks back to me, shrewd brown eyes studying me from head to toe. I'm fairly sure I couldn't appear any more harmless. My hair is thrown up in a messy bun, and I'm wearing a cream-colored pea coat, dark-blue skinny jeans, and brown leather riding boots. I look like I stepped off the pages of a Gap catalogue.

"I won't murder you," I say helpfully. "If anything, I should be worried about my own safety. Those heels look lethal."

Actually, *she* looks lethal. She's got black leggings on, a black coat, and black boots with those deadly four-inch heels. A red knit hat covers her head, with her dark hair streaming out from under it, and she's wearing bright red lipstick even though it's only noon.

She's such a badass, and I think I love her.

"I'm Summer," I add. "I transferred here from Brown, and I just moved into a townhouse in Hastings."

She purses her lips for a moment before answering. "I'm Brenna. I live in town too." She shrugs and marches to the passenger's side door. "Unlock it for real this time, crazy girl. I'll take that ride."

# 6
# SUMMER

"So, not that I'm complaining—trust me, I'm happy not to pay for an Uber or campus taxi—but do you always pick up random chicks in parking lots?" Brenna asks cheerfully.

I snort. "No. And FYI, this isn't a pick-up. I mean, you're gorgeous, but I like men."

"Ha. I like men too. And even if I did like women, you wouldn't be my type, Malibu Barbie."

"You've got the wrong coast—I'm from Greenwich, Connecticut," I shoot back, but I'm smiling because I heard the humor in her tone. "And no, I don't usually invite stranger danger into my life." I decide to be honest. "I'm doing everything in my power not to go home."

"Oooh. Intriguing. Why's that?" Brenna shifts in the passenger seat, angling her black-clad body so she's better able to study me. I can feel her eyes boring into the side of my head.

I keep my gaze on the road. It's two very narrow lanes, and there's a dusting of snow on the ground, so I'm driving carefully. I already have two fender benders on my record, both of which happened while driving in winter weather, when I didn't give myself enough room to stop.

"I moved in a few days ago," I tell her. "My roommates have been out of town—they went on a ski trip to Vermont or something. So I've had the place to myself. But they texted this morning to say they're on their way back." I suppress a nervous shiver. "They might even be there now."

"So? What do we have against the roomies? Are they assholes?"

*One of them is.*

"It's a long story."

Brenna laughs. "We're strangers who just committed to a car ride together. What else are we going to talk about, the weather? Tell me why you don't like these chicks."

"Dicks," I correct.

"Huh?"

"My roommates are guys. Three guys."

"Oh *hell* yes. Tell me more. Are they hot?"

I can't help but laugh. "Very hot. But it's a messed-up situation. I made out with one of them on New Year's Eve."

"And? I don't see the problem."

"It was a mistake." I bite my lip. "I had a crush on one of the other two, but I overheard him talking shit about me, and I was upset, so…"

"So you revenge-kissed his roomie. Gotcha."

There's no judgment in her tone, but I still feel defensive. "It wasn't a revenge kiss. It was…" I make an aggravated noise. "It was actually a very good kiss."

"But you wouldn't have done it if you weren't mad at the other one."

"Probably not," I admit, slowing down as we approach an intersection with a red light.

"What kind of shit was he saying?" she asks curiously.

My foot shakes on the brake pedal as I relive the hurt and embarrassment of walking out of the restroom and overhearing Fitzy's conversation with Garrett at the bar. It wasn't being called "fluff" that upset me, so much as the fact that he was standing there listing all the reasons why he would never, ever date someone like me.

"He told his friend that I'm surface level." My face heats up. "He thinks I've got zero substance, and that I'm a party girl, and he said he'd never go out with me."

"What the fuck." Brenna smacks her palm on her thigh. "Screw. Him."

"Right?"

"Oh my God, and now you have to live with the creep?" Genuine sympathy rings in her voice. "That's the worst. I'm so sorry."

"Yeah, it sucks. I'm…" Frustration jams in my throat like a wad of gum. "I'm mad, obviously. But I'm also super disappointed in him."

"Jesus, you sound like my father." She deepens her voice and mimics her dad. "*I'm not mad at you, Brenna. I'm just…disappointed.* Ugh. I hate that."

"Sorry." I giggle. "It's true, though. I am disappointed. I thought he was a nice guy, and I liked him. I was convinced he was going to make a move on me—he was sending out vibes, you know? And I totally would've done more than make out with him." I glance over sheepishly. "That's huge for me. I don't ever sleep with someone before I've been on a date with them. And even then, it's usually several dates before I put out."

"Prude," she cracks.

"Hey, I might burn down sorority houses, but I'm an old-fashioned girl at heart."

Brenna hoots in delight. "Okay—we *will* be circling back to that sorority-house comment, oh trust me, we fucking will. But let's stay on the topic at hand. So you don't typically give your flower to a boy until he proves that he's a prince, but you would've gladly offered this jerk your entire lady garden. Except then he revealed his true colors and you hooked up with his friend instead."

"Pretty much." I flash back to the moment Hunter Davenport stopped me from leaving the bar. I'd been making my way through the crowd toward the exit. Fitzy's comments to Garrett had been so hurtful, I was actually going to bail on New Year's Eve. But then I bumped into Hunter, and he said something to make me laugh. I don't even remember what it was. The next thing I knew, the count-down reached the last second, and Hunter pulled me into his arms and kissed me.

It was hot. He was a fabulous kisser and hard as a rock as he ground up against me. I can't say I regret it, because I really did enjoy it at the time.

But at the time, I also hadn't anticipated I'd end up living with the guy.

Dean arranged everything without consulting me first, though in all honesty there's no scenario in which I *wouldn't* have jumped at the chance to move into Dean's old house. Not only is it a million times better than the dorms, but finding anything else in Hastings would be insanely tough. Maybe a tiny basement apartment, but even those get snatched up fast. Available housing is hard to come by in a town this small.

The only downside is that I now have to live with the guy I kissed.

And the guy who, at one point, I'd desperately *wanted* to kiss.

And Hollis, but he's harmless because I haven't kissed him nor have I ever wanted to.

Brenna looks over. "Did y'all—"

"Y'all?" I tease.

She grins. "My mother was from Georgia. 'Y'all' is the only piece of the South I inherited from her."

"Was?"

The mood sobers slightly. "She passed away when I was seven."

"I'm sorry. That must have been rough." My life would literally be in shambles if I didn't have my mom. She's my rock.

"It was." Brenna quickly switches the topic back. "Anyway. Did y'all know you'd be living together before New Year's?"

"No way. I wouldn't have done anything—with either one of them—if I'd known. That's setting myself up for a whole lot of awkward. It's already going to be an adjustment living with three boys after spending two and a half years in a sorority house full of girls."

"Okay, but obviously the boys don't think it's awkward, otherwise they wouldn't have agreed to let you move in. They all agreed to it, right?"

"Right." Although, I'd actually only spoken to Mike Hollis, and exchanged a few texts with Hunter, who, blessedly, didn't bring up our make-out session. "I've been in contact with two of them. No contact with Fitz, though."

From the corner of my eye, I see Brenna's head whip in my direction. "Did you say Fitz?"

Uh-oh.

Panic tugs at my stomach. Does she know him? I guess it's not inconceivable that she might. Fitz isn't exactly the most common of nicknames.

Luckily, I'm presented with the perfect opportunity to change the subject, because we've just reached Hastings' idyllic Main Street.

"I can't get over how cute this town is," I chirp, avoiding Brenna's gaze by focusing on the shops and restaurants lining the street. "Oh, cool! I didn't know there was a movie theater." It's a lie. Of course I knew. It took me all of five minutes to explore Hastings and its "attractions."

"It doesn't offer a great selection. Only three screens." She points to a storefront just past the town square. "I'm meeting my friends at Della's Diner. It's right up there."

I haven't been to Della's yet, but I plan to. Apparently, it's a '50s-themed place where the waitresses wear old-fashioned uniforms. I heard they serve a gazillion different kinds of pie.

"The guy who was trash-talking you—his name is Fitz?"

Dammit. I was hoping I'd succeeded in distracting her. But she's back on the scent.

"Yes," I admit. "It's a nickname, though."

"Short for Fitzgerald? First name Colin?"

Shit.

I narrow my eyes at her. "You're not an ex of his or something, are you?"

"No. But we're friends. Well, friendly. Fitzy's a hard guy to be friends with."

"Why's that?"

"Mysterious, the strong, silent type, et cetera et cetera." She pauses for a beat. "He's also not someone I could ever see talking trash about a girl. Or anyone, for that matter."

My jaw tightens. "I'm not making it up, if that's what you're implying."

"Didn't think you were," she says lightly. "I can spot a liar from a mile away, and you sound genuinely beat up about this. I don't think you would've made out with the other one if—oh man, is Davenport the other one? Hunter Davenport, right? He's the one you hooked up with?"

I've never felt more uncomfortable in my life. I grit my teeth as I pull up in front of the diner, stopping at the curb without killing the engine. "Here we are."

Brenna completely ignores the fact that we've arrived. It's like she's talking to herself. "Yeah, of course it was Hunter. I can't see you hooking up with Hollis—he's so annoying. He'd probably be whispering the douchiest things the whole time."

I sigh. "So you know Hunter and Hollis too?"

She rolls her eyes. "I know all of them. My dad's Chad Jensen."

I blank on the name. "Who?"

"The head coach of the men's hockey team? I'm Brenna Jensen."

"Coach Jensen is your father?"

"Yup. He's—" Her jaw opens in outrage. "Wait a minute—did you say they were *skiing* this week? Those assholes! They're not allowed to be doing that in the middle of the season. My dad will kill them if he finds out."

Dammit, that's totally on me. I hadn't expected Brenna to know who I was talking about when I mentioned the ski trip.

"He's not going to find out," I say firmly. "Because you're not going to say anything."

"I won't," she assures me, but her tone is absentminded. She's busy staring at me again, this time in complete bewilderment. "I don't get it. How on earth did a sorority girl from Brown end up moving in with three hockey players? Who, by the way, are eligible bachelors with a capital B. Every puck bunny in a fifty-mile radius is in serious pursuit of a Briar hockey player, 'cause so many of them end up in the NHL."

"They're friends with my older brother. He played hockey here last year."

"Who's your brother?" she demands.

"Dean Heyward-Di Lau—"

"Laurentis," she finishes with a gasp. "Oh my God, I *totally* see the resemblance now. You're Dean's sister."

I nod uneasily. I hope to hell she's not one of Dean's former hook-ups. He was a major player before he fell for Allie. I don't even want to know how many broken hearts he left in his manwhore wake.

Brenna blanches as if she's read my mind. "Oh, no. Don't worry. I never went out with him. I didn't even go to Briar before this year."

"You didn't?"

"No. I did two years of community college in New Hampshire," she explains. "Transferred here in September. I'm a junior, but technically a freshman since it's my first year." She suddenly jerks in her seat as if her purse just bit her. "Hold on. Phone's vibrating."

I wait impatiently as she checks her phone. I need more details from this chick—ASAP. What are the chances that of all the random strangers I could've offered a ride to, I picked the daughter of Fitzy's hockey coach? And this might be her first year at Briar, but clearly she knows a lot about her father's players, including my brother, who she hasn't even met.

Brenna types out a quick text. "Sorry. My friends are demanding to know where I am. I should get going."

I glare at her. "Are you for real? You can't just drop the coach's-daughter bomb on me and then *leave*. I want every last bit of information you have on these guys."

She grins. "Well, duh. Clearly we need to hang out again. I'd invite you to have lunch with us right now, but I'm not an enabler."

"What's that supposed to mean?"

"It means you need to go home and face your roommates. Get the big awkward confrontation out of the way." She plucks my phone out of its dashboard stand. "I'm texting myself from your phone so you have my number. Come to the game with me tomorrow night?"

"Game?"

"Briar's playing Harvard. My dad expects me to be at all the home games and any away games that are within an hour's drive of campus."

"Seriously? What if you have other plans?"

"Then he cuts off my allowance."

"Are you—"

"Fucking with you? Yes." She shrugs. "If I'm busy, I don't go. If I'm not busy, I go. He doesn't ask much of me, and I love hockey and cute boys, so it's not exactly a hardship on my part."

"Good point."

Her phone buzzes again—this time from the text she's just sent from mine. "There. We're in each other's phones. We'll start planning the wedding next week."

I snicker.

"Thanks for the lift." She hops out of the car and starts to close the door, but then abruptly pokes her head back in. "Hey, whose jersey should I wear tomorrow night? Fitzy's or Davenport's?" She blinks innocently.

With a scowl, I flip up my middle finger. "Not funny."

"That was hilarious and you know it. See you tomorrow, crazy girl."

I watch enviously as she dashes into the diner. I'd love to be having lunch and eating pie right now. But Brenna's right—I can't keep putting it off.

It's time to go home.

# 7
# FITZ

THERE'S A SHINY AUDI IN THE DRIVEWAY WHEN WE PULL UP. MY shoulders tighten, and I hope Hunter doesn't notice the reaction. I don't glance at the driver's seat to gauge *his* reaction, because I'm sure he's thrilled to see Summer's car. At least I assume it's Summer's. I stowed my beat-up Honda in the one-car garage before we left for Vermont, so there's nowhere else she could've parked.

Besides, it's a fucking Audi.

Hunter parks the Land Rover behind the silver car and addresses us in a stern voice. "This stays between us."

"Obvs." Hollis yawns loudly and unbuckles his seatbelt. He slept like a rock in the backseat the entire drive home.

"I'm not joking. If this gets back to Coach…"

"It won't," Hollis assures him. "This trip didn't happen. Right, Fitz?"

I nod grimly. "Didn't happen."

"Good. But let's go over our story in case he asks at practice tomorrow." Hunter kills the engine. "We were in New Hampshire with Mike's folks. We chilled by the fire, sat in the hot tub, played Monopoly."

"I won," Hollis pipes up.

I roll my eyes. Of course he has to be the winner of this fictional Monopoly game.

"Naah, *I* won," I say smugly. "I bought Boardwalk and put eight hotels on it."

"Screw that. I owned Boardwalk."

"Nobody owned Boardwalk," Hunter grumbles. "We didn't play Monopoly."

He's right. We were skiing, aka the stupidest thing we could ever do, seeing as how we're midseason. But Hollis, Hunter, and I are not exactly the best influences on each other. We all grew up on the East Coast and love winter sports, so when Hollis suggested a secret ski trip over break, it sounded like too much fun to miss out on.

Coach will be livid if he finds out, though. As hockey players, we can't do anything that might jeopardize our bodies or our season. A drunken ski weekend in Vermont? Cardinal sin.

But sometimes you've got to prioritize fun, right?

And no, I didn't agree to the trip just to delay seeing Summer. Because that's pitiful and stupid, and I'm neither pitiful nor stupid.

So what if she hooked up with Hunter? She's not my type, anyway. And now I get to pay less rent. Win-win.

"Okay, so we've got the story straight? New Hampshire. Fire, hot tub, Monopoly, hot chocolate."

"Hot chocolate?!" Hollis screams. "What the hell! You're throwing a whole new plot twist into this. I don't know if I'll be able to remember."

I start laughing.

Hunter shakes his head at us. "You guys have been playing for Jensen a whole year longer than me—you of all people should know what'll happen if he finds out we were partying this weekend. The skiing's bad enough. The booze and weed might be worse in his book."

Hollis and I sober up. He's got a point. The last time a player was caught partying, he was kicked off the team. That player happened to be Dean, who took some molly at a party and then failed a piss test the next day.

Not that we did anything like MDMA this weekend. Just a

few beers, one joint, and a bunch of tricks on the slopes that we probably—fine, that we absolutely shouldn't have tried.

"Let's go in. Can't keep our new roomie waiting." Hollis is downright gleeful, his grin eating up his entire face.

Hunter gives him a dark look as he hops out of the Rover. "Hands off."

"No way. You can't call dibs."

"First of all, she's not a piece of meat. She's our roommate." Hunter flicks up one eyebrow. "But if we are calling dibs, I'm pretty sure mine was implied when I had my tongue in her mouth."

My teeth clench of their own volition.

"True." Hollis sighs in defeat. "I'll back off."

The muscles in my jaw relax as I snicker. He says that as if he ever stood a chance. Hollis is a good-looking guy, but he's a total bro, not to mention obnoxious. A girl like Summer would never go for him.

"Thank you," Hunter mocks. "That's so generous of you, Mike. Truly, I'm touched."

"I'm a good friend," Hollis agrees.

As we trudge up the front stoop, there's no mistaking the glint of anticipation in Hunter's eyes, which is to be expected. I saw his face when Dean called and said Summer needed a place to live. It was obvious he couldn't wait for a repeat performance of New Year's Eve.

Since I've got a practical head on my shoulders, I swallowed my feelings on the matter and warned Hunter that whatever happens with him and Summer, it can't affect our living arrangements because her name is on the lease now. He assured us it wouldn't.

As if he's already sure something *will* happen between them.

Whatever. I don't care if it does. Let them hook up. I've got better things to focus on.

I sling my duffel over my shoulder and wait for Hollis to unlock the front door. Inside, I drop the bag with a thud and kick off my boots. The others do the same.

"Honey, we're home!" Hollis shouts.

Laughter echoes from upstairs.

My pulse speeds up when her footsteps approach the landing. She appears at the railing in fleece pants and a Briar sweatshirt, her hair up in a messy twist.

Hollis' eyes glaze over. There's nothing indecent about Summer's outfit, but this girl could make a burlap sack look sexy.

"Hey. Welcome home!" she says cheerfully.

"Hey," I call up to her. My voice sounds strained.

Hunter shrugs out of his coat and tosses it on the hook. "Blondie," he drawls. "Glad you're here."

Hollis nods. "For real."

"Aw, thanks. I'm glad to be here."

"Hold on. You need a proper hello." Grinning, Hunter bounds up the stairs.

Her cheeks go a little pink as he draws her into his arms for a hug.

I wrench my gaze away and pretend to be really focused with the task of hanging up my jacket. I don't know if he kisses her or not, but Summer is still blushing when I force myself to turn back.

"Gonna get changed," Hunter says.

He ducks into his room, and Hollis wanders off to the kitchen. Which means Summer and I are alone when I reach the second-floor landing.

She watches me warily. "Did you guys have a good time?"

I nod.

"Cool." She edges toward her open bedroom door.

I peer past her slender shoulder and spot a perfectly made bed with a white duvet and about a hundred throw pillows. There's a neon-pink beanbag chair on the floor, along with a shaggy white rug. An open laptop sits on a small corner desk that wasn't there when Dean inhabited the room.

She's made herself at home.

*This is her home*, a voice reminds me.

"Thanks for letting me—" She corrects herself. "—for agreeing to have me as a roommate."

I shrug. "No prob. We needed a fourth."

She's still inching away, as if she doesn't want to be near me. I wonder if she's remembering how she practically threw herself at me on New Year's Eve and then ended up playing tonsil hockey with my teammate.

Not that I'm bitter or anything.

"Anyway..." She trails off.

"Yeah. I..." I start traveling backward too. "I'm gonna grab a shower. We got one last run in—ah, round of Monopoly," I amend, "before we left and I'm all sweaty."

Summer raises her eyebrows. "I didn't realize Monopoly was so strenuous."

Hunter snickers from his doorway.

I turn to glare at him, because he's the one who came up with the Monopoly alibi in the first place, but he's not there. He's moved past the doorway as he shrugs into a shirt.

"Board games are intense," I answer lamely. "At least the way we play 'em."

"Interesting. I can't wait for roomie game night, then." Her shoulder bumps the door as her backward journey ends. "Enjoy your shower, Fitz."

She disappears into her bedroom, and I lumber into mine. When my phone buzzes, I almost fall over with relief. I need the distraction before I start thinking too hard about how fucking awkward that whole encounter was.

The text on the screen makes me grin.

Still stuck at the 3rd gate! I fckn hate u, bro.

Rather than text back, I call my buddy. Morris is a fellow gamer, a good friend, and currently demo'ing the role-playing game I spent the past two years designing.

"Yo!" Morris answers immediately. "How do I get into the City of Steel, dammit?"

I snicker. "Like I'm going to tell you."

"But I've been stuck here since last night."

"I literally sent you the link last night. The fact that you've already made it to the city is wicked impressive." I shake my head. "I haven't checked the message boards today, but last I saw, none of the other betas were even close to passing the village level."

"Well, yeah. That's because I'm superior to them in every way. I'm the only one whose opinion matters."

"And your opinion so far?"

"This game is boss."

Excitement gathers inside me. I love hearing that, especially from a dedicated gamer like Morris, whose Twitch stream earns him a shit ton of money. Yup, people actually subscribe to watch him play video games online. He's that good, not to mention incredibly entertaining as he livestreams his virtual adventures.

Not to toot my own horn, but I'm a bit of a legend too. Not from livestreaming, but reviewing. Up until this year, I reviewed games for the college blog, as well as other hugely popular gaming sites on the web. But I stopped reviewing because it was a time suck, and I needed to concentrate on my own game.

*Legion 48* isn't the most complex of RPGs; it's not multiplayer and it follows a very scripted storyline rather than an open-world concept. With my schedule, it's hard enough to find time to play video games, let alone design them. But I'm in the process of applying for jobs at several game-development companies, and I needed to give them a taste of what I'm capable of in terms of design techniques. *Legion 48* might not be *Skyrim* or *GTA,* but all I need it to do is show these studios I'm not a total hack.

My greatest strength, I think, is that I did all the artwork myself along with the computer coding required to make the game functional. All of the art started out as rough sketches, was then drawn digitally, then turned into 3D assets. I can't even calculate how much time I spent on it, and that was nowhere close to how long it took to code the damn thing.

"Run into any bugs yet?" I ask Morris.

"Nothing major. When you speak to the dragon in the cave, the dialogue freezes up and then jumps to the next bit."

All right. Easy fix. A relief, because it took hours upon hours to refine and hammer out all the pesky bugs in the alpha stage. For nearly a year, the game was barely playable. The first round of beta testing shed light on more bugs I'd missed. Somehow, despite my grueling schedule, I debugged the game enough to make it fully functional and ready for this second and final round of beta testing. This time, dozens of gamers are playing, including many of my college friends.

"Hasn't crashed yet," he adds helpfully.

"Yet? Don't jinx it, man. I've sent this thing to half a dozen studios. If it crashes on them…"

"Hasn't crashed, period," Morris corrects. "Won't crash, ever. Now tell me how to open the third gate."

"Nope."

"But I'm dying to see the City of Steel. Is there an oracle I'm supposed to talk to? Why can't I find this key?"

"Guess you're not as good as you think you are."

"Oh, fuck off. Fine. Whatever. I'm gonna beat this thing and then call you to gloat."

"You do that." I grin to myself. "I'll find you online later. Jumping in the shower now."

"Cool. Ciao."

I strip out of my clothes and head for the bathroom, a spring to my step. Morris's enthusiasm for *Legion 48* managed to ease the tension plaguing my body.

But my muscles tense up again at the sound of Summer's laughter in the hall.

I gaze at my reflection in the mirror, noting the frustration in my eyes, the rigid set of my jaw. The harsh expression seems even harsher when paired with my tattoos—the two full sleeves covering my arms, and the chest piece that's done only in black. The piece is a bit faded now, though that almost gives it a cooler vibe. Not that I got tatted up because it's cool. I'm an artist. I designed all the tats myself, and whatever I can use as a canvas, I'll use. Including my own skin.

But when my face is surly, and my beard is growing out, and I'm brooding in front of the mirror, all the ink just makes me look like a thug.

If I'm being honest, "thug" is kind of what I was going for during my brief high school rebellion. I got my first tat—the dragon on my left arm—when I was hanging with the dudes whose go-to solution for solving problems involved their fists. Or brass knuckles. Don't get me wrong—they didn't pressure me to get inked. They just knew of a parlor that tattooed minors without their parents' permission. Because, truthfully, the first time was essentially a fuck-you to my folks. My sophomore art class had just put on an end-of-year exhibition, where Mom and Dad spent the whole time sniping at each other instead of supporting their kid. They walked right past my paintings, too busy arguing to notice my work.

So fifteen-year-old Colin, badass that he was, decided, *Fine. You guys are too busy fighting to appreciate my art, so I'll put it right where you can see it.*

These days, I do view the tats as an extension of my art, but I can't deny it didn't start out that way.

My shoulders tighten when I hear the low murmur of Hunter's voice. Followed by another laugh from Summer.

Guess he's picking up right where he left off.

# 8
# SUMMER

THAT WASN'T TOO BAD. I MANAGED TO EXCHANGE SEVERAL cordial sentences with Fitz without smacking him in his dumb face. Gold star for me! Except then take away my gold star and replace it with three rotten bananas because of the way my vagina responded to that dumb face.

It tingled.

Stupid vagina.

I *hate* that I still find him attractive after all the hurtful comments he made about me.

A knock on the door spares me from what probably would've been a solid hour of overthinking. Hunter saunters into the room and throws his lean, muscular body onto my bed.

"I need a nap."

My mouth quirks in a wry smile. "Sure, go ahead and make yourself at home."

"Aw, thanks, Blondie." He winks, and proceeds to get even more comfortable by sprawling on his back and propping his arms behind his head.

*Um, two tickets to the gun show, please.* His arms are incredible. He's changed into a wife beater that shows off defined biceps and broad shoulders. And his sweatpants ride low enough on his hips that I can see the smooth, tanned stretch of man vee. It's just as tantalizing as the gun show.

Hunter is hot and he knows it. His lips curve when he notices me checking him out.

Ugh, those lips. I still remember how they'd felt pressed against mine. He was a good kisser. Not too aggressive, not too eager, the perfect amount of tongue.

I wonder how Fitzy kisses.

*Like a jerk, Summer,* my inner Selena Gomez says firmly. *He kisses like a jerk.*

Right. Because he's a jerk.

"Why are you in my room, Hunter?" I ask, leaning a hip against my desk.

"Figured we should tackle the Big Talk right out of the gate."

I sigh ruefully. "Good idea."

"A'ight. Let's do it."

I graciously gesture toward him. "Men first."

He snorts. "Coward."

Laughing, I hop up and sit on the desk. "Honestly? I don't even know what to say. We made out. It wasn't a big deal."

His dark eyes zero in on my bare legs, which are dangling over the edge of the desk. It's obvious he likes what he sees, because his gaze turns molten. He reminds me a bit of Dean's friend Logan, and not just because they look similar with their dark hair and hard bodies. Logan radiates sexual energy. I don't know how to describe it, but there's just something so raw and dirty about him. Hunter gives off that same vibe, and I can't deny it affects me.

But just because we find each other attractive doesn't mean we have to do anything about it.

"I know we texted a few times after that night, but I felt like there was more to talk about. You never really told me what it—" He stops abruptly.

I wrinkle my forehead. "I never told you what?"

He sits up and drags a hand over his scalp. He's buzzed his hair since I last saw him, but it's still long enough to rake his fingers through. "I was about to ask you what it meant." He stares at me in horror. "I've become my worst nightmare."

I burst out laughing. "Oh, honey. It's okay—lots of men try to find meaning in New Year's kisses." I give him a pointed look.

He groans. "Don't rub it in, Blondie."

"Sorry, I had to. You were so cocky that night, acting like any girl you kissed at midnight would demand to have your babies." I stick out my tongue. "Well, who's the one who wants to have *my* babies? You!"

His shoulders shake with laughter.

I slide off the desk. "Tables have turned," I say in a singsong voice.

Hunter gets to his feet. He's taller than I remember, standing at well over six feet. Same with Fitz, but I suppose most hockey players have the height advantage. There's one guy on the Briar team who's five-nine, though. I think his name is Wilkins. One time I heard Dean raving about how tough he is considering his size.

"Don't worry," Hunter says. "I'm not thinking about babies just yet."

"No? What are you thinking about, then?"

He doesn't respond. Those dark eyes lower to my chest before flicking back to my face. I'm not wearing a bra. He definitely noticed.

And I'm definitely noticing that his sweatpants seem a bit tighter in the crotch area than they were two minutes ago.

When he notices *me* noticing, he coughs and angles his body slightly.

A sigh flutters out of my throat. "You're not going to make this weird, are you?"

Two ridiculously adorable dimples cut into his chiseled cheeks. "Define weird."

"I don't know. Be awkward? Tiptoe around me?"

He takes another step toward me. "Does it look like I'm tiptoe-ing?" he drawls.

My heart beats faster. Damn, he's smooth. "Okay. Then are you going to get all lovesick? Write poetry about me and cook me breakfast?"

"Poetry isn't my style. And I can't cook for shit." He edges closer, until our faces are inches apart. "I'm happy to make you coffee in the morning, though."

"I don't drink coffee," I say smugly.

His answering chuckle brings out his dimples again. "I can already tell you're going to make this hard for me, eh?"

"This?" I echo warily. "And what exactly is *this*?"

He slants his head, contemplating for a beat. "I don't know yet," he admits. His breath tickles my ear as he leans in to murmur into it. "But I'm kind of excited to find out."

Hunter's fingertips lightly graze my bare arm. Then, before I can blink, he's sliding out the door.

---

My new neighborhood is a vow of silence convent compared to the Kappa house at Brown. At one in the morning, the only sound beyond my bedroom window is the occasional cricket. No car engines, no music, no shrieky drunken sorority girls or loud-mouthed frat boys egging each other on during a rowdy game of beer pong.

I have to admit, I find it unsettling. Silence is not my friend. Silence forces you to examine your own mind. To face the thoughts you pushed aside during the day or the worries you hoped would go away, the secrets you tried to keep.

I'm not a fan of my own thoughts. They tend to be a jumble of insecurity, mixed with self-doubt, a splash of inner critic, and a sprin-kling of misplaced over-confidence. It's a fucked-up place, my mind.

I roll over and groan into my pillow. The muffled noise is like a blast of gunfire in the eerily quiet room. I can't sleep. I've been tossing and turning since eleven thirty and it's really starting to tick me off. I slept just fine when the guys were in Vermont. I don't get why their presence ought to change that.

Trying to force sleep is pointless, so I kick the comforter off and stumble out of bed. Screw it. I'm getting something to eat. Maybe it'll send me into a food coma afterward.

Since I sleep in nothing but panties, I grab the first item of clothing I find. It happens to be a thin white T-shirt that shows the outline of my nipples and barely covers my thighs. I slip it on anyway, because I doubt my roomies will be awake to see it. Hunter said they have a six a.m. practice.

But I'm wrong. One roomie is very much awake.

Fitzy and I both release startled noises when our gazes collide in the kitchen.

"Shit," I curse. "You scared me."

"Sorry. And ditto." He's sitting at the table, long legs resting on the chair beside him, a sketchpad in his lap.

Oh, and he's shirtless.

As in, not wearing a shirt.

I can't even.

I wrestle my gaze off his bare chest, but it's too late. Every detail has already been branded in my brain. The full-sleeve tats covering his arms. The black swirl of ink that stretches along his collarbone and stops just above his heavy pecs. His abs are so chiseled it looks like someone drew them on with a contouring brush. Like Hunter, he's all muscle and no fat, but while Hunter's chest triggered appreciation and some tingles, Fitz unleashes a flurry of shivers and a tight clench of need.

I want to put my mouth on him. I want to trace every line and curve of his tats with my tongue. I want to grab his sketchpad and whip it aside so I could be the one in his lap. Preferably with my lips glued to his and my hand wrapped around his dick.

God help me.

I don't get it. He's not my usual type at all. I've been surrounded by prep school boys my whole life, and that's what I'm typically drawn to—polo shirts, clean-shaven faces, and million-dollar smiles. Not tattoos and scruff.

"Can't sleep?" he says lightly.

"No," I admit. I open the fridge and scan the contents for something appetizing. "How about you?"

"I should've turned in about an hour ago, but I wanted to finish this sketch before bed 'cause I won't have time to do it tomorrow."

I settle on some yogurt and granola, glancing over at Fitz as I prepare a bowl. "What are you drawing?"

"Just something for a video game I'm working on." He snaps the sketchbook closed, even though I wasn't trying to sneak a peek at it.

"Right. Dean mentioned you're a gamer. I thought you just reviewed games, though. You design them too?"

"Only one so far. Working on a second one now," he says vaguely.

He obviously doesn't want to discuss it, so I shrug and say, "Cool. Sounds interesting." I perch against the counter and swallow a spoonful of yogurt.

Silence falls over the kitchen. I watch him as I eat, and he watches me eat. It's both painfully uncomfortable and strangely comfortable. Figure that one out.

So many questions bite at my tongue, most of them relating to New Year's Eve.

*Were you really not into me that night? Did I just imagine the interested vibes? Do you truly believe all those shitty things you said about me?*

I don't voice a single one. I refuse to reveal even a hint of vulnerability to this guy. He's not allowed to know how much his judgmental words hurt me.

Instead, I put him in the hot seat for something else.

"You weren't supposed to be skiing."

He blows out a quick breath. "No, we weren't."

"So why did you?"

"Because we're idiots."

I smile, then get mad at myself for smiling at something he said.

"Coach would freak if he found out. The other guys too, if I'm being honest. It was a real dick move on our parts," he says roughly. "So let's keep the ski trip between us, okay?"

Um…

I give him a sheepish look. "Too late."

"What do you mean?" His tone has sharpened.

"I accidentally became best friends with your coach's daughter earlier today. And I accidentally told her you guys went skiing."

He gapes at me. "Fucking hell, Summer."

I'm quick to defend myself. "Hey, Hollis didn't say it was a secret when we spoke on the phone."

Fitz shakes his head a few times. "How do you *accidentally* become friends with someone?" he sputters. "And why would our ski trip even be a topic of discussion? Did Brenna say if she was going to tell Coach?"

"She promised she wouldn't."

He curses under his breath. "That's no guarantee. Brenna's dangerous when she loses her temper. Never know what'll come out of her mouth."

"She won't tell," I assure him. "Like I said, we're best friends now."

His lips twitch as if he's trying not to laugh.

"I'm going to your Harvard game with her tomorrow," I add.

"Yeah?"

"Uh-huh." I finish my yogurt and walk to the sink to wash the bowl. "She's cool. We got along really well."

I hear him sigh. Loudly.

I glance over my shoulder. "What was that for?"

"It's in anticipation of all the trouble I envision you and Brenna getting into. I predict you two are gonna be terrible influences on each other."

I can't help but laugh. "That is a possibility."

He sighs again. "An eventuality. I can already see it."

Grinning, I turn off the faucet and set the clean bowl in the drying rack. My heart somersaults when Fitzy's footsteps come up behind me.

"'Scuse me, just grabbing a glass," he murmurs. One long arm stretches out toward the cupboard, inches from my cheek.

His scent tickles my nostrils. Woodsy with a hint of citrus. He smells so good.

I wipe my hands on a dishtowel and turn to face him. His breath hitches slightly, dark eyes flicking toward my chest before hastily dropping to the glass in his hand.

Oh right. My T-shirt is see-through. And my nipples are hard little buds thanks to the cold water my hands were submerged in a minute ago. Well, that's why they *were* hard. Now they're poking through my shirt for another reason.

A reason named Colin Fitzgerald, whose bare chest is so close I can touch it. Or lick it.

I think I might be in trouble. I'm still attracted to him. *Too* attracted to him. I'm not allowed to lust over someone who harbors such negative thoughts about me.

I breathe through my mouth to avoid his masculine scent, and dart away from the counter. My gaze seeks out a distraction, something to focus on that isn't Fitz's big, muscly, amazing chest. It lands on the fat paperback novel sitting next to the drawing pencils he left on the table.

"Oh!" My voice sounds overly loud. I quickly lower it before I wake Hunter and Hollis. "I love this series." I pick up the book and flip it over to skim the blurb. "Are you just starting to read it or doing a reread?"

When Fitz doesn't answer, I look over and glimpse the skepticism flickering through his expression. When he speaks, his voice is laced with the same doubt. "You've read the *Shifting Winds* books?"

"The first three. I haven't gotten around to number four yet." I hold up the paperback, which is well over a thousand pages. "I heard it's even longer than these ones."

"*Blood of the Dragon*? Yeah, it's double the length," he says absently. Still eyeing me uncertainly. "I can't believe you read this series."

A frown forms on my lips. "Why's that?"

"It's just really dense, and…" He trails off awkwardly.

It takes a second for the implication to sink in.

It's not that he can't believe I've read these books.

It's that he *doesn't believe* I've read these books.

Indignation rises in my chest and sticks to my throat, forming a hot lump. Well, why would he, right? In his eyes, I'm *surface level*. The dumb sorority girl couldn't possibly comprehend such lengthy, dense material! Hell, he probably thinks I'm illiterate too.

A growl rips out of my mouth. "I know how to fucking read."

He startles. "What? I didn't say—"

"And just because I don't have dragons and fairies and elves tattooed all over my body, doesn't mean I'm not allowed to read fantasy books—"

"Allowed? I didn't say—"

"—however *dense* they may be," I finish with a scowl. "But it's good to know your thoughts on the matter." With a tight smile, I drop the book on the table. *Thud.* "Goodnight, Fitz. Try not to stay up too late."

"Summer—"

I'm out of the kitchen before he can say another word.

# 9
# FITZ

Pregame skates aren't usually grueling, but this morning Coach wants to run a few shooting drills he anticipates will help us tonight. Harvard has been unstoppable this year. They're well on their way to a perfect season, and although I'd never say it out loud, I think they might be the better team in this matchup.

Coach must secretly think so too, because he pushes us harder than usual. I'm a sweaty mess by the time I lumber off the ice. My hair is plastered to my forehead, and I swear there's cartoon steam rolling out of my helmet.

Coach smacks me on the shoulder. "Good hustle, Colin."

"Thanks, Coach."

"Davenport," he says to Hunter. "Show me that same ruthlessness tonight, son. Shoot *through* Johansson, not around him. Feel me?"

"Got it, Coach."

We have thirty minutes to shower and change before a mandatory meeting in the screening room to review game tape. This will be our first of two games against Harvard this season, and we want to send a message. It's an away game, to boot, so it'll be extra tough— but extra sweeter if we can get a W in their arena.

In the locker room, I strip off my sweaty practice gear and duck into the shower area. The stalls are divided by partitions and have saloon-style doors that mean we can't see each other's junk, but chests are fair game. Stepping into the stall next to Hollis, I crank the cold water and dunk my head. I swear I'm still sweating even under the cool spray.

"Are we really not gonna acknowledge the fact that Mike shaved his chest?" Dave Kelvin, a junior defenseman, demands.

Laughter bounces off the acoustic tiles. I glance at Hollis and lift a questioning brow. I've showered, worked out, and gone swimming with the guy enough times to know that he usually has hair on his chest. Now it's smoother than a baby's bottom.

Nate Rhodes, our team captain this year, grins. "Home job or salon?"

Hollis rolls his eyes at the tall senior. "Home. Why would I pay someone to do something I can do myself? That's stupid." He twists around so he can wave at Kelvin. "And you? Get off your ivory horse, dude—"

"Ivory tower," I say helpfully.

"Whatever. We all know you wax your chest *and* your back, Kelvin. Hypocritical fucktard."

I snort and rub soap over my chest. My body temperature is finally dropping.

"I don't wax my back!" Kelvin protests.

"Yes you do. Nikki Orsen ratted you out, you back-hair motherfucker."

Nikki is a right-winger on the Briar women's team. She's a great player and an awesome girl, but she also happens to be a serious blabbermouth. You can't tell her anything you don't want anyone else knowing.

As Nate and a couple other seniors hoot loudly, Kelvin's face turns beet red. "I'm gonna kill her."

"Oh relax, princess," Hunter drawls. "Every dude you see on Instagram waxes some part of his body."

"Yeah, what's the big deal?" Hollis says. "There's no shame in manscaping."

"This is a safe place," Nate agrees solemnly.

"Exactly. Safe place. We all manscape here—or at least we all fucking should if we consider ourselves fucking *gentlemen*," Hollis chides.

Swallowing a laugh, I place the soap back in its tray and start rinsing off.

"Seriously, bro, what's with the makeover?" Matt Anderson pipes up. Like Kelvin, he's a junior D-man. The two of them were beyond shitty last year, but our new defensive coach, Frank O'Shea, has been working the D-men hard all season, and he's really whipped them into shape.

"Got a date after the game tonight," Hollis reveals.

"What, the chick has something against body hair?"

"Hates it. She swallowed a pube once, and it triggered her gag reflex so she threw up all over her boyfriend's dick. And then he started ralphing too because vomit makes him vomit, and they broke up right after that."

For one long moment, the only sound in the huge room is the rushing water.

Then it transforms into the weeping laughter of a bunch of buck-ass naked dudes.

"Oh my fucking god, that is the best thing I've ever heard in my life," Hunter moans.

"She told you all this?" Our team captain is doubled over, and I can't tell if it's tears or water streaming down his face.

"Said she wouldn't even consider boning down if a guy had body hair. That includes chest, arms, legs, so…" Hollis shrugs.

"You did your arms and legs too?" Nate squawks.

Hunter laughs harder.

"Women are nuts," Kelvin grumbles.

He has a point. Women are messed up. I mean, Summer told me off last night for no good reason other than me being surprised that she'd read *Shifting Winds*.

Apparently she took that to mean that I thought she couldn't read? Seriously?

Although...fine, if I look at it from her perspective, I can see why she overreacted. Maybe it did come off a bit like I was implying she wasn't smart enough for the series or that she was lying about reading it.

That wasn't my intention, though. Those books are legitimately tough to read. Hell, I barely got through them myself, and I've been reading fantasy religiously for years.

If she'd given me a chance to respond, I could've told her that. And I would've apologized for insinuating I didn't believe her.

But, just as I've always suspected, Summer is all drama. Ten measly words could have cleared it up—*I'm sorry, I didn't mean it like that, forgive me*—if she'd let me speak. Instead, she'd stomped off like a five-year-old.

I grab a towel and hastily wrap it around my waist. *Drama*, I reiterate to myself. I'm not interested in drama. Never have been, never will be.

So why can't I get her hurt expression out of my mind?

———

Briar's top-notch hockey facility is the land of luxury. We've got state-of-the-art equipment, well-ventilated locker rooms, an awesome shower setup, a lounge, kitchen, physio rooms, whirlpool—name it, and we've got it. The viewing room is especially sweet. It resembles a small movie theater, only with three semicircular rows of tables and huge padded chairs. At the bottom of the gallery, the coaches have an A/V setup similar to that of sports announcers, with an input for laptops and a video screen they can write on. When they highlight plays or circle players, their scribbles show up on the big screen too.

I plop down in the chair next to our goalie, Patrick Corsen. "Hey."

"Hey." He's staring at the screen, which is frozen on a shot of the Harvard arena. It looks like last week's game, Harvard versus Boston College. BC got creamed that day.

Harvard is definitely the team to beat this year. In the past, they were an easy divisional opponent for us, because Briar's always had the superior program. But this season they're on fire, with more talent on the roster than ever before. After last year's seniors graduated, the lowerclassmen who didn't get a chance to shine were given more ice time, and every single one of them has stepped up. Harvard's no longer relying solely on the skill of their team captain like they did last year. Jake Connelly is damn good, but he can't carry an entire team.

"Connelly's line is wicked fast," Corsen says glumly.

"Our line is faster," I assure him, referring to me, Hunter, and Nate.

"Fine. But their second and third lines are just as fast. Can you say the same about ours?" He lowers his voice. "Plus they've got a better D. Those two sophomores? Can't remember their names, but they're so good at keeping the puck out of their zone. Takes so much heat off Johansson."

Johansson is Harvard's goalie, and he's phenomenal. Truthfully, Corsen's right to worry.

"Kelvin and Brodowski aren't that strong," he mutters.

"No," I agree. "But Matty is." I nod toward Anderson, who's texting on his phone.

Like the Harvard boys, Matt stepped up after Dean and Logan graduated. He's now the leading scorer among the defensemen and one of our best penalty killers. He's also the only black player on the team, which he's damn proud of. He's entering the draft this year and eager to make his mark in a pro league that's predominantly white.

"True. Matty's an asset," Corsen relents, but he still sounds unhappy.

I get why he's worried. He's signed by LA and playing for them next season, so it's always a concern if your draft team sees you shit the bed. A lot of the time that guarantees you a spot on the farm team, though sometimes that's the better option, truth be told. That's what Logan is doing right now, playing for the Providence Bruins and developing his skills. Not everyone is like Garrett Graham, a born superstar. And not every college player is instantly ready for the pros.

Coach marches into the room and claps his hands. "Let's get started." He doesn't shout, just uses his speaking voice, but everyone snaps to attention as if he'd screamed like a drill sergeant. Jensen is the kind of man who just commands respect. He's also a man of few words, but the words he does use wield a lot of power.

"Take a good look at this kid," he orders. He presses *play* and the picture on the screen jumps to life.

A skater, jersey number 33, whizzes across the blue line. Coach pauses the frame, draws on his tablet, and a bright red circle appears on the player like a target.

"Junior, left wing," he says briskly. "Brooks Weston."

"The goon," a sophomore pipes up.

"So?" Hollis cracks. "We've got our own goons. We can take him."

"He's more than an enforcer," Coach Jensen tells us. "He's a goddamn instigator and a scourge to this earth."

We snicker.

"This little fucker has the superhuman ability to commit infraction after infraction without being called. And he's very, very skilled at drawing penalties from other guys. His specialty is provoking fights. End result is him usually coming out smelling like roses, while the other guy draws a major or, worst case, an ejection."

A mumble of general disapproval ripples through the room, even though I'm sure we've all been guilty at one point or another of trying to provoke opponents into committing an infraction. Some players do it habitually, though, using it as a strategy. Coach Jensen doesn't believe in this strategy. If it were up to him, the NCAA would take a much stronger stance on penalty gameplay.

"No matter what trash comes out of this kid's mouth, you don't let it get to you, you hear me?" He fixes us all with a deadly look.

"I'm not scared of some rich kid with a potty mouth," drawls Kelvin.

"How do you know he's rich?" Hunter asks in amusement.

"His first name is also a last name. That usually means his parents called him that to honor two filthy-rich grandparents."

"My first name is also a last name," Hunter points out.

"Yeah, and you're filthy rich!" Hollis chimes in, snorting with laughter. "Hell, you probably know this Wesley Brooke guy."

"Brooks Weston," someone corrects.

"I do know him," Hunter admits, drawing another snort from Hollis. "We both played for Roselawn Prep. He was a couple years ahead of me."

Coach nods. "Pain in the ass, those Roselawn guys."

"I literally *just* said I went to Roselawn," Hunter protests.

"I repeat—pain in the ass, those Roselawn guys."

Hunter sighs.

We spend the next fifteen minutes analyzing the first period of the Harvard/Boston College game. Coach is right. Weston Brooks or Brooks Weston or whatever the hell his name is, is a damn nuisance. He's aggressive as hell, getting away with highsticking three minutes in, and almost instigating a fight before the buzzer. Weston manages to taunt his opponent into a couple harmless shoves, but just as the BC player is about to lunge, a teammate yanks him back. Weston is chortling as he skates off.

I dislike him already.

When the second period starts, Harvard is leading two-zip. "Does Connelly's slap shot look a lot deadlier this year or is it just me?" Kelvin asks warily, his gaze glued to the screen.

"Oh, it's deadlier," Coach confirms. "And he's even faster now.

He's scored on every breakaway he's had this season." He points a finger around the room. "Don't let him rush the net. Understood?"

There's a chorus of "Yessir."

An aforementioned breakaway kicks off the second. Sure enough, Connelly dekes out four opponents, including two defensemen who literally look like they don't know where they are. It's like this old '90s show I binge-watched last year, where the main character time-jumps into random people's bodies in order to change history. Dude spends the first five minutes of every episode trying to figure out where the hell he is and whose body he jumped into.

That's what Connelly does to these defensemen. Their heads swivel around in confusion as if they were just dropped onto the ice in the middle of a hockey game. By the time they realize what's happening, Connelly has blown past them and is already taking a shot. The puck sails into the upper left corner of the net with laser precision, like an osprey diving into the ocean to pluck up its dinner. Coach pauses on the goalie's look of sheer frustration as the lamp lights behind him.

"Beautiful shot," Nate says grudgingly.

"Yes," Coach agrees. "And I don't want to see anything like it tonight, unless it's coming from one of you. Got it?"

"Got it," everyone answers.

We settle in to examine the rest of the tape. As Coach points out what he deems to be weaknesses on Harvard's team, we hang on to his every word. We're gonna have to exploit every single weakness if we want to kick their asses tonight.

# 10

# SUMMER

"Can you believe he said that?" It's been a whole day since my kitchen encounter with Fitz, and I'm still fuming.

"Yes, I can believe it," Brenna answers irritably. "I believed it when you told me during the first period, and I believed it during the second period, and now it's the third and I still fucking believe it, so will you please, for the love of little baby Jesus, just let it go?"

"Never," I declare.

Her response is a cross between a groan and a laugh. "Omigod, you're so stubborn. Have you always been this stubborn?"

"Yup. I am stubborn. I'll own that. But you know what I won't own?" I cross my arms tight to my chest. "Being illiterate. Because I know how to read!"

Brenna stares up at the rafters as if to ask the heavens for help. Or maybe she's meditating, though that'd be difficult to do in a packed arena. Plus, we need to stay vigilant, because we showed up late and got stuck sitting in a section overrun by Harvard fans. We're two black-and-silver dots drowning in a sea of crimson.

There are tons of other fans wearing Briar colors, but most of them seem to be congregated on the other side of the arena. Despite Brenna teasing me about it yesterday, we're not wearing Briar jerseys. I'm glad for that. We've already received more than enough dirty looks for not representing the Crimson.

"Summer. Honey. He didn't accuse you of being illiterate." Brenna's tone is one you'd use on a preschooler you're teaching to paint with watercolors. Barely checked patience.

"He implied I was too stupid to read *Shifting Winds*."

"Everybody's too stupid for *Shifting Winds*!" she growls. "You honestly think all those people who claim to love the series actually read the damn books? They haven't! Because they're fucking five thousand pages long! I tried to read the first book one time, and the dickwad author spent nine pages describing a tree. *Nine pages*! Those books are the worst. The absolute worst."

She runs out of breath, grinning when she notices me laughing my butt off.

"And that was my TED Talk about *Shifting Winds*," she says graciously. "You're welcome."

My good humor doesn't last long. "He was just so condescending, Brenna."

Her tone becomes cautious. "Was he? Or are you just extra sensitive to everything he says now, because of what he said about you being surface level?"

I bite my bottom lip. It's true. I am overly sensitive these days, especially about Fitz. It's just… I keep trying to perceive myself through his eyes, and the picture that forms isn't something to be proud of.

I see a ditzy blonde who got kicked out of one sorority and banned from another, who's always on academic probation, whose father had to call in a favor to get her into college, whose brother called another one in to find her a place to live.

I see a screw-up.

With a heavy heart, I say as much to Brenna, but a roar from the crowd drowns out her response.

Her gaze hasn't left the ice once during our conversation, and now she's shooting to her feet. "Are you blind, ref!" she screams. "That was tripping!"

A group of guys a few rows behind us start cackling at her outrage. "Hey, it's not our fault your shitty players can't skate without tripping over their own feet!" one of them mocks.

"Oh, you really want to go there?" She spins around and I smother a laugh.

Aside from her silvery-gray scarf, she's wearing all black again, plus the red lipstick I'm beginning to realize is her trademark. With her dark hair loose and her eyes blazing, she looks like a total badass. She kind of resembles Gal Gadot, the actress who plays Wonder Woman. Come to think of it, she resembles the original Wonder Woman too.

AKA she's frigging gorgeous, and the boys she's glaring at do a double take when they notice who they've been heckling.

"The only shitty thing I see is the huge dump your goalie just took on the ice," she taunts back.

I snort, a chortle breaking free.

"Take a look at the scoreboard, douchenozzles, and tell me what you see," she chirps, pointing to the screens above center ice.

The score clearly reads Briar—1, Harvard—0.

None of them follow her gaze. "Watch your mouth," one snaps.

"Watch yours," she snaps back.

"Your boys are pussies," he jeers. "Standing there begging for a call instead of taking it like a man. *Oh nooo, the bad man tripped me!*"

His buddies break out in gales of laughter.

"Don't make me come up there," Brenna warns, hands planted firmly on her hips.

"Don't tempt me. I don't fight chicks, but I might make an exception for you."

"I don't hit men, either," she says sweetly. "But luckily I don't see any men around here. Do you?"

"You bitch—"

I yank on Brenna's arm and force her to sit back down. "Relax," I order. I'm acutely aware of the death glares all around us.

"They're a bunch of jerks," she grumbles. "And that ref was a dick! Anderson was totally tripped. They should've called a penalty."

"Well, they didn't. And we're about three seconds away from getting assaulted, or thrown out. So let's move on, shall we?"

"Move on, huh? You mean, what *you* should be doing right now instead of obsessing over one trivial comment?"

I clench my teeth. "Sorry if it bothers me that one of the guys I live with thinks I'm nothing but a fluffy sorority girl."

"You know who else was viewed as a fluffy sorority girl?" she challenges. "Elle Woods. And you know what she did? She went to law school and showed everyone how smart she was, and then she became a lawyer and everybody loved her, and her slimy ex tried to win her back and she sent him on his way. The end."

I have to smile, though her recap of *Legally Blonde* isn't quite a parallel of my own life, since I won't be going to law school despite the fact that everyone else in my family has. Well, except for Dean. He followed his own path, deciding at the last minute to bail on law because he realized he'd rather coach hockey and work with kids. If my parents were rich snobs with sticks up their asses, they'd no doubt be horrified that Dean Heyward-Di Laurentis became a gym teacher.

Fortunately, my parents are awesome and supportive, and now Dean's paved the way for me to be able to veer off course too.

Once I decide what I want to do, that is. I love fashion, but I don't know if I want to design clothes, and fashion merchandising doesn't interest me much, either. My goal is to see how the rest of my college career plays out before I make any final decisions. And senior year we have work placement, so I'll get an even better idea of what I like or dislike.

"It doesn't matter how other people see you," Brenna finishes. "It's how you see yourself—" She stops abruptly, then curses up a blue streak as Harvard ties up the game.

"How do you like them apples!" her new archrival yells.

"How would you like an apple shoved up your ass!" she retorts, but her tone is absent-minded, and her gaze is still glued to the game. Her eyes fill with admiration for one brief moment before narrowing angrily. "Ugh. Connelly. Why does he have to be lightning on skates?"

"That's a bad thing?"

"It is when he's on the other team."

"Oh. Whoops." It's obvious I need to study the Briar roster. I only know Fitz, Hunter, Hollis, and a couple others I met in Brooklyn on New Year's. "So he's the enemy?"

"Damn right he is. He's dangerous. If he gets you one-on-one, you're screwed. Doubly screwed if it's a breakaway." She points to Briar's side of the rink. "And so is that jerk who's got Hollis pinned behind the net. That's Weston. We don't like him either."

"I went to school with a guy named Weston. He played hockey too."

Her head swivels toward me. "Swear to God, Summer, if you say that you're friends with Brooks Weston, I'm punching you."

I stick out my tongue at her. "No, you won't. And we're totally talking about the same guy—how weird is that? I didn't realize Weston went to Harvard. For some reason I thought he was on the West Coast." When I notice her glare, I grin. "Relax, we're not BFFs or anything, but we did hang out in high school. He's a fun guy."

"He's an evil demon goon."

"Doesn't make him any less of a fun guy."

"True," she says grudgingly. "I just don't like the idea of my friends fraternizing with the enemy." She raises her index and middle finger, then points them back and forth between her eyes and mine. "I'm watching you, Greenwich Barbie."

Smiling broadly, I lean in and smack a kiss on her cheek. "I love you. You're my soul mate."

"You're such a dork." Rolling her eyes, she refocuses her attention on the game.

Watching live hockey is such a rush. It's fast-paced, intense. If you take your eyes off the ice even for a split second, you might come back to a completely different game.

Harvard was on the attack before. Now it's Briar's turn. Our forwards rush toward Harvard's zone, but they're offside.

Brenna curses impatiently. "Come on, boys!" she shouts. "Get it together!"

"Can't get nothing together when you SUCK!" her heckler crows.

She gives him the finger without turning around.

There's a face-off to the left of the Briar net. The centers are coiled rattlesnakes ready to pounce as they wait for the puck to drop.

"Nate's the center," Brenna tells me. "That's Fitz on his right, Hunter on the left."

My gaze unwittingly shifts to Fitz. His jersey number is 55. I can't see his face because of his visor, but I can imagine the lines of deep concentration creasing his forehead.

The puck drops and Nate wins the face-off. He gains possession but passes the puck off immediately. To Fitz, who skillfully stickhandles it, deking out two opponents. It's hard to believe someone so big could be so graceful. His six-two frame flies into Harvard's zone, and excitement dances in the air for anyone wearing black and silver.

The puck was dumped behind the net and Fitz chases after it. He slams someone against the boards and wedges out the puck with his stick, then flicks a quick shot at the net. The goaltender easily stops it, but I don't think Fitz was trying or expecting to score. He was creating a rebound for Hunter, who shoots a bullet at the net.

The Harvard goalie stops that one too, just barely.

Brenna wails. *"Why!!"*

"Because we're better than you!" her new best friend sings.

It happens again—I turn my head for one measly second to glare at Brenna's heckler, and when I look back, Briar doesn't have the puck anymore. A Harvard player passes to Weston, who snaps it to Connelly, and I suddenly remember Brenna's warning about what happens if this particular player gets a breakaway.

"Get him!" I urge the Briar defenseman who's chasing after Harvard's captain.

But nothing can keep up with lightning. Connelly is too fast. He turns into Keanu Reeves, moving all Matrix-like, left and right, speeding away from his would-be defenders. If there was dust on the ice, every Briar player would be left in it.

Brenna moans and hangs her head. Connelly shoots. Brenna doesn't even look. I do, and I can't fight my disappointment as I watch the puck fly past Corsen's glove.

"GOALLLLLL!" a voice blares out of the PA. Seconds later, the buzzer goes off to signal the end of the game.

The Harvard fans erupt with joy as Briar loses.

———————

After the game, we don't immediately leave the arena. Brenna wants to say hi to her dad before he boards the team bus back to Briar, and I want to track down Brooks Weston.

I remember he used to throw the best parties in high school. My parents are cool, but they knew better than to let me or my brothers have more than a few friends over. Mr. and Mrs. Weston, on the other hand, were always out of town, so their son had the huge mansion to himself almost every weekend. His backyard was legendary. It was actually modeled after the yard in the Playboy mansion, grotto included. I'm fairly sure I made out with a guy or two behind the manmade waterfall.

"I'll meet you out front in ten," Brenna says. "And if you're dead-set on chatting up the enemy, at least try to get some trade secrets out of him."

"I'll do my best," I promise.

She disappears in the crowd. I thread my way toward the wide hallway outside the team locker rooms, where I encounter a handful of security guards and a slew of females. Brenna warned me that the hockey groupies linger after the games, hoping to catch the eye of a player. I remember this phenomenon from my brother's games too.

I stand a short distance away and shoot a quick text off to Weston, banking that he still has the same number from high school.

> Hey!! It's Summer H.D.L. Here w/ a friend and waiting for u outside locker room.
> Come say hi! Would luv to see u.

I include my name just in case he deleted my number. There's no reason he would, though. We're not exes. Didn't part on unfriendly terms after he graduated.

I decide to give him five minutes, and if he doesn't show I'll go find Brenna. But Weston doesn't disappoint. Barely two minutes pass before he's barreling toward me.

"Yessss! Summer!" He lifts me off my feet and spins me around happily, and I'm sure the groupies who were waiting for him are plotting my demise. "What are you doing here?" He seems thrilled to see me. I have to admit, it's good to see him too.

His dirty-blond hair is longer than it was in high school, almost to his chin now. But his gray eyes are just as devilish. They always had this gleam to them, like he was plotting something naughty. That's one of the reasons I never dated him, because he was (and I suspect still is) the definition of manchild. Plus, he went out with one of my friends, so girl code dictated he was off-limits.

"I go to Briar," I inform him after he releases me.

His jaw drops. "Are you shitting me?"

"Nope. Started this semester."

"Weren't you supposed to go to Brown?"

"I did."

"Ah, okay. What happened to that?"

"Long story," I confess.

Weston slings one big arm over my shoulders and lowers his voice conspiratorially. "Let me guess—partying and shenanigans were involved, and you were very politely asked to leave."

My outraged glare lasts about half a second. "I hate that we went to high school together," I grumble.

"Why? 'Cause it means I know you too well?" He smirks.

"Yes," I say grudgingly. "But I'll have you know, I wasn't even partying when the shenanigans happened." That's all I say on the subject, though. I'm still horribly embarrassed by the entire incident.

Only my parents know the whole story, but that's because I've never been able to hide anything from them. One, they're lawyers, which means they can extract information as skillfully as any Russian spy. Second, I adore them and don't like to keep secrets from them. Obviously, I don't tell them *everything*, but there's no way I could keep something as big as a sorority house fire from them.

"You have no idea how good it is to see you!" Weston says, hugging me again.

Oh yeah. The groupies hate me.

The temperature in the hallway becomes utterly glacial when another player approaches us. The covetous looks and hushed wave of whispers tell me that he's the one most of them were waiting for.

"Connelly, this is Summer," Weston introduces. "We went to high school together. Summer, Jake Connelly."

The superstar who won the game for Harvard. Oh boy. I really *am* fraternizing with the enemy. This is the guy Brenna hates.

He also happens to be incredibly attractive.

I find myself speechless as I stare into eyes the darkest shade of green I've ever seen. And I swear his cheekbones are prettier than mine. He doesn't look feminine, though. He's chiseled as fuck, like a young Clint Eastwood. Which I guess would make him Scott Eastwood? Oh, who cares. All I can say is…yum.

I manage to shake myself out of it. "Hi," I say, sticking out my hand. "What should I call you? Connelly or Jake?"

He gives me a long onceover, and I think he likes what he sees because his lips curve slightly. "Jake," he says, and briefly shakes my hand before pulling his long fingers back. "You went to high school with Brooks?"

I don't think I've ever heard anyone call Weston "Brooks" before. Granted, it's his first name. But even his own parents referred to him as Weston.

"Oh yeah, we go way back," I confirm.

"We used to party," Weston says, flinging his arm around me again. "Which is perfect, 'cause we're hitting up a party now. And you're coming."

I hesitate. "Oh, I…"

"You're coming," he repeats. "I haven't seen you in like three years. We need to catch up." He pauses. "Just don't tell anyone there that you go to Briar."

Jake's interest is piqued. "You're at Briar?"

"Yup. I know, I know, I'm the enemy." I glance at Weston. "Where's this party?"

"A friend's place west of Cambridge. It won't be too rowdy. It's a very chill crowd."

I haven't gone out since New Year's Eve, so the idea of being social and having a drink or two sounds appealing.

"I'm here with my friend," I say, remembering Brenna.

Weston shrugs. "Bring her."

"I don't know if she'll want to come. She's a rabid hockey fan, and by fan, I mean she roots for Briar and hates your guts."

He snickers. "I don't care if she roots for the devil himself. This isn't *Gangs of New York*, babe. We're allowed to socialize with people from other colleges. I'll text you the address."

When I notice Jake still watching me, I ask, "Are you sure you don't mind if we come?"

"Not my place," he replies with a shrug.

I don't know if he means it's not his place physically or not his place figuratively, as in he has no right to object. But I'll take it.

"Okay. I'll find my friend and meet you guys there."

# 11
# SUMMER

"This is blasphemy," Brenna hisses as we approach the front door of a detached house with a white clapboard exterior. She twists around, longingly glancing at the Uber that's speeding away from the curb.

I roll my eyes. "C'mon, let's go inside."

Her feet stay glued to the porch. "Don't do this to me, Summer."

"Do what?"

"Bring me into the den of Satan."

"Oh my God. And people say *I'm* a drama queen." I tug her toward the door. "We're going inside. Deal with it."

Despite what Weston said about it being a chill night, the place is overflowing when we walk in without ringing the bell. The music's so loud, no one would've heard the doorbell, anyway.

And despite Brenna's almost comical expression of horror, the party instantly puts a big smile on my face. I don't know what it is about music and merriment and crowds that never fails to lift my spirits. At one point in my life I thought about becoming an event planner, but I realized fairly fast that I don't actually like planning the parties—I like attending them. I get enjoyment out of putting together an outfit, picking a makeup palette, accessorizing. Making an entrance, and then wandering around to see what everyone else is wearing.

Maybe I need to be one of those interviewers who stands on the red carpet and admires the clothes. All I'd have to do is stick microphones in people's faces and ask who they're wearing. Damn. That actually sounds like it would be fun. But I think it's a bit too late to switch my major to broadcasting. I'd have to start all over again. Besides, I've never had much interest in being on camera.

"I don't like this. Look at these goons with their smug faces," she growls, jabbing her finger in the air.

At that exact moment, a tall guy with scrawny arms poking out of a Celtics jersey backs directly into her pointed finger. "Hey! What the—" His protest dies when he spins around and sees Brenna. "Forget I said that," he begs. "Please, *please* keep poking me. Poke me all night long."

"No. Go away," she orders.

He winks at her. "Come find me after you've had a couple drinks."

My jaw drops. "Ew. Now you definitely need to go away."

As Brenna and I brush past him, I search the crowd for Weston or Jake Connelly but don't see either one of them. I know Weston's here already, because he messaged me about ten minutes ago.

I take Brenna's arm and drag her toward what I hope is the kitchen. "I need a drink."

"I need ten."

I pinch the fleshy part of her forearm. "Stop being so melodramatic. It's just a party."

"It's a Harvard party. Celebrating a Harvard win." She shakes her head. "You're turning out to be the most disappointing best friend of all time."

"We both know you don't mean that. I'm terrific."

In the kitchen, we're greeted by a blast of raucous laughter. The cedar work island is covered with various alcoholic beverages and stacks of red plastic cups and surrounded by a crowd of people, mostly male. No Weston or Jake, but the noisy boys at the counter are all big enough that they're most likely hockey players.

Every single one of them sends an appreciative look in our direction, while the only females—two pretty blondes—narrow their eyes. Within seconds, they're dragging two of the guys away, under the pretense that they want to dance. I assume it's their boyfriends, and these chicks couldn't have been any more obvious that they viewed Brenna and me as threats.

I've got bad news for them. If they're *this* afraid their men will stray? It'll probably happen. That lack of trust doesn't bode well for their relationships.

A dark-haired guy in a gray Harvard hoodie checks us out and grins broadly. "Ladies!" he calls. "Come celebrate with us!" He holds up a bottle of champagne.

"Bubbly? Wow! You Hah-vahd boys are *so* fancy," Brenna drawls, but I don't think any of them pick up on her sarcasm.

Gray Hoodie grabs two empty glasses from a nearby cupboard—actual champagne flutes—and waves them at us. "Say when."

Brenna begrudgingly slinks toward him and accepts a glass. Over her shoulder, she defends her actions to me with, "I'm a sucker for champagne."

I hide a smile. Uh-huh. I'm sure she went over there for the bubbles and not the cute guy. At least, *I* think he's cute. He's got a mop of brown hair and a really nice smile. Plus, what I assume is a hard, ripped, lickable body underneath his sweatshirt and cargo pants.

God, I love athletes.

"Which one are you?" she asks him.

"What do you mean?"

"What name is on your jersey?"

He grins. "Ah gotcha. Number 61. McCarthy."

She narrows her eyes. "You scored the tying goal in the third."

McCarthy beams. "That was me."

"Sweet wrist shot."

My eyebrows soar. Wow. Is she actually complimenting him? I guess I'm not the only one who likes his smile—

"What's the matter, your slap shot doesn't have enough power behind it?"

Or not.

"Ouch," he says with a mock-pout.

I should've known better than to believe she'd give a genuine compliment to a Harvard player. Still, I can tell she's warming up to the party. Her hips, ever so slightly, begin moving to the dance beat blasting from the living room, and she seems more relaxed now as she sips her drink.

I'm about to take the glass McCarthy's holding out to me when my phone buzzes in my purse. And keeps buzzing. I fish it out, realizing it's a call. The display tells me it's Hunter.

"Keep the bubbly on ice for me. I need to take this call." I fix each guy with a stern look, holding two fingers up to my eyes as I drift toward the doorway. "Don't do anything stupid," I warn them.

"She's in good hands," McCarthy promises. "I'm a total gentleman."

"He's a virgin," one of his teammates says.

McCarthy nods solemnly. "I am."

Brenna narrows her eyes. "Are you actually?"

"Fuck no." He smiles again, and oh man, he has dimples. This guy is frigging adorable.

When I'm across the kitchen in a quieter spot, I answer the call. "Hey, what's up?"

"Where you at, Blondie?" Hunter demands. "Figured you'd be home by now."

"I ran into an old friend after the game and he invited us to a party."

In the living room, someone raises the volume of the drum and bass track that just came on, and I swear the walls start expanding and contracting like a beating heart. The music drowns out Hunter's response.

"Sorry, what? I can't hear you."

Suspicion fills the line. "Where exactly are you?"

"Cambridge. I told you, I ran into a friend from high school. Oh hey, you probably know him too. Brooks Weston?"

The silence that follows is thick with accusation.

"Hunter?"

"Are you kidding me right now? You're at a Harvard party?"

"Yes, and before you start lecturing me about fraternizing with the enemy, don't bother. I already got the speech from Brenna."

"This is unacceptable," he growls. "You can't party with the assholes who beat us tonight."

"Why not?"

"Because!"

I smother a laugh. "Here's the thing about sports, sweetie. Sometimes you win games and sometimes you lose them. It would be really petty—not to mention stupid—of you to hate every single player on every single team that's ever beaten you."

"We hate Harvard," he says stubbornly.

"They're not even your official rivals! That's Eastwood College."

"This is America, Summer. College hockey teams are allowed to have more than one rival."

My laughter spills over. "May I go now, Hunter? I'm ignoring Brenna because of you." Although a quick glance reveals that she's not missing me at all. She's giggling at something McCarthy is saying.

Den of Satan, my ass. She's enjoying herself.

"Fine, you can go." He sounds adorably grumpy. "But for the record, I wish you were here."

A strange warmth fills my tummy. This flirtation with Hunter is confusing. I liked kissing him, but I live with the guy now. And I also live with Fitz, who I'm still attracted to despite how badly I want to punch him in the dick.

Like I said, confusing.

"You could always come here if you want," I offer.

A loud snicker echoes in my ear. "To the fiery pits of Lucifer? No fucking way."

Jee-zus. Do all Briar hockey fans think Harvard is Dante's Inferno, or is it just the weirdos in my life? Harvard is a perfectly respectable school with a perfectly respectable hockey team that just happened to beat Briar tonight. Get over it, people.

"We're having peeps over, anyway," he adds. "That's the other reason I called, to give you a heads-up."

"Okay, cool. I'm—"

"Finally!" a familiar voice booms from the far doorway. "Where've you been!"

I grin as Weston strides into the kitchen. When I gesture to my phone and hold up a finger to indicate I'll be a minute, he shrugs and turns to his teammates. "Beer me."

"I have to go," I tell Hunter. "I'll see you at home."

———

Catching up with Weston is a blast. We hole up in a room off the main living area, which might've been a dining room at one point but is now a second living room with two overstuffed sofas, a couple of armchairs, and a massive glass coffee table. Weston's on one end of the couch while I'm perched on the arm of it. The music's not as loud in here, which means we don't have to shout as we fill each other in on what's happening with the classmates we'd lost touch with.

On the other side of the room, Brenna looks mighty cozy in McCarthy's lap. It's obvious he's super into her. He's got an arm slung around her and a hand resting on her thigh as they peer at something on her phone. I've glimpsed them kissing a few times since they sat down, and I've had to fight a smile each time.

There's no way I'm *not* rubbing this in her face later.

"Your friend is a smoke show," Weston tells me.

"Right? And she's fun to be around too." I find it hard to believe that Brenna and I met only yesterday. I feel like I've known her forever.

"Speaking of fun…" Winking, he leans toward the table and taps out a line of the white powder I was pretending not to notice.

I've been around cocaine more times than I'd like to admit. It's the preferred party favor for prep school kids with time on their hands and cash to spare. I tried it once at a party in junior year, but it wasn't my thing. I prefer the warm buzz of alcohol to that frenetic, wired sensation.

I'm not surprised to see Weston doing it, though—he always did enjoy his blow. So did most of the Roselawn hockey guys, for that matter. Dean once told me that coke and hockey players are synonymous, and now I'm wondering if any of the Briar guys dabble in it too. I hope not.

Weston snorts his line, then rubs his nose and shakes his head a few times as if trying to clear it of cobwebs. "Sure you don't want?"

"Not my jam," I remind him. I take a sip of my beer. "Don't you ever worry about drug testing?" My brother got fucked his last season thanks to a random drug test that was sprung on him.

"Blow leaves your system after forty-eight hours, babe." Weston rolls his eyes. "You'd have to be real dumb to get caught." He plants a hand on my knee, but there's nothing sexual about the gesture. "So how you liking Briar? Better than Brown?"

"Classes haven't started yet, so I can't say one way or the other. The campus is gorgeous, though."

"You living in the dorms?"

"No, I moved in with a few of Dean's friends. Actually, one of them is Hunter Davenport, your old Roselawn teammate."

"No shit! You're shacking up with Davenport?"

"Platonically."

"No such thing."

I'm about to argue when I feel a subtle shift of energy in the room. Jake Connelly has just entered, and let me just say, the man's got presence. He strides in holding a bottle of Sam Adams, stopping in front of the armchair opposite our couch. The guy currently occupying the chair shoots up instantly. Connelly calmly takes his place.

His dark-green eyes flick in Brenna's direction as he sips his beer.

Brenna is momentarily distracted from McCarthy. She takes in Jake's dark jeans, black Under Armour shirt, and Red Sox cap. "Connelly," she says curtly. "Good game."

He gives her a contemplative look. There was no sarcasm in her tone, but I think he senses the difficulty with which she voiced the praise. "Thanks," he drawls. Takes another sip of beer. McCarthy tries to get her attention by whispering something against her neck, but her eyes remain on Jake. And his remain on her.

"Where do I know you from?" he says thoughtfully.

"Hmmm. Well, are you able to hear any of your hecklers when you're on the ice? Because I'm usually the one screaming obscenities at you," she offers helpfully.

He sounds amused. "Got it. Briar puck bunny."

"Ha! They wish."

"You hang around the team. I've seen you."

"Got no choice." She tips her head in challenge. "My dad's the coach."

Jake is completely unfazed.

McCarthy, on the other hand? Utterly appalled. He jolts upright, causing Brenna to nearly fall face-first on the carpeted floor. Proving he's at least a gentleman, he regains his grip on her, then eases her onto the armchair before jumping to his feet.

"Why didn't you say something?" He turns to Weston in betrayal. "Why didn't you warn me?"

"Who cares, man. She's good people."

"I told her about my busted knee! Coach wasn't gonna put it on the injury report next week. What if she snitches to her father?"

"So?" Weston's still not concerned.

"So next thing I know, one of his goons is slashing my knee, you know, *oops! It was an accident*, and suddenly I'm done for the season."

"My dad runs a clean program," Brenna retorts, rolling her eyes. "No Tonya Hardings on the roster."

Weston snorts. Connelly grins, and damned if that doesn't make him even more attractive.

"Also?" she continues. "This isn't the CIA, and I've got better things to do with my time than spy on a bunch of college hockey players for my father."

McCarthy loses some of his bluster. "Yeah?"

"Yeah." She rises from the chair. "I came here tonight to chill with my friend, have a few drinks, and maybe fool around with a cute guy."

His expression becomes hopeful. "We can still fool around."

She throws her head back and laughs. "Sorry, big boy. That ship sailed when you practically threw me across the room because of my cooties."

A couple of his teammates whoop with laughter. Poor McCarthy is not as amused.

To my surprise, Connelly intervenes. "Don't listen to her, man. She was never going to hook up with you."

Brenna raises her eyebrows. "I wasn't, huh? I don't think you know me well enough to make that call."

He stares at her, his tongue coming out to moisten the corner of his mouth. It's extremely sexy. "You'd never sleep with a Harvard player."

She stares back for several seconds before capitulating. "You're right. Never in a million years." Her gaze shifts toward me. "Time to go, crazy girl. I'll get us an Uber."

Probably a good idea. I lean in to give Weston a kiss on the cheek. "It was so good to catch up," I tell him. "And thanks for the invite."

"Any time. Hopefully we'll hang out again now that you're in the Boston area."

"Absolutely." I stand up and glance at Jake. "Have a good night."

He just nods.

"Four minutes away," Brenna says, holding up her phone.

McCarthy is still standing close to her, not bothering to hide his disappointment. "You could stay…" He trails off, awaiting her response.

Secretly, I think she totally would've fooled around with him, Harvard be damned. Unfortunately, he really did blow it with his overreaction to her identity.

She takes pity on the guy, looping her arms around his neck and brushing her lips over his stubble-covered cheek. "Maybe in another life, McCarthy."

Smiling ruefully, he lands a lighthearted smack on her butt before she walks off. "I'm holding you to that."

On her way to the door, Brenna flicks the pithiest of looks in Jake Connelly's direction. His green eyes gleam with amusement as she disappears from the room.

Three minutes later, she and I are in the backseat of our Uber. Brenna addresses me in a grudging tone. "That wasn't too atrocious."

"See! I told you it would be fun," I tease.

Scowling, she jabs a finger in the air between us. "With that said, I'm totally telling my dad about McCarthy's knee."

I grin. "I wouldn't expect anything less."

---

Breanna decides to crash at my house when she finds out my roommates are having a party of their own. She confesses that she's a night owl and has a hard time falling asleep before three or four a.m. Me, I love a good after-party like I love my Prada boots, so I'm happy bringing her home with me.

To our dismay, everyone's gone when we walk through the door. My roommates are still up, though. Hollis and Fitz are on the couch, battling each other in a shooting game. Hunter is passed out in the easy chair, clad in sweatpants and a threadbare T-shirt with the sleeves cut off.

The only evidence of a get-together is the dozens of empty beer cans and the faint scent of marijuana that seems to be coming from Mike's direction.

"Get the fuck out of here," Hollis is growling at Fitzy. "Stop cornering me."

"Stop hiding in the same warehouse if you don't want me to find you."

From the doorway, I watch as the soldier on Mike's side of the screen faces down the barrel of a scary-looking gun. On Fitzy's side, it's clear he has Hollis completely trapped.

"Any last words?" Fitzy asks.

"I never learned how to ride a bike."

Fitz bursts out laughing. A deep, sexy laugh that rolls out of his muscular chest—and dies the moment he spots me.

"Holy shit, that was funny," Brenna tells Hollis as she saunters into the living room. "You actually said something that made me laugh. Like, *with* you and not *at* you."

He responds with a scowl. "Oh, hi there. How was Rome?"

"Rome?" she says blankly.

"Yeah. Rome." His dark look travels toward me. "Right, Brutus?"

I reluctantly turn to Fitz for assistance. "What the hell is he talking about?"

"*Et tu, Brute,*" he murmurs wryly.

"Davenport told us where you were," Hollis accuses. "So don't try to hide it."

"I wasn't going to," I say cheerfully. "Bee, you want a drink?"

"Obviously."

From the armchair, Hunter cracks one eye open. "Only thing

left is the bottle of Fireball," he mumbles, haphazardly gesturing to the end table.

I eye the whiskey bottle apprehensively. "Feeling spicy?" I ask Brenna.

"Always."

Grinning, I duck into the kitchen in search of shot glasses. When I come back, Brenna is nestled on the other side of Fitzy, trying to convince him and Hollis that she was coerced into attending the Cambridge party.

"It was terrible," she bemoans.

"Bullshit! She had the best time ever." I set the glasses on the table, then glance at my roommates. "It's okay if Brenna stays over, right?" I'm wondering now if I should've asked for permission.

But Hollis waves his hand dismissively. "Of course you're staying over," he tells her. "My bed is your bed."

Fitz snorts.

"Oh honey, I wouldn't touch your bed with a ten-foot pole."

"Speaking of poles…" He wiggles his eyebrows.

"Keep it in your pants, Michael."

"Aw, have some mercy on him. He needs it tonight," Fitz says, slinging one tattooed arm around her shoulder.

And no, I'm not jealous seeing that.

Why would I be?

I tear my gaze away and focus on pouring the Fireball.

"Why does he need my mercy?"

"Because he shaved his entire body for a woman and got stood up." Fitz looks like he's trying not to laugh.

From his chair, Hunter doesn't bother refraining. He chuckles, albeit sleepily. I think maybe Hollis wasn't the only one smoking weed tonight. Hunter has barely moved since we got home.

"Oh, dear." Brenna reaches across Fitz's big body and pats Hollis on the arm. "My apologies, sweetie."

I study him as I finish pouring. He's wearing jeans and long sleeves. Not a hint of skin. "On a scale of one to ten, how hairless are you?"

His lips curve. "C'mere and find out…"

This time Fitz reaches over, smacking Hollis on the back of the head. "Enough, dude. Even I'm starting to get skeeved out."

Brenna and I clink our glasses, raise them to our lips, and throw back the shots. The cinnamon-flavored liquid burns a path all the way to my stomach.

"Jee-zus!" I groan. My mouth and throat are on fire. "I forgot how potent this stuff is."

"Another one," Brenna orders. "I barely felt that."

With a snort of laughter, I pour two more shots.

As we drink our next round, I can feel Fitz's cautious gaze boring into me. I bet he wants to lecture me about the booze. Warn me to slow down. But he keeps his mouth shut.

"Oooh-kay, I definitely felt that one!" Brenna's cheeks are flushed now. She wastes no time whipping off her tight black sweater, leaving her in black skinny jeans and a lacy, barely-there camisole.

Hollis' blue eyes smolder. "Wanna go upstairs? To answer Summer's question, I'm a ten. Completely hairless…"

A giggle pops out of my mouth. Right. As if that's going to entice her.

"Absolutely not," she replies. She reaches for Fitz's abandoned Xbox controller. "What are we playing?"

"*Killer Instinct.*"

"Nice. I know this one. Let me play Hollis. I want to blow his brains out a couple times."

Hollis beams. "All I heard was 'I want to blow.' And my answer is yes. Blow away, baby."

Sadly for him, she sticks to virtually shooting him in the head half a dozen times. I'm not particularly fond of watching other people play video games, so I peruse Hollis' Spotify library on his open laptop, make a playlist, and spend the next hour rocking out by myself while Brenna takes turns facing off against Hollis and Fitz.

We down two more shots during that hour. And then another two, after Hollis insists there's no point leaving such a teeny tiny amount in the bottle. "This is Briar!" he shouts as if he's acting out a scene from *Gladiator*. "We finish what we start!"

I'm drunk enough that his speech makes perfect sense to me. So the three of us polish off the Fireball, while Hunter snores softly in the armchair and Fitz watches me with what I think is disapproval. I can't be sure, because my vision is a wee bit fuzzy.

And the room might be a wee bit spinny.

But that could also be because I'm spinning.

"I think it's time for bed." Fitz's low voice rumbles in my ear. He comes up behind me as I dance to a Whitesnake song from Hollis' metal playlist.

I was in the middle of a ponytail-swishing move, so my hair whips him in the face when I twirl around. He doesn't even flinch. Just plants one big hand on my arm to steady me before I topple over.

"I'm not tired," I inform him, shrugging his hand off.

Once again, I teeter on my feet. And once again, he grabs hold of me.

Only this time, he takes it a step further.

Before I can blink, my whole body is in the air. Fitz heaves me over his shoulder, and suddenly I'm staring at the back of his black T-shirt while my legs dangle over his broad chest.

I kick him. "Put me down! Oh my God, Fitz!"

"No."

I kick him again. Harder. "Put me down! Brenna, save me!"

"Babe, you've been solo-moshing to hair metal for the last hour," I hear her say. I can't see her, because Fitz is still caveman-handling me. "I think he might be right. I'll be up after this game."

I catch a glimpse of her amused face before Fitz marches us toward the stairs.

"Seriously," I growl. "Put me *down*."

"No." His arm is like an iron vise around the backs of my thighs.

"I mean it! I'm not some toy you can fling around! I'm a human being, and *I have rights!*"

All I get in response is a low chuckle.

I can't believe he's *carrying* me upstairs. Like I'm a six-year-old who's past her bedtime and needs to be banished to her Hello Kitty bunk beds. Gritting my teeth, I slam one fist against his shoulder blade. He doesn't even budge. We're halfway up the stairs. I try a different route and pinch his deltoid muscles. When that fails, I go for the lats.

He rears back as if he'd been shot, then curses in annoyance. "Stop that."

"I will if you put me down." I pinch him again, and again.

He shrugs his back and shoulders to try to shake my fingers off him. "For fuck's sake, Summer. No more pinching!" he yells.

"Oh, but you're allowed to grab me against my will?" I yell back.

We're both breathing hard. I feel beads of sweat form at the nape of my neck and between my breasts. It's hard work trying to pry myself out of his grip. He reaches the top of the stairs and charges toward my bedroom, swearing the entire way because I won't stop pinching his stupidly muscular back.

"When did you become the fun police?" I demand when he finally sets me down—a little rougher than necessary. My feet connect with the floor in a hard thud. "And what gives you the right to drag me upstairs?"

His brown eyes blaze at me. "You were three seconds from falling over and smashing your head on a piece of furniture. Probably knocking yourself unconscious too."

"Oh my God, why is everyone in my life so dramatic! I was just dancing!"

"*I'm* dramatic?" he roars, and I'm momentarily amazed because I don't think I've ever heard Fitz raise his voice. "You freaked out on me yesterday for no reason. You accused me of implying you can't fucking read."

"Because you were acting like a condescending asshole!"

"And you were acting like a brat!"

"And now you're acting like my father!"

"And you're still acting like a brat!"

We stop and glare at each other. He's visibly clenching his teeth. The cords of his neck are like overly tightened guitar strings. He looks like he might snap at any second. But after several beats, he releases a heavy breath and rubs his dark beard.

"I'm sorry about last night, okay?" he mutters. "I didn't mean to imply—"

"It's fine," I cut in tersely.

"Summer."

"What."

"I'm serious. I don't think you're stupid."

*That makes one of us.*

I banish the self-effacing thought to the bowels of my intoxicated mind. Somehow, even drunk off my face, I know better than to give him the satisfaction of seeing my insecurities.

I ball my fists and press them to my sides. Fitz is still watching me, no longer angry or frustrated, but contemplative. Even now, when I'm mad and aggravated by him, his presence affects me. My heart is pounding. My knees feel wobbly. Tingles dance along my spine and settle between my legs. When Fitz rakes his long fingers through his tousled hair, the tingles transform into a tight knot of need.

He turns me on so badly. I want those fingers on my body.

"I liked you," I blurt out.

His hand freezes in his hair. "What?"

"Nothing. Forget it. I'm drunk." I backpedal like my life depends on it, because Fitz isn't allowed to know that I was interested in him, or that he hurt me. Telling him means admitting I'd heard every derisive word he'd spoken about me.

A line cuts into his forehead. "Summer…"

"I said forget it. You're right, it's time for bed. Thank you *so* much for escorting me upstairs." The sarcasm oozes like molasses. "Now will you please get out of my room?"

He hesitates for a second. Then his shoulders roll up and stiffen, and he gives a curt nod. "Goodnight."

I let out a frazzled groan the moment he's gone.

Dammit. Me and my stupid mouth. I really need to stop blurting out exactly what's on my mind all the time.

---

A loud thump followed by an even louder curse jolts me awake the next morning.

I'm a light sleeper, so the slightest noise can pull me from a state of deep slumber into wide-awake panic mode. Wild-eyed, I sit up and check the time on my phone. It's seven-thirty. On a Sunday.

Which one of my roommates is making such a ruckus? I must know this in order to know who I'll be murdering.

They better not wake Brenna. I assume she's asleep next to me, but when I look over, I realize I'm alone. I swear she'd said she'd be right up last night.

"Dammit," someone mutters.

Brenna's voice.

I fling the blankets off and jump out of bed. I open my door at the same time two other doors swing open. Fitz and Hunter appear in their respective doorways, sporting boxers and some serious bed head.

All three of us gape when we notice whose room Brenna is exiting.

She freezes like a forest animal that just heard a twig snap. She's wearing nothing but her camisole and black bikini underwear. Her jeans are slung over one arm, and her hair is '80s-rock-level disheveled.

She meets my eyes and shakes her head in warning. "Not one word."

I don't think I'm capable of words. My tongue is on the floor, rendering me speechless.

Brenna is doing the walk of shame out of Mike Hollis' room?

This is unfathomable to me.

Hunter opens his mouth, but she silences him with a low growl. "Not. One. Word."

Fitzy shakes his head in resignation, turns around, and closes his bedroom door.

"I'll call you later," Brenna murmurs as she passes me on the way to the stairs.

I nod wordlessly.

She's gone a few minutes later, the sound of a car engine telling me she arranged for a ride home.

"Wow," I say.

To my surprise, Hunter follows me into my room and throws himself on the bed. His abs bunch up and ripple as he gets comfortable. "That was unreal," he says drowsily.

I stare at him. "Is there a reason why you're lying in my bed?"

"Not really." He rolls onto his side, thrusting out one long, muscular leg. He cuddles with my pillow and lets out a contented sigh. "Night."

Unbelievable. He's fast asleep within seconds, but I don't even have the energy to kick him out. It's too early in the morning, and I've only gotten about four hours of sleep.

So I do what any tired twenty-one-year-old woman would do.

I crawl into bed with the half-naked man who's taking up residence there.

Hunter makes a soft noise and then flings an arm over me, drawing me closer. At first I resist, going stiff. Then I relax, allowing the tension to seep out. It's been so long since I've spooned with someone, and it's…

Dammit, it's nice.

# 12
# FITZ

MONDAY IS THE FIRST DAY OF THE NEW SEMESTER AND I'M UP before the birds. The sky is a navy-blue brushstroke across a black canvas. A tiny glimmer of light begins to peek through the darkness as I stare out the kitchen window waiting for my coffee to brew. I'm looking forward to my classes today. I've heard nothing but phenomenal things about Cinematography for Games, and Fundamentals of 2D Animation sounds bomb.

I'm a double major in Fine Arts and computer programming—which my old man never fails to lecture me about. He thinks it's an unnecessary burden, that I should focus only on the latter. "Computers are the future of art, Colin," is his go-to argument.

He has a point; graphic design does operate mostly in a digital sphere these days, with people drawing directly on their computers or tablets. I'm guilty of it myself.

But for me, there's nothing better than feeling the firm surface of a sketchpad under my hand, hearing the scrape of a pencil or the rasp of charcoal moving across the page. Drawing on paper and painting on canvas is so ingrained in me that I can't imagine ever relying solely on technology.

I'm sure eventually museums will display only digital screens instead of canvases, and maybe it makes me a dinosaur, but that notion is a real bummer to me.

Since my first class isn't till ten, and practice isn't till eight, I have plenty of time to monitor the beta progress of my game. I take my coffee upstairs and settle at my desk. Or, what Hollis likes to call Space Command Central.

My gaming setup *is* a bit intense for a college student, complete with three hi-def monitors, a programmable keyboard, a fully customizable gaming mouse, and a graphics card that cost more than I'd like to admit. But frickin' worth it.

I reach for the black-and-neon-green headphones hanging off the external speakers and slide them on. I watch a couple of streams, then check the private message board I set up for my beta group. Access to the game was by invite only, so the only people playing *Legion 48* are the ones I chose and approved. On the chat feed, there are a few requests for cheat codes that make me roll my eyes. I skim those and search for usable data. The point of this version is to get the bugs fixed so that the final product is fully functional.

Nothing jumps out at me. I sip my coffee as comments and questions pop up on the screen, the feed scrolling itself with each new line of text. I'm not surprised to see so many of the players online this early. Chances are, they never even went to bed.

When I hear footsteps in the hallway, my head jerks warily toward the door. Someone enters the hall bathroom and closes the door. A few minutes later the shower comes on.

I wonder if it's Summer. Part of me hopes it isn't and that I'll be able to escape the house and go to practice without seeing her at all. Every interaction she and I shared yesterday had been beyond awkward. And don't get me started on the night before, when I had to fireman-carry her drunk ass upstairs.

Her drunk, very fine ass. I'm talking smoke show, unbelievably firm, mouthwateringly round, I-want-that-ass ass.

*I liked you.*

I've been trying not to dwell on the three words she'd hurled my way. She'd been wasted when she said them, and I don't put much stock in alcohol-fueled declarations.

More footsteps echo outside my door. This time I know for sure who it is—Hollis. He's mumbling to himself about how badly he needs to piss.

I'm suddenly reminded of Brenna making that same walk down the hall. Hollis couldn't shut up yesterday about their hookup, acting like he'd scored a winning lottery ticket. I guess that's not far off the mark, since I'm fairly certain this is the first time Brenna's hooked up with one of us. Normally she avoids us like the plague, though I don't know if that's because she doesn't like hockey players or because she's smart enough to know what Coach would do if one of us ever touched his precious daughter.

Hollis, sadly, isn't smart. Fearless, yes. But not smart. Because if Coach ever finds out what he did, he'll tie him up naked and spread-eagled to the net and practice his slap shot.

"Eeeeeeeeee!"

I almost fall out of my chair as an ear-splitting scream pierces the quiet house. My blood runs cold and I'm on my feet in a heartbeat, lunging for the door.

My brain goes caveman on me.

Summer scream.

Summer danger.

Save Summer.

Fists up, I throw myself into the hall and then skid to a stop when the bathroom door flies open. A boxers-clad Hollis is unceremoniously dumped at my feet.

"No!" Summer shrieks. "You can't just come in here when I'm in the shower! That is UNACCEPTABLE!"

Oh boy.

She stumbles out, her blonde hair soaked and dripping water all over her wet, golden skin. Soapsuds run down her bare arms, and it's obvious she grabbed the wrong towel because this one is too small—the top of it barely contains her breasts and the bottom barely covers her thighs. If the white terrycloth slides one inch in either direction, we'll all be in trouble.

My mouth goes bone dry. Her legs are impossibly long and they're so fucking sexy I can't help picturing them wrapped around my waist.

I gulp. Hard.

Meanwhile, Hollis looks dazed. "I was just taking a leak," he protests.

"I was in the shower!" she screeches. "And I locked the door!"

"Lock's broken."

"Now you tell me that!"

He rubs his eyes. "Don't see the big deal here, babe."

"*Don't* call me babe."

Hunter's door swings open. "What the hell is going on?" His eyebrows shoot up when he takes in the scene. "What did you do?" he growls at Hollis.

"I didn't do anything," Hollis grumbles.

"He walked in on me in the shower!"

"I was just pissing! It's not like I got *in* the shower with you."

"That's not the point!" She points at the bathroom door. "See that room? It's a sacred room! It's a temple, Mike! It is meant for one person, and one person alone. Like solitary confinement."

"So is it a prison or a temple?" the bonehead asks.

"Shut up," she snaps. "And listen to me, Hollis. Unlike you, I don't have a penis."

"Well, thank God for that."

"Hollis," I warn in a low voice.

He slams his mouth shut.

"*I* am a woman," Summer continues. Her fingers tighten over the top of the towel to keep it in place. "I'm a woman living with *three* men, and I have a right to privacy. I have a right to take a fucking shower without you barging in and pulling your dick out!"

"You didn't even see my dick," he argues.

"That's not the point!" She throws her arms up in frustration.

And just like that, the towel drops.

Oh sweet mother of Moses.

I catch one glimpse of full, creamy tits with pale pink nipples. One incredible, tantalizing glimpse, before Summer slaps a hand and forearm across her chest. She manages to catch the towel before it falls, using her other hand to hold it over her lower body.

Hollis looks stunned.

Hunter's eyes are on fire.

Me, I'm doing everything in my power not to look at her. I focus my gaze on a random spot above her head and speak in a surprisingly steady voice. "It won't happen again, Summer. Right, Hollis?"

"Right," he assures her.

I nod in approval. "First thing we'll do is get the lock fixed—"

"Why are you talking to the ceiling?" she demands.

Swallowing a groan, I force myself to meet her eyes. Those big green depths reflect nothing but unhappiness and embarrassment back at me. She might be a drama queen, but she's right. She's living with three dudes and she deserves her privacy.

"This is the worst bathroom ever," she moans miserably. "There's no counter space. The lighting is so terrible I can't do my makeup. And now I can't even be alone when I'm taking a shower?"

"Summer," I say softly. She looks like she's going to cry, so I slowly walk toward her.

*Don't touch her. Don't touch her. Don't touch her.*

I touch her.

Just my fingertips on her shoulder, but the contact sends a hot shiver up my spine. "I'll fix the lock. I promise."

Her body relaxes as she exhales. "Thank you."

She spins around and marches into the bathroom. The door slams in our faces. A moment later, the shower comes back on.

Hunter and I exchange a quick look before turning to frown at Hollis.

"What?" he says defensively.

"Dude, you have two sisters," Hunter accuses. "How do you not understand bathroom etiquette? Me and Fitz are only children and *we* know goddamn bathroom etiquette."

"My sisters and I never shared a bathroom." With an irritated huff, he stalks toward my room.

"Where are you going?" I demand.

"To use King Colin's john." He scowls at me. "Or would you rather I piss downstairs in the sink?"

I quickly hold my arms out in a welcoming gesture. "It's all yours, bro."

----

2D animation is as fun as I expected it to be. Afterward, I leave the computer lab with my two buddies, Kenji and Ray. Since they're major gamers, they were at the top of my list for beta testers, and they can't stop talking about *Legion 48* as we head outside.

"It's brilliant, Fitz," Kenji is saying as he zips up his parka.

I pull a black wool hat over my head and shove my hands into a pair of gloves. I feel like January is never going to end. I swear it's like the planet goes into some fucked-up time loop every year to make January a hundred days long. And then the loop snaps apart and the rest of the year flies by in about four minutes.

"Brilliant," Ray echoes.

We push open the exit doors and are greeted by a gust of icy wind. Frickin' January.

Despite the cold, I can't contain a burst of excitement. "You're really not having any major issues so far?"

"None whatsoever."

"Come on, there's got to be something."

We descend the wide steps toward the frost-covered sidewalk. The Fine Arts buildings are clustered together on the west side of campus, so almost all of my studios and lecture halls are located here.

"I'm telling you, there's nothing," Ray says.

"Nada," Kenji agrees.

My phone vibrates in my pocket. I pull it out and frown at the words *Private Caller*.

Kenji and Ray are still engaged in an animated conversation about the game, so I signal that I'm out and they take off walking.

"Please hold for Kamal Jain," a brisk female voice snaps in my ear.

I freeze for a beat, then give a hasty laugh. "Right. Nice try—"

But she's already clicked off.

This has to be a joke. Yes, I did apply for a position at Orcus Games, the billion-dollar game studio owned by legendary geek-god Kamal Jain. But if this woman actually works for Orcus, I highly doubt she'd be transferring me to the founder and president of the company. That's like Mark Zuckerberg taking customer services calls at Facebook.

I'm half a second from hanging up when a new voice fills the line.

"Colin, hi! Kamal. So I'm sitting here looking at your résumé. Gonna be honest with you, Colin—you were a no for me."

My pulse quickens. Either I'm hallucinating, or that's seriously Kamal Jain on the line. I've seen hundreds of interviews with the guy, and I'd recognize his fast-paced, nasally voice anywhere.

"NCAA hockey? I won't lie, brother. It was an easy pass, on account of the jock thing. I mean, most jocks I've met don't even know the difference between Java and C-Sharp."

I'm glad he's not in front of me so he can't see the frown that creases my lips. I'm sick to death of the dumb jock stereotype. It's so archaic, not to mention completely false. Some of the most intelligent people I know happen to be athletes.

I keep my mouth shut, though. This is Kamal Jain, for chrissake. He designed his first multiplayer RPG at the age of fifteen, self-published it, and then saw it take off to rocket levels of popularity. He sold the game for five hundred million dollars, used the money to start his own company, and has been raking in the cash since then. This kind of trajectory in the gaming industry is virtually unheard of. The creator of *Minecraft* has nothing on this guy.

"But one of my interns came to me this morning, told me I needed to play this game of yours. Got to tell you, Colin, as far as code goes, it's more simplistic than I'd like—though let's get real, to me anything is simplistic if I haven't coded it myself. What got me? The assets. Oh lordy lordy, the graphics! All you?"

It's hard to keep up with Jain's rambling, but somehow I manage to answer, "Yes. All me."

"Visual Arts major at Briar."

"Double major," I correct. "Computer programming as well."

"Ambitious. I like it. Don't like the hockey background much, but I assume you're done with that, seeing as how you're applying to work for my studio. No plans to go pro after graduation?"

"No, sir."

A high-pitched laugh pierces my ear. "Sir? Give up that habit right now, Colin. Call me Kamal, or KJ. I prefer KJ, but whatever makes you more comfortable. All right. Let me look at my calendar." Papers rustle over the line. "I'm in Manhattan next Friday. I'll tell the pilot to make a stop in Boston first. We'll meet at the Ritz."

"Meet?" I echo in confusion.

"I personally interview every potential designer, and I do it face-to-face. You're on a shortlist with six other candidates. This will be competitive," he warns, but there's a note of glee in his voice. I get the feeling he might enjoy pitting candidates against each other. "So, two weeks from now. Friday. Yes?"

"Yes," I say immediately. Working for Orcus Games would be a goddamn dream. It was my top choice, and I honestly didn't expect an interview. Like he said, it's competitive. Everyone wants to work for Kamal Jain, self-made billionaire.

"Good. I'll have my assistant email you the details. Looking forward to meeting you, brother."

"Looking forward to it too."

I'm shaking my head in amazement as I hang up. Did that really just happen? I have a job interview with Kamal Jain?

Holy shit.

I open my text window to send a message to Morris, but before I can start typing, my phone rings again. Not a private caller this time, but my father.

As always, uneasiness starts circling my gut. You never know what you're gonna get with my folks.

"Colin," he barks when I pick up. Dad has this brusque, no-nonsense way of speaking that comes off as rude if you don't know him, and grating if you do.

"Hey, what's up? I only have a sec before my next class," I lie.

"I won't take up much of your time. Just wanted to tell you that I'm bringing Lucille to your home game this weekend. She's been dying to see you play."

Lucille is my dad's new girlfriend, though I don't imagine they'll date for more than a few months. The old man goes through women with a speed that is both impressive and disgusting.

On the flip side of that, Mom claims to have not dated anyone since the divorce, and that was twelve years ago. And while Dad has no qualms bragging about his conquests to me, Mom equally has no issue bemoaning her life of celibacy. It's Dad's fault, of course. He shattered her trust in all of mankind, emphasis on the *man*. And according to him, Mom is to blame for his revolving door of girlfriends, because he too can never trust again.

My folks are exhausting.

"Nice. Looking forward to seeing her." Still lying.

For a moment, I consider telling him about my interview with

Kamal Jain, but I swiftly decide that needs to be done in a joint email to both my parents. If I tell one before the other, the world will end.

"Will your mother be at the game?" He says the word *mother* as if it's poisonous. "If so, you should warn her that I'm bringing Lucille."

Translation: you should make a point of telling her so I can rub it in her face that I'm seeing someone.

"She's not coming," I answer, happy to defuse that bomb.

"I see. You must be very disappointed."

Translation: she doesn't even care enough to watch your games, Colin. I love you more!

I suppress an annoyed sigh. "It's fine. Neither of you need to come to my games. Anyway, I have to go. I'll see you this weekend."

The moment we hang up, the pressure weighing on my chest eases slightly. Dealing with the folks takes an actual physical toll.

"Colin, hey!"

I turn to find Nora Ridgeway approaching. Nora was in two of my art classes last year, and this semester we have Advanced Figure Drawing together. She's a cool chick. Double major like me, in Visual Arts and Fashion Design.

"Hey," I greet her, eager for the distraction. It always takes a few minutes for the tension to completely drain from my body after a parental encounter. "Class isn't until two. You know that, right?"

She smiles. "Don't worry, I'm aware." She nods toward the building across the lane. "I've got History of Fashion in ten minutes. I saw you over here and just wanted to come and say hi." As she talks, her breath comes out in a visible white cloud.

"You need a hat," I tell her, noting that the tips of her ears are red.

"Eh, I'll live."

I can see why she doesn't want to cover her hair. Cut in a pixie cut, it's jet black except for the ends, which are bright pink. She's got a cool indie vibe to her that I've always appreciated. Plus, she has tats, a definite checkmark in the pros column for me.

"How was animation?" she asks. "My friend Lara is taking that course, and she was so pumped about it."

"It was awesome." I grin at her. "I guarantee it's more fun than History of Fashion."

Nora lightly punches my arm. "No way. Clothes are way more interesting than computers."

"Agree to disagree."

"And this course is taught by a *legend*." Her light gray eyes sparkle in the winter sun as they fill with excitement. "Erik Laurie."

My blank look makes her laugh.

"Former fashion editor for *Vogue*, *GQ*, *Harper's*. And he's the co-founder and former editor-in-chief of *Italia*, probably *the* most innovative fashion magazine for men. He's like the male version of Anna Wintour."

I draw another blank.

"Editor-in-chief of *Vogue*, and total goddess. She's my idol. And so is Erik Laurie. He's teaching two classes at Briar this year, *and* he's the director of the year-end fashion show. I'm beyond excited. We're going to learn *so* much from him."

I wonder if Summer is in Laurie's class today. I can't remember if she's majoring in Fashion Design or Merchandising. I suppose History of Fashion lends itself to either one, though.

And speak of the devil.

Summer appears on the cobblestone path, bundled up in a knee-length coat and a thick red scarf looped around her neck and hair. Her easy gait stutters for a step when she notices me. The moment our eyes lock, I remember her tiny towel sliding off her delectable body. That split-second glimpse of her wet, naked tits. A fleeting, dick-hardening tease.

I don't call out a hello or raise my hand in a wave. I'm waiting for her to initiate the greeting. Only, she doesn't. A few seconds tick by. Then she frowns at me and keeps walking. I don't know if I feel offended or ashamed. Maybe I should've greeted her first.

"Do you know her?" Nora has realized my attention's been diverted. Her suspicious gaze rests on Summer as she awaits my response.

"Yeah. She's a friend's sister," I say vaguely, deciding not to mention that we're roommates. I feel like that'll just open a conversation I'm not in the mood to have.

Nora relaxes. "Oh, cool. Anyway, I have to run, but I'm thinking maybe it's time we grab that elusive drink we've been talking about for a year?"

I laugh. "Maybe we should." We'd talked about it last year in Color Theory, but my schedule makes it hard for me to date. We played phone tag for a while, and by the time I finally had a free evening, Nora was dating someone else.

Clearly she's single again. "Do you still have my number?" she asks.

"Still got it."

She looks pleased by that. "How about tomorrow night at Malone's? Text me during the day to confirm?"

"Sounds great."

"Perfect. See you then." She squeezes my arm briefly, then hurries toward the same building Summer just disappeared into.

I guess I have a date tomorrow night.

# 13
# SUMMER

As I get comfy in my seat in the History of Fashion lecture hall, I try to remind myself that I'm all about girl power. We live in a society where too many women tear each other down instead of raising each other up. That's absurd to me. We need to empower one another, teach future generations of girls that it's important to stand together. Once upon a time, we had a common goal and a common enemy. We were burning bras and fighting for the right to vote.

Now we're body shaming each other on social media and blaming the mistress if our man cheats.

I don't consider myself a radical feminist. I don't believe men are evil demons from hell and should be purged from society—I think men have lots of good things to offer the world. Their dicks are fabulous, for one.

It would just be really nice if we could show some female solidarity like we used to.

But I know what's stopping us: jealousy. We're too frigging envious of each other, and envy is such a crippling feeling. It causes us to say things and behave in ways that we're secretly ashamed of, or at least I am. I regret nearly all the things I've said and done out of jealousy. I've also been on the receiving end of it from other girls. Some of them resented me for my looks. Others assumed I was going to be a bitch to them because of said looks, so they attacked first.

In spite of that, I've always tried to keep a smile on my face and be nice to everyone, even the haters. Ironically, a lot of the haters in high school ended up good friends of mine once they stopped linking me to their own insecurities.

So yes, I'm pro girl power. Ladies doing it for themselves. I am woman, hear me roar.

Yet I hate this girl Nora with the heat of a thousand suns.

She was talking to Fitz before class. Now she's sitting with two other chicks, talking *about* Fitz. I know her name is Nora because one of her friends called her that, and since I'm only two rows behind them, every word she utters floats toward me, clear as a bell.

"…just *so* cool. And wicked smart. And he's *so* talented. You should see his paintings."

"Doesn't hurt that he's hot as fuck," her friend teases her.

"Those tats," the other friend sighs.

I guess they've all seen Fitz's tats somehow? I now loathe the friends too.

"*So* hot," Nora says, pretending to fan herself.

And I'm *so* ready to accidentally throw something at her, because she's *so* annoying with her overuse and overemphasis of the word *so*.

"We're having drinks tomorrow night."

The flames of hatred in my stomach are doused with an icy bucket of reality.

He asked her out?

"Holy crap, this date is finally happening?" One of the friends claps with delight.

"Yes! I'm *so* excited."

Okay. So Fitz invited her on a date. She's pretty, has a great sense of style. Why shouldn't he go out with her?

And why should it bother me if he does?

*Because…*

Because, well, because she's obviously a bitch. I don't want Fitz going out with a bitch.

*She's not a bitch. That's your jealousy talking.*

*No,* I stubbornly argue with myself. She absolutely gave me a couple of dirty looks before she joined her friends. I didn't imagine that. So there's some bitch in her, at least.

*And there's a lot of bitch in you right now.*

"Fuck off," I order myself.

A few seats down in my row, a guy with longish black hair shifts his head in my direction. He arches a bushy eyebrow at me.

I raise my hand in a friendly wave. "Just ignore me. I've decided I'm going to be the crazy lady who talks to herself in class."

He laughs. "Noted."

Nora turns at the sound of my voice, narrows her eyes, and then turns back.

I hate her.

*You're being insane.*

"Did we not just determine that I've chosen a path of insanity?" I say out loud, though mostly it's to mess with my row-mate.

Bushy Eyebrows glances over again. "Oh wow. You weren't kidding."

I grin. "I'm done now. I promise."

In front of me, Nora's friends are grilling her for more details about her impending date.

"Just drinks?"

"Just drinks," she confirms. "Do you honestly think I'd ever agree to a first-date dinner after Eight-Course Ethan?"

The girls break out in laughter. "Oh my God! I forgot about him!"

I tune them out as they reminisce about the time Nora got stuck on an expensive, four-hour dinner date when she was ready to bail before the first course. It's an entertaining story, but I'm too busy trying to combat my unwanted jealousy.

Fitz can date whomever he wants. Besides, I have no right to be jealous. I cuddled with Hunter the other night. Granted, we didn't do anything but spoon, but it felt nice lying there with a warm male body pressed up against me. And if Hunter had made a move, I can't say with absolute certainty that I wouldn't have reciprocated.

The doors at the base of the lecture hall swing open, interrupting my thoughts. The man who enters the room needs no introduction, yet he still approaches the podium and greets us as if none of us have ever picked up a fashion magazine.

"Good morning! I'm Erik Laurie and I'm sorry to inform you that you will be enduring my unbearable presence for the next four months."

Laughter ripples through the hall.

"Just joshing," he says with a hearty chuckle. "I'm a fucking delight."

I smile along with everyone else in the room. He's establishing himself as the cool, fun prof right off the bat. I like that. He also looks a lot younger than his photos. Possibly because he usually sports a thick blond beard in those pictures, and today he's completely clean-shaven, revealing the baby face underneath.

I know he's in his mid-thirties, though. And his fashion sense is so on point I almost purr out loud. The clothes are Marc Jacobs—I recognize the retro blazer from Marc's fall collection. The shoes… Tom Ford, I think. I'd have to get a closer look to be sure.

"Welcome to the History of Fashion, ladies and gentlemen."

His voice is smooth and velvety, turning every girl's face into a real-life heart-eyes emoji. For some reason, he doesn't have the same effect on me. Objectively, Laurie is an attractive man, but something about his angular, symmetrical face doesn't do it for me.

Our new professor doesn't miss the female attention he's garnering. He winks at two girls in the front row as he rests his forearms on the podium. For the next ten minutes, he lists his impressive credentials, not revealing anything I didn't already know.

He's had an insanely prolific career for his relatively young age, and it's evident he has a genuine passion for what he does. When he's done reciting his résumé, he talks about what we can expect from his course. We'll be examining the global influence of fashion, how it's taken shape over the years, and how certain eras and historical events have impacted the concept and implementation of style.

Laurie has a way of speaking that captures your attention. He tells us that rather than a formal lecture, today he just wants to "chat" about why we love fashion and who inspires us. He kicks it off by confessing that his idol growing up was Ralph Lauren, then proceeds to spend five full minutes fan-girling about Lauren.

After he's done, he passes the torch to us. Bushy Eyebrows, who introduces himself as Ben, surprises me by proclaiming his love for Versace. Judging by his hobo-chic style, I would've pegged him as an Alexander McQueen enthusiast. But Ben goes on and on about Versace until our prof finally grins and asks for another volunteer.

Since I've never had any problems speaking in class, I raise my hand.

Laurie studies me from the podium. "And your name is?"

"It's Summer."

"No, sweetheart, it's winter. Have you not looked outside?"

Nora and her friends titter behind their hands. A few other students giggle as well. Me, I roll my eyes, an action that brings another grin to Laurie's face.

"Get that joke a lot, eh?" He waves a hand. "All right. Tell us who inspires you."

I answer without hesitation. "Chanel."

"Ah, yes." He nods his approval. "Gabrielle Bonheur Chanel. Also known as Coco. Do you know how she got the nickname, Winter?"

Cue more giggles.

I'm not sure how I feel about Professor Comedian, especially since he keeps flipping between two personalities. One second he's suave and confident, the next he's Mr. I'm Just Gonna Crack Jokes Because I'm One of You!

It's disorienting.

"She got the nickname when she was a cabaret singer," I answer. "She tried to make a go of it as an actress, failed, and went into fashion."

"Finding unimaginable success," he concludes.

"That's one of the reasons I love her. When her original plans fell through, she didn't give up. She chose a different path, succeeded, and became an icon. Her brand has been around for nearly a century. It survived the Second World War—"

"Yeah, because she was a Nazi collaborator," Nora pipes up in a snide voice.

I ball my fists and press them to my thighs. Is she for real right now? Interrupting me so she can insult a fashion legend?

"And you are?" Laurie prompts.

"Nora Ridgeway." She shrugs. "And it's common knowledge that Chanel was shady. Documents that were recently declassified speculate her wartime activities were downright despicable."

Our professor does not disagree. "Yes, that is what's being alleged. And when she reentered the fashion world after the war, there was indeed a lot of anger about these claims. Yet the brand recovered." He tips his head. "Why do we think that is, Summer?"

"Because…she…" I bite my lip in thought. "Because she was *fashion*. She pioneered the little black dress, for Pete's sake. People accused her of being too conservative, but honestly I think she revolutionized the industry. She showed the world that fashion isn't just about wearing a nice dress or tailored suit to a dinner party—it's a way of life." I pause, scanning my memory. "There was this famous quote of hers about how fashion is everywhere—'It's in the sky and in the streets, it's in how we live and what we do.' That's a philosophy I believe in."

He nods. Many of my classmates are nodding too. Nora, however, scowls at me over her shoulder and then stiffly faces the room again.

Whatever. I don't care if she doesn't like me. She tried to make me look like a fool for respecting Chanel, and it backfired on her. Tough shit.

"Very well said," Laurie tells me before sweeping his gaze over the room. "Who's next? I want to know who inspires you."

The next hour flies by, and I'm less than thrilled when we're dismissed. I was dreading this moment, even more so now because I know I impressed Erik Laurie. I really don't want him to lose all that good will toward me when I tell him about my learning issues.

As I navigate the aisle, I hear Nora speaking to her friend. "I'll meet you outside. I want to tell him what a huge fan I am."

Oh great. Now if I go talk to him, Nora will think I'm trying to one-up her.

"Summer," Laurie calls from the front of the room. "A quick word?"

Okay. At least it doesn't look like I'm the one initiating the contact.

But I think this might be worse.

Nora stops in her tracks. Her eyes burn into my back like hot coals as I hurriedly descend the steps.

"It's nice to officially meet you." Smiling, he extends a hand.

I give it a shake. "Nice to meet you too, Professor Laurie."

"Call me Erik."

"Oh. Um. We might need to work up to that. I feel weird first-naming authority figures."

He chuckles. "Fair enough. How about Mr. L until you warm up to Erik?" He winks at me, and his tone holds a flirtatious note, but I'm starting to think this is just him being friendly. I saw him winking at several other girls throughout the lecture.

"Mr. L, it is." I hesitate, readying myself for the awkward part. "I don't know if you had a chance to speak to Mr. Richmond. He's serving as my academic advisor this year."

"I did, actually. Rest assured, he advised me about your learning difficulties, and I do plan on sitting down with you to discuss it further. But we'll need to do that during office hours." He studies me for a moment. "I was impressed with you this morning. You're a very eloquent speaker."

"And a very terrible writer."

"Hey, you could say that about plenty of individuals. And there are ways around it. Like I said, we'll talk during office hours, but I do believe I can make alternate arrangements for you. Perhaps a lower word count for the midterm, supplemented by an oral element?"

A tiny smile lifts the corners of his mouth at the word *oral*. I know he's referring to an oral presentation, but the accompanying smile triggers my ick meter. Either he's skirting a dangerous line between his authority and his female students, or he's just overly friendly. I really hope it's the latter.

"You can check the department website for my availability, but I think the sooner we sit down and hammer this out, the better."

"I agree."

He reaches out and squeezes my hand. "And, please, continue to speak out in class the way you did today. I appreciate students who are as passionate as I am about this topic."

Another wink.

Or maybe he's not winking, and that's just his eye? Is there a possibility that this is how he blinks, one eye at a time? I have no clue, and I don't care to find out. Nora is still glaring at me. And Laurie is still holding my hand.

I awkwardly slide my palm out of his grip. "I'll do my best. And I'll check your office hours when I get home. Thanks, sir—I mean, Mr. L."

"That's better."

He winks. Or blinks. Who the fuck knows.

I practically sprint toward the exit, ignoring Nora's thunderous expression.

Outside, I shiver from the cold as I pile all my winter clothes on. I didn't want to do it in the lecture hall under Laurie's gaze. The man might be a legend in the fashion world, and he did seem nice enough, but I got such a weird vibe from him.

Ugh. I don't know. Maybe I'm reading too much into it.

Since this was my only class for the day, I'm free as a bird, so I text Brenna asking if she's on campus. She's quick to answer.

**BRENNA:** Library
**ME:** Just finished class. Wanna grab lunch at the diner?
**BRENNA:** Yessss. Come get me?
**ME:** Kk. 10 min
**ME:** Be prepared to discuss MH or I won't let you in my car!

This time, there's a delay in her response. Shocking. I texted her a bunch of times yesterday begging her to tell me exactly what happened between her and Hollis, but she refused to discuss it.

**BRENNA:** MH?

Seriously? She's going to play dumb?

**ME:** Mike Hollis. AKA king of the bros. I want all the deets today or else this friendship is over.
**BRENNA:** I'll miss u
**ME:** You think I'm bluffing? I've cut friends off for not tagging me in Insta posts. I'm ruthless, Bee.
**BRENNA:** Don't believe u
**ME:** Arggghhh! Come on, please?? I can't take it anymore. I must find out 1) his dick size and 2) WTF WERE U THINKING

After another long pause, she responds with: Fine. You win.

Despite my threats, I don't push Brenna to talk about Hollis during the drive to Hastings. We discuss our classes instead, and I confess that I'm feeling a tad uneasy about my professor.

"I got a pervy vibe from him," I say as I search for street parking.

"What's his name?"

"Erik Laurie."

"Never heard of him."

There's no reason why she would, unless she follows the fashion world closely, which I know she doesn't. I give her a quick rundown of his credentials before describing the chronic winking.

"Maybe he doesn't understand the concept?" she suggests. "Like, to him, winking could be another form of smiling. So if you give him a compliment, he says *Thanks!* Wink. And when he greets people, he goes, *Nice to meet you!* Wink."

I bite my lip to stop from laughing. "Are you fucking with me right now?"

"Of course I am. Nobody is that dumb. Winking is flirting. Everyone knows that."

"So he was flirting with me?"

"Probably?" She rolls her eyes. "And if you try to tell me this is the first time a prof has ever flirted with you, I won't believe you."

"No, it's happened before," I admit. "But I wasn't expecting it from this one. He's so respected in the industry."

Her loud snort echoes in the car. "Right. Because well-respected men can't possibly be douchebags. Do we need to have a talk about the current climate in Hollywood?"

"No, let's not go there." I find a spot and squeeze my Audi into it.

Five minutes later, we're seated across from each other in one of the retro, red vinyl booths. Brenna orders a coffee, black. I order a mint tea with lemon. Somehow that sums up this friendship of ours. Appearance wise, I'm all about light colors and nude makeup, while Brenna prefers smoky eyes and black everything. In terms of personality, I'm more carefree, she's edgier, but we're both a little nuts. It's a hoe-mance for the ages.

"Okay, I've let you avoid it for long enough," I announce after the waitress takes our order. "Are you ready?"

She wraps both hands around her coffee cup. "Hit me."

For more than a day, my overflowing curiosity has been contained by a dam named Brenna. Now that she's broken, there's no stopping the flood.

"Is he a good kisser? What's our penis situation like? Did he go down on you? Did you sleep with him? Why did you do this? Is he annoying in bed? Do you regret it? Is he—"

"Omigod!" Brenna exclaims. "I am not answering *any* of that."

I get one last question in before the buzzer. "Do you have a boyfriend now?"

"No, but I have an ex-best friend," she says sweetly.

I ignore that. "Speaking of your boyfriend, he walked in on me in the shower this morning."

That momentarily distracts her from whatever murder plot she's devising about me in her head. "What?"

"Hollis walked in on me showering."

She perks up. "Nice. So I don't need to punish you for referring to him as my boyfriend. The universe did it for me."

"It was so embarrassing." I fill her in on the morning's theatrics, ending with the grand finale: my towel dropping in front of three boxers-clad college boys.

She purses her lips. "You just described the setup for a porno, so I assume the scene ended with you jacking them all off?"

"No, you brat. It ended with Fitz promising to fix the lock. Which was nice of him," I force myself to add.

"See? I told you, he's a good guy."

"Are you sure about that? Because I saw him outside my lecture hall earlier and he didn't even say hello. He looked right at me and then ignored me."

"Maybe he didn't see you."

"Did you miss the part where I literally just said he looked at me?"

She lets out a sigh. "He's really not as bad as you think, Summer." Under her breath, she mumbles, "Hollis, on the other hand…"

I pounce like a jackalope. Well, if a jackalope pounces, that is. And if I knew what a jackalope was. "If Hollis is such a bad guy, then why'd you sleep with him?"

"Because I was drunk. And we didn't sleep together."

"As I recall, you weren't wearing pants yesterday morning…"

"I'm not sure if you learned this in sex ed, but it *is* possible to be naked with someone and not have sex." She throws me another bone by relenting. "He's not a terrible kisser."

"Are you going to hook up with him again?"

"Absolutely not."

Our food arrives, and Brenna is extra speedy about taking a huge bite of her club sandwich. I suspect it's so she doesn't have to talk.

I pick at my chicken Caesar salad with my fork, my appetite easing slightly as I remember what else happened today. "Some girl in my History of Fashion class asked Fitz out."

Brenna answers while chewing. "Really? Who?"

"Nora something or other. This little indie chick with pink hair." I take a tiny bite of my salad. "He said yes."

"How do you know he said yes?"

"I heard her telling her friends."

"Okay." Brenna swallows and sets the sandwich on her plate. "I'm not sure what the proper response is—do you want me to be happy for Fitzy that he's gettin' some, or outraged on your behalf because you still have a thing for him?"

"I don't have a thing for him," I object instantly.

"Doth protest, et cetera et cetera."

I glare at her. "Of course doth protest. I'm not attracted to guys who think I'm fluff."

"Mmm-hmmm. So you're saying if he called you up right now and said, *Hey Summer, I'd like to take you on a date and possibly show you my penis at the end of it?* You're telling me you'd say no?"

"One hundred percent."

"Bullshit."

"Fitz can date every woman at this college for all I care. He blew his chance with me."

"Bullshit."

"He did."

"Bullshit."

I growl in aggravation. "You're such a child."

"Right. *I'm* the child. Just admit you still like him."

"Sure, if *you* admit you enjoyed fooling around with Hollis," I challenge.

It's a stalemate.

Brenna shrugs and resumes eating. I keep picking at my salad. My appetite is completely gone now, because the knowledge that Fitz is going out with another girl bothers me much more than I thought it would.

---

In high school, I was a cheerleader, captain of the dance team, and co-captain of the girls' swim team. The latter meant that I didn't just hang out with hot football players, but hot swimmers as well. The boys with the lean muscles and smooth, aerodynamic bodies. So I'm not at all fazed the next evening as I lounge on the couch next to a very hairless Mike Hollis.

The bare arm resting haphazardly on the cushion between us and the bare legs up on the coffee table don't have a single hair on them, yet somehow this doesn't take away from his masculinity. Hollis might be annoying, but he does have sex appeal, I'll give him that.

Also, he and I—and this slightly horrifies me, as I'm not sure what it says about *me*—have a lot more in common than I ever could have imagined. In the past hour, I've discovered that he prefers tea to coffee, isn't ashamed to say he loves Harry Styles' solo album, and is as obsessed with the movie *Titanic* as I am. It's currently playing on one of the movie networks the guys subscribe to. We landed on it at the halfway point, and the film is now gearing up for all the epic, devastating moments.

"We might need to turn it off before the real shit goes down," he warns me. Then he snickers at his own pun. "Goes down, get it? Like the ship."

"Yes, Mike. I got it." I lift my socked feet on the table, nudging his left foot with my right one. "And we can't turn it off. The ending scenes are the best ones."

"Babe. Please. I'm not in the mood to cry tonight."

Laughter bubbles in my throat. His serious expression tells me he's not even joking. "Which part gets you? Mother reading to her children? Old couple on the bed?"

"All of the above. And don't get me started on Jack's senseless death. Goddamn unnecessary."

I nod wholeheartedly. "There was room for two on the door."

"Damn right there was. It was even myth-busted. He didn't have to die."

When my phone chimes, I tear my gaze off young Leonardo DiCaprio's beautiful face. Though really, his face is as beautiful now as it was then. He's an ageless wonder.

I read the incoming text from Hunter, who'd gone out tonight with a few guys from the team. I stayed home because Brenna had been supposed to come over and hang out. I have a feeling that's the only reason Hollis stayed behind too. But she canceled at the last minute, hence why Hollis and I are alone.

Fitz isn't home either, but I'm trying very hard not to dwell on why that is.

"Hunter wants to know if you want him to bring you some chicken wings," I tell Hollis.

"How is this a question?"

"Is that a yes?"

"What do you think?"

"I think it's a yes," I say irritably, "but I'd like to be sure."

"I won't even justify his question with an answer."

I swear one day I'm going to murder this guy. I text Hunter a yes to the wings, then send a message to Brenna.

> **ME:** Due to you ditching me, I'm chilling with your bf tonight and he is mighty annoying.
>
> **BRENNA:** Didn't mean to ditch u, GB. Forgot about study group.

It takes a second to figure out "GB" means Greenwich Barbie. Grinning, I type back, All good. J/k anyway. Well, not about the annoying part. Because he is.

> **BRENNA:** Very much so. And he's not my bf.

She punctuates that with the middle finger emoji. Just to mess with her, I turn to Hollis and say, "Brenna says hi."

His blue eyes light up. "Legit? Tell her to give me her number already. I'm tired of begging for it." He stops, his gaze dropping to the phone in my hand. "Better yet, how about you give it to me and I'll tell her directly?"

Oh my God. She won't even let him have her precious phone number? Poor guy. I want so badly to laugh, but I think it might hurt his feelings.

"Sorry, sweetie," I say lightly. "Can't do that. It's against hoe-code."

Despite his disappointed expression, he leans over and drops a solemn pat on my shoulder. "I respect that. We all need to live by a code." His attention returns to the film. "Jesus fuck, Kate Winslet looks so hot wielding an axe."

I snort out a laugh. We watch as Kate wades through knee-deep water to rescue a handcuffed Leo. "See, rich girls can be badasses," I tell Hollis.

"If that's your way of offering to break my handcuffs with an axe, I graciously decline. In no way do I trust your aim."

"No? How's this for aim?" Lightning fast, I grab a peanut from the can of mixed nuts we've been passing back and forth and flick it at him.

It hits him smack in the forehead and bounces off with an actual *ping*.

I curl over, inconsolable with laughter. "Why…did…it…make…that…sound?" I wheeze, trying to catch my breath. My stomach hurts from the force of my giggles. "Mike! Do you have a metal plate in your forehead?"

Hollis is as perplexed as I am. "Dude. I didn't think I did. Now I just want to call my mom and ask."

I'm still howling when the front door creaks open. I expect Hunter to appear with a platter of chicken wings, but it's Fitz's broad body that fills the doorway. Almost immediately, my laughter dies.

He went out with Nora Ridgeway tonight. Hollis was teasing him about it earlier when Fitz came downstairs in nice jeans and a light blue button-down.

Oh, and no beard.

That's right. He shaved for her. And unlike Professor Laurie, whose beard removal made him appear prepubescent, Fitz is all man with or without the facial hair. If anything, the clean-shaven look emphasizes his masculine features more—the hard slash of his jaw, the sexy mouth, dimpled chin. I almost fainted with desire earlier when I realized he's got a cleft in his chin.

"Hey. What's so funny?" he asks gruffly, glancing from me to Hollis.

"My skull is made of metal," Hollis replies. "How'd your date go?"

It's barely ten thirty. I wonder if his early return is a good sign, but Fitz squashes that notion by saying, "Pretty good."

I promised myself I wouldn't ask a single question about his stupid date.

My mouth doesn't feel like obeying.

"I'm surprised you went out with a fashion major," I blurt out.

He shrugs, leaning one shoulder against the doorframe. "She's also a Visual Arts major. Her medium's abstract painting."

Of course it is. Nora seems like the kind of girl who'd throw a glob of black and pink paint on a canvas and then stand there pontificating about how the "piece" represents anarchy and/or the inequality of women.

"I see. So you spent the whole time discussing Monet and Dalí, I suppose?" I meant to tease, but the words sound almost like an attack.

Fitz senses it too. His eyes narrow. "We talked art, yeah. Is that a problem?"

"Of course not. Why would it be?"

"I don't know. Why would it?"

"I just said it wasn't." My teeth clench as I reach for my water bottle. I have a hard time swallowing on account of my tense jaw, but I manage. "I'm glad you two share similar interests. Imagine how dreadful it would've been if she spent the whole night babbling about the Kardashians." I cap the bottle, hastily adding, "Not that there's anything wrong with the Kardashians." I adore Kim and the crew. I think they're all savvy businesswomen, if I'm being honest.

"I love the Kardashians," Hollis chimes in.

"If you say one word about their butts," I warn.

"I like the show," he assures me. "It's funny."

"Liar. No way you watch the show."

"Bible."

I gasp. "Oh my God. Okay. We'll discuss the current season later." To Fitz, I say, "Sounds like a super-fun date. All that art talk. Real deep."

He props one hand on the door jamb. "Any reason why you're being a bitch right now?"

What?

"Whoa," Hollis murmurs.

I gape at Fitz. My hand trembles around the water bottle. Did he seriously call me a bitch? I don't think I've ever heard that word exit his mouth before. And for it to be directed at *me*? Hurt and anger war in my stomach, making it churn.

The anger wins out.

Slamming the bottle on the table, I get up and advance on him. "I can't believe you just said that."

"Really? So *you're* allowed to sit there and make snarky comments, but it's unfathomable for me to call you on it?"

"Guys," Hollis interjects.

"I wasn't being snarky," I snap.

"You were mocking Nora," he snaps back. "That's snark in my book. And this isn't the first time you've been bitchy toward me, Summer. You honestly think I haven't noticed?"

"Noticed what? That I don't particularly want to be around you?" I plant my hands on my hips. "I wasn't trying to hide it."

"Exactly. You've been openly bitchy."

"Stop calling me a bitch!"

"Stop acting like one!"

"Guys," Hollis chides.

"Why are you always yelling at me?" I growl at Fitz. "I never hear you yell at anyone else."

"Because nobody else drives me *insane* like this." He angrily drags both hands through his hair. "One minute you're all smiles and hugs on New Year's, the next you're—"

"We are *not* discussing New Year's," I interrupt. "Not after what you—" I stop abruptly.

A crease appears in his forehead. "After what?"

"After what?" Hollis echoes curiously.

"I just told you, we're not discussing it."

"Discussing what?" Fitz demands. "I still have no clue what you're talking about. What is it I supposedly did?"

I slam my lips together.

He searches my face for a few seconds. Then his eyes take on a gleam of determination. Oh no. I'm starting to recognize that expression.

"You know what, we're dealing with this right fucking now." He takes a menacing step forward. "'Scuse us, Mike."

"Naw, man, this was just getting good!"

I hold up my hands in a defensive pose as Fitz edges toward me. "Don't you dare," I caution. "Don't you fucking—"

I'm being flung over his shoulder before I can finish that sentence.

Un-frigging-believable!

*"How is this happening again?"* I shriek.

My protests fall on deaf ears, because Fitz is already carting me up the stairs.

# 14
# FITZ

I won't lie. Having an angry, squirming Summer wriggling in my arms is just the teeniest bit of a turn-on.

Okay fine. I'm rock hard.

In my defense, I didn't start this argument off with a boner. I was genuinely pissed at her. I still am. Only now I'm also aroused.

So sue me.

"Put. Me. Down." Summer snarls out the words, and each sharp sound sends another bolt of heat to my cock.

Something is really wrong with me. I just spent the past three hours with a girl who dolled herself up for me, who batted her lashes and touched my hand and all but held up a cardboard sign that said *FUCK ME, COLIN!*

I didn't experience so much as a dick twitch.

And now here I am with Summer, who's wearing baggy plaid pants and a long-sleeve shirt, who's shouting obscenities at me, and my dick is raring to go.

"You thought I was a bitch before?" she says threateningly. "Well, how about now!"

She resorts to her go-to move: pinching my butt.

But the sting of pain only turns me on. I kick her bedroom door open. "Did anyone ever tell you you're a brat?"

The moment I set her down, she takes a swing at me.

Startled laughter lodges in my throat. I easily block her fist before it can connect with my solar plexus. "Stop that," I order.

"Why? Because it makes me a brat? Oh, and a bitch too, right? And a drama queen…and a sorority girl…what else…" Her cheeks redden with what appears to be embarrassment. "Oh, yes. I'm surface level. That's what you think, right? That I'm fluff?"

My stomach sinks like a stone.

Dick's not doing great, either—one look at Summer's stricken face and my hard-on says "peace out."

Her fingers, which were clenched so tightly before, slowly uncurl and go limp. Noting my expression, she gives a bitter laugh. "I heard everything you said to Garrett at the bar that night."

Aw hell. Guilt ripples through my entire body before settling in my gut, an eddy of shame. "Summer," I start. Then stop.

"Every word," she says quietly. "I heard every word you said, and not a single one was very nice, Colin."

I feel like such an asshole.

Most of my life I've made it a point not to be cruel to others. Not to talk trash about anyone—to their face or behind their back. Growing up, all I saw from my parents was negativity. Nasty jabs directed at each other. *Your father is a piece of shit, Colin. Your mom is a lying bitch, son.* Over the years they'd calmed down, but it didn't happen fast enough. The toxic environment they'd created had already done its job, teaching me the hard way how damaging words can be. That there's no taking back the poison once you've spewed it.

"Summer," I try again, and stop again.

I don't know how to explain my actions without revealing just how badly I'd craved her that night. I'd been looking for negative traits because I was having a good time with her. Because she was making me laugh. Turning me on. I wanted her, and it was messing with my head, so I started picking apart everything I perceived to be a flaw.

"I'm sorry you heard all that," is what I finally choke out.

And I know immediately that it was the wrong thing to say. Sitting on the edge of my bed, she peers up at me with sad green eyes.

Jesus. Her expression. It's like an arrow to the heart.

"I'm not fluff." Her words are barely a whisper. She clears her throat, and when she speaks again, it's in a strong, even tone. "Yes, I have a stupid amount of energy. Yes, I enjoy shopping, and I'm obsessed with clothes. Yes, I was in a sorority, and yes, I like to dance and have fun with my friends." She exhales in a fast rush. "That doesn't make me superficial, Fitz. And it doesn't mean there isn't more to me beneath the surface. Because there is."

"Of course there is." Taking a ragged breath, I sink down beside her. "I'm so sorry, Summer. I didn't mean to hurt you."

"You know what really hurts? That you just assumed there was nothing more to me than parties and shopping. I'm a loyal friend. I'm a good daughter, a good sister. You'd spent, what? Ninety minutes in my presence? And you think you know the whole story?"

The guilt travels upward to coat my throat. I try to gulp it down, but it only thickens, like a layer of tar coating the pavement. She's absolutely right. Even though I was using those perceived flaws of hers as deterrents, it doesn't change the fact that they occurred to me in the first place.

I *did* make the assumption that she's just a party girl and there's nothing more to her, and I'm ashamed of myself for it.

"I'm sorry," I say roughly. "None of what I said was right. Or deserved. And I'm also sorry about calling you a bitch downstairs. Your behavior *has* been bitchy, but now I understand where it was coming from. I'm so sorry."

Summer goes silent for a long beat. A foot of space separates us, but she might as well be sitting in my lap, that's how aware of her I am. The heat of her body, the rise of her tits beneath her shirt as she inhales, the heady scent that's so uniquely Summer. Her thick, gold-spun hair is cascading over one shoulder, making my fingers itch to touch it.

"I was having a good time with you that night." Her tone is flat, disappointed. "It was fun talking to you. Teasing you about being a curmudgeon." She pauses. "Curmudgeon doesn't quite fit anymore, though. I think 'dick' works better now."

My heart squeezes because it's true. "I'm sorry." Apparently that's all I'm capable of saying.

"Whatever." She waves a dismissive hand. "That's what I get for developing a crush on someone who isn't my usual type. I guess… Well, I guess that's why we have types, right? You're drawn to certain people, and they're drawn to you. But you didn't have to be mean, Fitz. If you weren't interested, you could have told me instead of trashing me to Garrett." Her hands become fists again, pressed tight to her thighs.

"I don't usually do that." I hear the torment in my voice. I'm sure she does too. "But, that night—"

"I get it," she interrupts. "You didn't want to be with me."

Shame once again seals my throat until I can scarcely draw a breath.

"But for the record, there's more to me than you think." Her voice cracks. "I have substance."

Oh my fucking God, this girl is ripping my heart out. I've never felt so bad about anything in my entire life.

"I know people who sit around and ponder the meaning of life, their purpose, the universe, why the sky is blue, anything they can question. But that's never been me. I'm good at other things, like listening when someone needs me. I'm…"

*Sunshine*, I finish silently.

Just like her name, Summer is sunshine.

Rather than fill in the blank, she switches gears. "And despite what you may think, I can hold a conversation that doesn't involve shoes or designer clothing. I might not be able to write you a five-thousand-word dissertation about Van Gogh and every tiny little brushstroke he did, but I can explain the joy that art and beauty bring to the world." She rises to her feet, somewhat stiffly. "Anyway. I'm sorry I was rude about your new girlfriend."

"She's not my girlfriend," I mutter. "We went on one date."

"Whatever. I'm sorry I mocked your date. For what it's worth, she's in my history class, and she didn't particularly make a good first impression on me."

I bite hard on the inside of my cheek. "I really am sorry about New Year's. Truly. I didn't mean any of that shit."

She gives a resigned smile that once again cuts me to the core. Then she shrugs and says, "Yes, you did."

---

Typically, clearing the air is supposed to ease relations between two people.

For Summer and me, it produces the opposite effect.

In the days following our confrontation, we keep our distance, tiptoeing around one another and speaking only out of necessity. There isn't any malice behind it, just extreme awkwardness on both our parts. I suspect she still thinks I'm an ass for saying what I said, and I still feel like one.

To make matters worse, she and Hunter have been hanging out a lot. A few times, I've caught them sitting real close to each other on the couch. No PDA or overtly sexual vibes, but it's clear they enjoy each other's company. Hunter flirts with her every chance he gets, and Summer doesn't seem to mind.

I mind.

I mind a little too much, and that's why I'm holed up in my bedroom on Sunday night after our win against Dartmouth instead of partying downstairs with my teammates. And we beat Suffolk yesterday too, so technically it's a double celebration.

But I'm not in the mood to watch Hunter hit on Summer. Plus, my entire body feels like one giant bruise.

The Dartmouth game was a rough one. Lots of hits (not all of them clean), lots of penalties (not all of them called), and one groin injury to a Dartmouth defenseman that made my balls shrivel and retreat like a frightened turtle. Needless to say, I'm tired, sore, and cranky.

The music blasting downstairs keeps trying to drown out the playlist pouring from my computer speakers. It's a weird mix of bluegrass and indie rock, which for some reason lends itself well to this free draw exercise I'm currently putting myself through. Sometimes, when I'm creatively blocked, I'll lie on my back, sketchpad on my lap, pencil in hand. I'll close my eyes, breathe in and out, slow and steady, and allow my pencil to draw whatever it wants.

My high school art teacher urged me to try it one day, claiming it's as effective as meditation in clearing the mind, opening the creative floodgates. She was right—whenever I'm blocked, free drawing does the trick.

I'm not certain how long I lie there, sketching with my eyes closed, but by the time I register that my pencil's no longer sharp and my wrist is cramping, the music in the living room has ceased, and my own playlist has restarted itself.

Shaking out my wrist, I slide into a sitting position. I stare down at my sketch and discover that I've drawn Summer.

Not the season. The girl.

And not the girl with the dazzling smile. Not the laughing Summer, or the Summer whose cheeks go brighter than Red Delicious apples when she's pissed at me.

I drew the Summer whose green eyes shimmered with pain as she'd whispered the words, "I have substance."

On the page, her full lips are frozen in time. But in my mind, they're quivering as she takes a shaky breath. The sketch hints at the tears clinging to her lower lashes, conveying an air of vulnerability that tugs at my heart. But the tight set of her jaw tells you she won't go down without a fight.

I suck in a breath.

She's completely and utterly perfect for the character in the new game I'm designing. I've been working on the assets for the past few months but haven't found any inspiration for the female lead, and it's been slowing my production.

I stare at the sketch for nearly five minutes before forcing myself to close the pad and put it away. The moment my brain snaps out of art mode and into I'm-a-living-breathing-creature mode, I realize not only do I have to piss like a racehorse, but I'm hungrier than that horse and could probably eat it. My stomach rumbles so loudly I'm surprised I didn't notice the hunger pangs until now.

I take care of the bladder issue first, then go downstairs to scrounge up some food. From the staircase, I hear a wave of laughter from the living room and Hollis' voice saying, "*That's* what I'm talkin' about!" Usually when Mike Hollis sounds this excited about something, it's either the most horrifying thing in the world or unimaginably awesome. No in between with that guy.

Curiosity has me following Mike's voice instead of turning toward the kitchen. When I approach the doorway, I feel like I've been transported back to the eighth grade. A bunch of people are still over. Including my team captain, Nate, who's rubbing his hands gleefully, urging the bottle on the table to stop in front of him.

Yes, I said bottle.

Either I'm hallucinating, or my college-aged friends are playing Spin the Bottle. They're on the floor or sitting on various pieces of furniture in some semblance of a circle. Clearly Summer was the spinner, because she's leaning forward from the couch, watching the bottle. Meanwhile, all the single dudes in the room are watching *her*. Beyond hopeful.

The green Heineken bottle slows, just passing Nate and Hollis. It nearly lands on Jesse Wilkes's girlfriend Katie. It spins another fraction of an inch, glides to a stop. And points directly to the living room doorway.

At me.

# 15
# SUMMER

AND THIS IS WHY GAMES LIKE SPIN THE BOTTLE AND 7 MINUTES in Heaven stopped being cool after middle school.

Because when you're twelve and thirteen, you're allowed to kiss random boys without worrying about the consequences.

When you're an adult, there are *always* consequences.

For example, if I have to kiss Colin Fitzgerald right now? Everyone in this room is going to see how hot I am for the guy.

"Let me spin again," I blurt out. "Fitz isn't even playing."

Katie, a pretty redhead with a wide Julia Roberts-esque mouth, wags a finger at me. "No way! I just had to kiss Hollis—in front of my *boyfriend*!"

"I wasn't threatened," Jesse says easily. "I mean, it's Hollis."

"Hey," Mike protests.

"That's not the point," Katie argues. "All I'm saying is, you kiss whoever the bottle points to. No exceptions."

My gaze shifts to Fitz. He's sporting what I like to call Exploding Ovaries attire—gray sweatpants that ride oh-so-low on his trim hips, and a tight white T-shirt that shows off his tattooed arms. This fucking guy. He's a total ten.

Actually, let's make that a nine. I'm deducting one point for the fact that he looks like he wishes he could hop into a transporter and teleport to Siberia.

His less than enthused expression raises my hackles. Really? The idea of kissing me is *sooooo* repulsive to him? After our showdown earlier this week when I called him out on his nastiness, he should be clamoring to curry favor with me.

Asshole should be *begging* to kiss me.

Fitz inches backward. "I'm, ah, gonna grab some food."

From the other end of the couch, Hunter drawls, "Good idea." His tone is light, but there's a hint of darkness behind it.

Like me, Hunter hadn't seemed too pumped to play this game, although I didn't see him complaining when he got to French the insanely hot Arielle ten minutes ago. Arielle's the only other single chick here. Katie and Shayla are both taken, but apparently their boyfriends (Jesse and Pierre, respectively) don't mind sharing their girlfriends for the sake of the game.

"Freeze!" Katie orders when Fitz tries to take a step.

He freezes.

"I'm sorry to have to break it to you," she informs him, "but Summer will be kissing you now."

Oh my God. Where's Brenna when you need her? If she were here, she never would've allowed Katie and Arielle to convince us to play this silly game. Brenna would've laughed in their faces and challenged everyone to a shot contest instead, which I'm sure would've resulted in lots of kissing anyway. Just not on-the-spot, being-forced-to-kiss kissing.

But nope, Brenna had other plans. Bitch.

"I'll spin again," I insist. At this point, I'll gladly kiss anyone else, even Hollis. Or one of the girls.

To my shock, Hollis sides with Katie. "Naw, babe, a rule's a rule." My reluctant, unhappy expression only hardens his resolve. "This'll be good for you guys." He glances toward the doorway, where Fitz is frowning at him. "All you two do is fight. Time to kiss and make up."

Aggravation rises inside me. "Come on, Hollis."

"See! Even better," Katie says happily. "You two need to clear the air."

"With your tongue," the dark-haired Arielle agrees solemnly.

Nate, the captain of the hockey team, snorts in amusement. Why can't I kiss *him*, dammit? He's tall and built and has amazing, vivid blue eyes.

Before I can blink, Katie is tugging on my hand. My jaw drops as the tiny redhead, who can't be more than five feet tall, muscles me onto my feet and gives me a little shove.

"You are freakishly strong," I growl down at her. And I do mean *down*—I'm almost a head taller than this girl, yet she's still able to manhandle me.

She grins. "I know."

Fitz's wary gaze sweeps the room. "How drunk are you guys, exactly?" He raises a brow at his team captain. "Since when do we play kissing games?"

Nate shrugs and lifts his beer bottle. "Only live once, right?" he says easily.

"All right, babes." Katie claps her hands. "Kiss and make up."

I give an outraged squeak when there's another hard push on my back. I stumble forward, and I'm two seconds from smacking my nose on the doorframe before Fitz's strong hands steady me.

His touch sends a bolt of heat through my body, and my breath catches in my throat when I notice that his eyes have softened. Actually, no. They may have lost their hard edges, but they're certainly not soft. They're heavy-lidded now, gleaming with unexpected heat.

Then he blinks, and the fire is replaced by exasperation.

"Let's just do this so they shut up," he murmurs so only I can hear. "She won't let it go."

He means Katie, and I think he might be right. Tonight's my first time meeting her, but within five seconds of being introduced, I concluded that she's a bossy little firecracker. Don't get me wrong, she's fun. But I feel like if you're friends with Katie, she always has the final say about everything.

"Fine," I murmur back. "No tongue."

I see the merest hint of a smile. "No promises."

I barely have time to process the unexpected teasing remark before Fitz cups my chin with one big hand. I vaguely register a loud whistle—I think it comes from Hollis. And then it gets drowned out by my pounding heartbeat as Fitz's lips gently touch mine.

Oh.

Oh wow.

I didn't expect him to start off so tender. In front of everyone. But he does. His thumb sweeps over my cheek as his mouth moves ever so slowly over mine. He's got the softest lips I've ever felt, and he uses them with confidence. I shiver when he increases the pressure, sealing his lips tight to mine. And then the tip of his tongue slicks over my bottom lip, and I jolt as if I stuck my finger in a live socket.

The moment our tongues touch, I'm gone. A low hum of desire buzzes between my legs, crackling up to my breasts and hardening my nipples. I completely surrender to his kiss. I let his tongue sweep into my mouth. I let his fingers dig possessively into my waist, his warm breath to heat my mouth, his sexy scent to infuse my senses.

I can't stop myself—I press one hand to his rock-hard chest. The other, I curl around the nape of his neck. The baby-fine hairs there tickle my palm. His left pec quivers beneath my palm, and I can feel his heartbeat. It's hammering as fast as mine.

When I feel him start to pull away, a frantic, helpless sensation surges through me. I tighten my grip on his neck and kiss him harder. My tongue tangles with his, and I swallow the husky sound he makes. I hope nobody else heard it.

Because that beautiful desperate sound belongs to me. It's all mine. I want to memorize the seductive resonance and replay it over and over again later, when I'm lying alone in bed, when my hand slides between my legs as I touch myself to the memory of this kiss.

Oh fuck. I'm so turned on. My legs are shaking. My panties are soaked.

I force myself to wrench our mouths apart. What takes even more willpower is not looking at him. I'm terrified of what his expression will show me, so I avoid it by glancing over my shoulder at our audience.

But I feel it. Like a molten-hot brand scorching the center of my spine.

I pray to God that our friends can't see through the careless mask I quickly arrange on my face. "There," I chirp, my smile overly bright and my voice way too cheery. "We kissed and made up. Whose turn is it now?"

---

Here's the thing about kissing. Some kisses are a prelude to sex. Some happen out of boredom. Some make your body tingle, others might leave you feeling nothing at all. But what all those kisses have in common? They're just kisses.

They're not THE KISS.

The one that lingers in your mind for hours, even days, after it's over. The one that has you randomly touching your lips and breaking out in a warm, fluttery shiver as you remember the feel of his mouth on you.

And it doesn't have to be some epic production, either. It doesn't need to take place in front of the Eiffel Tower at sunset with majestic horses in the background and the aurora borealis shimmering up above (making a miraculous appearance in Paris).

The last time I experienced THE KISS, it happened behind a bale of hay at my friend Eliza's ranch in Kentucky. I was sixteen and in love with her older brother Glenn, but he'd been dating the same girl for ages. That summer, when I tagged along with him and Eliza to visit their grandmother's ranch, he and his girlfriend finally (finally!) broke up. And Glenn finally (finally!) noticed me.

He kissed me to the sound of horses snorting and the smell of manure. It was clumsy and furtive, and yet it was a kiss I never forgot. We went back to Connecticut and dated for seven months. I lost my virginity to him and thought we'd get married and have babies, but then his ex-girlfriend decided she wanted him back and now *they're* married and have babies.

Good for Glenn. I don't think I would've been happy with him in the long run. Me living on a ranch in the middle of nowhere? Hard pass.

I hadn't experienced another kiss like that since him, though. Until yesterday.

Fitz gave me THE KISS. It lasted less than a minute, occurred in front of a dozen people during a juvenile game of Spin the Bottle, and yet? It has consumed my mind from the second I went to bed last night to the moment I opened my eyes this morning. I undoubtedly dreamed about it, too, though I can't remember.

I also can't allow myself to dwell on it anymore. Fitz only played along to placate Katie, and he disappeared right after it was over. For me, it might have been THE KISS, but for him it was just…a kiss.

What an unbelievably depressing thought.

Luckily, I've got plenty of distractions today, though they're not exactly the good kind. First off is another meeting with Mr. Richmond, who's as curt and condescending as he was the last time we met. Froghole's lips curl in distaste when I tell him I've decided to design a swimwear line for the fashion show.

I guess fake British people don't like swimming.

Once again when I leave his office, I'm torn between never wanting to see him again and desperately needing to dig into every corner of his life to discover whether the accent is real.

On my way out of the admin building, I text Brenna with my continued suspicions.

> **ME:** Swear to god he's not British!
> **BRENNA:** Who?
> **ME:** Assistant dean aka academic advisor. I told u about him last week
> **BRENNA:** Right. OK. We MUST investigate.
> **ME:** ikr?? How do we proceed?
> **BRENNA:** I was being sarcastic. There needs to be a way to convey that over text. I mean, I thought the capital-letter MUST implied sarcasm, but I guess not??
> **ME:** I'm being serious, Bee
> **BRENNA:** That's the sad thing
> **ME:** How do I find out where he was born? His LinkedIn profile says he went to Columbia U in NYC. He didn't even go to school in England!
> **BRENNA:** 1) Lots of peeps come to USA as international students 2) You're insane 3) We still on for the game Sat?
> **ME:** Yeah we are. And thanks for ALL your help
> **ME:** You got that was sarcasm, right?
> **BRENNA:** Fuck off.

After a ten-minute walk across campus in the bitter cold, I knock on Erik Laurie's office door for my second meeting of the day. Despite my winter clothing, I'm colder than an icicle. My teeth are chattering, and I swear I have frostbite on my nose.

"Oh boy. You brought the cold in with you." Laurie mock-shivers as he lets me into his office. It's surprisingly spacious, with a brown leather couch against the far wall, a big desk in the center of the room, and a gorgeous view of the snowy courtyard.

"I'm keeping my coat on, if it's all right with you," I say wryly. "I'm chilled to the bone."

"As much as I'd love to see what dazzling and fashionable outfit you're wearing underneath all those layers, I'll let it slide." He winks. "This time."

A familiar uneasy sensation ripples in my belly. It's the second week of classes and Laurie has been nothing but friendly to me. But every time I'm around him, my creep-o-meter goes haywire. The winking hasn't stopped, either. He flashed no less than ten winks to various female students yesterday.

"Sit down." He gestures to one of the plush visitor's chairs as he settles in his own chair. "Let's discuss the midterm first."

Nodding, I sink into the chair. We'd already emailed back and forth a few times about how he's going to accommodate my learning issues. There are two major papers required for this course, but I'll only be turning in one, the midterm. For the final essay, I've been given permission to do a seminar in front of the class, where I'll have to lead a discussion on a topic that Laurie assigns me.

On Monday, he handed out a list of themes for the midterm, and I chose what I believe will be the easiest one to write. Now he just needs to approve it.

"Have you decided on a topic? I want to make sure you're comfortable with your decision before you start writing."

His genuine concern thaws some of my wariness toward him. Despite the chronic winking and occasional creepy vibe, he does seem like a good professor. One who cares about his students.

"I'd like to do the one about New York fashion. I think I can find a lot to say about the topic. I'm planning on starting an outline tonight."

"All right. Perfect. And you have my email address, so you can contact me if you get stuck or if you want me to look over your thesis."

"Thank you," I say gratefully. "I might take you up on that."

Laurie smiles broadly. "Good. Now, moving on, I need to see your proposal for the fashion show."

"I've got it right here." I reach into my messenger bag and pull out the leather portfolio that holds my sketches, a brief write-up of my swim line, and the comparative photographs he requested. "I included images from some lesser-known swimwear designers who I've been inspired by lately." I slide the portfolio across the desktop.

Laurie's expression shines with approval as he flips through the photos. "Kari Crane," he says with a nod. "I was in the front row for her debut in Milan."

"You were?"

"Of course. I never miss a Fashion Week."

"I go to Fashion Week in Paris and New York," I tell him. "But not usually Milan."

Laurie flips to the next designer. "Now these are intriguing. I love Sherashi's use of beadwork in these halter tops."

He seems to know every single designer on the planet, and I'm somewhat awed by that. "Me too. I also love how she infuses her own culture into her line."

"Bollywood meets French Riviera. It's brilliant."

"Yes. Exactly." I can't help but beam at him. And he hasn't winked or flirted in the past five minutes, which is a relief. "For my line, I want to play around with a combination of classic and modern, with some boho-chic thrown in the mix."

"Interesting. Let me take a look at your sketches." Concentration creases Laurie's forehead as he studies the drawings I've enclosed. "These are quite good, Summer."

I flush. I'm not the best artist when it comes to portraits or landscapes, but I've always had a knack for drawing clothes. When I was younger, I filled entire sketchbooks with what I considered the perfect outfits or styles.

"Thank you." I hesitate as he studies a series of sketches featuring men's trunks. "I know swimwear isn't going to be as difficult to design as, say, formalwear, but I'm really passionate about these. And obviously I can include more pieces in the show so that my workload is comparable to the other students'."

"I'm not worried about that," he says absently, moving to another sketch. When he finishes examining each one, he looks up with a pleased smile. "I'm on board with this."

Excitement stirs inside me. "Really?"

"Oh, yes. I can't wait to see what you come up with." And just when I thought we were done with it, he winks. "I'm especially curious about who you'll line up to model these designs."

Ew. Way to ruin the moment.

"You're a tall girl," he adds. "You should think about walking the runway yourself. I have no doubt you look incredible in a bikini."

Double ew.

"Um, yeah, I've never been interested in modeling." I get to my feet and gesture to the portfolio. "So do I have your approval to move forward?"

"Absolutely." He hands the leather book back to me.

"Great. Thanks. I'll see you in class."

I'm relieved to leave his office, even if it means shivering my ovaries off in the cold again. Every time I start to think he's harmless, he triggers that dreaded creep-o-meter.

Outside, I'm blasted by a gust of frigid wind. *I hate you, January. Just die already.* I begin my journey across campus, checking my phone as I head for the parking lot where I left my car. I find a missed call from my mom, along with a text that makes me smile.

Call your parents, Summer. I miss my girl.

My heart expands with love. Ugh, I miss them so much. I've barely spoken to them since the semester began. I've been busy, but so have they. Dad recently started jury selection for a high-profile murder trial, and Mom has been visiting Nana Celeste in Florida.

I return Mom's call but get her voicemail. I try my dad instead.

He picks up right away. "Princess! It's about time!"

"I know, I'm sorry. I've been swamped. Also, I can't believe I caught you out of court."

"Barely," he admits. "I'm only available because the prosecutor requested a five-minute recess. His next witness is late."

"That's unacceptable!" I exclaim, only half joking. "Don't let them get away with it, Daddy. Have them charged with contempt of court."

He chuckles. "Not how it works, sweetheart, but thanks for the concern. How's school going?"

"Good. I just had a meeting with my independent-study advisor. I'm designing a line of swimwear for the final show."

"What about your other classes? How are you handling the workload?"

I give him a quick rundown of what I'm studying this term, admitting that it hasn't been too challenging yet. "But I am writing an outline for an essay tonight. Wish me luck."

"You don't need luck, Princess. You're going to kick this essay's butt."

He has such faith in me, it makes me want to cry. Not once, in my entire life, had my parents ever called me stupid. But I know they must've thought it. How could they not when I kept coming home with failed tests for them to sign? When all my written work was covered with red edits, comments scribbled all over the margins?

"But if you are having trouble, let me know. Maybe I can speak to David—"

"No," I cut in, my tone firm. He means David Prescott, the dean. Well, I'm not having it. "Dad. You need to stop talking about me with Prescott and asking for favors. The assistant dean already hates me because he thinks I got preferential treatment—wait, forget all that," I interrupt myself. "If you're so eager to grant favors, I need one from you."

He laughs. "Do I even want to know?"

"Can you find out where Hal Richmond was born?"

"Who?"

"Briar's assistant dean. He has a British accent, and I'm convinced it's fake."

There's a beat.

"Princess." Dad sighs. "Are you torturing this poor man?"

"I'm not torturing anyone," I protest. "I just have my suspicions and I would love you so, so much if you could verify his place of birth. It'll take you all of five seconds, you know it will."

His laughter rumbles in my ear. "I'll see what I can do."

---

My spirits are still high when I sit down later to outline my midterm. Mom got ahold of me before dinner and we spent an hour on the phone catching up. And all three of my roommates are out for the night, so I can work in silence. With my ADHD, even the slightest distraction can set me back. I get sidetracked far too easily.

My essay topic is how New York fashion evolved in the first half of the twentieth century, and the factors that led to each transformative incident. It's a bit daunting because I'm dealing with five decades of fashion, marked by major events like the Great Depression and World War II.

In high school, my special-ed teacher—oh gosh, it makes me want to throw up saying that. It's frigging mortifying. Anyway, the teacher assigned to me had an arsenal of tips to help me better organize my thoughts. Like making flash cards or using sticky notes to jot down various ideas. Over time, I figured out it worked best to write one idea per note, and then arrange them until they all flow together to form one coherent train of thought.

To begin my midterm's outline, I sit on the floor of my room with my supplies lined up and ready for use: highlighters, Post-It notes, erasable pens. I'm wearing thick wool socks and sipping on a big cup of herbal tea. I got this. I'm a rock star.

I start off by writing decade headings on each yellow note—1910s,

'20s, '30s, '40s. It'll probably be easier to organize the paper chronologically. I know I have a ton of research ahead of me, but for now I rely on what I know about those time periods. Up until the Great Depression, I'm pretty sure bright colors were all the rage. I write that down on a sticky.

Roaring '20s, we're looking at flappers. Another sticky gets written.

Women's fashion favored a boyish look for a while—I think maybe that was the '30s? I stick another note to the floor. But I feel like the '30s also produced a lot of feminine, frilly tops? And speaking of frilly tops, I saw like five of them at the Barneys on Madison over the break. Are they back in style?

Oh, and I forgot to tell a girlfriend from Brown about Barneys! They're having a super-secret VIP sale on Valentine's Day weekend. She's going to lose her mind when she finds out.

I grab my phone and shoot a quick message to Courtney. Her response is instantaneous.

**COURT:** OMG!!!!!!
**ME:** I know!!!
**COURT:** We're going, right?
**ME:** OBVIOUSLY!!

We text back and forth in pure excitement, until I suddenly realize I've spent ten minutes talking about a clothing sale instead of doing my work.

Grrr.

I take a deep breath and force myself to concentrate. I list as many trends as I can think of, then nod in approval. There. Now I simply need to go into detail about each one and explain the societal factors and events that shaped fashion over time.

Wait. Is that my thesis?

*No, you idiot. You still have to come up with one.*

I bite my lip harder than necessary. My inner critic is, frankly, a total bitch. My old therapist was always preaching about self-love, urging me to treat myself kindly, but that's easier said than done. When you have one major insecurity that rules your life, your subconscious doesn't let you forget it.

Loving yourself is hard enough. Silencing the inner critic borders on impossible. For me, at least.

I inhale a slow, steady breath. It's fine. This is fine. I don't have to think up a thesis right this second. I can gather all the information first, and then once I begin to piece it together, a general hypothesis will form.

But there's so much information. A mere five minutes of Googling on my laptop leaves me overwhelmed with facts. And the more I read, the broader the topic becomes. I have no idea how to narrow it down, and the panic hits me like a fist to the stomach.

I take another breath, but it's quick and choppy, and I don't think any of the oxygen actually enters my lungs.

I hate this. I hate this essay, and I hate myself.

My eyes feel hot. They start to sting. I rub them, but the act of touching them unleashes the tears I'm trying to suppress.

*Stop crying*, my inner critic scolds. *You're being ridiculous. It's just an essay.*

I try again to draw air into my lungs. My brain begins to scroll through the exercises my counselors and parents encourage me to do during a panic attack: I repeat that I'm going to be okay. I visualize giving myself a big hug. I think of Nana Celeste (who always calms me). But the scrolling stops when my gaze drops to the sea of yellow stickies on the floor, the jumble of thoughts that make up my nutty brain.

Another choked sob slips out.

"Summer?"

I freeze at the sound of Fitz's voice. It's followed by a soft knock on my door.

"You okay?"

My breath escapes in a trembling wheeze. "F-fine!" I manage to answer, and cringe at the crack in my voice.

He hears it too. "I'm opening the door now, okay?"

"No," I blurt out. "I'm fine, Fitz. I promise."

"I don't believe you." The door eases open and his handsome, worried face appears.

He takes one look at me and curses roughly. Before I can blink, he's kneeling beside me. One warm hand grips my chin, forcing my gaze to his. "What's wrong?" he demands.

"Nothing." My voice shakes again.

"You're crying. That's not nothing." His eyes drop to the dozens of notes stuck to the floor. "What's all this?"

"Evidence of my stupidity," I mumble.

"What?"

"Nothing."

"Stop saying nothing. Talk to me." His thumb rubs a gentle line up my wet cheek. "I'm a good listener, I promise. Tell me what's wrong."

My lips start quivering. Dammit, I feel another wave of tears coming. And that makes me angry again. "I can't fucking do this, that's what's wrong."

I fling a hand out and sweep the Post-It notes away. Some of them remain stuck to the hardwood, while others fly across the room or slide under the bed.

Fitz plucks one of the notes and reads it. "Is this for a paper you're working on?"

"Midterm," I whisper. "Which I'm going to fail."

Letting out a breath, he shifts positions so he's sitting. He hesitates for a beat, before reaching for me.

Maybe if I wasn't feeling so vulnerable at the moment, I would've been strong enough to push him away. But I'm weak and I feel defeated, and when he holds out his arms, I climb into his lap, bury my face against his chest, and allow him to comfort me.

"Hey," he murmurs, running a soothing hand up and down my back. "It's okay to be overwhelmed by school. We all stress about it."

"You get stressed?" I ask in a small voice.

"All the time."

His fingers thread through my hair, and I suddenly feel like a child again. My mom used to stroke my hair whenever I got upset. Sometimes my brother Nick did too, if I scraped a knee or bumped my head thanks to whatever daredevil stunt I'd attempted that day. I was a rambunctious kid. Hell, I'm a rambunctious adult.

The warmth of Fitz's strong body seeps into me. I press my cheek to his collarbone and voice an embarrassed confession. "I have a learning disability."

"Dyslexia?" His voice is thick with understanding.

"No. It's more of a cluster of symptoms related to ADHD. I have a very hard time concentrating and organizing my thoughts on paper. I was on medication for it when I was a kid, but the meds gave me terrible headaches and made me nauseous and dizzy, so I went off them. I tried taking them again in my teens, but the same symptoms kept happening." I give a harsh, self-deprecating laugh. "My brain doesn't like the meds. Unfortunately, that means it's up to me to focus my thoughts, and that's really hard sometimes."

"What can I do to help?"

I jerk up in surprise. "What?"

His gaze is earnest, shining with sincerity. Not even a hint of pity there. "You're having trouble with your midterm, so how can I help?"

I'm a bit dazed. Awkwardly, I slide off his lap and sit cross-legged beside him. The moment we're no longer touching, I miss the warmth of his body. For a fleeting moment, THE KISS floats into my mind, but I swat it away like a pesky fly. Fitz hasn't mentioned the kiss, and right now he's not looking at me like he wants to stick his tongue in my mouth.

He looks genuinely eager to help me.

"I don't know," I finally answer. "I just... There's so much information." Anxiety fills my stomach again. "We're talking fifty decades' worth of fashion. I'm not sure what to focus on, and if I can't condense all the info, this paper will be like fifty pages long, and it's only supposed to be three thousand words, and I don't know how to streamline all the ideas, and—"

"Breathe," he orders.

I stop and do what he says. The oxygen clears my brain a little.

"You're letting yourself get carried away again. You need to go one step at a time."

"I'm trying. That's the point of the stupid sticky notes, to break it all down."

"How about talking it out? Does that ever help?"

I nod slowly. "Yeah. Usually I'll dictate the points and ideas and transcribe them afterward, but I'm not at that stage yet. I was trying to get the basic premise down when the panic struck."

"Okay." He stretches out his long legs in front of us. "Then let's talk about the basic premise."

I bite the inside of my cheek. "I appreciate the offer, but I'm sure you have better things to do with your time. Like draw. Or work on your video game." I shrug weakly. "You don't have to help me with my essay."

"I wouldn't be doing it for free."

I narrow my eyes. "You want me to pay you?"

His eyebrows shoot up. "What? No. Of course not. I just meant..." He takes a quick breath, avoiding my gaze. "I need your help with something too."

"You do?"

He glances over again, oddly sheepish. "How about an exchange? I'll help you with this midterm—the outline, the thesis. And, as you write it, I can proofread and help you organize ideas. And you help me out by..." He mumbles the rest—"Letting me draw you."

This time it's my eyebrows taking flight. "You want to draw me?"

His head jerks in a nod.

"Like one of your French girls?" Heat scorches my cheeks. Is he saying he wants to draw me naked?

Oh my God.

Why does the idea kind of turn me on?

"What French girls?" he asks, confused.

"Are you sure you weren't secretly watching *Titanic* with me and Hollis the other night?"

He snorts. "Ah, the naked portrait. Forgot about that scene. And no, you wouldn't be naked." His voice thickens at that, and I wonder if he's imagining the same thing I am.

Me. Lying naked in front of him. My body on full display.

My breath quickens as the vision takes a dirty turn. Suddenly Fitz is naked too. Naked and hard. His tattooed biceps flexing as he lowers his long, muscular body on top of me and—

He coughs, and I don't miss the flash of heat in his eyes. "You'd be fully clothed," he says. "I'd be basing a character in my game on you. Well, on your appearance. I've had a tough time figuring out what this woman looks like, and…" He shrugs awkwardly, and it's insanely adorable. "I think she might look like you."

My jaw falls open. "You want to base a video game character on me? That's so cool. What's her name?"

"Anya."

"Oooh, I like that. It's very elfin princess."

"She's actually a human."

I grin. "You should reconsider. That's totally an elf name."

He grins back, then gestures to the mess on the floor. "Do we have a deal? I help you out, you let me sketch you?"

"Yes," I say immediately. It takes a second to realize that all traces of defeat and despair have left my body. I feel rejuvenated, and the gratitude filling my chest threatens to overflow. "Thank you, Fitz."

"You're welcome."

Our gazes lock. I wish I knew what he was thinking. I wish

he'd bring up our silly Spin the Bottle kiss so I could figure out his feelings about it.

I wish he'd kiss me again.

His throat bobs as he visibly swallows. He licks his lips.

Arousal courses through my body. Oh God. Is he actually going to do it?

*Please*, I beg silently. With any other guy, I'd probably take the bull by the proverbial horns. As in, put my literal hand on his literal penis.

Not with Fitz, though. I'm terrified of putting myself out there again, not when the bitter taste of his rejection on New Year's Eve still clings to my throat. I still want him, yes. But I'll never admit it unless he makes the first move.

He doesn't.

Disappointment crashes into me when he breaks the eye contact. He clears his throat, but his voice is still full of gravel as he says, "I'll go get my sketchbook."

# 16
# FITZ

"STRIP."

Spending time with Summer is…a challenge. And that's coming from me, a guy who plays hockey at the college level for a Division 1 school. I can honestly say that my grueling athletic career is a walk in the park compared to the sheer grit it takes maintaining a friendship with Summer Di Laurentis.

First off, it's impossible for me to forget about the kiss we shared. Maybe she's been able to put it out of her mind, but it sure as hell hasn't left mine. Which means every time I've looked at her mouth these past few days, I've been reminded of how good it felt pressed against mine.

Second, I'm still attracted to her, so usually when I'm admiring that mouth, the fantasy doesn't stop with a harmless kiss. Her lips and tongue have played a starring role in so many dirty fantasies that I've taken to jerking off in the shower every morning to the thought of her.

Third, jerking off to her every morning makes it hard to look her in the eye when we hang out.

And lastly, when you're friends with Summer, she does things like waltz into your bedroom and order you to strip.

"No," I answer.

"Strip, Fitzy."

I cock one eyebrow. "No."

"Oh my God, why won't you take your clothes off!"

"Why are you asking me to take my clothes off? I'm not one of your French girls," I growl.

She keels over laughing. Summer has this way of completely losing herself in fits of laughter. It usually involves tears, doubling over, and furiously rubbing a stitch in her side. When she laughs, she does it with her entire body and soul.

Needless to say, I like provoking that response from her.

"I don't want to draw you," she says between giggles. She straightens and plants both hands on her hips. "I'm trying to *help* you, you stupid jerk."

I swallow a sigh. I deeply regret telling her about my job interview with Kamal Jain tomorrow morning. It came up last night during our nightly sketching/study session, a routine we've had going for the past four days. When she asked what I planned on wearing, I shrugged and said, "Maybe jeans and a blazer?"

To which she'd gazed at me in horror and retorted, "I'm sorry, sweetie, but that's not a look you can pull off. Justin Timberlake, he can rock it like a hurricane. But you? No way." Then she'd dismissively waved her hand. "Don't worry. I'll take care of it."

I wasn't worried, and I hadn't asked her to clarify what she meant by "taking care of it."

I regret not asking, because now it's eight o'clock on Thursday night and Summer just dropped half a dozen garment bags on my bed and demanded I undress.

"I'm not trying on clothes for you," I say stubbornly.

"I told you, this isn't for me!" she grumbles in frustration. "It's for *you*. I'm doing you a huge solid right now, Fitz. Do you know how many thousands of dollars' worth of clothes are in those bags?"

I scowl. "I don't care how much they cost. I want to wear my own stuff."

"What stuff?" She charges to my closet door and throws it open.

"You mean this stuff? A bunch of T-shirts. Jeans and cargo pants. Some sweaters, a couple of button-downs, a whole lot of sports jerseys, and more wife-beaters than any man should ever need to own."

"And the suit I wore to my Uncle Ned's funeral," I say helpfully. "I could wear that if you want."

"I do not want." She rifles through the hangers. "Everything you own is either black or gray. What do you have against colors, Colin? Did red bully you as a child? Did green steal your girlfriend? Black, gray, gray, black, black, oh look! More black! This is insanity. I'm literally going insane looking at your closet." Summer spins around, glaring. "You're going to let me dress you for the interview, you hear me? It's my right, now that we're best friends."

"Best friends?" I sputter with laughter. "I agreed to no such thing."

"If I decide something, then it's the law." She sticks out her tongue. "You have no say."

Gone is the teary-eyed girl I'd comforted mere days ago, and I have to admit it's nice seeing her smiling and beaming at me. Directing all her innate sunlight at me instead of eyeing me with dark caution and cloudy uncertainty.

"Come on, Fitz. Please? Just try on a few outfits. If you don't like them, I'll send them back."

"Send them back to who?" My stomach churns. "Please don't tell me you bought these." I'm not good with accepting gifts, particularly expensive ones.

"Oh no. That would make a huge dent in my trust fund. My parents would murder me." She shrugs. "A friend of mine sent them over as a favor. She's the stylist for an actor."

"Which actor?" I can't help but ask, curiously eyeing the bags.

"Noah Billings."

"Never heard of him."

"He's on a CW superhero show. He's about your size, maybe a

tad shorter. Most of these have been tailored to him, but we'll see what we can do. Anyway, Mariah said you can borrow whatever you want, as long as we pay for it to be dry-cleaned before we give it back. So now shut up and strip, sweetie. I want you to look great tomorrow. I mean, this is huge."

She's right. It *is* huge. A job at Orcus Games would be a dream come true.

"You're right," I concede. "I can't look like a scrub."

"I'm sorry, did you say I'm right? As in, you're wrong?"

"Yes, Summer. You're right. I need to make a good impression." I sigh in defeat. "Let's see what's in those bags."

She squeals loud enough to make me flinch. Man, that's a seriously high pitch she's got there. "You won't regret this. This is going to be so much fun."

Clapping happily, she does a few spins, her blonde hair whipping around her slender body. She punctuates the excited dance with a little jump where she kicks out both legs and then lands directly on the tips of her bare toes.

"Whoa," I blurt, genuinely impressed. "Where'd you learn to do that?"

"I took six years of ballet." She marches to the chair and picks up the first garment bag.

Right, I remember she'd mentioned ballet had been one of her interests. "Didn't stick with it, eh?"

"I told you, I get bored easily." She unzips the bag and extracts a hanger that holds a...

Gray sweater.

"It's a fucking gray sweater," I accuse. "You know, like the one hanging five feet away from us? The one you were just criticizing?"

"First of all, it's not gray. It's slate—"

"It's gray."

"Second of all, it's Tom Ford—is the one in your closet Tom Ford? I didn't think so. Third of all, shut up and come touch this."

I'm scared she'll smack me if I don't, so I do what the lady orders. I can't help but whistle as my fingers encounter the softest wool I've ever felt. "It's nice," I relent.

"Perfect, so we'll try it over this…" She checks the second hanger. "Oooh, over this Saint Laurent shirt. Actually, no… You know what? I don't think we even need a shirt underneath. I feel like the sweater might be thick enough that your nips won't show. We'll pair it with these trousers. Turn around."

"Why?"

"I want to see your butt."

"No," I say indignantly.

"Turn around."

I turn around because I don't feel like losing another argument, but I throw in a silky reply just to unnerve her. "Do you like what you see? You can give it a squeeze if you want."

She makes a squeaky noise. "Are you *flirting*? That's highly inappropriate."

"Says the woman staring longingly at my ass."

"Keep telling yourself that," she replies, but I don't miss the breathy note in her voice. "Okay. We'll try the trousers, but Noah Billings' butt isn't as muscular as yours. These might show off a little too much ass."

"Is there such a thing?" I ask solemnly.

Summer grins. "Touché. All right. Let's see how this looks."

I'm about to remove my shirt, when I realize she's still standing there watching me. "What, I don't get any privacy?"

"You're just taking your shirt off. It's not like you're getting naked."

Yes, but it still feels kind of…intimate. I shrug the thought away. If we were at the beach, I'd have no qualms going bare-chested. I'm being a pussy right now.

I peel my T-shirt over my head.

Summer's green eyes widen. Appreciation heats her expression, and damned if that doesn't inflate my ego like a helium balloon. It only gets bigger when she lets out a breathy noise that speaks directly to my dick.

"I love your tattoos," she informs me.

"Yeah?"

"Uh-huh."

Her gaze is glued to my naked torso. Holy shit, if she keeps looking at me like that, I might not be able to stop myself from touching her. It's already been a Herculean effort for me to draw her every night without giving in to every carnal urge that's begging me to fuck her.

But I can't. Not unless she makes the first move. I already blew my chance thanks to my behavior on New Year's. My hypercritical words had hurt her, and just because she'd accepted my apology doesn't mean I can assume she's into me now. The fact that she referred to us as "best friends" is probably a good indication of where I stand.

I've been friend-zoned.

"Permission to approach the chest?"

A hasty laugh pops out. "Permission granted?"

She steps forward for a closer examination of the ink on my arms and chest. "Did you design these yourself?"

"Yeah."

"My God, Fitz. You're so good."

Embarrassment creeps up my throat. I don't take compliments well. Never have. So I make a noncommittal sound that hopefully she interprets as a thank you.

"You're really into the fantasy imagery, huh?" She focuses on my left biceps. "This sword is badass. Is it based on Sir Nornan's glass sword in *The Glass Forest*? No, wait, the sword doesn't show up until the third book."

"*Weeping Devils*," I confirm, naming another title in the *Shifting Winds* series. Nerves make me pause, because I don't want to rock the boat again. "Which one is your favorite?" I quickly add, "It's not a trick question, I promise. I know you read them."

"If you want to get technical, I didn't read them—I listened to the audiobooks. I'm obsessed with audiobooks," she reveals. "And to answer your question, I'd have to go with the first book. First book is always the best."

"Agreed."

She touches something on my shoulder. "Ohhh, this is so pretty. This cluster of roses." Her impish gaze lifts to mine. "Not very manly," she teases.

I'm too distracted to respond or take offense, because her fingertips are still tracing my bare flesh. Air gets trapped in my throat. The sweet scent of her shampoo tickles my nose, along with a hint of her signature perfume.

I find myself asking, "What perfume is that?"

"Chanel No. 5." Her lips curve in a smile. "The only scent a lady should ever own."

"I'll take your word for it."

My body weeps from the loss of contact when she withdraws her hand. "Enough chit-chatting, Fitzy. Put this on."

The next thing I know, she's shoving the sweater over my head. I feel like a child as I slide my arms into the sleeves and poke my head through the neck hole. I swear Summer's fingernails scrape my abdomen as she drags the shirt down.

A shiver races up my spine. I'm turned on.

Like, really turned on.

Shit, and now I have to take my pants off, and I'm wearing boxer-briefs that perfectly outline my cock. She's totally going to notice.

*Ding.*

Summer's phone chimes with an incoming text. Oh, thank you, Jesus. As she turns to check the message, I hastily kick my sweatpants off and slide into the crisp black trousers. Making sure her gaze is occupied, I do a quick rearrange of the dick region so it's not as pokey. When Summer turns back to me, I hope I resemble a man who *isn't* harder than granite.

She whistles softly. "Oh, I like this, Fitz. It's super sharp. Here, look." She angles the closet door so I'm able to see my reflection in the full-length mirror.

I'm pleasantly surprised. I clean up nice. "Sweet," I say. "Let's go with this."

I register her disbelieving expression in the mirror. Then she barks out a laugh. "Colin," she says between giggles. "Are you always this naïve?"

I wrinkle my forehead. "What do you mean?"

"It means this is the first outfit you've tried on." She pats my arm as she brushes past me, chuckling under her breath. "We're just getting started."

"Started with what?" comes a suspicious voice.

We turn to find Hunter in the doorway.

A thread of discomfort wraps around my insides. Hunter's been keeping his distance from me since Sunday night. He hasn't stated outright that the Spin the Bottle thing pissed him off, but I get the distinct feeling it did.

In my defense, I wasn't even playing the damn game, and I wouldn't have kissed Summer at all if Jesse's bossy girlfriend hadn't insisted. I know better than to argue with Katie.

Besides, if Hunter's upset that Summer and I kissed, he can man up and talk to me about it.

"Listen to this," Summer tells him in an amused voice. "I brought six garment bags of clothes for Fitz to try on. You know, for his interview tomorrow. He's only tried one outfit." She points at the Ford and Saint Laurent combo. "And he thinks…" She looks like she's going to explode with laughter. "He thinks we're done now."

I expect Hunter to give her a blank look. But my teammate snickers at me, obviously in on the joke. "Naïve bastard." He strides into my room and sprawls on the bed. "This is gonna be fun." He winks at Summer. "Go get Hollis. Tell him to make some popcorn."

"On it." She's already hurrying out the door, yelling, "Mike!"

"Traitor," I grumble at Hunter.

He merely grins. "You gave an heiress from Connecticut permission to dress you for an interview. You really think I'm going to miss this show?"

I sigh. I guess I could put my foot down and declare this travesty over, but clearly Summer is having fun, and this is the first time in days that Hunter's actually seemed at ease with me. Maybe I was imagining his aloofness, and he doesn't care about the kiss at all.

"Listen, about you and Summer," he hedges.

I spoke too soon.

"She said you're helping her with her midterm."

"Mmm-hmmm. I am." I pretend to be preoccupied with the left sleeve of my sweater, examining it as if it holds all the secrets to the universe.

"And then there was the whole, ah, kiss thing on Sunday." From the corner of my eye, I see him run his fingers through his dark hair. "So I'm just gonna come out and ask. Is there something between you guys? You hooking up?"

"Naah, we're not." Man, this sleeve is damn fascinating. "We're just friends."

"You sure about that?"

I force myself to look him in the eye like a mature adult. "In case you forgot, I was walking by minding my own business when that bottle landed on me. Neither of us wanted to follow through, remember?"

"True." He's nodding slowly. "You guys did look really uncomfortable."

Did we?

I try not to frown. Because what *I* remember is how her lips set my entire body on fire. I remember her tongue rubbing against mine and sending an electric shock straight to my balls. I remember breathing in her addictive scent and almost passing out with need.

But Hunter saw discomfort. Interesting.

Maybe that's why Summer hasn't raised the subject of the kiss even once since it happened. Fuck. Am I actually in the friend zone?

"I think she's awesome, Fitz." He shrugs. "I wasn't joking about the whole dibs thing when we got back from Vermont. I'm into her."

He shoots a glance toward the doorway, as if he's worried Summer might be standing there. But he relaxes when her and Mike's laughter echoes from downstairs.

"And I think she's into me," he continues. Another shrug. "I mean, we made out on New Year's. We've cuddled."

They've *cuddled*? The stab of jealousy I feel hurts more than I expect.

"I'm planning on asking her out." He tips his head, watching me carefully. "Is that going to be a problem?"

What the hell am I supposed to say to that? Yes, it's gonna be a problem? What if I did say that? What then? Would we have to duel for Summer's honor?

"Like I said when we discussed her moving in, as long as it doesn't affect our lease, I don't care what you do." It's very, very difficult to utter these words, but the alternative would only create problems I'd rather not deal with at the moment.

If Summer was ripping her clothes off and begging me to screw her, maybe my answer would be different.

But she's not.

# 17
# FITZ

I grew up in the suburbs outside of Boston, so the odds of me ever seeing a tornado were about as good as the chances of my parents getting back together.

This morning, I finally get to witness one.

The tornado's name is Kamal Jain. He bursts into the hotel bar in a blur of gray and black, offering fleeting glimpses of white teeth and brown skin and stubby fingers that he waves at the server as he flies past her.

The vortex grinds to a halt to reveal the short, stocky figure of Kamal Jain, and it takes serious effort to keep my jaw hinged because it turns out he's not wearing gray and black.

It's slate and charcoal, as Summer would say.

And it's the same fucking outfit I tried on last night. The first one, which Summer advised me to forsake in favor of what I'm wearing now: dark-blue Ralph Lauren jeans, a Marc Jacobs dress shirt with no tie, and brown Gucci loafers. Summer would be proud that I remembered each designer's name and can link it to his corresponding clothing item.

Thank God I didn't go with the first outfit, or this interview would've started off a touch awkward.

"Colin!" Kamal greets me with enthusiasm, pumping my hand in a shake that lasts the entire time he speaks. "So good to meet you!

Look at you—you're huge! You look way smaller in the picture I have of you. In person you're a giant!"

"Picture?" I say blankly.

"My assistant grabbed your hockey mug shot off the net. Is it called a mug shot? I don't know. How tall are you? Six-one? Six-two?"

"Six-two—"

"Six-two, I bet. I'm five-eight, just a little fella with a big bank account, right?" He guffaws at his own joke. "Let's grab a seat?"

"Sure," I say, although I doubt he hears me. It seems like Kamal Jain mostly talks to himself, and you're just along for the ride.

The Ritz bar resembles one of those gentlemen's cigar clubs you see in the movies. A few round booths span one wall, but for the most part it's padded leather armchairs tucked throughout the room to provide the illusion of privacy for patrons. There's even a roaring fire in the fireplace, a real one, which crackles as the server leads us past it.

We settle in a pair of chairs in the corner of the room. Kamal orders a vodka tonic. It's ten thirty in the morning, but I don't comment on it. No way am I criticizing my potential employer's morning beverage selection. Also, I'm a bit starstruck, so speaking might be a challenge in general. I've seen this man's face on the cover of magazines. I've followed his career for years. It's surreal to be sitting across from someone I've admired from afar for so long.

"Thank you for coming all this way to see me, Mr. Jain," I start.

"Mr. Jain! We already discussed this, man—call me Kamal or KJ. 'Mister' gives me the heebie-jeebies. Too authoritarian for my liking."

"Sorry. Kamal." I decide to be upfront with the guy. I suspect he might appreciate it. "I'm sorry. I'm almost embarrassed by how hard I'm fan-boying right now."

He gives a loud laugh. "Oh, trust me, I can relate. One time I met Stan Lee at a comic book convention, and I almost came in my pants. Swear to God, I felt a tingle in the dingle."

I stifle a snicker. "Well, luckily you were able to control yourself," I say helpfully.

"Barely! That man's a legend. I'm divorcing my parents and hoping he'll adopt me."

The snicker slips out. I already knew from the interviews I've seen with him that Kamal has no brain-to-mouth filter. But experiencing it in person is a whole other spectacle.

"Is that a Marc Jacobs?" He gestures to my shirt. "Great fit, bomb cuffs—pricey. Hope you didn't clean out your savings account for li'l ol' me. You're in college, you can't afford frivolous purchases yet, Colin. I'll get my assistant to send you a check of reimbursement."

"Oh, that's not necessary—"

"All right," he interrupts, "I've got four more minutes. Let's do this fast."

Four minutes? He literally just sat down.

I wonder what it's like to be SO IMPORTANT that you fly to Boston for a five-minute meeting before having to board the old company jet again.

For the next three minutes, Kamal launches questions at me as if he's firing an interview rifle. They seem to have no rhyme or reason. Jumping from one topic to another before I can blink and only allowing me about ten seconds to answer before firing again.

*Who are your artistic influences?*

*What's your favorite movie?*

*Do you eat meat?*

*Would you be willing to work weekends if needed?*

*What do you think of* No Man's Sky?

*Would you consider yourself a jock?*

In fact, the jock issue comes up in at least three questions. I get the distinct sense that Kamal is anti-athlete. Bullied by a jock or two in high school, I suspect.

I can't tell if I answered a single question correctly, or to his liking. Whereas Kamal moves and talks like a tornado, the interview itself is a tsunami, slamming into me without warning and retreating just as fast.

Before I can blink, he's shooting to his feet and pumping my hand again. "Can you be in Manhattan in a few weeks?"

"Um, I'm not sure. It depends on my game schedule—"

"It's a Thursday night—you play on Thursdays?" He frowns. It's evident that the biggest strike against me right now is hockey.

"No, but…" I wrinkle my forehead. "What's in Manhattan?" Have I gotten the job? Am I supposed to start working that day? My cover letter clearly stated I couldn't start until after graduation.

"I'm hosting a fundraiser at the Heyward Plaza Hotel. It's to raise awareness for autism. No, it's a kids-with-leukemia event. Autism is in April," he babbles. "April Autism Awareness—my fucking team loves their alliteration. I've invited the other candidates I'm considering. Only three others now. Two didn't impress me in the face-to-face."

And I did? I'm legit baffled. I can't fathom how he was able to judge me one way or the other, given the length of the interview and the absurdity of his questions.

"It's between the four of you now. The leukemia event will let me gauge how you network."

Aw crap. I'm not good at networking. At all.

"Plus, it'll be fun as fuck. Open bar, lots of ladies. You have a plus one if you've got a girl at home, but I recommend leaving her at said home…" He winks, and I hide my distaste.

It's no secret that Kamal is a womanizer. According to an article I read, he almost married his college sweetheart about ten years ago but didn't go through with it because she refused to sign a prenup. Since then, he's been photographed "canoodling" with a Leonardo DiCaprio-amount of supermodels, along with several actresses and heiresses.

"My assistant will email you the invitation. If you don't RSVP, I'll assume you're removing yourself from the running." He slaps my shoulder. "But nobody is that stupid, so…" He grins widely. "I'll see you next month."

He tornadoes out of the bar in another blur of motion, leaving me standing there alone. Two seconds later, the server returns with a tray holding Kamal's vodka and my coffee.

She stares at me in confusion. "Oh. Your party had to leave? Do you still…?" She lifts the tray slightly. "The tab's already been paid."

I look at the coffee cup, then at the glass tumbler. Screw it. Who cares if it's early.

I reach for the vodka tonic and down it in one long swig.

---

"Five minutes," I tell my friends later that night. We're all jammed in a booth at Malone's. Directly under a speaker too, which means I have to raise my voice to be heard over the Drake track blasting in the bar. "It lasted *five* minutes. I checked my watch."

"Time is money," says Hollis.

"I don't even know how the interview went," I say with a loud groan. "Seriously. I got no indication one way or the other if he even liked me."

"Of course he did," Summer says firmly. She's on the other side of the booth, sandwiched between Hunter and Matt Anderson. "He wouldn't have invited you to the fundraiser if the interview had gone poorly."

"Time is money," Hollis says again.

Nate knocks him on the back of the head. "Cut it out with that nonsense. Just 'cause Fitzy met a billionaire today doesn't make you a billionaire by association."

"If he wasn't serious about hiring you, he wouldn't have flown all that way to meet you in person," Matt points out. "He woulda sent an underling."

"Not necessarily," I counter. "He was a poor kid from Detroit when he designed his first game—he actually stole a lot of the parts he needed to build his own computer. The company is his baby. I think he takes a hands-on role as often as he can."

"Either way, we're here tonight to celebrate that you caught the eye of a major game designer and that's amazing," Summer declares. "Even if you don't get the job, it's an honor that you were even considered."

"Let's toast!" Hollis pipes up, raising his pint glass. "Time is money!"

Nobody participates in his toast, but I take pity on the guy and tap my Sam Adams bottle against his glass. It was Hollis' idea to go out and celebrate, and as much as I don't like being the center of attention, I'm touched that he's so supportive of me. I think he's more thrilled than I am at the possibility that I might snag a position at Orcus Games.

Luckily, the bar isn't too crowded tonight, probably because we didn't have a game. Malone's tends to be a Briar hockey bar, though we do get the occasional football player in here. Typically, though, the football guys prefer their off-campus houses to the very pathetic Hastings nightlife. They're notorious for their house parties. Me, I prefer the bar. Means I don't have to clean up after anyone. Plus, the beer is cheap and Friday nights they have half-price wings.

"Oh, fine," Summer relents, raising her glass to Mike's. "Time is money!"

She flashes me a wink and a smile, and my insides promptly melt like butter on a hot pan. She has the kind of smile that makes a man want to start writing very bad poetry. Dazzling and genuine and as beautiful as the rest of her.

I've been in a permanent state of semi-hardness since we got here. When we left the house, Summer looked like a snowman, bundled up in a parka with a fur hood, gloves, scarf, the whole winter shebang. Then we got to Malone's, where she unzipped the coat and removed the rest of the gear to reveal skinny jeans that cling to her impossibly long legs and a boner-inducing crop top. The top is a halter-style one that leaves both her back and midriff completely bare. It's amazing.

"Brenna texted she's here," Summer says, checking her phone. "Do you guys see her?"

"My Juliet has arrived!" Hollis says happily.

Hunter snickers. "Dude. She's not interested."

"Really? Because I seem to remember her looking very interested when she walked into my bedroom last week…and looking very satisfied when she walked out of it…" He waggles his eyebrows.

Summer flicks one of Matt's French fries at Hollis. "One—no locker room talk, please. Two—Hunter's right."

"I'm always right," Hunter says.

"Where is she…" Summer twists around, flashing the bare expanse of her back.

Jesus. It's as pretty as the rest of her. Delicate shoulder blades. Smooth, tanned skin.

My semi turns into a fully as I envision kissing my way down the bumps of her spine until my lips reach the top of her perfect ass. I'd use my hands to squeeze it. Hmmm, and what would I do with my mouth…maybe I'd nibble on one of her firm, round ass cheeks.

Motherfucker. Thank God the booth's table covers my lower body, because I'm hard as a rock now.

"Why are you guys hidden in the corner?" Brenna demands when she finally appears. "How am I supposed to ogle all the hot men if I can't see them?"

"You can ogle me," Hollis offers.

She ignores him and scopes out the seating situation. When she realizes neither side of the booth can accommodate her, she shrugs and grins at me. "Guess you can be my chair, Fitz."

My mouth opens to voice a protest, but it's too late. She's already plopping onto my lap.

Brenna's eyes widen.

She squeaks in surprise, and I curl my fingers around her hip and shoot her a warning look. If she says one word about the erection pressing against her left butt cheek, I'll be the target of my teammates' ragging until the end of time.

"What is it?" Summer asks in concern.

Brenna recovers quickly. "Sorry, didn't mean to alarm you. I think I'm sitting on your phone, Fitz." She makes a big show of shifting around, then slides her hand in my pocket and pulls out my phone. "This was digging into my butt."

"Hot," Hollis says.

She ignores him again, probably because she's focused on fishing her own phone out of the pocket of her black hoodie. The sweatshirt is half unzipped, revealing the tops of a black lacy bra. Only Brenna would wear a zip-up with nothing but a bra underneath.

She texts something one-handed, and I stifle a resigned sigh when my phone buzzes. I nonchalantly read the message.

**BRENNA:** Please tell me that boner isn't because of me!

The sigh slips out.

When she raises her eyebrow, I quickly type, No.

**BRENNA:** OK good. It was there before I sat down so I assumed it wasn't me. Just making sure, tho. You and I aren't meant to be, sweet Fitzy. I'd eat you alive

Ha. She'd eat any man alive. And for some reason, I feel the stupid need to justify why I have a boner. Or rather, had, because the poor fella has retreated like a Confederate soldier.

**ME:** Chick sent me some nudes right b4 u got here. I'm a guy. Shit happens

**BRENNA:** Think about Hollis. That always kills my desire

I laugh out loud, causing everyone to look in my direction.

"What's so funny?" Summer asks lightly.

I set the phone on the table and pick up my beer bottle. "Nothing. A friend just sent me a funny meme."

"Your mean your girlfriend?" Summer's tone doesn't sound as light and airy anymore. A darker note threads through it, something I can't quite decipher.

Nate looks surprised. "You have a girlfriend? Since when?"

"Is she hot?" asks Hollis.

Brenna wads up a napkin and throws it at him.

He catches it easily. "Hey, it's a valid question."

She sighs. "It's never a valid question when it comes from you."

"She's pretty," Summer says grudgingly.

I'm a bit lost. I thought this was a joke conversation, but obviously she's referring to a real person. Suddenly it occurs to me. "Oh, you mean Nora?"

Summer's mouth flattens in a thin line. "Yup."

"You don't sound like a fan," Nate says, lips twitching in humor.

She shrugs, reaching for her vodka cranberry. She takes a demure sip, and I see every guy in the booth eyeing her lips. "I think she's condescending. And she was rude to me because I admire a Nazi sympathizer."

Hunter chokes on his beer mid-sip. "I'm sorry—what?"

"Chanel," Summer explains. "Chanel's my idol, and Fitz's girlfriend—"

"Not my girlfriend—"

"—wouldn't shut up in class about how Chanel was a wartime criminal." Summer juts her chin stubbornly. "Allegedly."

Nate snorts.

"How dare she," Brenna says mockingly.

"Wait, this is your girlfriend?" Matt asks me.

"No. We went on one date," I say in aggravation. "I doubt there'll be a second one."

Summer's contemplative gaze fixes on me. "No?"

I shrug. "Probably not."

Nora and I have texted a few times since we went for drinks, but to be honest I'm not feeling the click. Nora's really nice, but the chemistry isn't quite there. I'm usually a believer that two dates are required before you completely write someone off. People are always nervous on the first date. Maybe Nora was anxious, and that's why the conversation felt so stilted.

When she suggested we go out again, I said yes, but I haven't followed up on it. Now I'm not sure if I will. The fact that I jerk off every morning to fantasies of another girl kinda tells me everything I need to know about my feelings for Nora.

"Okay, clearly our server is never coming back," Brenna announces, sliding off my lap. "I'm going to order a drink at the bar."

"I'll come with you," Summer offers, and Matt gets up to let her out of the booth.

We all turn to admire the two girls as they walk away. Two pairs of skinny jeans means two amazing asses for us to salivate over, and the sleek bare skin of Summer's back is an added bonus. It means she's not wearing a bra, and my mouth turns to sawdust as another dirty image flies into my brain—Summer's naked tits jiggling softly with each sultry step she takes.

Nate gives a low whistle. "Da-yum. They really are the hottest girls in this place."

"Everyone wants to kick our asses," Matt agrees, smiling ruefully.

"Eh. We can take them," Hunter assures him. That's not an exaggeration. Summer and Brenna might be the hottest girls in the bar, but we're the biggest guys in the bar.

From the corner of my eye, I see the girls approach the counter. Another shadow crosses my peripheral. I glance over and hide a frown. Some guy in a black polo shirt is chatting up Brenna, who touches his forearm and says something that makes him guffaw loudly.

"She is smokin'," Hollis says with a heavy, soul-sucking sigh. His blue eyes are locked on Brenna.

"Aw, why so glum, chum?" Nate mocks.

"Yeah, you should be wearing a perma-smile because that

gorgeous chick actually fooled around with you," Hunter pipes up. "That's probably how Jesus felt when he turned water into wine."

Matt and Nate snicker.

Hollis flips up his middle finger, but he doesn't offer his characteristic douchebag response. He simply picks up his glass.

I lift one eyebrow. "What, you're not gonna say that it wasn't a miracle because you're such a stud, et cetera, et cetera?"

Rather than answer, he chugs the rest of his beer, as if he needs the liquid courage to speak his next words.

"Guys. I think maybe she only hooked up with me that night because she was bored."

Everyone goes dead silent.

Hunter's the first to laugh. I can't help it—I do too. Then Nate and Matt join in.

Hollis buries his face in his hands. When he lifts his head, he's scowling. "You guys are the most unsupportive assholes I've ever met."

"Dude, she cuts you down every time she sees you," Hunter finally says, but I don't miss the way his tone has softened. He's trying to let Mike down gently.

I feel bad letting Hunter do this alone, so I speak up too. "It's not gonna happen," I tell Hollis.

"It might," he protests.

We all look to the bar again. Brenna flips her long, dark hair over one shoulder. She's still with the frat boy. I can tell he's in a frat not just because of the polo shirt, but because a couple of his friends have joined him, and one is wearing a hoodie with the Sigma Chi logo on it. The other one is talking to Summer.

I notice Hunter's shoulders stiffening as he watches Summer and the guy. Luckily, the bartender finally gives the girls their drinks. I didn't see any money exchanging hands, which tells me the male barkeep is as enamored with them as everyone else in this bar.

They return with a second vodka cranberry in Summer's hand,

and a bottle of Harpoon in Brenna's. This time Brenna squishes in beside and not on me, while Summer settles next to Matt on the end instead of between him and Hunter. Hunter flicks a contemplative look at her.

"Frat boys are the worst," Brenna tells us as she raises her beer to her red-painted lips. "They have a sense of entitlement that really pisses me off. Even the poor ones."

"Are there poor ones?" Nate cracks.

"Of course. Anyone can pledge." She rolls her eyes. "You just have a better chance of getting in if you're rich."

Summer shrugs. "Those guys weren't too bad."

Jealousy stabs at my gut. Luckily, Brenna's reply ensures that I don't have to worry about Summer going home with one of those dudes.

"Polo Douche tried to slide his hand in my shirt and cup my boob, Summer."

Her eyebrows fly up. "Seriously? Oh my God. Gross." She shakes her head. "I thought the one in the salmon shirt was really nice."

"Pink," Hollis grumbles at her. "Just fucking say pink, Summer."

"There are different shades of pink, Mike."

"Yeah? Name ten."

"Fine." Like a pro, she starts listing hues. "Salmon, rose, blush, fuchsia, watermelon, flamingo, cerise, bubble gum, magenta—"

She's on number nine when a blur of red and yellow rushes up to the booth.

I barely have time to blink before a pale arm flings out and a waterfall of liquid rains down on us. The intended target was Brenna, who receives the bulk of it, but Hollis, Nate, and I are victims of secondary splashing.

Brenna's jaw falls open as a furious blonde glares down at her. "What the—"

*"Keep your hands off my man!"*

# 18
# SUMMER

BRENNA IS SOAKING WET. DESPITE HER INITIAL SHOCK, SHE RECOVERS quickly, reaching for a napkin to wipe her face. "Who exactly is your man?" she asks calmly.

The blonde points to a spot about ten feet to her right. She's got long fingernails, painted bright fuchsia (or pink, as a naïve Hollis would say) and one sharp talon directs my gaze to the polo shirt-wearing guy who was hitting on Brenna. The attempted boob-grabber.

"Him?" Brenna's disdain is written all over her gorgeous face.

"Yes."

"Funny. He didn't mention he had a girlfriend when he was offering to take me for a spin in his Lambo."

Hollis snickers.

"You're a liar. Davey would never do that." The girl is still spitting mad, cheeks redder than the crimson tank top she's got on. Her top clashes with her nails. I hate that. "He said you were throwing yourself at him."

Brenna's lips curve in a mocking smile. "Of course he did. His ego was bruised. But if I'd agreed to blow him in his fancy sports car after you went to bed tonight? I guarantee you never would've known he talked to anyone but you."

"Truth," Hunter drawls.

I hide a grin. She's absolutely right. The only reason this loser even mentioned the existence of another woman to his girlfriend is because he needed his ego stroked. He probably knew she'd go apeshit on Brenna and stake a claim on her man, which makes him feel nice and wanted after Brenna laughed when he suggested they hook up in his Lamborghini.

Brenna gets to her feet. Her face is dry, but the front of her sweatshirt is still sopping wet. The clear liquid doesn't reek of alcohol, so I suspect it was just water. With an annoyed breath, Brenna unzips the wet hoodie and peels it off her slim shoulders.

"Oh my fucking God," Hollis groans, arousal darkening his eyes.

She's wearing nothing but jeans and a lacy black bralette that's more crop top than bra, and not much skimpier than what the blonde has on. She won't get kicked out of Malone's for indecent exposure, but she's definitely about to be responsible for every hard penis in our vicinity.

*Even Fitzy's?* a voice taunts.

I try to swallow my jealousy. I do *not* like the idea of Fitz getting hard for Brenna, no matter how incredible her boobs look in that bralette.

But a quick glance across the booth at Fitz reveals a harsh expression and sneer of distaste as he eyes the polo-shirt guy, who's now creeping toward his girlfriend. Fitz's big hands aren't quite fists, but they're curled on the tabletop. He's on guard and not liking this escalating situation.

"Hey, sweetheart?" Brenna says to the blonde. "Your man is a fuckboy with a capital F. Drop him now before he hurts you worse."

"Did you just call Davey a fuckboy!" is the outraged response. "You'd be *lucky* to have someone like him! If he tried to get with you, and you said no, then you're a stupid bitch."

Brenna's brown eyes twinkle. "First you're mad because you think I tried to steal him from you. Now you're pissed because I turned him down. Pick one injustice and commit, sweetie."

I can't help but laugh. The blonde glares daggers at me.

"But if you want, I'd be happy to bang him," Brenna offers. "His technique was wicked clumsy when he tried to grab my breast. I could probably teach him a few things."

"Slut," the girl spits out.

"Right. I'm the slut, not him."

"You wouldn't know a good man if he walked up and smacked you in the face."

"Neither would you, apparently."

Hunter chuckles.

The girl's face is so red, I almost feel bad for her. Almost.

"Stupid slut!"

Just like that, I officially reach the maximum amount of *slut* I'm willing to hear.

I shoot to my feet. "Enough with this slut bullshit," I snap at her. "Do you realize how many decades you set us back every time you call another girl a slut? We've spent years fighting to not be viewed as sexual objects or be judged and shamed if we happen to enjoy sex. It's bad enough that men still do this to us. When *you* do it too, it sends the message that it's fair game for women to be treated this way."

"Shut up," is her comeback. "You're a slut too!"

I cross my arms tight to my chest. "Say that again. I dare you."

She flashes a smug smile. "You're. A. Slut."

I might have let it go. I really might've. If she hadn't stepped forward and flicked her razor fingernails against my cheek in a mocking, dismissive gesture that turns my vision into a haze of red.

I launch myself at her.

"Catfight!" Hollis yells, jumping out of the booth.

I'm too busy tackling the blonde to chastise Hollis for the enjoyment he's receiving from this. Straddling her, I get one good punch in before her own fist flies out and connects with the corner of my mouth. I taste a burst of copper on my bottom lip, lick it away, and grab a hunk of her hair. She wails when I give it a sharp pull.

"What the hell happened to girl power? Did you never listen to the Spice Girls?" I growl in her face. "What's wrong with you?"

She slaps at me with her taloned hands. "Get off me!"

Her wish is granted, because suddenly I'm being heaved off her body. Strong arms wrap around my waist to keep me away from her. She jumps to her feet and pounces again. "You broke my nail!" she screeches at me.

Davey grabs her and tugs her backward. She clings to his arm as if it's the last remaining lifeboat on the *Titanic*.

I frown at the sight. "Your loser boyfriend tried to grab another girl's boob—how is *that* not what you're mad about?"

Holding his girlfriend protectively, Davey announces to the world that he's a dumbass by picking this exact moment to join the conversation.

Because only a dumbass would point at Brenna and say, "Look at what she's wearing! She was asking for it!"

*Oh no he di'int.*

I lunge forward again, but those big arms lock tighter around me. They belong to Hunter, I realize. But even if I'd been able to charge, I'm nowhere near as fast as Fitz. One second he's seated, the next he's got Douchebag Davey by the collar.

"She was asking for it?" Fitzy hisses. "Did those words really just come out of your filthy, rapist mouth?"

Davey gasps for air. "I didn't mean it like that—"

Fitz slams the frat boy against the brick wall next to the booth. I swear I feel the entire room shake. Malone's has framed sports memorabilia hanging on the walls, and several photographs of hockey players I don't recognize crash to the beer-stained floor. I hear the crunching of glass beneath Fitz's Timberlands as he shifts his feet.

A server comes flying over, but she's a tiny woman and no match for a six-two, enraged Colin Fitzgerald. His dark eyes spit fire as he literally dangles Davey a foot off the ground with one hand around the guy's neck.

Concern flutters in my tummy. Shit, this isn't good. Fitz is strangling the—

Nope, he's punching him. With his free arm, he takes a powerful swing that lands a bone-cracking blow to Davey's nose. Fitz releases him, and Davey crumples to the sticky floor, blood pouring out of his nostrils.

"I'm having you arrested for assault!"

"Go for it." Fitzy sounds amused by the threat, and there's something so insanely sexy about that. "Saves Brenna a phone call to the cops. She can press charges against you at the same time."

I cannot take my eyes off his face. His jaw is sharper than steel. His mouth is hard and dangerous. And his arms are… Oh sweet Lord, his muscles are coiled with tension, taut with rage, and his tattoos seem to ripple across his skin as he presses his sculpted arms flush to his sides. The dragon on his left biceps looks as if it's about to take flight and rain fire on the world. Fitz is as primal as the creature on his arm. He looms over the fallen Davey. Big and broad and radiating raw, masculine power.

I've never wanted to fuck anyone more.

"Good idea," Brenna pipes up, smiling at Davey. "Not sure if you knew this, but groping a girl in a bar is considered sexual assault in this state."

Her words succeed in making him go pale. His bloody nose paired with cheeks devoid of color gives Davey a ghoulish air. He stumbles to his feet and tries to push past Fitz.

Fitz is a wall of muscle. Muscle walls don't budge.

"Colin," Hollis murmurs.

After a few beats, Fitz moves out of the way to let Davey pass.

"Come on, Kerry," Davey mumbles to his girlfriend. "These fuckers aren't worth it."

He says this as if he'd been the one with the upper hand on Fitz and not the other way around.

"Slut," is the blonde's parting insult to me.

I swallow a sigh. Some people never learn.

"I'm sorry," comes Fitz's rough voice. He's speaking to the wait staff. "I'll pay for the damages."

"No," I blurt, stepping forward. "I will. I started the fight. It's my fault."

The fact that Fitz doesn't argue the point or insist on paying tells me he feels the same way about where the blame lies. One look is all it takes for me to glimpse the barely checked accusation in his eyes.

Oh, he blames me, all right.

I wait for him to scold me. Or maybe throw me over his shoulder as he's prone to doing. Instead, he curses under his breath, grabs his jacket, then mutters, "I'm out."

Disbelief spirals through me as I watch him stalk away. I'm frozen for a beat. Then I tear my gaze off him and grab my Chanel purse from the booth seat.

Nate and Matt are trying to help the flustered waitress clean up the broken photo frames, while Hollis is murmuring something in Brenna's ear.

That leaves Hunter. I toss him the Chanel and say, "I've got cash—can you pay whatever needs paying? I want to check on Fitz."

Without giving him a chance to reply, I dart toward the exit.

Outside, I'm quick to realize my mistake. I forgot that it's winter. My coat is inside, and I'm wearing a shirt that doesn't have a back. Goose bumps break out on my exposed skin when the chilled air kisses it. I run as fast as my Prada boots and sense of self-preservation will allow. The heels aren't that high, but a layer of ice covers the ground beneath them.

I catch up to Fitz in the parking lot behind Malone's, as he's unlocking his car.

"Wait," I call out.

At the sound of my voice, his broad frame tenses. "Go back inside, Summer. You'll freeze to death."

I hurry over to him. "Not until I make sure you're okay."

"I'm fine." His tone is terse.

"Your knuckles are bleeding." Alarmed, I grab his hand and rub one big knuckle. The pad of my thumb comes back stained with a reddish tinge.

"Screw my knuckles. Your goddamn lip is bleeding."

I wipe my mouth with the heel of my palm. "She didn't split my lip," I assure him. "It's a scratch from her demon nails."

He doesn't even crack a smile. "Go back inside," he repeats. "I'm leaving."

Something about his expression raises my hackles.

Well, not something. I know exactly what's bothering me—the disapproval shining in my direction.

"You're pissed because I tackled that girl?" I demand.

"Of course I'm pissed." He slams the driver's door and marches toward me. "What the hell were you thinking?"

"I was defending myself and my friend," I snap. "I don't know about you, but I don't particularly enjoy repeatedly being called a slut."

"And I don't particularly enjoy bar brawls," he retorts. His breath hangs in the frigid air before dissipating.

"Right, and I'm a habitual bar brawler!" I clench my teeth. Because I'm cold and they won't stop chattering, but also because I have the craziest urge to bite him. Maybe I am a brawler.

"Whatever," he says flatly. "I don't want to be put in that position again, okay?"

"What position?"

"Where I have to defend your honor."

My jaw drops. "I didn't ask you to! You're the one who decided to throat-grab that jerk. Granted, he had it coming—"

"He wouldn't have opened his fool mouth if you hadn't attacked his girlfriend," Fitz cuts in. He shakes his head at me, scowling deeply. "I don't like to fight, Summer. I learned a long time ago that problems don't need to be solved with fists."

"He groped Brenna," I remind Fitz. "He deserved a fist."

I can tell from his inflexible expression that he doesn't agree. In Fitz's mind, I forced him into a bar fight, end of story.

I turn on my heels. "I'm going back inside."

"No."

With an incredulous look, I spin around. "Are you serious right now? I'm doing what you want! You keep telling me to go inside."

"Changed my mind," he barks. "I'm taking you home. You've caused enough trouble for one night."

"*I* caused trouble! What about the maniac who dumped water all over Brenna? Or her sleazy, gropey boyfriend? I cannot believe you're blaming *me* for anything that happened in there!"

He takes a step forward and I whip both hands up in a martial arts pose. I took three months of karate when I was twelve. I can take him.

"If you throw me over your shoulder, I will scream my bloody lungs out," I warn. "It's not my fault you decided to punch someone tonight. Deal with the consequences of your own actions."

Dark eyes blaze at me. "I wouldn't have to deal with these consequences if you hadn't gotten your panties in a knot over some silly girl who wasn't worth your anger."

Just like that, my body reacts as if someone cranked my internal arousal meter up to *Danger: Orgasm Imminent*. A guy as sexy as this one isn't allowed to say the word panties. Because now I'm imagining a variation of that sentence. In my head, I hear his deep voice rumbling, *"I want to rip your panties off with my teeth, Summer."*

"Don't you fucking look at me like that."

My gaze jerks toward his. Okay, the words aren't the same, but the growly rasp is exactly what I'd heard in my head.

"Like what?" I ask weakly. My pulse has gone from zero to a million in a split second, making my knees wobble.

"You know what I'm talking about." He hisses out a breath. "And you need to stop it."

"Stop what?"

He groans. A frustrated, animalistic groan that sends a bolt of heat between my legs before spreading outward to set every square inch of my skin on fire. I'm no longer feeling the cold. I could be buck-naked in the Siberian tundra, and I'd still feel like I was going up in flames. I thought I'd known what lust felt like, but I was wrong.

"Stop playing with my damn mind." The words are tortured, shaky. "One day you're flirting with me, the next you're cuddling with Hunter."

Guilt pricks into me. Crap. I forgot about the night Hunter and I snuggled. Fitz knows about that?

"One day you're calling us best friends, the next you're standing in front of me looking like you want my dick in your mouth."

My core clenches with an ache so powerful I almost keel over. Oh my God. That is a visual I do *not* need right now.

He shakes his head before dropping his gaze to his scuffed boots. "I don't like mind games and I definitely don't like drama," he mutters.

"Fitz." Wariness curls around my throat. "What are you actually mad about right now?"

His jaw clenches tight. For a moment I don't expect him to answer, but then he mumbles, "You could've gotten hurt in there."

Surprise jolts through me. *That's* what this is about? He was worried for my safety?

"But I didn't," I assure him. "Trust me, I know how to handle myself. I'm scrappy."

"I've noticed."

I shake my head irritably. "Why couldn't you say that from the start? *Summer, I don't like the idea of you getting hurt.* There. Easy. Instead, you shout at me like a maniac and then act like there's something wrong about me thinking you're hot when you're angry?"

Slowly, he lifts his head.

I suck in a breath. He levels me with a hot, needy look that has me desperately squeezing my legs together. The throbbing is back, and it's worse now. Nobody has ever looked at me this way.

"You think I'm hot when I'm angry?"

"Yes, I do. You were sexy-shouting and it got me going. So sue me." I glare at him. "Just because you're not attracted to me doesn't mean I'm—"

"Not attracted to you?" he interrupts incredulously, and the next thing I know he's snatching my hand and placing it directly on his crotch. "Feel this? This is what you do to me. You make me hard. Constantly."

He presses my palm tighter to his body, and a moan gets stuck in my throat. I'm mesmerized by the thick ridge beneath my hand. He's impossibly big. I mean, I guess I expected it. He's a big guy. Tall, muscular, huge shoulders. Big hands... But that isn't always a reliable indication of wiener size. I dated a tight end once with bear paws and size fourteen shoes and a teeny little ding dong. The kind of penis that makes you cry real tears because it's so depressingly disappointing.

Fitz? He doesn't disappoint. I wish I could wrap my fingers around him, put my mouth on him. But his stupid pants are on, so I settle for rubbing the tantalizing length of him. Just slightly, and yet the fleeting contact is enough to summon a deep, tormented moan from his throat.

"You think it's fun walking around with this damn thing all day long? You so much as breathe in my direction, and you do this to me. You're on my mind twenty-four-seven."

"But..." I swallow. "You think I'm fluff."

"For fuck's sake. Are we back to that? I only said that shit to Garrett because I was trying to convince myself not to get involved with you."

I falter. "Really?" I experience a burst of hope...until the last thing he said registers, bringing a flicker of hurt. My hand drops from his groin. "Why didn't you want to get involved with me?"

"Because you drive me crazy. Wanting you is exhausting, Summer. Being around you is exhausting." He throws his hands up before dragging them through his messy hair. "I'm an introvert, and you're the very definition of social. And exhausting. Did I mention you're exhausting?"

I frown. "I don't—"

"Everything okay out here?"

We both whirl around at the sound of Hunter's voice. Our roommate strides across the lot, my parka slung over one arm. He holds it out for me, and, despite the heat still coursing through my blood, I take the coat and shrug it on.

"Thanks," I tell Hunter. "And everything's fine." I'm dying to look at Fitz, but I'm afraid of what I'll see.

He solves the dilemma for me by walking to his car. "Make sure Summer gets home safe," he says.

Not even a backwards glance.

A moment later, his huge body disappears into the driver's seat, the engine sputters to life, and he peels out of the lot without even waiting five seconds to defrost his windshield.

Tears sting my eyes. I blink hard and fast, but they still manage to break free. The adrenaline from the bar fight (both my fight and Fitz's) is suddenly sucked out of my body as if someone stuck a vacuum hose on me. It leaves me feeling weary.

Hunter draws me toward him, wrapping one arm around my shoulders. "Hey, don't cry, Blondie."

I bite my lip, blinking faster to ward off the tears. "Sorry. Adrenaline crash, I think."

"I get it." There's humor in his tone. "I mean, you did kick someone's ass tonight."

"Barely."

His free hand reaches for one of mine. He lightly caresses the inside of my palm with his thumb. "That was so badass of you, by the way. Defending Brenna like that."

At least someone thinks so. "Thanks."

He chuckles softly. "Though I'm pretty sure that catfight gave Mike enough spank-bank material for at least a year."

I make a face. "Oh God, I hope not."

Hunter's callused fingers graze my palm before linking through mine. Holding his hand is both comforting and unsettling, but I don't have the strength to pull away. I'm currently using most of my energy to try to make sense of everything Fitz said before his abrupt departure.

I drive him crazy.

He finds me exhausting.

He wants me, but he doesn't want to want me.

"Blondie," Hunter says roughly.

"Hmmm?" My mind continues to race, making it hard to concentrate. Or rather, making it hard*er* to concentrate. My ADHD already gives me a handicap.

"Next Saturday," he starts.

"What about it?"

"We don't have a game." He hesitates. "Do you want to go out that night? Grab some dinner?"

It's my turn to hesitate. There's no mistaking his intentions. He's asking me on a date. And maybe if Fitz wasn't in the picture, I'd—

*Are you fucking kidding me right now!* my inner Selena Gomez shrieks.

Wow. A rare F-bomb from her. Inner Selena is usually far more proper and composed. She doesn't let the exasperating behavior of men affect her pure, elegant way of living her life.

But she's absolutely right. I have one guy who doesn't want to want me, and another one who's proud to declare that he does—and I'm leaning toward the *first* one?

Why? Really. Why. Why is this even a choice? Hunter is gorgeous. He's a great kisser. And he's actually making an effort to be with me instead of running away every chance he gets.

I like Fitz, but he's too confusing. He thinks *I'm* playing mind games? He's gone from telling Garrett he'd never date me, to comforting me about my midterm and offering to help me, to confessing he's attracted to me and then saying I'm too exhausting to be with.

Uh-huh. *I'm* exhausting.

I want a man with clear intentions. A man who makes an effort and is excited to spend time with me. A man who actually *wants* to want me.

If he has to fight himself to be with me, then chances are he'd never fight for *me* if it came down to it.

What woman would ever choose somebody like that?

I rest my head on Hunter's shoulder and allow the warmth of his body to seep into my tired bones. I squeeze his hand and say, "I'd love to have dinner with you."

# 19
# SUMMER

IN THE PAST, I'VE FELT JUDGED BY MY FEMALE FRIENDS. MY CIRCLE in high school was super competitive, which inevitably led to trash-talking, backstabbing and outright in-your-face betrayal. Even with the girls I (more or less) trusted, I'd try not to share every aspect of my life. That's probably just a good rule to live by, though. Always keep part of yourself hidden.

Fitz is very good at that, but he does it to the extreme. And me, I haven't mastered it completely. I'll still share certain personal details with my friends, like whether I kissed someone. Who I'm interested in. Whether I enjoyed or hated a date.

But admitting that I went from essentially giving one guy an over-the-pants hand job to agreeing to go out with another one? Um. No. If I'd confessed that to any of my high school friends or Brown sorority sisters, the slut rumors would already be traveling across campus. And don't get me started on all the sub-tweets and social media bullshit I'd have to deal with.

Typically, I'd have no problem confiding in my mom, but this time I'm too embarrassed to confess what happened. How do I even phrase it? *Hey Mom, I put my hand on a guy's dick yesterday. Discuss.*

But for the first time in my life, I think I actually found a friend with whom I'm comfortable providing all the dirty little details that other friends would pass judgment on. I have the utmost confidence that Brenna can be trusted and won't try to make me feel bad about my actions in some catty, passive-aggressive way.

So, I don't regret telling her everything.

I do, however, regret telling her while we're sitting in public.

"You touched Fitzy's dick?!" she shouts.

Awesome. I probably should've called her after it happened last night. But I needed to mull. And I was mulling this morning too. And this afternoon. It wasn't until we arrived at the Briar arena tonight that I decided I need advice. Brenna and I don't even ask each other to go to home games anymore. We just assume that we are. Tonight I get to meet some of her friends, though, which I'm excited about. We're meeting them at Malone's for drinks after the game, and she's promised me they're really cool chicks.

"Would you keep your voice down?" I order, looking around to make sure nobody is paying attention to us.

"How on earth did that happen?" she demands. "You left the bar to check if he was okay after the fight. Did that require grabbing his junk? Was it under the boxers?" She gasps. "Was there sucking?"

I choke on a wave of laughter. "Over the pants. And I told you, it was just touching. Maybe some rubbing."

Her bottom lip sticks out. "So no bare dick?"

"No bare dick."

"Pity. I bet his bare dick is phenomenal."

The girls in front of us titter, alerting me to the fact that we've uttered the phrase "bare dick" one too many times. The braver of the two looks over her shoulder at us, and I give her a sheepish smile.

She smiles shyly in return. I think they're both freshmen. They still have that air of innocence to them.

Beside me, Brenna lowers her voice. "How was it?"

"It was intense."

"I meant size, Summer. How was the dick? Big? Small? Long? Thick? Happy? Sad?"

I bury my face in my lap, shaking with laughter. When I've calmed down, I ask, "How can a dick be sad?"

"Trust me, I've seen some sad sausage." She waves a hand, flashing her red-painted nails. "Fine, we can discuss measurements later. What was intense about it?"

"I don't know." I gulp as I recall the naked passion glittering in his eyes. "It just was. But then it got annoying."

She frowns. "How so?"

"He kept going on about how he wants me but doesn't want to want me. It was…" I think it over. "Insulting," I conclude.

"I'll bet. You don't want Mr. Resistance. You want a guy who shouts from the rooftops how lucky he is to have you."

"Exactly." I love that we're on the same page about this. I feel like too many girls fail to remember one vital truth: we deserve someone who gives us one hundred percent. Half-assed effort isn't effort. Half-assed love isn't love. If a man isn't all in, then we need to be all out.

"So, yeah. It got weird, and then Hunter interrupted us, and Fitz drove off." I avoid her gaze. "And then I agreed to go on a date with Hunter next Saturday."

"On Valentine's Day?"

*"It's Valentine's Day?!"*

My screech causes every single person in our vicinity to stare in our direction. Brenna quickly waves her hand again. "Nothing to see, folks. Enjoy the game," she chirps.

"Oh my God, do you think he knew it was Valentine's Day when he asked me out?" I hiss.

"I doubt it. Most guys don't pay attention to that kind of stuff."

"She's right," a familiar voice confirms.

I turn in time to see Brooks Weston flopping down in an empty seat behind us. Jake Connelly is with him, lowering his broad body onto the neighboring seat. Jake's dark hair is swept away from his chiseled face, and I can't tell if it's windblown or slicked back with gel, but either way it looks hot. Both guys wear hoodies conspicuously lacking the Harvard logo or colors.

Because *that's* not suspicious.

Sharing my thoughts, Brenna flicks a cagey glance at them. "Scoping out the competition?"

Weston nods, unabashed. "Absolutely. We play you again in a couple of weeks." He winks. "Correction—we beat you again in a couple of weeks."

"You wish. We've got home-ice advantage," Brenna reminds him.

Weston simply grins.

She glances at Jake. "What about you? Don't feel like taunting us about how you're going to kick our asses?"

He cocks a brow. "We are going to kick your asses. I don't see the point in rubbing it in." Jake focuses on me. "And to answer your question, I doubt he knew the date. V-Day isn't something we usually mark on our calendars, unless we've got a girlfriend."

"Girlfriend?" Brenna echoes, her tone dry. "From what I hear, you don't know the meaning of that word."

The smile he gives her is seductive as hell. "You been asking around about me?"

"Nope. Your puck bunnies just like to talk." She shrugs. "Apparently you never go out with the same girl twice."

"So?" Somehow, he's able to inject cockiness, sheepishness, and pure sex into one measly syllable.

I speak up before Brenna can. "Do you think I should give him a heads-up about what day it is?" I ask the boys.

"Depends," Connelly replies.

"On what?" I've completely abandoned the game being played on the rink below us. I twist around in my seat, desperate for some male advice.

Jake licks his bottom lip. I'm not sure if it's intentional or if his lips are dry. But again, looks hot either way.

It's a bit alarming, this strange fascination I have with the guy.

I don't want him for myself, but I'm wholly aware of the sex appeal he radiates. Maybe I'm feeding off Brenna's energy? Despite her constant mocking of him, I've noticed that her gaze always lingers on him a bit longer than necessary.

"Depends on whether you want to fuck him or not," Jake explains.

"True," Weston agrees. "If you want to bang him, don't tell him. Chances are he'll bail if he knows the date. Unless you want him to bail?"

"I don't know," I confess.

There's no denying that Hunter is incredibly attractive. He's easy to talk to, he makes me laugh, turns me on. But Fitz does something to my stomach. Saying he gives me butterflies would be an understatement. And he does something to my heart too. Damned if I can tell you what that *something* is, but rest assured he does it for me.

Crap. Maybe agreeing to go out with Hunter was a mistake. Here I am preaching about deserving someone who gives me one hundred percent—well, doesn't Hunter deserve the same?

As long as Fitz is on my mind, even if he's only taking up a teeny corner of it, is it fair of me to date someone else?

I don't say this out loud, because I don't want to reveal to these Harvard guys that I'm torn between my two roommates. But deep down I suspect there's not much of a competition there. I wanted Fitz from the moment I met him last year. I think those might actually be the first words I spoke to Dean's girlfriend. I pointed at Fitz and said, "I want him."

And this isn't about me being a spoiled brat and needing a shiny new toy. Fitz isn't a pair of Louboutin pumps or a Valentino clutch.

And it's not about me wanting him simply because he's been making me chase him.

And while it may have begun as a physical kind of wanting, that's changed.

I think I might want more now.

Fuck.

---

The game is surprisingly low scoring. We're playing Eastwood, our conference rival, and they're damn good at keeping the puck out of their zone. Whenever the Briar guys cross the blue line, they need to take full advantage of the opportunity, and they haven't been doing it so far in the first two periods. Plus, Eastwood has this goon on their team that's driving me nuts. He's already instigated several scrums, but nothing to warrant the attention of the refs.

"Man after my own heart," Weston cracks from behind us. He says this after the goon once again gets a few good shoves in on a Briar player before skating away.

"Figures you'd fall in love. A goon always recognizes the goon in another," Brenna says sweetly.

Weston reaches out and ruffles her hair good-naturedly. "I wear my goon badge with pride, babe."

On the ice, the Eastwood goon just stole the puck from Matt Anderson after slamming the defenseman against the boards. He takes possession and flies toward our net, his teammates skating fast in tow.

"Ugh! I hate this guy!" Annoyance has me jumping to my feet. "Go away!" I shout at him. "Nobody wants you here!"

Jake and Brenna snort in unison, then frown at each other as if any sort of united reaction is unacceptable.

Weston taps the back of my knee. "Hey, you know who that is, right?"

"No." I can't see his jersey number or his name. I just know I hate him.

"It's Casper Cassidy. From Greenwich Prep," he replies, naming the high school that my brother Dean attended.

I went to Greenwich for freshman year, but I transferred to Roselawn because I couldn't handle the workload. Greenwich places a lot more importance on academics than Roselawn does. In fact, in the prep-school circuit, Roselawn has a rep for being a party school.

The kids are rich enough to buy their way into college, so nobody is too concerned about getting straight As.

Despite the fact that my dad pulled strings to get me into Briar, I'm at least proud to say I was admitted to Brown all on my own. My GPA wasn't something to write home about, but I made up for it with my extra-curriculars and community service.

"Are you kidding me?" I marvel, trying to spot the goon again. There are too many jerseys battling it out behind the net. "That's Casper Cassidy? Did he have some sort of growth spurt? He looks enormous."

"No, he was always that big," Weston argues.

I twist in my seat again. "I played 7 Minutes in Heaven with him at a Greenwich party, and he fingered me in a closet. Trust me, he was not that big."

Connelly starts to laugh. "You're really something else, Di Laurentis. No filter whatsoever." He tips his head. "Doesn't embarrass you at all to admit that, huh?"

"Nope."

"Why should she be embarrassed?" Brenna challenges. "What, you don't think girls are allowed to hook up?"

Jake's mouth hitches in a wry grin. "Jensen, I think no matter what I say, you'd still argue the point."

"That's not true."

"You're arguing right now."

"Because you're annoying me."

"What a coincidence," he mocks. "You're annoying me too."

A collective gasp from the crowd interrupts their bickering. I'd turned away, so I'm not certain what happened, but I stumble to my feet when I glimpse the blood.

"Oh shit, that's Fitz," Brenna says. "What the hell happened?" I guess she hadn't been watching, either.

The freshmen in the row ahead help us out. "He took a shot to the face," one girl says.

"What!" My heart jumps to my throat.

"He laid out to block Cassidy's shot," Weston explains. "Puck was deflected."

"But he's wearing a visor," I protest.

"Visor's probably what cut him," Jake says wryly.

"He's fine," Weston says. "Doesn't look too bad."

Now that the whistle has been blown and the players have skated away from the net, I can clearly see the red drops staining the white surface. It's not as much blood as I thought. But still.

My panicked gaze seeks out Fitz. He's on the Briar bench. His head is being tipped back by a woman I assume is the team doctor. She's pressing a square of gauze to the outer edge of his right eyebrow. Not his eye, then. Relief flows through me.

Fitz is arguing with the doc. His mouth is moving, and his body practically vibrates with frustration. He wants to go back on the ice, but the woman keeps shaking her head. She readjusts the gauze, and my stomach churns when I glimpse the river of blood pouring down the side of his face.

"He needs stitches," Brenna says unhappily.

Fitz flings a gloved hand toward the scoreboard, I assume to point out the game clock. There are eight minutes left in the third. Clearly he's determined to keep playing. The doc once again shakes her head, unyielding. Then Coach Jensen shouts something at them, and Fitz stands up.

With my heart still lodged in my throat, I watch as he's ushered away. He slams an angry glove against the boards before disappearing in the tunnel that leads to the locker rooms.

I'm already marching toward the aisle. "Later, spies," I call to the Harvard boys. To Brenna, I issue a sharp order. "Come on, Bee."

I expect her to object, insist we need to watch the rest of the game, but she surprises me by following me down the steps. Outside the rink doors, I gaze imploringly at her. "Can you sneak me into the locker room? Or the medical room? Whatever you call it. I want to make sure he's okay."

She nods, her eyes softening. "Sure. I've got you."

In the hallway, she takes the lead, while I scramble to keep up with her brisk pace. When we reach a door that requires a keycard, Brenna whips one out of her purse and holds it to the scanner. It turns green and off we go. Being the coach's daughter comes with perks, apparently.

The doctor who'd been arguing with Fitz exits the locker room at the same time we approach it.

"Hey, Alex," Brenna greets her. "How's Fitzy?"

"Physically? He's fine. I stitched him up." The woman—Alex— rubs the bridge of her nose. She's visibly aggravated. "But his attitude could use an adjustment. Your dad said he's done for the night."

Brenna nods. "Makes sense. We're ahead by two." She gestures to me. "You mind if Summer pops in to see him?"

Alex scrutinizes me for a moment. She's a short, stocky woman with sharp features and a narrow jaw, but there's kindness in her eyes. Finally she nods. "Be quick," she tells me. To Brenna she says, "If your father asks, I never saw either of you."

"You rock, Alex." Once the team doc disappears around the corner, Brenna gives me a cheeky grin. "I'll stand out here and keep watch. If someone comes, I'll hoot like an owl."

I swallow a laugh. "Solid plan," I reply, reaching for the door handle.

When I enter the locker room, I find it completely empty. No Fitz, only sleek benches, padded lockers, and a faint whiff of sweat and old socks. In all honesty, the room smells a hell of a lot better than other locker rooms I've been in. Briar's hockey facility boasts the kind of ventilation system other teams probably have wet dreams about.

The sound of rushing water captures my attention. I glance toward the wide doorway across the room. Wisps of steam float out of it, but I don't see any light. There's nothing but darkness beyond that doorway.

"Fitz?" I say warily.

A beat.

Two.

Then his equally wary, albeit muffled, voice replies with, "Summer?"

"Yeah, it's me. I'm coming in, okay?"

I cross the threshold and am greeted by a cloud of steam. It takes a second for my eyes to adjust to both the darkness and the haze, for me to make out the bulky figure in the stall nearest the door. I'm not sure why I don't turn on the light. I guess because he didn't. If he wants to take a shower in the dark, who am I to stop him?

I inch my way toward the stall. In the shadows I glimpse the swirl of his tats and the ridges of his abs. Cotton fills my mouth when it occurs to me that he's naked. The only barrier between Fitz's naked body and myself is a short swinging door. All I have to do is nudge that partition, and I'd get an eyeful of—

"What are you doing in here?" His gruff voice interrupts my thoughts.

"I wanted to make sure you're all right. How's the eye?"

"Fine," he grunts.

He turns the shower off and steps toward the little door. My heart rate triples. Water drips down his bare chest, rippling over his tattoo and trickling between his defined pecs. One muscular arm reaches out, and I forget how to breathe. Is he—

Reaching for the towel on the hook behind my head? Yes, he certainly is.

I gulp hard, hoping to bring some moisture to my arid mouth. Fitz wraps the towel around his waist and exits the stall, but rather than go into the other room, he stays put. We stand there in the darkness, facing each other. The air is still hot and muggy from the steam, but now it's also thick with tension.

The sexual kind.

The *"holy shit, this guy is looking at me like he's already inside me"* kind.

I try to ease backward, but my knees knock together. I honestly didn't think it through when I decided to check on him. He'd just left the ice in the middle of a fast-paced, demanding game. He's in pain because he took a puck to the face. He's probably still hopped up on adrenaline.

He's dangerous.

I don't fear for my safety. But I fear for my sanity.

Shadows dance across his masculine features. I catch a glimpse of his tongue dragging over his bottom lip. Long fingers scraping over his wet hair. Then he speaks in a gravelly voice that sends a hot shiver up my spine.

"You should leave."

My pulse hammers in my throat. It's all I hear, the relentless *thump-thump* of my heart. "What if I don't?" I find myself asking, and we both hear the breathy note in each word.

He moves closer. Slowly. Deliberately. Until he's completely backed me up against the tiled wall.

"If you don't go? Then I'll probably kiss you," he says bluntly.

My mouth is so dry I can't answer him. I swallow, once, twice. It's pointless, though. There's nothing to swallow. No saliva, just the sawdust that's coating my throat. My heart beats even faster. I swear it's going to give out on me any second.

He dips his head, and his next words rumble in my ear. Low and silky. "What do you think, Summer? You want me to kiss you?"

It's the sexiest question I've ever heard in my life, voiced by the sexiest guy I've ever met in my life. I find the strength to lift my head so I can meet his eyes. It's too dark to fully make out his expression, but I don't need to. I know exactly what he's feeling right now. I'm feeling it too.

Hot, uncontrollable lust.

"Yes or no," he whispers.

I finally find my voice. "Yes."

# 20
# FITZ

I'M GONE FOR THIS GIRL.

So gone.

I should be urging her to leave the locker room. My teammates could come barreling in at any second—there wasn't much time left in the third period before Doc Alex forced me to leave the ice so she could stitch me up.

But although common sense tells me this isn't a good idea, I'm helpless to stop it. My surroundings disappear. When I inhale, I breathe in nothing but Summer and Chanel No. 5.

Fuck it. I need this too much. She needs it too, otherwise she wouldn't have said yes.

I curl one hand over the back of her neck and thrust the other one through her hair. It feels like silk between my fingers.

"Colin," she whispers, and the sound of my name on her lips is what spurs me to action.

I lower my head and press my lips to hers, and she makes the sweetest sound in the world. A soft, desperate moan. Then she deepens the kiss and it's my turn to moan. When our tongues meet, I feel like I've been struck by a Taser gun. A jolt of electricity sizzles right down to my dick. Fries my brain. Makes my hands shake.

She tastes like cola and mint, and her lips are so damn soft. We stand there in the dark, her tongue in my mouth, my fingers in her hair. One of her legs comes up and hooks around my waist. And I don't know if it's intentional or not, but her foot nudges the edge of my towel, causing the terrycloth to slide to the floor.

Her mouth abruptly leaves mine. "Your dick's out," she informs me.

I choke on a laugh. "Yup."

"Cool." Humor colors her tone. "Just making sure you know."

Our gazes lock as she flattens one palm against my bare chest. Meanwhile, my hard-on is impossible to ignore. It's like a sharp sword between us, poking her in the belly.

Her fingertips drift lower. Only an inch, hovering over my abs. Despite the steam still hanging in the air, I shiver.

Her hand stops moving. "Are you cold?"

"No," I say thickly.

I'm enjoying her slow, torturous exploration of my chest. Delicate fingers caress my abdominal muscles before skimming even lower.

"Remember the night we met?" she murmurs. "When I teased you about showing me your dick?"

A laugh slips out. "How could I forget?"

Her head slants, sending her silky hair cascading over one shoulder. "You said you don't go around showing it to just anyone."

"I don't."

"So I'm special."

"Very much so."

Her fingers wrap around the base of my aching cock. The instant she makes contact, a shudder rolls through me, and moisture forms at my tip. Jesus. I'm leaking. That's how turned on I am.

She slides her hand up and down a few times. And then she actually tugs me forward by the dick and crushes her lips against mine again.

I grunt, thrusting into her closed fist. My tongue fills her mouth and we exchange the hottest kiss I've ever experienced. Once again I'm lost in the fog. I'm lost in her. I barely feel the pain in my eye anymore. Right now, I'm kissing Summer and she's stroking my cock and I'm in frickin' heaven.

When I drag my hands up her body to cup her tits over her thin V-neck sweater, I promptly lose the ability to think straight. Even through her bra I can feel her nipples, hard little buds that make my mouth tingle with need. I've always been a boob guy, and I desperately wish I was sucking and nibbling on her tits. The fantasy has me groaning loudly against her lips. She strokes me faster, and just when I think it couldn't feel any better, she pushes my hands away and sinks to her knees.

"Let me make you feel good."

I gaze down, but it's hard to see her expression. It's too dark. But I feel every last sensation when her warm, wet mouth engulfs me.

"Oh fuck," I grind out.

She sucks me all the way to the root, then licks her way back up. Her tongue teases my tip before gliding along the underside of my shaft, and I almost black out.

"God…fuck, that's good…"

Her answering moan vibrates all around me. I swear I feel it in my toes. She takes me deeper and sucks harder, pumping me with her hand while she torments me with her tongue.

In the back of my mind I hear alarm bells. *Stop this*, they warn. But stopping is impossible when Summer's blonde head is moving up and down on my dick. My fingers tangle in her hair, but I don't seize control. I let her go at her own pace, trusting that she'll get me where I need to be.

And she does. As the suction tightens and her pace quickens, my balls throb and the tip of my dick tingles and then I'm there. "Coming," I choke out.

She doesn't release me. I bite the side of my thumb to stop from groaning out loud as I rock my hips and shoot in her mouth. She swallows every drop while I shudder in pleasure bordering on pain.

When Summer rises to her feet, I pull her close and rest my chin on her shoulder. Still shaking from that climax.

"I needed that," I say hoarsely.

"I know you did." She plants a kiss between my pecs and brings her hand back to my dick, petting it softly.

I break out in shivers. "You're killing me."

Her laughter tickles my collarbone. "Sorry. I just really like touching you." She pauses. "I should probably go."

"Yeah."

"I don't want to."

"I don't want you to."

I feel her trembling as she kisses me again, this time the fleeting brush of her lips over my shoulder. "What just happened here, Fitz?"

*You blew my dick and my mind?* I almost say. But I know what she means. She wants to know what this means.

"I—"

"*Hoo-hooo! Hoo-hooo!*"

My head snaps up in alarm. Was that an owl?

"Oh shit," Summer blurts out. "That's the signal."

"Signal?"

"Yeah. Brenna is in the hall. I asked her to keep an eye out and make sure nobody catches me in here."

She's barely finished speaking when we hear the voices. And the footsteps. A lot of voices, and a lot of footsteps. My teammates are coming down the tunnel.

Summer snatches my fallen towel off the ground and hurriedly wraps it around my waist. Her fingers brush my dick, and I swallow a groan. I'm still hard.

I take a breath and nod to a doorway on the far end of the showers. "The PT room is in there. It leads to the coaches' offices, and there's another exit to the arena from there."

The footsteps grow louder, accompanied by animated male

voices and raucous laughter. My teammates sound happy, which means we won.

"Summer," I say when she doesn't move. "You gotta go. And you better do it fast, before the boys get in here and start pulling their dicks out."

She hesitates. "We need to finish this conversation."

"We will," I promise. "At home."

Her teeth dig into her lip. "Brenna and I are meeting friends at the bar."

"Then we'll talk at the bar. Or afterward. Right now, you need to go."

Summer nods. She stands on her tiptoes, gives me a kiss on the cheek, and then she's gone.

---

I'm a pussy. I don't go looking for Summer after the game, and I don't go to Malone's. I also don't go home.

Like an asshole, I get in my car and drive to Boston.

My friend Tucker bought a bar in the city this past fall. I helped him with the reno, getting it ready for its big opening in November. Doesn't surprise me that the only person I want to confide in right now is Tuck. He's easy to talk to and has a good head on his shoulders. Gives really smart advice too, and right now I'm desperate for some advice.

I'm reaching the freeway exit when my phone rings. My car is an older model and doesn't have the Bluetooth feature, so I'm forced to use speakerphone. If it wasn't my mother's number flashing on the screen, I'd probably press ignore. But ignoring Mom is never a good idea.

"Colin! Sweetie! Are you all right?" Her greeting holds a hefty dose of concern.

"I'm fine. Why wouldn't I be?"

"Your Uncle Randy was at your game tonight, and he just sent me a phone picture of your face!"

"You can just say 'picture,' Ma. You don't have to specify 'phone.'"

"But he sent it from his phone to my phone."

"Yes, but—" I stop myself from continuing. *Pick your battles, man.* My mother isn't an old lady and therefore has no excuse for her total lack of knowledge about anything tech-related. But she's also set in her ways and arguing with her is pointless.

She still uses a BlackBerry, for chrissake.

"I promise, I'm fine. Got stitched up and now I'm good as new."

"How many stitches?"

"Only two."

"Okay." The worry leaves her tone. Unfortunately, it's replaced with anger. "This is all your father's fault."

Here we go again.

"How do you figure?" I don't know why I'm playing along. I already know the answer.

"Because he forced you into hockey."

"He didn't force me. I love hockey."

I may as well be speaking to my car windshield. "What a selfish prick that man is," she gripes. "Come on, Colin. You don't think it's pathetic that a grown man is trying to live vicariously through his son?"

My jaw tenses. No use in asking her to stop, though. Or vice versa. The pair of them never stop. "In other news," I say in an attempt to steer the topic into safe territory. "My job interview went well."

"You had an interview?" She sounds startled.

"Yup." I quickly fill her in on Kamal Jain as I get off the freeway and stop at a set of red lights. "I guess he'll make his decision after this fundraiser thing in New York."

"There's no decision to be made—you're *clearly* the best candidate," she replies with the kind of unshakeable confidence only a mother can feel toward her son.

"Thanks, Ma." I turn onto the street that houses Tuck's bar and click my blinker to claim the last available parking spot at the curb. "I just got to my buddy's and need to parallel park. I'll call you later this week."

"Sounds good. I love you." Does she? Sometimes I wonder.

"Love you too."

We hang up, and I experience the same sense of overwhelming relief as when I got off the phone with my father last week.

I hop out of the car and glance at the neon signs lighting the front of Tucker's bar. And there's actually a line at the door. Business is obviously booming. Good for Tuck.

As I approach the sidewalk, I send him a quick text.

**ME:** Dude, I'm outside your bar. Not gonna make me freeze my nuts off in this line, are ya?

Three dots appear as he types a response.

**TUCK:** I'm upstairs. Come up. And 4 future—tell bouncer ur name and he'll let u in. Ur on the perma guest list

Sweet. I'm a VIP.

I bypass the front door and walk to the side of the building, where a narrow door buzzes open the moment I reach it. I know Tuck is staring at me on a camera right now. I helped him set up the system, which he can control entirely from his smartphone. It makes it easier to get in and out of this place. Plus, he takes security seriously. His baby girl and baby mama are the most important things in the world to him.

"Hey," I say when I reach the second-floor loft.

Tuck greets me with baby Jamie on his hip. "Gaaah!" she shrieks when she sees me.

I can honestly say she's one of the most beautiful babies I've ever seen. The kid belongs in diaper commercials and on baby food jars. She inherited the best of both her parents, who are disgustingly attractive to begin with, especially Sabrina.

Jamie's pink rosebud mouth opens, and she gives me a huge gummy smile. Her arms flail in my direction.

Tuck sighs. "She's such a little attention seeker."

"Aw, I don't mind." I hold out my arms, and the six-month-old practically somersaults into them. "She's gotten so big, man."

"I know. Swear to God, I turn around for five seconds and I look back and she's doubled in size."

Jamie wiggles happily in my arms, her chubby hands instantly seeking out the stubble on my face. She loves textures and is fascinated by colors. The last time I saw her, she was in total awe of my tats.

"Are you sure you don't mind that I stopped by?" I ask as he shuts and locks the front door.

"'Course not. You're welcome here any time, man."

"Where's Sabrina?"

"Study group."

"So late?" It's almost ten o'clock.

"Yup. That woman works her butt off." Deep pride resonates in his voice.

Sabrina is in law school, and, truth be told, I have no idea how she manages to be a mom while studying to be a lawyer. Fortunately, she and Tuck have help—his mother moved up here from Texas in December. Apparently she lives in an apartment a few blocks away.

"How's your mom liking Boston?"

"She hates the cold with all her heart."

I grin. I imagine that February in Texas is a tropical paradise compared to these frigid New England winters.

"But her place has a gorgeous view of the Charles. She says it's pretty to look at, and she gets to see her granddaughter whenever she wants, so she's happy. We all are."

"Sounds like you've got a good arrangement going on."

Tucker nods. He looks so blissed out as he stares at his daughter, who's still running her teeny fingers all over my chin. She squeals every time she encounters a stubbly whisker. "Want a beer?" he offers.

"Sure. But just one. I'm driving back tonight."

"We've only got cans. Jamie's really grabby lately, and she knocks shit off the counters when we walk by. I've had to pick up broken glass enough times that we just decided, fuck it. We're a beer-can family now."

"Cans are fine," I assure him. Still holding the baby, I accept the can of Peak IPA, and we wander over to the couch.

The apartment features an open-concept layout with the living room on one side, kitchen on the other, and dining area in the far corner. Floor-to-ceiling windows offer a decent view of the small playground across the street, and a hallway off the dining room leads to the bedrooms. I helped Tuck renovate one of those rooms into a nursery for Jamie, and as I settle on the couch cushions and reposition her in my lap, I wonder why she's not currently in that nursery.

"Shouldn't she be asleep?"

"I was getting ready to feed her. Actually, she was screaming her lungs out about thirty seconds before you got here. She literally just settled."

"Liar. This beautiful angel could never scream her lungs out," I retort as I tickle one of Jamie's socked feet. "Look at how sweet and calm she is."

Jamie chortles in delight.

"Fuck off. She's acting sweet and calm because we've got company. She's a little terror in real life. Aren't you, darlin'?"

The baby gazes at her father with pure adoration.

Tuck immediately caves. "I take it back," he tells his daughter. "You're not a terror. Fitz, entertain the princess while I prep her bottle."

That's no hardship. I bounce Jamie on my knee and tickle her tummy over her pink onesie while she makes the cutest noises. Damn, this kid is frickin' cute.

"So what's going on?" Tucker calls from the kitchen. "It's not like you to show up out of the blue. Especially on game night. That shot to your eye looked brutal, by the way."

"You saw it?"

"Yeah, I was flipping between your game and Garrett's. His is still on. Second period."

"G's playing tonight?" I look over at the TV, but a commercial for laundry detergent is flashing on the screen.

"Yeah. He has a series of road games coming up. Playing LA tonight."

"What's the score?"

"Two all. G's looking good."

"One of those goals his?"

"No. One assist, though."

"Sweet." I'm thrilled for the success Garrett's been having in his rookie season with Boston. He's so frickin' talented, and he also happens to be a genuinely decent guy. A bit cocky, sure. Definitely a smartass. But he's got a big heart, and he's a good friend.

"Dammit, Fitz." Tuck's southern drawl rears its head as he chastises me. "You managed to distract me again. Why aren't you celebrating tonight's W at Malone's?"

I shrug. "Wasn't in the mood for people."

"Okay. Then why aren't you at home?"

*Because one of my roommates gave me a BJ tonight, and I don't know how to act around her.*

"I…It's complicated." I keep my gaze on the top of Jamie's head. "Dean's sister lives with us now."

"I heard." Tucker's tone is cautious. "How's that working out?"

*Well, she gave me a BJ tonight, and I don't know how to act around her.*

"Pretty good." I keep my own tone vague and smatter kisses on Jamie's soft cheek, making her giggle again. But it isn't long before my baby shield is taken away from me.

"You ready, little one?" Tuck drawls. "Mama pumped this yummy goodness out just for you."

I snort loudly.

At the sight of the bottle, Jamie's face lights up. A few moments later, she's sucking happily on a nipple. With a pillow propped under his elbow and a contented baby in his arms, Tuck grins at me.

"She still into you?" he asks.

"Jamie? Yeah, she loves me."

He rolls his eyes. "I'm talking about Summer Di Laurentis. I remember last winter she had a thing for you. Is that still the case?"

"Yup."

"I see." He looks like he's trying not to smile. "What about you? Do you return the sentiment?"

After a reluctant beat, I dip my head in assent.

His smile breaks free. "Then what's the problem? You worried about how Dean's going to react?"

"No. I…" I puff out another breath. "I don't know if I want to go there."

*Then you probably shouldn't have let her blow you tonight.*

Maybe not, but clearly I don't possess any control when it comes to Summer. She makes me do the most uncharacteristic things. Well, she doesn't *make* me. It just happens. I let her blow me in the *locker room*, for chrissake. Anyone could've walked in on us, and for a dude who hates PDA, drama, and attention, a public hookup definitely doesn't top my bucket list.

And it's funny—because wasn't I telling myself the other night that if Summer was throwing herself at me, then I'd be challenging Hunter's claim to her? Well, there's no misinterpreting her intentions toward me anymore. I haven't been friend-zoned. Her actions tonight proved that.

But rather than stake a claim, I ran away.

I drag both hands though my hair, which is getting too long for my liking. I prefer it out of my eyes when I'm drawing. "Hunter has a thing for her too," I tell Tuck.

"Oh."

"Yeah. And she kissed him on New Year's."

His reddish brows shoot upward. "Oh?"

"But tonight..." I stop.

"Tonight what?"

"She showed up in the locker room after I got stitched up and we kissed." I pause. "And maybe a bit more."

"Define more."

"She sucked my dick in the showers."

Tucker jerks in surprise, and the nipple pops out of Jamie's mouth. She squawks in outrage.

"Aww, I'm sorry, baby girl," he croons. "It's okay, keep eating. Daddy was being a big doodlehead."

"A doodlehead?" I snicker.

"Oh shush. You're an even bigger doodlehead. You hear that, little one? Your Uncle Fitzy is the king of the doodleheads." He nudges her lips with the bottle's nipple and she latches on again. Then he frowns at me. "This happened tonight?"

I nod.

"And instead of sticking around to talk to the girl who suc—" His gaze drops to his daughter. He promptly rephrases. "—the girl who did stuff to your body, you came here instead?"

Guilt sears into me. Fuck. I'm such an ass. That beautiful, amazing girl knelt on wet, uncomfortable tile for me tonight and rocked my world. I should be blowing up her phone with apologies right now.

To Tucker, I manage a quick nod.

"I never took you for a coward."

"I'm not usually one," I say gruffly.

Tucker grabs a small blue cloth from the end table and wipes the corner of Jamie's mouth, where a bit of milk has drizzled out. He gazes at her with so much love that I actually feel a spark of envy. I wonder what it's like to love somebody that much.

"I don't know how to handle this, Tuck. Summer wants to

talk—about 'us,' I'm assuming—and I have no clue what to say to her."

A crease appears in his forehead. "You don't know how to let her down, you mean? Are you saying you don't want to be with her?"

My teeth dig into my cheek. "Not sure about that, either. She's just... She's too much, man."

"Too much," he repeats. "What does that mean?"

"She's too everything." A helpless sensation tightens my throat. "She's too beautiful. She's got too much energy. She's too open." I let out a groan. "Everybody is drawn to her. Everybody. She walks into a room and all eyes instantly home in on her, and not simply because she's hot. Summer's one of those girls, the high-profile ones who attract attention. She can't help it. It's her orbit—you get sucked into it."

"And that's bad because?"

*Because I've never been so drawn to anyone and it kind of scares the shit out of me.*

"Because I don't want to be a high-profile guy," I say instead. Tuck wouldn't understand this fear I have about Summer. Emotions don't scare him. He knew he wanted to be with Sabrina from the second he met her, and his certainty that they belonged together and relentless pursuit to win her heart were damn near incomprehensible to me.

"Being with someone like her means putting myself in the spotlight. And there'll always be some kind of drama. The other night she started a bar fight," I grumble. "Summer doesn't know the meaning of the word *low-key*. Everything she does is over the top, flashy, extravagant. That's not me."

"No," he agrees, before offering a dry smile. "But letting a chick go down on you in the locker room isn't typical of you either, so... You must like her a helluva lot if you took that kind of risk tonight."

He's right. Stifling a groan, I drop my head in my hands for a long, torturous moment. "I'm in her orbit, man," I mumble into my palms.

He chuckles. "So whatcha gonna do about it?"

I lift my head. "I have no fucking idea."

# 21
# SUMMER

So I guess nobody talks about oral sex anymore? We just perform it on each other and hand out orgasms willy-nilly and it never gets discussed again? Is this the world we're living in? If so, I'm going off the grid. I'll build a shack in the middle of the woods where there isn't a penis in sight.

*Forest animals have penises, Summer.*

"Oh, shut up, Selena," I mumble. "I love you, but I don't need this today."

My row-mate Ben glances at me, sighs, and then returns his gaze to the front of the lecture hall. He's grown accustomed to my cat-lady ramblings. I'm not certain if that's a good thing or a bad one.

It's been two days since the locker room incident, and Fitz has been completely MIA. Gone in the afternoons (holed up in the painting studio, according to Hollis), hasn't had dinner (or any meals, for that matter) at home, and both nights he's come back around midnight and proclaimed to be SO TIRED when I tried to talk to him.

You know what I have to say to that?

Fuck you very much, Colin Fitzgerald. That's the last time his dumb penis goes anywhere near my sacred mouth. A girl's got to have standards.

Brenna echoes that sentiment when I text her after class with a Fitz update.

**ME:** Still no mention of the BJ. Last nite he said he had a migraine and locked himself in his room. This morning he left for practice at 5am. Snuck out like a thief in the night

**BRENNA:** Men are garbage

**ME:** They're pure trash

**BRENNA:** Trash garbage

I send her the poop emoji, because I can't find a garbage-bag emoji and poop is an adequate alternative.

**BRENNA:** All seriousness—I'm sorry, GB. Never thought Fitz was trash garbage, but people are full of surprises

**ME:** So are Dumpsters

**BRENNA:** lolololololol

I grin to myself as I slide my phone into my tote. The Prada bag smells like delicious new leather, a scent that never fails to cheer me up. It showed up on my doorstep yesterday morning courtesy of UPS and Nana Celeste. I swear that woman can sense whenever her grandbabies are upset. It's like she possesses internal radar that shouts "Quick! Call Prada!" if one of the grandkids so much as gets a paper cut.

Not that I'm complaining about my gorgeous new tote. I'm not a crazy person.

I descend the steps toward Laurie's lecture podium. It's not his office hours, but he agreed to see me after the lecture so I could start writing my midterm today instead of waiting till Wednesday for him to approve my thesis.

And the good thing about Erik Laurie teaching History of Fashion as well as serving as my independent-study advisor is that

I'm able to kill two birds with one stone—I can get my thesis green-lit and give him an update on my swimwear line in one shot.

I still can't quite explain it, but the man continues to creep me out. Everyone else adores him, especially the girls. They laugh at all his jokes. They tolerate his winking disorder.

And then there's me, who leaves every encounter with him feeling like I need a shower. He reminds me of that intolerable character from *Harry Potter*—Gilderoy Lockhart, only the film version of him that Kenneth Branagh knocked out of the park. Laurie isn't as flamboyant, but, like Lockhart, he comes off as a vain egomaniac who wants everyone to love him.

Or rather, who assumes they already do.

I know it's a harsh assessment, and I try to push it out of my mind as I approach my professor.

"Winter!" he teases. "I enjoyed your thoughts in class today."

"Thanks."

He shuffles a few papers, then glances beyond my shoulder and nods at someone. I turn and realize Nora is waiting a discreet distance away.

"There's another student I need a progress report from, so this will be quick," he informs me.

Thank God. The quicker, the better.

He reads over my thesis for the midterm, suggests two minor tweaks, and signs off on it. Once that's out of the way, I fill him in on the fabric order I placed. The Fashion department has a decent selection of free fabrics for students to use, but we're also able to buy our own if we choose to do so. Since several of my bikini tops are crochet, I had to order a more lightweight yarn that doesn't stretch or shrink if it gets wet. Laurie approves of the choice, nodding in agreement when I explain the reasoning behind it. I conclude by giving him an update on the models I plan to recruit.

He throws his head back in laughter when I mention I'd like to ask some football players to model the men's line. "That's a great idea, Summer. That'll definitely sell some tickets. And for the women's pieces?"

"I'm not sure yet."

He winks. "So you haven't changed your mind about modeling one of the swimsuits yourself?"

Ugh.

Why.

Just why, Gilderoy.

I force a laugh. "Nope, still not interested."

"What a shame. All right, let's touch base at the end of the week." He rests his hand on my shoulder before giving it a light squeeze.

And either I imagine it, or his fingertips graze the nape of my neck when I turn to walk away.

Disgust crawls up my spine. It takes a serious effort not to Usain Bolt out of the lecture hall. Instead, I move at a normal pace and act as if I'm not completely repulsed by the potential neck graze.

"Nora, I'll be with you in a minute," Laurie tells her, stepping away to answer a call on his cell.

"He's all yours," I murmur to Nora.

She makes a sardonic noise under her breath. "Doesn't look that way from where I'm standing."

I turn to frown at her. "What's that supposed to mean?"

She checks to make sure Laurie is still on the phone, before sniping, "Don't you get tired of using your looks to get ahead?"

"What are you talking about? I'm not using anything."

"You've got Laurie wrapped around your little finger. He drools every time you walk in the room. He acts like every word you say is worthy of a Pulitzer. I swear, if he wasn't already on his feet, he'd give you a standing ovation every time you opened your mouth."

I clench my jaw so tight my teeth start to hurt. "It's not like I'm asking him to do that. I'm actually interested in the material we're discussing."

"I'm sure you are." She rolls her eyes, tucking a strand of pink-streaked hair behind her ear. "Maybe if you spent less time flirting and more time learning, you wouldn't have gotten kicked out of your last school."

"Uh-huh. Have a good day, Nora."

My hands are trembling as I stalk off. She is such a nasty person. I can't believe Fitz liked her enough to go out with her.

I wonder if she gave him a blowjob and he ignored her afterward too.

The reminder floods my belly with the heat of embarrassment. Sexual acts don't generally embarrass me, not even the ones in high school that occurred when I wasn't quite sober. But Fitz has made it this way for me. By not even acknowledging that it happened, he's caused me to feel like there's something shameful about what we did.

I try to push the negative thoughts from my mind as I exit the building. Once again, it's cold outside. I swear, February's even chillier than January. But at least it's shorter.

Still, I don't know how much longer I can take this. I might skip out for a week and fly to our place in St. Bart's, write my essay while lying on a beach chair and sipping pina coladas. Hmmm. Actually not a bad idea.

On the walk to my car, I scroll through my phone contacts. I really do need to secure my models. I require twelve bodies. Six males, six females. Brenna would laugh in my face if I asked her to put on a bikini and strut down a runway. But I do know some girls who might say yes. My Kappa sisters. Or rather, former sisters, but that's semantics.

Sorority girls crave attention, and most of them have no issue with skimpy clothing. Besides, I have a feeling Bianca might agree out of guilt alone. I think she genuinely felt bad about the way Kaya handled the whole living situation last month.

I don't have Bianca's number, so I pull up my profile on MyBri, the college social network. She's not on my friends list, but you don't have to be friends with someone to message them. I send a quick note explaining what I need, then close the app.

For the men, I hadn't been kidding about the football player angle. Nobody wants to see Speedos and swim trunks on scrawny guys with their ribs and hipbones jutting out. Gotta have the abs, baby.

I call my brother, who actually answers despite it being the middle of the school day. "Hey," I greet Dean. "You're not teaching a class?"

"Snow day," he replies.

"Aw, it's snowing over there? We got a few flurries this morning, but it's cleared up." I pray that whatever blizzard has hit New York doesn't decide to pop over to Massachusetts.

"Yeah, the weather's shit here. What's up, Boogers? What do you need?"

"Are you still friends with any of the Briar football players, or did they all graduate?"

"I still talk to a few."

There's a skip to my step as I reach my Audi. "Perfect. Can you get me an introduction?"

"What for?" he asks suspiciously.

"I need models for my fashion show. I was hoping to recruit some hard bodies."

He snorts in my ear. "If even one of them says yes, I expect a front-row ticket to the show so I can get my heckle on."

"Deal. Most of them live on the same street in Hastings, right? Elmway? Elmhurst?" I remember Brenna pointing it out when we passed the neighborhood on the way home from a Briar game.

"Elmhurst," he confirms. "Rex's house is your best bet. He lives with a bunch of clowns who like to show off their muscles."

"Perfect. I've got some time now, so I figured I'd drive over. Can you give me one of their numbers?"

"There's no fucking way you're going to a football house alone." Horror drips from his every word. "Let me call one of my boys and ask them to meet you there. I was just texting with Hunter, so I know he's around."

His overprotectiveness makes me roll my eyes. But I suppose it's sweet. "Fine. Tell him I'll see him in thirty."

———————

But it's not Hunter's Range Rover that pulls up behind my Audi thirty minutes later. It's Fitz's beat-up sedan.

My brother sent Fitz to meet me?

*Ha.*

If Dean had so much as an inkling of what Fitz and I did in the locker room this weekend, he never would've dispatched him to Elmhurst Avenue.

I don't know which one of us looks more uncomfortable as we approach each other. Fitz's hands are shoved in his coat pockets, and his eyes don't quite meet mine as he says, "Hey. Dean sent me."

"I figured." My tone is probably harsher than necessary, but—

*It is absolutely necessary!* Selena assures me. True. He did come in my mouth and run away.

"You, ah, had class this morning? History of Fashion?" he says awkwardly.

He's making small talk?

Is he for real?

"Yes, Fitz, I had class," I say. I shift my tote to my other shoulder and march toward the driveway of the detached Victorian we've parked in front of. According to Dean, there are, like, eight football dudes living here.

"How's the essay going?"

I stop in the middle of the paved drive. "You mean the one you agreed to help me with?" I can't help but snipe.

Unhappiness clouds his expression. "I'm sorry. I know I dropped the ball. I've been..."

"Busy?" I supply.

"Yeah."

"And don't forget about the headaches," I say sarcastically. "All those terrible, terrible headaches you've been suffering from."

Fitz lets out a quick breath. He lifts his hand to run it through his hair, then halts when he remembers he's wearing a Red Sox cap.

"Don't worry," I mutter, gulping down the bitter taste in my mouth. "I've got the essay covered."

We resume our walk up the driveway. His legs are longer than mine, so he shortens his strides to match my pace. "Are you sure? Did your prof approve the thesis? Give you any notes?"

At the mention of Laurie, I momentarily forget that I'm pissed off at Fitz. "He made a few suggestions, but I was so eager to leave, I didn't fully listen to what he said. I'll read over what he wrote in the margins when I get home."

Fitz studies my face. His own expression is inscrutable. "Why were you eager to leave?"

"Honestly? He makes me uncomfortable."

A frown tightens the corners of his mouth. "In what way?"

"I don't know. He's very friendly." I pause. "A little too friendly."

"Has he tried anything?" Fitz demands.

"No. Oh no, he hasn't," I assure him. "I…I don't know. Maybe I'm being overly sensitive. I get a weird vibe from him, that's all."

"Always trust your gut, Summer. If something feels off, it usually is."

"My gut isn't exactly the most accurate barometer," I say flatly. "I mean, it told me to track you down in the locker room this weekend, and look how *that* turned out."

At the mention of what went down this weekend (me. I went down this weekend. On him), Fitz's expression fills with regret. "I'm…" He clears his throat. "I'm really sorry about that."

I don't know how to respond, because I can't figure out what he's apologizing for—that he disappeared after I blew him, or that it happened in the first place.

"You're sorry," is what I finally say.

"Yes."

I wait for him to expand on that. When he doesn't, my anger returns in full force, spurring me to brush past him and stomp to the front porch.

The door flings open before I can even ring the bell, and a huge black guy with a shaved head appears in front of me. In a split second, the excitement in his eyes transforms into grave disappointment. "It's not the pizza!" he shouts over his shoulder.

"Motherfucker," someone curses from inside.

The big guy peers past me. "Fitzgerald? That you?"

Fitz reaches the porch. "Hey, Rex. How's it going?"

"Shitty. I thought your girl was the pizza guy, but she ain't got pizza."

"Sorry." I'm trying hard not to laugh.

Fitz seems to be doing the same. "You realize it's barely noon, right?"

"You saying you can't eat pizza at noon? Boy, you can eat pizza whenever you want to eat pizza. Noon, midnight. Dinner time. Breakfast time. It's fuckin' pizza."

"It's fuckin' pizza," I echo solemnly. Then I stick out my hand. "I'm Summer Di Laurentis. I forced Fitz to bring me here because I need a favor."

"I'm intrigued. You're forgiven for the pizza snafu." Rex holds the door open for us. "Come inside. I'm cold." We enter the house, and he gestures to the scary amount of coat hooks and shoe racks in the front hall. "Ditch your gear. We're playing Madden. You want next round, Fitz?"

"Naah, I don't think we're staying that long. Are we?" he asks me.

I shake my head. "I'll be quick. I need to get home and work on my paper."

We follow Rex into a massive living room with a U-shaped sectional that is currently bearing the weight of four football players. I estimate about eight or nine hundred pounds of muscle.

"Fitzgerald!" one of them exclaims. He waves his game controller. "You want in?"

"Another time," Fitz answers.

Rex flops down in an easy chair and gestures to the only other free chair. "Sit down, cutie. Summer, you can stand." He laughs loudly at his own joke before saying, "Kidding. Fitz, your ugly ass can remain standing."

I sink down on the chair he indicates and find myself drowning in brown leather. This is the biggest armchair on the planet. I feel like a toddler trying to sit in the big-people chair.

Rex introduces me to his teammates, and it's hard to keep up with all the names and positions he spits out. Turns out they're all offensive players—two tight ends, a running back, and a wide receiver. Rex is also a receiver. "Lockett, Jules, Bibby, C-Mac. This is Summer Di Laurentis. She needs a favor."

"I'll do it," one player says instantly. Jules, I think. He's really cute, with chin-length dark hair, dimples, and a diamond stud in one ear.

I grin at him. "You don't even know what I'm asking."

"Doesn't matter. Ain't none of us gonna say no to a face like yours," drawls C-Mac, who has dreadlocks and the cutest babyface I've ever seen. If it weren't for his tree-trunk biceps and huge pecs, I'd think he was fourteen years old.

"Girl, for real. You could be asking me to let you wax my balls and I'd say yes." This comes from Lockett, the smallest guy in the room. And by small, I mean he's probably five-eleven instead of six-five, and one-hundred-and-eighty-pounds instead of two-fifty. As in, a normal-sized human male.

"Oh." I swallow my laughter. "Well. I mean, that's a big commitment."

Rex snorts.

"If you agree to help me, there is a chance I'll be handling your balls, though."

"What!" Fitz sputters, turning to scowl at me. "Dean said you just needed models."

"Dean?" Lockett leans forward, recognition filling his dark eyes. "Oh shit. Dean Di Laurentis? Heyward-Di Laurentis? You're Dean's sister?"

"Yup. And I need six models for my fashion show," I explain to the football players. There are only five of them in the room, but if at least two or three agree, I'm sure they could recruit the number I need. "We'll have to take measurements and do some fittings. And like I said, I might accidentally touch your junk. Sorry in advance."

"*Never* apologize for touching a man's junk," Rex tells me.

Bibby, a tight end with a bushy red beard, looks curious. "What would we be modeling?"

"Swimwear."

"Dibs on the Speedo!" Lockett says immediately.

C-Mac's hand shoots up. "Dibs on the thong."

I'm surprised at how easy this is. But in case they're pulling my leg, I offer more details to judge their sincerity. "The show is a month from now, right before spring break. I'm still in the design stage, but if I get a commitment from you, we'll take measurements in the next few days and start fittings in a couple of weeks. We'll also do some runway coaching—"

"I don't need runway coaching," Lockett interrupts. "I've watched *America's Next Top Model*."

"Same," Jules chimes in. "Tyra's got nothing on me."

I bite my lip to keep from laughing. Yup. These are exactly the guys I need. "So you're in?" My gaze conducts a sweep of the room. "All of you?"

Everyone nods. "We'll be there," Rex promises.

"She needs one more, though," Bibby says. He glances over at me. "I'll ask Chris."

I have no idea who Chris is, but I reply with, "Sounds good. Thank you."

He shrugs. "Anything for a Di Laurentis."

Rex nods fervently. "Your brother used to chill here all the time. He was good friends with a lot of our seniors."

"I know." Before I can stop it, a lump of sorrow rises in my throat. "Beau's death hit him pretty hard."

It hit me pretty hard too, but I don't say that out loud. Beau Maxwell played quarterback for Briar for three seasons and died in a car accident last year. After I'd heard the news, I'd locked myself in my room at the Kappa house and cried my eyes out. Dean doesn't know this, but Beau and I made out once. It was a stupid drunken thing, and we both swore we'd take it to the grave because neither of us wanted to deal with my brother's wrath.

My heart squeezes painfully as I realize that Beau really did take our secret to the grave.

"Beau was good people," Rex says gruffly, and the mood in the room grows somber.

"Anyway." Fitz clears his throat. "We should be taking off."

"I'll start a group chat for us on MyBri," I tell the guys. "And thank you so much for doing this."

They don't let me leave right away—first, each one has to swallow me up in a bear hug, while Fitz watches with resigned eyes.

"Does every single hetero male on this planet fall in love with you on sight?" he mutters when we're outside again.

"No. Some fall in lust." I spare him a pithy look. "And some fool around with me and then pretend it never happened."

He halts about five feet from our cars. "I'm not pretending it didn't happen."

"No? So you're avoiding me for no reason, then? Just for funsies?" Gritting my teeth, I bulldoze past him.

He catches up to me as I reach the Audi. "Summer. Come on. Wait."

"Wait for what?" I snap. "For you to decide that I'm worthy of your time and attention?"

His brown eyes widen. "What—"

"Isn't that what it boils down to?" I cut in, bitterness staining my tone. "I'm not someone you want to spend time with."

"That's not true."

"Fine. I'll amend that. I'm okay to hook up with, but I don't deserve a conversation about it afterward."

"Stop saying those words," he growls. "Worthy. Deserve. That's not what this is about."

"What's *this*?" I burst out, my frustration levels skyrocketing. "Seriously, Fitz. What *is* this? You rub up against me outside Malone's, and then you drive away. I get on my knees for you in the locker room, and then you disappear for two days. I have no clue how you feel about me at all. So forgive me for assuming that you don't want me." My mouth twists in a humorless smile. "Why would I ever think that, right?" Sarcasm creeps into my voice. "I mean, a guy runs for the hills after I blow him. That means he's super into me, right?"

Guilt flickers in his eyes at the mention of the blowjob. But he remains maddeningly silent.

I grind my molars together. Soon they'll turn to dust, that's how pissed off I am. "I have a date with Hunter this weekend," I find myself declaring.

That gets me a response. A muscle in his jaw twitches, and then he mutters, "Since when?"

"He asked me last week." I hit the key fob to unlock my car. "And you want to know why I said yes? Because it was really frigging nice to be asked on a date by someone who isn't, I don't know, ashamed of me."

Fitz exhales slowly before speaking. "I'm not ashamed of you," he murmurs. "I'm just…"

"You're what?"

"I'm bad at expressing myself."

"Bullshit. You're the most articulate person I know."

"Not when it comes to sharing feelings." He sounds as discouraged as I feel.

"Feelings? Oh, you mean you have those?"

Every muscle in his face goes taut. It's the only outwardly discernible sign that my accusation upset him. His expression is completely shuttered. "I'm not good at this shit, Summer." The words are hoarse, strained.

"Good at what?" I clench my fists in exasperation. "It's not that hard, Colin! You either want to be with me, or you don't." My fingers tremble on the door handle. "So which is it?"

He hesitates.

He actually hesitates.

A ball of hurt clogs my throat. I gulp it down best as I can. "Wrong answer," I mutter, and then I get in my car and slam the door.

# 22
# SUMMER

A FEW DAYS AGO, FITZ WAS THE ONE AVOIDING ME. NOW WE'RE avoiding each other.

If he's in the living room with Hollis and Hunter, then I'm in my bedroom. If I'm in the kitchen, then he's somewhere else. Our townhouse turns into a pathetic game of Musical Chairs: The Room Edition, as we do everything in our power not to share the same space or breathe the same air.

But maybe that's a good thing. Maybe I shouldn't be anywhere near him. Because when I am, I'm either touching his dick or sucking it, and I refuse to let that happen again.

As usual, Fitz and the guys have already left for practice by the time I'm ready to head to campus. I have another check-in with Hal Richmond this morning. Yay. Fun times. Can't wait.

I drive to Briar and park behind the admin building, but I don't get out of the car yet. I'm fifteen minutes early, and damned if I'm going to spend any extra time with Froghole. Instead, I crank the heat, load up an old playlist, and start singing along to One Direction's "No Control."

I'm still humming the same song ten minutes later on the way to the dean's offices. Man, why did 1D ever break up? They were so frigging magical.

"Get back together already," I moan, at the same time that a dark-haired girl rounds the hall corner.

She jumps in surprise. "Sorry, what?"

I wave my hand flippantly. "I was talking to 1D. They need to get back together."

She shakes her head, visibly saddened. "I know. It's heartbreaking."

As much as I'd love to spend the rest of the day—hell, the rest of my life—discussing the huge hole that the loss of One Direction left in my soul, I force myself to keep walking. I can't afford to be late. Each time I see Froghole, I swear he's even more condescending. It's like he goes home every night and practices all the things he can say to make me feel like dog poop under his shoe.

Today, he doesn't disappoint. The patronizing attitude makes an appearance before my butt even hits the visitor's chair, as he asks how my dad's golf game with Dean Prescott went this past weekend. "Must be nice being able to fly to Florida just for the day to get a round in." His tone isn't overtly sarcastic, but his eyes tell a different story.

I stiffly reply that I don't keep track of my father's golf or travel schedule, and proceed to give him an update about each of my courses.

When we get to History of Fashion, Froghole leans back in his plush chair and asks, "How are you liking Professor Laurie? You know, he received several plum offers to teach at the other Ivys, but he chose Briar partly because of me."

"Because of you," I echo, hoping my skepticism doesn't show on my face.

"My mum attended North London Collegiate with Anna Wintour. Fancy that, right?" His fake accent becomes more pronounced. At least, I still think it's fake. My dad never got back to me with proof of Froghole's birthplace.

"Fancy that," I say with a faint smile.

"Anyhow, they've remained in touch over the years. Anna made an appearance at Mum's birthday celebration last year. Erik tagged along, and I convinced him that Briar would be the best fit for someone of his renown."

"Cool." I honestly can't think of anything else to say.

"I assume you're enjoying his course?"

"Sure. It's fine."

"Just fine?" He tilts his head. "Based on the feedback we've received thus far, it sounds like it's a smashing success."

"The class itself is interesting." Hesitation washes over me as I debate whether to go on.

Maybe I should say something about the winking. And the touching. The shoulder squeezes, the hand caresses. His fingers on the back of my neck.

But Mr. Richmond already doesn't like me very much, and I'm not sure what his reaction would be.

*Tell him.*

My mom's voice fills my head, urging me to be direct. I know that's what her advice would be. Mom never holds anything back.

"I enjoy the subject matter," I continue, before stopping to take a deep breath. "But...Professor Laurie..." I exhale in a rush. "He's a bit creepy, if I'm being honest."

Richmond narrows his eyes. "Creepy?"

"Yes." My mouth suddenly feels dry, but my palms are clammy. I wipe them on the front of my jeans. "He touches my hand a lot, and my shoulders, and his gaze stays on me a little too long—"

"You must be misunderstanding," Richmond interrupts. "Erik is a friendly chap. That's one of the reasons everybody adores him."

I bite my lip. "That's what I thought at first—that he was just being friendly. But I think it's more than that. I don't like it when he touches me. I find it inappropriate—"

"Summer," the assistant dean interrupts.

"Yes?"

"As a beautiful girl, I'm sure you've grown accustomed to being admired, perhaps often enough that it's led to the assumption that when someone is acting in a friendly manner or paying extra attention to you, there's an admiring or sexual connotation to it—"

My jaw falls open in shock.

"However, I'm certain that you're misinterpreting whatever signals you believe Professor Laurie is sending." He leans forward in his chair and clasps his hands on the desktop. "Do you realize that throwing around statements such as these could seriously threaten and potentially destroy someone's career?"

My own hands aren't damp anymore. They're dry as dust, and I curl them into tight fists on my lap. "I'm not trying to destroy anyone's career. I…"

"Would you like to lodge a formal complaint? If so, we can begin the process right now. You should be aware, however, that it can often be a lengthy process, as well as difficult for all parties involved."

My eyes start to feel hot. "I, um…"

Impatience lines his forehead. "Summer. Will you be lodging a formal complaint against Professor Laurie?"

After a long moment of indecision, I say, "No."

"I see." Richmond rises from his chair. "Well, do let me know if you change your mind. Until then, I advise you to be prudent before making these kinds of accusations—"

"I wasn't making accusations," I protest. "You asked what I thought of him, and I told you he makes me uncomfortable."

Richmond rounds his desk. "I'll see you next week, Summer. Let me walk you out."

---

Later in the afternoon, I'm still smarting over Froghole's dismissive behavior. But at the same time, I'm also starting to question myself. The descriptions I'd given Richmond sound kind of flimsy when I replay them in my head.

*He touches my hand a lot, and my shoulders, and his gaze stays on me a little too long.*

That doesn't exactly scream "highly inappropriate behavior!"

The more I think about it, the more I wonder if maybe my original assessment of Laurie was correct, and he's simply a very friendly man. The fact that Richmond openly admitted that Laurie is known for being a "friendly chap" only makes me doubt myself more. If the assistant dean doesn't think Laurie's friendliness is anything to be concerned about, maybe I shouldn't either?

Ugh. I honestly don't know.

"Ow!"

Madison, the sophomore whose measurements I'm taking, jerks in discomfort, alerting me to the fact that I'd cinched the tape way too tight around her boobs.

"Sorry," I say hastily, loosening the hold. "Let me finish with the bust, and then we're all done." I look over at Bianca, who's sprawled on the ornate couch flipping through the latest issue of *Vogue*. "Thanks so much for agreeing to do this, by the way. I think it'll be a blast."

"Thanks for asking us. I'm super excited," Bianca admits.

"Me too!" Madison bounces on the heels of her socked feet. "I can't believe you convinced the football team to walk the runway in Speedos."

"Not the whole team. Just six of the players." I wink at her. "Six very hot players."

Her expression lights up. "Oh my God. I can't wait for the after-party."

When Bianca messaged me to say she and five sisters were down to model in my show, I'd sweetened the pot by telling them they were all invited to the after-party. Not the official Briar-hosted one, but the after-*after*-party with the football team. I already got Rex to agree to host us. All I had to say was "sorority girls" and he was on board.

"I can't wait to see the final designs," Bianca gushes. "The pics you sent of the sketches are so hot."

"Yeah, they're boss," Madison agrees.

"Thanks. I'm excited to see them on you guys." I jot down

Madison's bust measurement and then roll up the measuring tape. I tuck it and my little notepad into my Prada tote. "All right. Perfect. I've got everything I need. Next time I'm here, we'll do a proper fitting and—"

"What the hell is going on?" Kaya appears in the doorway, suspicion darkening every inch of her pretty face.

"Hey, Kaya," I say cheerfully.

Bianca warily gets off the couch, while Madison scurries out of the room like an animal that's just sensed a thunderstorm brewing.

Kaya glares at me. "What are you doing here?"

"I came to take some measurements." I sling my purse strap over my shoulder and root around inside the bag for my phone.

"What for?"

"For none of your business," I chirp.

Bianca makes it Kaya's business quickly enough. "Some of the girls and I are walking in Summer's fashion show."

"Well," I hedge in, "it's not *my* show. The Fashion department does this every March."

Kaya ignores me. She's too busy staring Bianca down. "Why would you walk in her fashion show?"

Bianca falters for a beat. "Because it sounded like fun."

"So fun that you didn't think to ask me if *I* wanted to do it too?"

I arch an eyebrow at the huffy girl. "Would you like to model in my show, Kaya?"

"Absolutely not."

It's hard not to roll my eyes, but somehow I manage to restrain myself.

"I just feel like I should have been informed about this before you agreed," she says stiffly. "I'm the president of this sorority, Bianca. Anything a Kappa does has the power to reflect poorly on me."

"Chill out, Kaya. It's just a fashion show, and it will look *great* for the house, I promise. We're helping out a fellow student. Nationals likes it when we show community spirit."

"How many of you said yes?" Kaya demands.

"Six of us."

"Six? Oh my God. I can't believe you all agreed and not a single person told me!"

"Because it had nothing to do with you."

I edge toward the door. "Um. I'm going to take off now—"

"After everything I went through with Daphne! You *know* how upset I was when I found out she was going behind my back, and now you're doing the same thing?"

"No one is going behind your back," Bianca coos. She gives me a look that says, *Get out of here while you can.*

I make my escape, fleeing through the front doors of the house that, instead of Kappa Beta Nu, should be called DAPHNE KETTLEMAN WAS HERE, because holy shit did that girl leave her mark on this place.

As I'm unlocking my car, "Cheap Thrills" blares out of my purse. I fish out my phone and flip it over to check the screen.

Hunter.

I answer with an overly bright, "Hey."

"Blondie. Hey."

The sound of his husky voice triggers a rush of guilt. Saturday night is fast approaching, and I've been stalling in telling him it's Valentine's Day. Because he'll either want to go anyway, or reschedule, and I don't even know if I want to keep the date.

"So. I was just informed that I scheduled our date on Valentine's Day." He snickers. "My bad."

I laugh in relief. "Okay, thank God. I was going to say something about it, because, yeah…I don't know if V-Day is the best idea for a first date."

"No, I totally get it. That's a lot of pressure."

"We should probably reschedule," I say, even more relieved now. Maybe I can put this off indefinitely, or at least until I figure out how I feel about him.

Hunter throws a wrench in that plan by suggesting, "How about tonight?"

I gulp. "Tonight?"

"Yeah. No game, and I don't have plans. Do you?"

"No." Crap. Why did I say no? Now there's no reason for me not to go.

"So let's do it. Dinner?"

"Sure," I concede.

"Cool. I'll pick you up at your place."

Another laugh pops out. "That was so lame."

"I know." He chuckles. "Should we leave around seven?"

"Sounds good." I hope he doesn't hear the note of uncertainty in my voice.

"Later, Blondie."

After we hang up, I instantly call my mother.

"Sweetie!" She sounds overjoyed. "You caught me at a good time. I just got out of a meeting."

"I'm having man problems!" I blurt out.

There's a second of silence, and then, "Okay, baby. Hit me."

Laughter bubbles in my throat. I love this woman. "I have a date with one of my roommates tonight. Hunter. He went to Roselawn, but he was a year behind me."

"All right…" I can practically see the deep furrow between her eyebrows as she absorbs my words. "Are you nervous about the date?"

"No, not really. But…" I let out a breath. "I kissed my other roommate." Among other things. But what she doesn't know won't hurt her.

"You kissed him before the date?"

"No, I didn't kiss the one I'm going out with. Well, I did, but that was a while ago. On Saturday I kissed the other one."

"Hunter."

"No. Fitz."

"Fizz?"

"Fitz!" I sputter. "Colin Fitzgerald. Mom, keep up."

"Sorry, Summer, but maybe I'd have an easier time keeping up if your love life wasn't like an episode of *The Bachelor*."

"*The Bachelorette*," I correct. "Okay. Pay attention. Hunter is the one I'm having dinner with tonight. Fitz is the one I kissed."

"I see. And you have feelings for both of them?"

"Yes?"

"Is that a question?"

"No? I mean, I don't know. I really don't know."

"Well, I'm not sure what to say to you, sweetie. You're skimping on both the context and the details. I suppose pick the one you like more?"

"Mom! That doesn't help at all," I grumble. "Whatever. I'll figure it out on my own." I mimic her crappy suggestion. "*Pick the one you like more.* Come on, Mom. Get it together."

Her laughter tickles my ear. "Hey, it's all I've got. Call me later. Let me know how everything shakes out."

Wonderful. Usually my mother dispenses the sagest advice in the world. Today she gives me nothing. Even grammatically incorrect fortune cookies offer better solutions than *pick the one you like more*.

Besides, it's not a matter of liking. Half the time I'm not sure I even like Fitz. He drives me bananas most of the time. But I'm drawn to him, and he's on my mind constantly, a lot more than Hunter is.

In all honesty, I wouldn't be considering going out with Hunter if Fitz came up to me and said, "Let's do this."

But Fitz *isn't* saying that. He isn't saying anything, except that he's "bad at expressing feelings" and "not good at this shit."

What the hell am I supposed to do with that? Beg him to magically be good at "this shit"? Forget that.

Hunter is a great guy, and we get along so well. What's the harm in getting to know him better?

*You'll be leading him on.*

Not necessarily. Maybe we'll have so much fun on the date that my feelings for Hunter will eclipse my feelings for Fitz.

*Or that won't happen at all, and you'll be leading him on.*

Do I keep the date or cancel it? I have no idea what to do.

I'm still debating it when I take a shower later. A worry-free shower, thanks to the new lock Hollis installed on the bathroom door.

I'm still debating it as I dry my hair and get dressed. I pair a dove-gray sweater dress with black stockings and Jimmy Choo lace-up combat boots, black suede.

I'm still debating it when Hunter calls out from downstairs that he's warming up the car.

And I'm still debating it when Fitz enters my bedroom without knocking and levels me with two husky words.

"Don't go."

# 23
# SUMMER

"W-what?" The question comes out in a fast, quavery squeak, as my heart stutters mid-beat.

Fitz's long, muscular body advances on me. I find myself moving backward. Moving away from him, because his intensity is a bit terrifying. Usually his eyes are a normal shade of brown. Right now, they're dark chocolate and liquid fire. The heat of them sears right through me.

I move until I can't move anymore—because my butt meets the wall. Fitz doesn't stop until his body is a mere inch from mine. If I inhale, my breasts would rise and probably bump his chest.

"Summer." His voice is low, tormented.

His rough fingertips graze my cheekbone. I can scarcely breathe. My worried gaze flicks toward my bedroom door. It's ajar. Hunter or Hollis could walk by at any moment and see us.

"Don't go with him tonight." It sounds like the words are being ripped out of his throat.

My pulse quickens. Fitz's lips are so close to mine I can almost taste him. His chest tat peeks out the top of his worn, gray T-shirt, and I have to fight the urge not to reach out and run my fingers over the faded ink.

"Don't go with Hunter," he rasps, those molten eyes locking onto mine.

I find my voice again, though it's shakier than I'd like. "Give me a reason not to."

He visibly swallows.

I silently implore him. I can't speak the words for him, but if he doesn't want me to go out with Hunter, then he has to tell me why. He *needs* to tell me why.

He doesn't. A muscle in his jaw tics, but still he doesn't speak.

"What the hell is going on, Fitz? Because it kinda feels like this is you wanting to have your cake and eat it too. We hooked up, and then you pushed me away. You don't get to make demands now about who I go out with—I owe you nothing. You had your chance."

"I know," he finally says, sounding as confused as I feel.

Clearly when he stormed into my room, he didn't have a damn thing rehearsed other than "don't go with Hunter." Well, that's not enough for me.

"I know I messed up." Remorse swims in his eyes. "Avoiding you after what happened in the locker room was so fucking stupid. And selfish."

"No kidding."

"I'm sorry for that," he says hoarsely. "I really am. And I'm not trying to have my cake and eat it too. Or at least I'm not doing it intentionally. All I know is that I feel sick about the thought of you going out with him tonight."

I wait for him to elaborate. As usual, he doesn't.

"Then tell me why I should stay here, Fitz! And don't say it's because you're hard twenty-four-seven because of me. We can't hook up anymore, okay? I'm not interested in a fling with you. I get the feeling you don't do flings, anyway."

"I don't," he says hoarsely.

"Then what is this?" Frazzled, I gesture between us. "Why shouldn't I date Hunter?"

"I'm not saying you can't."

"You're not saying anything at all!" I remember the open door and quickly lower my voice. "What do you *want*, Colin? Just tell me how you feel."

We stare at each other for what feels like an eternity. I can't pick out a single emotion in his expression. He's so good at that, placing a veil over his eyes. He guards his thoughts and emotions with the dedication of a Secret Service agent. Hell, he'd probably rather take a bullet than show anyone what he's feeling.

And whether he means to or not, he's playing games with me. I like games—the ones you play at parties, with friends. When it comes to my love life, I'm not interested in having to guess what the other person is feeling or thinking.

"I have to go," I mutter.

He makes a frustrated noise under his breath. "Summer."

But I'm already marching out the door.

And he doesn't stop me.

---

Needless to say, I'm more than a little distracted when Hunter pulls out my chair at the nicest restaurant in Hastings. It's called Ferro's, and it comes highly recommended by both Allie and a friend of hers, Grace Ivers. Grace is Logan's girlfriend, and apparently they eat at Ferro's all the time.

I can't deny that Hunter looks hot tonight. His tight ass fills a pair of trousers very, very nicely, and he recently got his hair buzzed. I prefer shorter hair on guys.

While I check him out, he's doing the same to me. His sultry gaze admires me from across the table. "That's a great dress, Blondie."

I manage a smile. "Thanks." Can he tell that I'm preoccupied? Or worse, can he tell I'm upset? Because I am. I'm still so shaken from that encounter with Fitz.

Why couldn't he just tell me how he felt? Why do I have to pry the details out of him like I'm trying to extract a splinter from under my fingernail? Talking to Fitz is painful and frustrating and I don't fucking understand him.

I don't even notice the waiter coming by to take our drink order until Hunter says, "Summer? Vodka cran?"

I hastily shake my head. "Water for now," I tell the waiter. After he leaves, I explain my choice to Hunter. "I haven't eaten in hours. I don't like to drink on an empty stomach."

"Yeah. Makes sense." He watches as I unroll my napkin.

It's a fancy cloth one, and my hands tremble slightly as I smooth it over my lap.

A crease lines his forehead. "What's wrong?"

I swallow. "Nothing's wrong. It's just been a long, somewhat crappy day."

"You had to see your academic advisor, right? How'd that go?"

"Not great. Richmond hates my guts." My cheeks hollow as I grind my teeth together. I force myself to stop. "He pretty much baited me into saying one of my professors creeps me out and then scolded me about how I shouldn't be making accusations."

"Accusations?" Hunter sounds alarmed. "What's this fucker done?"

"Nothing," I say quickly. "Really, he hasn't done anything. But he creeps me out, and he's kinda handsy. I told Richmond about it and, like I said, got scolded."

The waiter returns with our waters and asks if we're ready to order. Neither of us has even opened the menu yet, so Hunter says we need more time.

We pick up our menus. I try desperately to concentrate on the app list, but my brain is still back in my bedroom with Fitz.

Hunter releases a heavy sigh.

I lift my head. "Are you okay?"

"Me? I'm fine." He gives a wry shake of his head. "You, on the other hand? Doesn't seem like you're fine."

I offer a feeble assurance. "I am."

"Summer, I've been living with you for a month now. I'm pretty good at deciphering your moods. You're extra distracted tonight."

"I know. I'm sorry." I clasp my hands in my lap. "I…"

He hesitates for a long moment, then asks, "What's going on between us?"

Misery burns my throat, stings my eyes. I don't know how to explain what I'm feeling, because I don't *know* what I'm feeling.

My heart drops as I realize I'm in the exact position Fitz was in twenty minutes ago. The position I put him in. Demanding access to his thoughts. Insisting he tell me how he feels about me.

Maybe he truly doesn't know. God knows I can't quite describe what I feel for *him*. Yet I'm expecting him to, what, fight for me? Declare his undying love for me? And now here Hunter is, asking me what's going on between us, and I cannot for the life of me answer the question.

"Summer," he says roughly.

I clamp my teeth over my bottom lip. I don't like disappointing people, but I'm not sure there's much of a choice at the moment. "I think I have to go," I whisper.

Hunter doesn't respond.

I lift my gaze to his. There isn't an iota of surprise in his eyes.

"Is it Fitz?" The words are curt, low.

Despite the guilt and shame weakening my body, I force myself to say, "Yes."

His hard gaze slices into me and then through me. I couldn't even hazard a guess as to what he's thinking right now. And I'm not sure what he's going to do. Drop his napkin on the table and calmly exit the restaurant? Lose his temper and call me a heartless bitch?

He does neither. He scrapes his chair back and walks over to help me out of mine.

"Come on. I'll take you home." He tosses a twenty on the table, way more money than necessary for two waters we didn't even drink.

Trying not to cry, I follow him to the door.

Neither of us says a word on the drive home. It's awkward as hell, and it only gets worse when Hunter stops in the driveway but doesn't kill the engine.

"You're not coming in?" I ask, then curse myself for giving voice to the stupidest question in the world. Of course he's not coming in. I just rejected him. It's not like he's going to sit on the couch with me while we watch 1D music videos on YouTube together.

"Naah." He taps his fingers on the steering wheel. He seems wired with energy, or maybe he's impatient for me to get out of the car. "I can't be in there right now. I'm gonna go out, find a party." He shrugs. "Don't wait up."

"Text me if you decide to stay out all night so I don't worry?"

For the first time since I told him I was interested in Fitz, he reveals a flash of anger. With a cynical smile, he says, "I'm pretty sure you'll be too busy to care what I'm doing tonight, Summer."

Guilt pierces into me. "Hunter…"

*Don't be like this*, I want to say, but how can I blame him? I agreed to go on a date with him, and ten minutes into it I told him I wanted to be with somebody else. That's a crappy thing to do to someone, and I don't know how I'll ever make this up to him.

"Thanks for driving me back," I whisper.

"Of course."

I reach over and gently touch his shoulder, and he winces as if I've hurt him. And I realize I have, only not physically. I hadn't known he'd liked me this much. I thought it was more of a flirtation on his part.

I pull the door handle and slide out of the Rover. I've barely taken a step before Hunter reverses out of the driveway. He drives off in a cloud of exhaust that burns my nostrils before floating away in the evening air.

I feel awful as I let myself into the house. I guess Hollis went out, because he's not in the living room, and his bedroom is empty when I pass the open doorway. I ignore my own room and walk to the master. No light spills into the hallway from beneath the door, but I know Fitz is home because his car's in the driveway. Unless he went somewhere with Hollis, but I guess I'll find out.

I take a breath, gather my courage, and knock softly.

No response.

Crap. Maybe he did go out.

I hesitate, just for a second, before turning the knob and easing the door forward. The room is bathed in shadows. I squint in the darkness and make out a bulky figure on the bed. He's not under the covers, but a fleece throw is haphazardly draped over his lower body.

"Fitz?"

The mattress shifts. "Summer?" he says sleepily.

"Yeah. I'm back."

He makes a drowsy sound, a cross between a moan and a rumble. It's so frigging cute. "How long was I asleep for?"

"Not long. It's barely eight."

"You left thirty minutes ago." There's a lot of confusion in that statement.

"Yes."

"And now you're back."

"Yes."

"Why?"

I close the door and then approach the foot of the bed. "I'm not sure yet. But…I have three questions for you." I take a breath. "Could you please, just this once, try to answer them? I don't expect a speech or anything. A yes or no would suffice." I seek out his eyes in the shadows. "Please, Fitz?"

The throw rustles as he slides into a sitting position. "What do you want to know?" he asks gruffly.

With a shaky exhalation, I ask, "Do you still think I'm surface level?"

"No. I don't." Sheer sincerity.

I nod slowly. "Did you plan on running away after I sucked you off in the locker room?"

"No. I didn't." Genuine regret.

I swallow. "Are you as tired of fighting this attraction between us as I am?"

"Yes. I am." Pure need.

My hands tremble as I grasp the hem of my dress and drag the soft wool up my body and over my head. This is crazy. But crazy is kind of my middle name.

Fitz makes a choked noise. "Summer?"

I ignore him. I keep my stockings on because the hardwood floor is damn cold. Underwear stays on too, but I unclasp my strapless bra and let it drop to the floor.

He gives a sharp intake of breath.

I climb onto the bed and slide under the throw with him.

"You're not wearing a shirt," he rasps.

"Nope."

"Why not?"

I move closer so that our lips are inches apart. "Why do you think?"

# 24
# FITZ

Summer is in my bed. Not the season. The girl. The beautiful, topless girl who just woke me up from a nap and told me she's tired of fighting her attraction to me.

I know there's more we need to talk about. I all but begged her not to go out with Hunter earlier, and she'd still walked out the door. And I'm sure she has questions for me, questions I'll undoubtedly have a difficult time answering. Not because I don't want to, but because I'm scared to.

Summer scares me. She always has. She makes me want to open up, and that's not a normal urge for me.

And speaking of urges, she unleashes a pretty basic one when she brings her fingertips to my lips and gently strokes them.

I inch closer, doing everything in my power not to look at her tits. Don't get me wrong—I'm dying to. But I'm about to offer her an out before this gets out of hand, and if she takes it, I'd rather we stopped before I get too attached to those tits.

"Are you sure?" I whisper.

"One hundred percent." A note of vulnerability enters her voice. "Are you?"

I can't stop a laugh from flying out.

Summer's entire body stiffens. "Are you kidd—"

"No," I say quickly, "I'm not laughing at you. I promise. It's just...am I sure? Fuck, Summer, I jerk off to the thought of you every single day. I can't get you out of my head, and it only got worse after you gave me a blowjob. Now I jerk off *twice* a day."

She responds by kissing me senseless.

Yeah, neither of us is going to stop this. It's been a long time coming. A long fucking time.

Our clothes come off. I'm not sure how or when, but suddenly I'm naked and rolling on top of her, one leg sliding between both of hers, my lower body grinding against her softness. Her mouth is fused to mine, and she lifts her hips, shamelessly rubbing herself on my dick, straining to get closer.

My tongue prods the seam of her lips. She parts them on command, granting me access. When I swirl my tongue over hers, she gives a desperate moan that vibrates through my body. I chuckle and retreat, nibbling her full lower lip before peppering kisses along her jaw.

When I reach her neck, she slants her head and my mouth latches onto her flesh, sucking gently. She whimpers and rocks harder against me.

She tries to reach between us to grab my dick, but I gently swat her hands away. "Nuh-uh," I murmur. "You're always the one making me feel good. It's my turn."

And then I proceed to tease the living hell out of her. Forget drugs—you want a real high? Suck on Summer's perfect tits. Kiss the surprisingly sensitive spot right below her belly button and watch her hips arch as her pussy seeks the heat of your cock.

My stubble scrapes the underside of one round, perky breast as I lick my way back up to toy with her nipples some more. I spend an obscene amount of time kissing and licking her, while she grabs my head to keep me in place. Ha. Like I'm going anywhere. I suck one nipple hard enough to elicit a loud moan from her lips, then flick my tongue in feather-light movements over each hard bud until Summer's hips begin to thrash again.

"Fitz," she begs. "No more teasing. I need…"

I slide down and bury my face between her legs. "This what you need?" I groan against her flesh.

Her ass shoots off the mattress.

Chuckling, I grasp her hips to steady her before teasing her with my tongue. Every long, lazy lick summons from her a whimper or a moan or a breathy sigh. When I push one finger inside, her inner muscles greedily clamp around it, and the top of my dick nearly blows off. Oh man, she's amazingly tight. My brain goes hazy as I capture her clit in my mouth and suck on it, while my finger languidly moves inside her.

"Oh my God," she says in a choked voice. "Don't stop. I'm getting close—"

I stop.

"Why!" Summer wails.

I drag my tongue over my lips. Fuck, she's all I can taste. "Not yet," I say, sitting up.

"What gives you the right to decide that?" she huffs. "It's my body, Colin!"

"It's my tongue," I say with a cheeky grin.

"I want to come."

"Don't we all."

"Arrrgghh!" Her cry of frustration triggers my laughter. "I hate you, you know that?"

"No you don't."

"I'm going to die if I don't have an orgasm." Her tone is grave. "Like, actually die. And then you'll have to explain to my father how my death could've been prevented if only you'd finished going down on me. My *father*, Fitz. Is that really what you want?"

I press my lips together to fight another wave of laughter. This girl is the best. The goddamn best. "Tell you what," I say thickly. "Why don't we compromise?" I open the bottom drawer of my nightstand and produce a condom. "We can both come, and nobody has to die."

"Greatest idea ever."

She watches as I rise on my knees to suit up. I gaze down at her, and my breath catches. Her cheeks are flushed, green eyes glittering with arousal, chest heaving with every labored breath. I've never seen a sexier sight.

Her breathing gets choppier. "Why aren't you in me?"

Good question.

I lower my naked body over hers and slide into her in one achingly slow stroke. *Oh fuck.* It's the best feeling in the world. It's…a sense of belonging I've never felt before. And my chest expands in the strangest way when I look at Summer and see the way she's looking at me in return.

I think she's feeling it, too.

The bedsprings squeak when I start to move. Slow, shallow thrusts, filling her only to withdraw each time she tries to pull me in deeper.

"More," she begs.

"No."

My restraint impresses even me. I'm dying to quicken the tempo. Dying to find release. But I also never want this to end. I never want to lose this sensation of sheer *rightness.*

So I drag it out, my hips thrusting and releasing so carefully that beads of sweat break out on my forehead. When Summer tries to hook her legs around my ass, I reprimand her by biting her neck and withdrawing completely.

"Dammit, Fitz…please. Please, please, *please.*"

I've reduced her to begging. Hell yeah.

A husky laugh rumbles out of my chest. "I think I like torment-ing you." To punctuate that, I glide my cock into her again and slowly rotate my hips.

She clings to my shoulders, her tits crushed against my chest. Her nipples are like sun-warmed little pebbles that dig in to my flesh. Her pussy grips me tight enough to bring black dots to my vision.

"I need to come."

It's that one shaky word—*need*—that causes me to give in. Need, not want. I've tortured her long enough.

With an agonized groan, I thrust as deep as I can, and off we go. The sex becomes hard and fast and dirty. This time I let her wrap her legs around me, and the new angle means I'm rubbing against her clit with each downstroke. She comes first, and I'm not far behind, and then we're both gasping with pleasure and rocking together as if we've done this a hundred times before.

Maybe I black out, because when the pleasure finally ebbs, I'm on my back and Summer is lying on top of me, and I can't remember how we got in this position. The spent condom is by my left knee. I don't remember removing it, either. With my last remaining burst of energy, I pick it up, tie it off, and drop it on the nightstand.

Summer rests her cheek on my collarbone. "Your heart's beating so fast."

"So's yours." The rapid flutter of her pulse vibrates against my chest, almost in time to my own erratic heartbeat. I tangle my fingers in her hair.

She sighs happily. "I like cuddling naked with you."

"Me too," I say gruffly.

"I like having sex with you." Her breath heats my left nipple, making me shiver. "I like you, period. I like you a lot."

"I…" My mouth goes dry. I almost say '*ditto*' and then realize how dismissive that sounds. So I say the next best thing—nothing.

Because that's how I roll.

Summer senses the shift in my demeanor. I know she does, because she releases a quiet sigh. But to my surprise, she doesn't lose her temper the way she has the other times I haven't offered the sweet words and reassurances she clearly needs.

"I had an epiphany earlier."

I stroke her hair.

"Did you?"

"Mmm-hmmm. I keep expecting you to be open about your feelings and make yourself vulnerable in front of me, and maybe that's not fair." She absently runs her fingers over my abdomen, leaving goose bumps in her wake. "I have to remember that not everyone is like me. I say whatever's on my mind."

"Saying what's on your mind isn't the same as sharing what you feel," I point out.

"I do that too."

I laugh. "True."

She goes silent, and I can practically hear her brain working. "I don't share *everything*."

Curiosity tugs at me. "You keeping secrets from me, eh?"

"Not just from you. I keep secrets from everyone."

I doubt it. Like she said, Summer's one of the most open people I've ever met. "Uh-huh. Such as?"

"Ha. I'm not revealing anything unless I know I'm getting something in return." She props up on one elbow. "I'll make you a deal. Give me one thing. One vulnerable, real moment. And if you do, I'll…" She purses her lips for a second. "I'll tell you why I started the fire in my sorority house."

*That* gets my attention. It's the first time she's admitted that she'd intentionally set the fire.

"Deal," I tell her. "But you have to go first."

"I knew you'd say that." She crawls forward and reaches for the fleece blanket that's balled up at the foot of the bed.

"Are you cold?" I ask.

"Of course I'm cold. This is New England." She wraps the blanket around her shoulders and returns to sit close to my side.

Me, I'm sprawled on my back, buck-naked, and my body is still on fire. I tend to run hot.

"Okay, you have to promise not to tell anyone." I don't miss the chord of embarrassment in her voice. "The only people I've told are my parents."

"What about Dean? And your other brother?"

"Nicky and Dicky think I got drunk at a toga party and knocked over a candle," she admits.

"And that's not what happened?"

Summer shakes her head.

The plot thickens… "So what did happen?"

"You have to promise, Fitz."

Her green eyes are more serious than I've ever seen them. "I promise."

She brings her hand to her mouth and begins chewing on her thumbnail. First time I've ever seen her bite her nails. It's alarming, and I don't like it. Gently, I reach up and capture her hand. I bring it down to my chest, where I cover it with my palm.

"There was a toga party," she finally says. "That part is true. And I was drunk, but not as drunk as my brothers believe. The Kappa house has a huge enclosed porch, right off the sitting room. Actually, I guess it wasn't really a porch. More like a sunroom. It was an addition to the mansion, and there was this massive wall of windows, with thick drapes." She shrugs wryly. "Highly flammable drapes, as it turned out."

"Oh boy."

"Yup." She tries to chew on her other thumb, so I steal that hand too and clasp it to my chest. "I'm pretty much the only one who used the sunroom. It wasn't well insulated, so it was usually super cold. I'd go and sit out there, mostly when I was in a crappy mood and needed to be alone. Anyway, there was a toga party. We were cohosting it with the Alpha Phi frat, and a few of the frat members were in my Sociology class. The TA gave our midterm papers back that morning, so the guys were talking about their grades and I overheard them." Her tone turns bleak. "I guess they all aced it. Meanwhile, I got an F."

I swallow a sigh. "Ah, babe. I'm sorry." The term of endearment slips out before I can stop it, but I'm not sure Summer even notices.

Shame darkens her eyes. "I plagiarized it."

The revelation stuns me. "Are you serious?"

"Yeah." Her voice cracks. "I didn't realize it was considered plagiarism, though. I paraphrased from a bunch of websites and didn't source them properly. Anything with a direct quote, I cited. But not the other references. I stuck them in the bibliography, but I guess I didn't do it right." She rubs her eyes, and when she looks at me, there's misery clouding her expression. "I was already having so much trouble with that paper, Fitz. It was a mess. I went in for extra help, but it wasn't enough. I emailed the TA and asked for more help, but he was a total dick and told me he'd accommodated me as much as he could. And, well, you saw what happens when I get overwhelmed."

Sympathy fills my chest. "I'm sorry."

"I turned in the paper knowing I'd get a shitty grade, but I didn't expect an F. And when I tried to talk to the TA after class and explain that I hadn't intentionally plagiarized, he gave me the 'too bad, so sad' speech and said I could appeal the grade with the college if I wanted, but that he doubted they'd overturn it."

When I let go of her hands, Summer cinches the blanket tighter to her body. "Fast forward to the party. The frat boys were bragging about their grades, and I was standing there in a ridiculous toga feeling like a complete moron. I was..." She groans softly. "I was so frigging tired of being the village idiot, you know? Just knowing that my paper was upstairs on my desk, with that big red F and the word 'plagiarism' written on it in capital letters. I was pissed. And I just wanted to, I don't know, eliminate all the evidence of my stupidity."

My heart splinters at her stricken tone, then cracks in two when I see her eyes. Jesus. She actually believes what she's saying. She truly thinks of herself as stupid.

"So I went upstairs and grabbed the midterm, and then went down to the sunroom and lit a match. There was a big ceramic bowl on a table under one of the windows. I tossed the burning essay into it." She sighs. "I honestly thought it would burn itself out. It probably would've, if it weren't for the drapes and the fact that someone left the window open." She shakes her head in amazement. "Of all the nights for someone other than me to be in there, right?"

I have to chuckle.

"So," she continues, "the breeze fanned the flames and the drapes caught fire and the sunroom was no more."

"Did it seriously burn to the ground?"

"No. I mean, the outer wall was completely destroyed and needs to be rebuilt, but the part that was attached to the actual mansion remained intact." She hangs her head in shame. "When the fire department came, I lied and said I knocked over a candle when I was dancing on the table. Like, 'Oops, I'm just a drunk sorority girl in a toga!' They labeled it an accident, my parents wrote hefty checks to the sorority and the school, and I was very nicely asked to leave."

"Wow." I sit up against the headboard and pull her toward me. She's cocooned in fleece, so I run a comforting hand over her scalp. "Let me get this straight," I say gently. "You'd rather people think you're a drunk party girl than know that you got an F on a term paper?"

"Pretty much." She tips her head so she can meet my eyes. "But it sounds really ridiculous when you say it out loud."

I cup her cheek, sweeping my thumb over her lower lip. It trembles when I make contact with it. "You're not stupid, Summer. You have a learning disability. There's a difference."

"I know that." The lack of conviction in her tone thoroughly troubles me, but she doesn't give me a chance to probe any deeper. "There. Now you know something truly embarrassing about me. It's your turn."

When I don't respond right away, she pokes her hand out of the blanket and laces her fingers through mine.

"Share something, anything. You promised me something real, Fitz."

I did promise. But that doesn't mean it's easy for me to give it to her. "I…" I grumble with frustration. "I'm not holding back on purpose," I tell her. "It's just…a habit."

"A habit." Her forehead creases. "Holding back is a habit?"

"Yes. I don't talk about what I'm feeling."

"Why not, though?"

I shrug. "I don't know. I guess I…got used to whatever I said being used against me."

"What on earth does that mean?"

Discomfort creeps up my spine, until the back of my neck feels cold, tight. The instinct to flee is strong, but so is Summer's grip on my hand. I draw a breath.

"Fitz?" she prompts.

I exhale. "My parents went through an ugly divorce when I was ten. My dad cheated. Though if you ask him, it's because my mom drove him to it. Either way, they couldn't stand each other back then, and they can't stand each other now."

"I'm sorry. That sounds rough."

"You don't know the half of it. Until I turned twelve, they had joint custody. And then Dad started dating some woman Mom despised, so she decided to sue for full custody of me. Dad got pissed and decided *he* deserved full custody. And that's when the head games began."

"Head games…?"

"The custody battle was even uglier than the divorce. They used me to hurt each other."

Her eyes widen. "How so?"

"Whenever I was alone with Dad, he'd try to coerce me into saying bad shit about Mom. She did the same thing. If I complained to Dad that Mom wouldn't let me play ball hockey with my friends until I cleaned my room, suddenly there'd be a social worker coming by and asking me if I felt 'socially isolated' by my mother. If I told Mom that Dad let me eat sugary cereal before bedtime, a different social worker would show up interrogating me about everything Dad fed me. It was all being documented too. Every word I said went right back to the lawyers."

"Oh my gosh, that's awful."

"They were throwing out accusations of neglect, emotional abuse, 'nutritional deprivation.'" I shake my head in disapproval. "And I couldn't tell them how I felt about it. About anything at all, in fact. Otherwise the blame game would start."

"The blame game?"

"If I was sad about something? *It's your father's fault.* If I was mad? *Your mother's fault.* I was nervous about the school play? *It's because your dad didn't run lines with you.* If something scared me? *It's 'cause your mom's raising a pussy.*" I let out a breath as I remember how exhausting it was to have a single conversation with them. Hell, it's equally exhausting now.

"Did you go to court and tell the judge which parent you wanted to live with?" Summer asks curiously. "Wouldn't that have solved the whole custody battle?"

"You'd think. I did go to court. Well, it was more of a conference room with a bunch of tables, but there was a judge."

I cringe even thinking about it. I remember holding a social worker's hand as she led me into the room and asked me to sit down. My parents were seated next to their respective lawyers. Mom was pleading at me with her eyes. Dad gave me that encouraging look that said, 'I know you'll make the right decision.' Everyone was staring at me. It was fucking brutal.

"The judge asked me to describe my routine at each of their houses." I absently rub Summer's knuckles. "She asked me questions about what I ate, whether I enjoyed playing hockey—a bunch of questions that made me realize they'd told the lawyers everything I'd ever said to them. And then the judge asked me who I wanted to live with."

Summer's breath hitches. "Who did you pick?"

My lips twitch in amusement. "I pleaded the Fifth."

Her jaw drops. "You were twelve, and you pleaded the Fifth?"

"Yup. I think I saw someone do it on *CSI* or some shit." I snicker. "The judge said I couldn't do that and urged me to pick. So I said both. I wanted to live with both." I offer a wry smile. "She awarded them joint custody, which was what they'd started off with. She said she felt it was better for my mental and emotional wellbeing to spend equal time with both of them."

"Did things get better after that? Did your parents settle down?"

"Nope. They kept trash-talking each other to me. Still do to this day, though not as bad as before."

She frowns. "How'd you deal with it when you were growing up?"

"By becoming invisible," I say roughly. "I mean, there was one rebellious phase where I got my first tat behind their back and dared them to pay attention to me, but mostly I hid in my room. As long as they couldn't see me, they weren't able to poison me against each other."

"I'm sorry you had to go through all that."

I shrug.

"You're doing it again," she teases with a smile. "Okay, listen. I know you're used to having your feelings twisted into something negative, but I promise you, anything you tell me will stay in our sacred trust circle. I will never, ever report it to the judge."

I find myself smiling back. "I'm sorry. Bad habit. I'll try to break it." I shoot her a stern look. "But only if you promise to stop being so hard on yourself. You've got to stop telling yourself you're stupid."

"I'll try," she says, and I suppose I can't ask for more than that. "Are you hungry? I never ended up having dinner."

I want to ask her why not, what happened on the date with Hunter, but I tamp down the urge. I really don't want to kill the mood by bringing up another guy. That can wait till tomorrow.

I want tonight to be about just me and Summer.

# 25
# SUMMER

"My French girls have got nothing on you," Fitz informs me three nights later.

From the floor of his bedroom, I lift my gaze off the papers in my lap and stick my tongue out at him. And then I realize he's not joking. A mixture of awe and appreciation shines in his brown eyes as he stares at me.

"You're stunning," he insists.

"Stop," I order. "You're going to make me blush."

"Yeah right. Compliments don't make you blush. You love 'em."

Well, sure. I do. But the intensity on his face is a tad unnerving. We've gone back to our he-draws-me-while-I-write-my-essay routine, but usually he doesn't say much while he sketches, and he certainly doesn't throw around words like "stunning."

I tend to do most of the talking, reading bits of my paper aloud to him and trying to vocalize my thoughts before I put them down on the page. His presence helps my concentration, if I'm being honest. It's as if it creates a sense of accountability for me. The midterm is due in a few days, but I'm actually feeling good about it. Not saying it's A-material, but I'd be perfectly content with a B or C.

Fitz studies his sketch. His biceps flex as he shifts one arm and scrapes the pencil over the page to add another detail.

Lord, he is hotter than a five-alarm fire. In appearance, and in body temperature, I'm discovering. He stripped off his T-shirt ten minutes into our study/sketch session, taunting me with his ripped chest. I honestly don't know how my ADHD brain has managed to remain focused on my schoolwork.

"Stunning," he says again, this time mumbling it under his breath. "I can see why other women are threatened by you."

I feel the blush rise in my cheeks. "Nobody's threatened by me. You're nuts."

"No? Remember the girl at the bar?"

"She was threatened by Brenna, not me."

"Naah, it was both of you." He examines his drawing again. "Jesus. I can't get over it. You're beautiful, but it's the kind of beauty that's so…unattainable. It's otherworldly."

I snort. "That's very poetic of you, sweetie."

But inside, Selena Gomez and I are doing an entire cheerleading routine's worth of cartwheels and flips. Nobody has ever called me *otherworldly*. I think I like it.

When footsteps echo in the hall, we both stiffen. And this is something I *don't* like—the awful cloud of tension that's fallen over our household. If we're in my bedroom or Fitz's, the tension fades away. The conversation flows, and there's an ease between us that I've never experienced with another guy before.

Anywhere else in the house, the thundercloud looms.

Hunter's hardly spoken a word to us since Thursday night. We've been tiptoeing around him, and even Hollis, who's fazed by nothing, admitted that Hunter's brooding is getting to him. I don't know how to make the situation better, though. Hunter needs time to get used to the idea that Fitz and I are…dating, I guess?

We haven't given it a label yet, but I'm in no rush. I know he likes being with me, and that's all that matters at the moment. Besides, it's not like I could raise the subject on Valentine's Day weekend. That's pressure with a capital everything for a guy.

In fact, we barely even acknowledged that yesterday was

Valentine's Day. We watched *Titanic* with Hollis, then went upstairs and made out for a bit (not with Hollis).

Beyond his door, I hear the footsteps travel down the stairs, then grow muffled. The TV switches on in the living room. We both relax. Must be Hollis, then. Hunter hasn't hung out in the living room in days.

"Okay, I think I'll write the conclusion tomorrow. My brain needs to recharge." I set the laptop and notebook on the hardwood and pick up the leather portfolio that contains everything related to Summer Lovin', the cheesy name I've chosen for my swimwear line.

I'm holding my first fittings with the models in a few days. Nearly all my pieces are done—I sewed most of them myself in the Fashion department's sewing rooms. Brenna kept me company for a couple hours yesterday, mockingly calling me Home Ec Barbie. The crochet bikinis, I had to outsource; I'm working with an awesome seamstress in Hastings. Once I tailor the swimsuits to my models, we'll do a final fitting to iron out any kinks, and then we're good to go.

"I need to redo this one pair of briefs," I say absently, flipping through my designs. "My seamstress says the cut is too high for a man. I'll draw a couple other options and see what she says."

"Draw?" There's a funny note to his voice.

I glance over, confused by the astonishment in his eyes. "Yes, draw. How do you think I designed these swimsuits? I did sketches of them."

"Sketches." Fitz is staring at me as if he's never seen me before in his life.

"Yes. Sketches. What's wrong with your face?"

He shakes his head a few times, as if it's stuffed with cobwebs. "I'm just…I can't believe you can fucking *draw* and this is the first I'm hearing about it."

I arch my eyebrows. "What, you're the only one in this house who's allowed to draw? That's a bit arrogant, don't you think?"

Fitz flings his sketchbook aside and shuffles over to me. "I gotta see this. Show me."

I snap the portfolio closed and hug it to my chest. Before, I would've gladly shown him the sketches. Now, with his eager eyes and grabby hands, I feel an anvil of pressure weighing on my throat.

"It's a bunch of bikinis and swim trunks. Nothing fancy," I insist.

"Lemme see."

My cheeks heat up. "No. You're, like, the most talented artist in the world." He showed me pictures of some of his paintings— mostly dazzling fantasy worlds and dystopian landscapes—and his art blew my frigging mind. "I draw *clothes*."

"Garments can be really difficult to draw."

"Uh-huh. No need to humor me."

"I'm serious. Clothing has elements that a lot of artists tend to overlook. There are shadows and creases in the drape of the garment, in the way certain fabrics fold." He shrugs. "Can be challenging."

"I guess." I still think he's humoring me, but his earnest expression has me relinquishing the sketches.

Fitz doesn't say a single word as he scrutinizes each one. I try to see the drawings through his eyes, but it's hard to tell what he thinks. The figures are at their most basic. Faceless, with long limbs that aren't anatomically correct, because it doesn't matter. They're only there to display the garments.

"These are great," he tells me, then spends a long time examining a one-piece with a plunge neckline that reveals my pencil-drawn model's perfectly round boobs.

"Nice tits," he remarks.

I fight a laugh. "You know they're not real, right?"

"They're not? Right on. I support a woman's choice to get a boob job. Whatever makes her happy."

"You're hilarious."

He looks at the sketch again. "Did you use your own tits for reference?" he drawls.

"Come on. Those are way bigger than mine."

His seductive gaze drops to my chest. I'm still sporting the dress I wore to campus today, and its high neckline and long sleeves don't offer much in terms of cleavage. But Fitz is ogling me as if I'm completely topless. "I don't know... Yours are pretty big."

"I'm a C cup. That's average."

"That is not average."

"Mmm-hmmm, and you know the universal boob size average because...? You personally polled every woman in the world?"

"No, but there's this thing on the Internet, Summer. It's called porn. Have you heard of it?"

My laughter can't be contained this time. I have so much fun with this guy, it's unreal.

"I'm so turned on right now," he adds. "Just so you know."

"Because of my cartoon lady's bigger-than-average boobs?"

"No, because you're an artist. You literally just became a hundred times hotter to me."

Rolling my eyes, I gather my stuff and get to my feet. "I'm going to put all this back in my room. You said you wanted to watch something on Netflix—are we still doing that?"

"Like hell we are."

The growly timbre stops me from taking another step. When I notice his expression, a shiver rolls through me.

He's looking at me as if I'm his next meal.

"You're smoldering," I inform him.

Fitz walks over and takes my school stuff from my hands. Without a word, he sets the entire pile on the bed. Then he returns.

He's unzipping his pants as he walks.

My breath gets stuck in my throat. Oh my God.

Saliva floods my mouth. He's got a rocket in there. I want it. To my dismay, he simply reaches a hand inside his undone pants and does some rearranging, tucking his hard-on under the waistband of his boxers.

My jaw opens. "Are you kidding me? You unzipped your pants just to hide your sweet penis from me?"

He chokes out a laugh. "My sweet penis can wait a few minutes."

"Wait for what—"

His mouth is on mine before I can finish. A loud moan slips out, which he swallows with his soft, hungry lips. "Quiet," he murmurs, even as his tongue scrapes over mine in a dirty, dirty kiss. "Mike's downstairs. And my door isn't locked."

"Should we lock it—"

He cuts me off with another kiss. I guess he's confident in our roommate honoring the privacy code.

With his lips glued to mine, he nudges me backward. My butt bumps into his desk, and a pair of earphones crash to the floor. Fitz ignores that and slips one hand underneath my dress. I shiver when his fingers graze my inner thigh. His knuckles briefly rub my damp panties, and then he moves the fabric to the side and the pad of his thumb presses on my clit.

The air leaks out of my lungs in a squeaky rush.

"Feel good?" he whispers in my ear.

"What do you think?"

He smiles, and it's filthy and adorable at the same time. His hand glides over me. The heel of it now tends to my swollen clit while his middle finger teases my opening. Every nerve ending in my body crackles to life. I never, ever want this to stop.

Fitz bends and kisses the column of my throat. I'm sure he can feel my pulse throbbing there. His mouth is hot on my neck when his finger slips inside. He doesn't go too deep. Instead, he curls it and rubs a sweet spot inside me.

"So wet," he croaks.

Yup. I am. And I can barely stay upright. Luckily, he's gripping my butt with his other hand, holding me steady while he expertly fingers me. The pleasure builds to an excruciating point, until I'm swaying on my feet even with his strong grip on me.

He laughs huskily. "Hop up on the desk."

I almost cry when he withdraws his finger, but I follow his orders and find an available surface, which is hard because there are computer monitors and gaming equipment all over his desk.

The second my ass connects with the solid wood, Fitz bunches the hem of my dress between his fingers. The calluses on his palms rake my bare legs as he drags the fabric up to my waist. His hungry gaze focuses on my pink bikini panties. Before I can blink, he's tugging them off and tossing them aside.

I'm completely exposed to him now, and he eyes me like a man who's just discovered a secret treasure.

"No teasing tonight." There's a note of desperation in my voice. "Just fuck me."

He chuckles and goes to get a condom from his drawer. He eases his cargo pants and boxers down his hips until his penis springs free and slaps his washboard stomach.

"You are so sexy," I breathe, staring at his thick erection.

The pressure between my legs intensifies. He's so big and so male and I've never wanted anybody the way I want him.

Licking his lips, Fitz covers himself with the condom. When he grips the base of his erection, anticipation ripples through me.

I spread my legs wider.

Heat flares in his eyes. He steps into the cradle of my thighs and guides himself inside me.

And that's when the door swings open and Hunter stumbles into the bedroom.

# 26
# FITZ

"AW, WELL, THIS IS COZY."

Summer and I freeze as Hunter makes a not-so-graceful entrance, staggering into my room without warning. And we have no choice but to remain frozen, because my ass is bare and my dick is buried deep inside her.

But Hunter doesn't know that yet. From his vantage point, it looks like Summer is sitting on my desk and I'm standing between her legs. Bare-assed, sure, but I don't think he's picked up on that.

He is noticeably drunk. I'm talking wasted. His broad, muscular body weaves and lurches as he wanders around my room. His gaze briefly connects with mine, and I can see him struggling to focus his eyes. They're hazy with intoxication. He finally stops at the foot of the bed, then spreads his arms and lets himself fall backward onto the mattress. He lands with a thump and starts to laugh.

He rises on his elbows and grins at me. Still hasn't noticed that my ass is hanging out. "Fuckin' hell, Fitz, your bed is way more comfortable than mine. Lucky bastard."

Summer's hands tremble on my waist. She slowly slides them off and flattens them on the desktop. Her pussy spasms around my still-hard cock. I don't know if it's intentional or involuntary, but I choke back a groan all the same.

"I just came from this party at Sigma Cow. Chow. Chi. Sigma *Chi.*" He's slurring now. "And my buddy was like, what do you mean you're pissed at Fizzy? You grow a vagina or something?"

Summer shifts, and I give her a warning look. I'm waiting for the right moment to pull out. And it can't be when Hunter's gaze is on me like white on rice.

It takes several seconds to find my voice. "Dude, can we talk about this later? Maybe in private?"

"What are…" Hunter trails off. His eyes narrow. Then he laughs. "Are you inside her right now?"

"Get the fuck out," I growl.

His shoulders shake with laughter. "You are. Jesus. That's kind of hot."

Screw it. Despite his gaze boring into me, I withdraw from the heat of Summer's body and hastily tuck my dick in my pants, condom still on. Summer shoves her skirt down and hops off the desk. Two red splotches stain her cheeks.

"Aw, you didn't have to stop on my account."

"Hunter," I say flatly.

"What?" He raises his hands in a gesture of innocence. "We're roomies. Sometimes roomies watch each other fuck."

Summer exits my room without a backward glance. I don't blame her. I see the tight set of her shoulders, but I know she's not pissed at me. Hell, she's probably not pissed at Hunter. If anything, that's nothing but sheer embarrassment tensing her body.

"Hello to you too, Blondie," Hunter calls after her, but gets no response. Shrugging, he stumbles back to his feet. "Didn't waste any time, did ya, Fitz? How long after I dropped her home did it take for you to dick her down?"

I bite back my anger. He's drunk. And as much as I hate to say it, he has a point. "Let's talk when you're sober, all right?"

"Let's not." He shakes his head, continuing to laugh under his breath as he weaves toward the door. "You and Blondie do your thing. I'll do mine. And they all live happily never ever. I mean, after. Happily ever after."

I frown at his retreating back. "Hunter."

"Mmmm?"

"Are we good?" I ask warily.

He glances at me over his shoulder. "No."

———

I do my best to keep my distance from Hunter after that, especially around the house. It's the least I can do. On one hand, Summer and I didn't do anything wrong—it's not like she was officially dating him. But Hunter had made his intentions clear to me. He'd staked a claim, and I'd trampled over it. But at the time, I hadn't thought Summer and I were possible. I thought I'd been friend-zoned.

But that's neither here nor there. You can't change the past. You can only try to better the future.

In this case, it means giving Hunter his space, which Summer and I both agree is probably for the best right now.

If it were Hollis or Tuck, maybe I'd handle the situation differently, talk to them, try harder to fix shit. But Hunter and I, while friends, aren't super close. He's got a great sense of humor and he's fun to be around, but the truth is, I don't know him very well.

So I maintain the distance. I thought it'd be harder to do, considering we live together, but Hunter isn't around much in the days following our confrontation. I can't completely avoid him, though, because we're forced to interact during practice.

Harvard is still leading our conference. We play them again in a few weeks, so Coach Jensen and Coach O'Shea are working us even harder these days. On Wednesday morning, we run several one-on-one drills, followed by a three-on-three mini-game—Jesse, Matty, and me, versus Hunter, Nate, and Kelvin.

Hunter and I take center. As he gets into position, I glimpse his determined expression and know this ain't gonna be pleasant.

I'm not wrong. He gains possession and skates off. When he tries to pass the puck to Nate, it's intercepted by Matt, who snaps it over to me. I fly toward the blue line and dump the puck, catching up to it again behind the net. I barely get my stick on it before I'm slammed into the boards. The hit is harder than necessary, and so is the elbow to the ribs, courtesy of Hunter.

He flashes a humorless smile and steals the puck from me. Then he's gone.

*Motherfucker*, that hurt. But fine. Whatever. I let it slide. He has a right to be angry, and it's better he let out his aggression on the ice rather than off it.

Here in the arena, it's controlled violence. Which is one of my favorite things about hockey. It might be stupidly primal, and maybe it makes men as dumb as women claim we are, but sometimes it's nice to release our pent-up aggression in a place where we can't get in trouble for it.

As practice continues, the encounters between me and Hunter get more and more physical. Our teammates start to notice. Nate whistles softly when I give Hunter a bone-jarring crosscheck. I swear I hear the breath leave Hunter's lungs.

"Save it for the game," Nate urges after the whistle blows.

We line up for another face-off. Hunter's eyes are blazing at me. He didn't like that check. Well, I didn't like his elbow in my ribs, but what can you do.

This time I win the faceoff. Jesse and I flip the puck back and forth as we plan our attack. Lazy and predatory. Hunter's line doesn't like being toyed with, and just as they go on the attack, Jesse snaps the puck to me and I take my shot. Corsen stops it with his stick, then passes to Hunter.

I chase after him, and we wind up behind my net. Elbows are thrown. One hits me in the center of the throat. For a second I actually can't breathe. I gasp for air, but my windpipe isn't working. I feel like I'm choking.

Hunter doesn't care. He gives me a shove as he skates away, and I manage to catch my balance before I fall. That throat move? No way.

I skate after him, the game all but forgotten. "What the hell was that?"

A hush falls over the rink. I hear the hiss of Nate's skate blades as he comes to a stop a few feet away from us.

"It was a clean hit," Hunter says.

I growl. "Nothing clean about that."

"No? Sorry, then. My bad."

His careless tone grates on my last nerve. "Whatever, bro. If knocking me around makes you feel better, go for it."

"Aw, how generous of you, giving me permission to throw down. Totally makes up for the fact that you're fucking the chick I like."

Yup, he went there.

Nate skates closer, his stick dangling loosely from his glove. "C'mon, guys, we got work to do."

We ignore him.

"Look, Summer and I have been dancing around each other for more than a year. I had a thing for her before I ever knew you."

"Funny, you didn't mention having a thing for her when I told you that *I* did."

I can feel our teammates watching us, which gives rise to the familiar prickling sensation that means all eyes are on me because I've just been dropped into drama I can't avoid.

I push past him, but he grabs a handful of jersey.

"Let's not do this here," I mutter.

"Why not? You don't want everyone to hear what a dick you are?"

"Hey, ladies!" Coach shouts. "We don't have all day. Get your asses back to the bench."

Hunter reluctantly obeys. I happily do, because being the center of attention makes my skin crawl.

Coach announces we're running more battle drills. The first drill involves two players out of the corner—one needs to drive the net, the other has to stop him. From the bench, I watch as several pairs battle it out. Then it's my turn, and I'm not at all surprised when Coach announces I'm up against Hunter. Maybe, like me, he's hoping Hunter will release all his hostility and leave it on the ice.

The second the whistle blows, Hunter uses every dirty trick in the book to keep me trapped in the corner. I finally break free and get a shot off, but the sophomore goalie, Trenton, easily captures the puck with his glove and then tosses it in the air with a grin.

"Run it again," Coach demands.

So we do. Once again manhandling each other in the corner. I manage to gain possession and drive the net, but before I can shoot, pain jolts up my arm as the fucker two-hands me in the wrist.

"What the *fuck* is wrong with—"

I don't get to finish the sentence. The next thing I know, I'm flat on my back, the wind completely knocked out of me.

His gloves drop. A fist slams into my chest. My helmet slides off, and another fist connects with my jaw. I hear the cheers and shouts of our teammates. Some are egging us on, others trying to break it up. Someone tries to pull Hunter off me. It doesn't quite work, but it gives me the opportunity to ditch my own gloves and unleash a few decent retaliation blows. But then Hunter punches me again, and I taste blood in my mouth.

Breathing heavily, we take a few more swings at each other, until Nate launches himself between us and forcibly shoves us apart. A couple of the other seniors come up and grab hold of each of us to stop us from attacking again.

"Well? You ladies work it out?" From his perch near the home bench, Coach Jensen sounds utterly bored.

O'Shea looks like he's trying not to laugh. "Hit the showers," he tells us.

I look down and notice the red droplets staining the ice. It's my blood—I didn't draw a single drop from Hunter. But I'm grati-fied to note that his cheek is beginning to swell. He'll have a bruise tomorrow. I'll have a split lip. Not quite even, but at least I left *some* damage.

I meet his hard gaze. "I'm sorry, man."

I think he's scraping his teeth together, because his cheeks keep hollowing in and out. "Yeah." He shrugs. "I think you actually mean that."

"I do."

We stare at each other. Hunter's legs slide apart as he gets ready to skate, and the seniors tense, prepared to break us apart again. But he doesn't move toward me—he skates backward for several feet, eyeing me in thought.

Then he offers another shrug and rotates his body, leaving his discarded gear scattered on the ice behind him. He glances over his shoulder at me. "Don't worry, Fitz. I'll get over it."

I'm not so sure about that.

# 27
# FITZ

**THREE WEEKS LATER**

Six half-naked football players compete in a twerking contest while "It's Raining Men" blasts out of the wireless speakers.

No, that's not the setup for a raunchy joke.

It's what Hollis and I come home to on this chilly Tuesday morning. We'd just finished practice and then grabbed breakfast at the diner in Hastings, because Summer said she needed the dining room and living room for her final fittings.

Hollis' jaw falls open as he takes in the scene before him. "Is this the wrong house?" he asks me.

"Yeah, Rex!" Brenna is shouting from her spot on the armchair. She waves a dollar bill in the air, while Summer and a girl I don't recognize laugh uncontrollably from the couch.

The star wide receiver of the Briar football team shakes his ass before sauntering over to Brenna and proceeding to give her a lap dance.

"Nope," I hear Hollis mutter. "Nope, nope, nope."

A second later, he's in front of the entertainment unit, powering off the speaker.

The music stops.

Rex's dance comes to an abrupt end. At first the big guy looks disappointed, but then he notices me in the doorway and says, "Fitzgerald! Whadda ya think?" He points both index fingers at his Speedo.

Well, technically not a Speedo, but a Summer Lovin' original. Rex is wearing navy-blue briefs with silver stripes on the sides, and when he does a full turn, I grin at the S stitched on his ass.

"It's nice," I tell him. But it's a bathing suit, and I have no opinion one way or the other about bathing suits. I've owned the same pair of trunks for like five years.

Summer rolls her eyes. "Don't bother with Fitzy. He doesn't understand fashion." She gets up from the couch and approaches Grier Lockett. "Don't move for a sec. Something's not right with this seam."

And then my girlfriend drops to her knees in front of another man's junk and starts fondling him.

"Summer," I say politely.

She pokes her head from around Lockett's crotch. "What is it, sweetie?"

"Do you need help jacking him off?"

Rex and the others break out in gales of laughter. Summer gives me the finger, and my jaw drops when she reaches around and pats Lockett on the butt.

"Okay, take these off and put on real clothes. I'm gonna need to take that apart and restitch it."

Lockett hooks his fingers under the waistband.

"In the bathroom!" she squeaks before he can yank his trunks down. "Jesus!"

"Well, you're no fun." Pouting, Lockett lumbers out of the living room.

"The rest of you can get dressed too. Everything looks great." She turns to address Rex, who I know is the unofficial leader of the offense. His quarterback, Russ Wiley, might be the actual captain, but I hear Russ is an egomaniac. Rex, meanwhile, is universally loved.

"So we're all set for next week? The show starts at nine, but I'll need you guys there at least an hour before."

"Don't worry, cutie. We'll be there with balls on."

"Bells," Brenna's friend corrects from the sofa.

Rex fixes her with a stern look. "Audrey. When I say balls, I mean balls."

She snorts and goes back to checking her phone.

"Are you sure the timing is okay?" Summer presses. "I heard Bibby mention something about a team-building retreat, but isn't it the off-season?"

"It is," Bibby grumbles.

Jules, another wide receiver, rolls his eyes. "Coach is making us attend this hippie-dippie bullshit course because we fell apart in the playoffs."

"Because Wiley fell apart in the playoffs," Lockett corrects, referring to their quarterback.

I don't miss the disappointment in their expressions. Before this season, it had been a while since Briar had produced a football team with a good record. The fact that they'd ranked so high this year only to lose in the postseason must kill them.

"He thinks we have trust issues," Jules says. He shrugs. "So we've been sentenced to five days of forced camaraderie."

Brenna raises her eyebrows. "Five days? That's savage."

"We get back on the day of the show," Rex says. When he notices Summer's worried eyes, he ruffles her hair reassuringly. "But we'll have plenty of time to spare. The bus is dropping us at campus around seven-thirty, eight."

Summer nods with relief. "Okay. Perfect."

As the players leave the room to change into their street clothes, Summer gathers her supplies and tucks them into the huge sewing case on the coffee table. Audrey is now chatting with Lockett, who returns in track pants and a Patriots hoodie. And in the armchair, Brenna is now bent over her phone, her long hair forming a dark curtain around her face.

"Who are you texting?" Summer asks her.

"Nobody."

But it's clearly somebody, based on her secretive tone and the quick glance she flicks in Hollis' direction. The cloud of hurt in his blue eyes is unmistakable, and sympathy tugs at my gut. I don't think he's given up on the idea of him and Brenna yet, but it's been about a month since they hooked up, and it's evident she's not looking for a repeat.

"I'm making a coffee," he finally mutters, tearing his gaze off Brenna. "Want one, Fitz?"

"No thanks." I had two cups at Della's and I'm still wired.

The moment he disappears into the kitchen, Summer launches an interrogation. "Spill, Bee. Who is he? Do I know him?"

Brenna shrugs. "You met him once."

Summer continues watching her like a hawk. "Who is it?" I'm pretty sure she's holding her breath as she awaits Brenna's response. When she doesn't get one within three seconds, she blurts out, "Is it Jake Connelly?"

My head swivels toward Brenna. "Are you fucking kidding me?"

"God, no. It's not Connelly. He's such a prick."

"Then who!" Summer demands. "Just tell me. Otherwise I'll steal your phone and—"

"Relax, crazy girl. It's Josh, okay?"

"Who?"

"McCarthy," Brenna clarifies.

Summer gasps. "The Harvard guy? Oh my God. How do you even have his number?"

"He messaged me on Facebook. Wanted to apologize for losing his shit when he found out who my dad was." Brenna offers another shrug. "We're just fooling around, though. Nothing serious."

I don't miss how she discreetly slips the phone into her purse, as if a part of her is worried Summer might actually try to snatch it from her. And there's no more discussion after that, because the rest of the guys file into the room and exchange their goodbyes with Summer. Brenna and Audrey announce they're taking off too, so our front hall turns into a can of sardines as eight people (six of them enormous football players) put on their coats and boots and various winter gear.

"Hey, Summer." One of the players hesitates at the door. He's got a mop of curly brown hair and a shy expression. "Are there any tickets still available? I checked online and it said the show's sold out."

"It is, but all the designers get a block of tickets to give away. I think I have about five left. How many do you need, Chris?"

"Just one. It's for my girlfriend, Daphne."

Summer freezes. And I mean freezes. She was in the process of reaching up to tuck some hair behind her ear, and her arm literally stops midair. Then it drops abruptly to her side, and at least five seconds tick by as she stares at Chris, whose body language displays some serious discomfort.

"Do you mean… Did you ever go out with a Kappa named Kaya, by any chance?"

Chris shoves his gloved hands in his pockets. "Yeah, I dated Kaya. But that was a long time ago." He frowns. "I'm with Daphne now."

"Daphne Kettleman?"

He looks startled. "Yeah. You know her?"

Summer's entire body seems to vibrate with excitement. "No. I don't know her."

Since she moved in with us, I've witnessed this girl get excited about many things.

Her Prada boots.

One Direction.

Leonardo DiCaprio.

Sex.

But I've never seen her face light up the way it does during this conversation about Daphne Kettleman. Whoever that is.

"Oh my God. Okay. I'm sorry. I'm freaking out right now." She's practically bouncing on her feet. "I can't wait to meet her. Tell her I'm a huge fan. Oh my God, tell her we need to chill at the after-party."

Chris gives her a strange look.

As he should. I'd be weirded out too if, for no discernible reason, some crazy blonde lost her shit at the thought of meeting my girlfriend.

"Um. Sure. I'll tell her." He starts backing away, then mutters a hasty goodbye and flees.

"Because that wasn't fucking weird," I tell Summer.

She beams at me. "You don't even know. Daphne's reputation precedes her." And then she babbles on about Daphne and alcohol poisoning and someone stealing Daphne's clothes, and I follow her up the stairs and try to keep up until my eyes finally glaze over.

We enter my room and I lock the door, shutting Summer up the only way I know how—by kissing her.

But kissing her never fails to lead to a raging hard-on, which she notices instantly. "It's nine o'clock in the morning, Fitz. How are you always so horny, no matter what?"

"My cock can't tell time."

She laughs, a sweet melody that makes my dick sing along with anticipation. I kiss her again, and we're naked in no time at all, making out on the bed with our legs tangled together and our hands busy exploring.

As her fingers roam my bare chest, she releases a happy sigh. "There should be a law stating you're not allowed to wear a shirt ever."

"There should be a law stating you're not allowed to wear anything ever." I ease out of her grip and kiss my way down her centerfold body until I reach my favorite place on earth.

I go down on her until she's clawing at the sheets and begging me to get inside her, but rather than climb on top of her, I sprawl on my back and tug her on top of *me*.

"Ride me," I tell her, and she's happy to oblige.

In a heartbeat, I've got a condom on and there's a beautiful woman grinding on my dick. Pain stings my pecs as she digs her nails into my skin, her pelvis moving in slow, seductive strokes. The teasing tempo doesn't last long, though. Soon her pace increases and she's riding me in earnest.

I lie back and admire the view, her perky breasts swaying as she moves, the flush rising in her cheeks. She bites her bottom lip, and I can see in her eyes that she's close. She's got that fuzzy, blissed-out look that I love, and when she cries out and collapses on top of me, her orgasm pushes me over the edge. I wrap my arms around her as she milks every last drop of pleasure from my body. I can only manage short, ragged breaths, and it takes a few minutes before my brain is able to function again. I open my eyes to find Summer grinning at me.

"You okay?" she teases.

I groan. "I can't feel my legs."

"Oh, you poor baby." She strokes my shoulders and kisses a spot between my pecs. "How can I make it better?"

"You just did."

I groan at the loss of her when she climbs off me. And I'm still sporting a semi, a fact she wastes no time commenting on when she returns from the bathroom.

"Oh good!" Her eyes light up. "You'll be ready to go again soon."

I roll onto my side. "Damn, woman, one orgasm isn't enough for you? You have incredibly high expectations."

"I require at least two." She jumps on the bed and nestles in front of me so that she's my little spoon. "I'm kidding. I'm good for now. That was incredible."

"Mmm-hmmm," I agree. I sling an arm around and hold her tight. I'm feeling sleepy all of a sudden. "Wanna take a nap?"

"Mmm-hmmm." She sounds drowsy too.

My eyelids flutter closed. I feel myself starting to drift, my mind starting to fade, when suddenly I remember something. "Hey. Babe."

"Hmmm?" She snuggles her ass closer to my groin, and the heat of her body seeps into me.

"Thursday night."

"What about it?"

"It's the fundraiser. The one Kamal Jain wants me to go to. His assistant emailed me the details this morning. It's at your hotel."

That gets her attention. "The Heyward Plaza?"

"Mmm-hmmm." I run my fingers over her hip. Her skin is so fucking soft. "I have a plus one."

"Hmmm?"

I laugh. "I feel like we can have an entire conversation with just hmmms and mmm-hmmms."

"We should try it when I'm not in an orgasm coma."

"Deal." I press a kiss on the nape of her neck. "You wanna go to the fundraiser with me?"

"Hold on. You're inviting me to a fancy party where I get to dress up and be social? What the hell is wrong with you? That's *so* not my scene."

I sigh. "You're right. That was a stupid question."

"Of course I'll go. But I have one condition."

"Hmmm?"

"I get to pick your outfit."

"Well, yeah." My shoulders tremble with laughter as I wrap my arms tighter around her. "I'd never dream of picking my own."

# 28
# FITZ

"WE'RE GOING TO BE LATE," I TELL SUMMER'S CLOSET. I'D LIKE TO tell Summer herself, but she's been locked up in the cavernous walk-in for the past two hours.

At first I didn't mind, because it gave me the opportunity to explore the penthouse, which I didn't have a chance to do when I came here with Dean once. The place has a sleek, modern design, and it's luxury to the max. I'd poked my head into their library, and then had to duck right back out, because I'd require about three full days to thoroughly examine the contents of the enormous, walnut-paneled room.

I can't believe real people actually live here. And not even full time; Summer's parents split their time between this surreal apartment and their mansion in Greenwich. I'm afraid to even see pictures of the latter. I hear it has a skating rink in the backyard.

It's a stroke of luck that Kamal Jain's fundraiser for leukemia is being held in one of the ballrooms downstairs. That means Summer and I didn't have to spring for a room in this insanely priced hotel. Nope, we're staying for free in the penthouse. Though that's not a detail I plan to reveal to Kamal. I feel like he wouldn't like the idea that I'm staying somewhere better than him, assuming he's at this hotel. For all I know, he's boarding his private jet after the shindig and flying to a villa in the Mediterranean.

"I'm almost ready," Summer's muffled voice replies.

"Define almost," I call back.

"Three minutes, give or take five minutes."

Laughter bubbles in my throat. This girl.

We got in last night, and we've been having a blast so far. I ate her out on the pool table, which was hot. She blew me on her California king mattress, and then we snuggled in bed and binged a show about child killers. Summer agreed to watch it with me in exchange for—ugh. I don't even want to think about it. But I may or may not have agreed to watch the latest season of *The Bachelor* with her. Summer has that effect on me. My first instinct is to say yes to anything she asks, because I want to make her happy.

We've spent almost every waking hour together for the past three weeks. She sleeps in my bedroom. Her makeup clutters my bathroom counter. Every morning she rumples her bedsheets to make it look like she's still sleeping in her own room. I think it's for Hunter's sake, but he's not an idiot. He knows.

No matter how quiet we think we're being when we have sex, I have no doubt both Hunter and Hollis are well aware that we're sleeping together.

But short of moving out, or asking Summer to, I don't how to make the situation with Hunter any better. And at the moment, I need to focus on impressing Kamal Jain.

"Summer," I grumble. "Your three minutes are up. I know the event is right downstairs, but I think it'd make a bad impression if we were late to—"

My vocal cords seize, all coherent thought flying out of my brain.

Summer's closet is clearly a magical portal. She entered it wearing Lululemon pants, wool socks, and one of my hockey hoodies.

She exits it looking like a goddess.

A slinky silver dress is plastered to her body, hugging every tantalizing curve. A slit goes up to her thigh, revealing one long, tanned leg, and her silver stilettos add about another four inches to her already tall frame. Her golden hair is up in an elegant twist held together by an ornate clip that sparkles under the light fixture overhead. It takes me a moment to realize that her hairclip is sparkling because it's encrusted with diamonds.

Summer notes my expression. Her makeup is subtle except for her bright red lips, which curve into a smile. It's really fucking hot.

"You like?" She spins in a circle and her shimmery dress swirls around her ankles.

"I like," I say gruffly.

"How much?" She plants a hand on her waist, cocks her hip, and thrusts a leg out in a pose that makes me groan. My dick twitches at the sight of her bare thigh emerging from the dress's slit.

"I like a lot." I clear the gravel from my throat. "How 'bout me?"

She scrutinizes me from head to toe. Completely unnecessary considering she's the one who chose every scrap of fabric on my body, from the Tom Ford shoes to the crisp black suit jacket to the navy-blue dress shirt with only the top button undone. Summer said that as hot as my chest tattoo is, she doesn't want it peeking out tonight. Apparently, she's been to this leukemia fundraiser before (why am I not surprised?), and she warned me that the crowd will consist of a lot of old people with very deep pockets—and very closed minds.

"You look sharp, babe. Super professional. Oh, and sexy."

I laugh. "Perfect. Sexy is what I'm going for. I plan on sleeping with Kamal Jain to get the job."

"Let me know how that works out for you."

The penthouse has an elevator requiring a key that only Summer's family has access to. As we ride it downstairs, she takes her phone out of her silver clutch and opens Instagram. "Let's take a selfie," she announces, and the next thing I know she's pulling me into frame and snapping a dozen photos of us.

"You're the worst," I tell her, because she knows I hate selfies.

She beams at me. "I think what you mean is, I'm the best."

I snort. "My bad. That's exactly what I meant."

We reach the lobby. Summer's heels click on the marble floor as she glides across it. The Heyward Plaza is hands down the fanciest hotel I've ever seen. I can't fathom that Summer might inherit it one day.

She smiles and waves at the concierge. "Evening, Thomas."

The white-haired man gives her a warm smile in return. "Evening, Miss Summer. Try not to cause too much trouble tonight, will you?"

I snicker under my breath.

"Thomas has worked here for more than twenty years," she explains as we enter another hallway that holds another elevator bank.

"Really?"

She nods. "I was a baby when he got hired, so he pretty much watched me grow up."

"Ah. So he's had a front-row seat to all your troublemaking."

"Oh yeah. My Greenwich friends and I used to sneak into the city and come to the hotel, and I thought I was bribing him to keep quiet by slipping him hundreds." She makes an outraged face. "And then I found out he was double-crossing me."

I snort. "Ratted you out to the parents, huh?"

"Every single time. But they never said a word. I didn't realize they knew about it until years later, after I left for college. My parents are really cool," she admits. "If I wanted to cut a day of school to go shopping with my friends, they didn't mind as long as I was safe and didn't make it a habit."

The elevator shows up, and we walk inside. Summer presses the button for the "Heather Ballroom." There are four other ballrooms on the list, all named after flowers. The Lily, the Rose, the Heather, and the Dahlia. Fancy.

The doors ding open, and we're met by a crescendo of noise—a symphony of glass clinking, high heels clacking on hardwood, the hum of conversation, laughter.

Summer links her arm through mine as we approach the massive arched doorway of the ballroom. Beyond it, I see elegantly dressed people milling around in an elegantly decorated room. The stage is set up for a live band, but they're not playing at the moment. Round tables with pristine tablecloths and ornate centerpieces are scattered on either side of the shiny dance floor. I don't see anyone eating actual meals, but the waiters thread their way through the crowd carrying trays of hors d'oeuvres.

This totally isn't my scene. A sea of gowns and tuxedos swells before me, fingers and earlobes and wrists sparkling and gleaming like the front window of a lighting store. And I thought Summer's diamond hairclip was flashy. I gape as I spot a middle-aged woman wearing ruby earrings that are so enormous, her earlobes are actually stretching due to their heft.

"Is that him?" Summer whispers in my ear.

"Yup." I'm not surprised that she's picked Kamal out of the crowd. Despite his small stature, he's got a big personality.

He holds court across the room near the largest of the three bars in the ballroom. Wild hand gestures and animated facial expressions accompany whatever long-winded anecdote he's regaling his audience with.

We stand there watching as his half-dozen admirers all burst into laughter. "Must be a great story," she remarks. "Or it's boring as fuck, and they're just sucking up to him because he's a gazilliotrillionaire."

I laugh. My girl has a way with words. Especially ones she makes up. "Could go either way."

"Well, let's say hello. He's the reason you're here, right?"

"Right."

Anxiety tickles my stomach as we approach the bar. The second he notices me, Kamal breaks off midsentence, his expression lighting up. He slaps the arm of the old dude beside him and says, "Gonna have to excuse me, brother. My guest has arrived." He disengages from the group and strides toward me. "You made it!"

"Thanks again for inviting—"

He's still talking, as he always does. "Was worried about you, man! Everyone else got here before the doors were even open, saw them lurking in the lobby like a bunch of creeps, but hey, better early than late, huh?" There's a bite to his last statement.

"You can blame me for our tardiness," Summer says sheepishly. "I held us up."

Kamal does a double take, as if he's suddenly realized I'm not alone. He scrutinizes Summer from head to toe, and there's nothing subtle about the way he does it. His eyes linger on her cleavage. They linger even longer on the diamonds in her hair.

"And who might you be?" he finally asks.

"I'm Summer." She extends one delicate hand. "Colin's girlfriend."

Kamal's eyebrows soar. He takes her hand, but rather than shake it, he brings it to his lips and kisses her knuckles. "Pleasure to meet you."

Her smile looks forced. "Likewise."

He releases her hand and turns to address me. "You never mentioned you had a girlfriend."

I shrug awkwardly. "Well. Yeah. It didn't exactly come up in the interview."

"No reason why it should have," Summer says lightly. "Job interviews are about the candidate's résumé, not their personal life. Right?"

"Right," Kamal echoes. Once again, his tone has a bite to it. And his expression is darkening by the second.

I can't figure out the source of his displeasure, but the longer he looks at Summer, the more his demeanor changes. I swear I see the corner of his mouth curl in a slight sneer. I guess the source is Summer? But I couldn't tell you why.

———————

"Is it just me, or is this really uncomfortable?" Summer hisses in my ear an hour later. She'd dragged me onto the dance floor and looped her arms around my neck, leaving me no choice but to rest my hands on her hips and pretend I know how to dance.

I understand her motivation, though—it was the only way to unglue ourselves from Kamal's side. He hasn't let us out of his sight since we arrived. That's not to say he hasn't been mingling. He has, only he's been dragging me and Summer along with him to every conversation. The other job hopefuls trail behind us like baby ducklings, and I feel bad for them because he isn't paying them a lick of attention. He seems utterly fascinated by Summer, yet at the same time I sense animosity rippling beneath the surface.

"It's not just you. He's acting strange."

"No, he's acting like a dick." She bites her lip. "I feel like he's judging us. I can't really explain it…" She trails off.

I know precisely what she means. I've felt it too.

The song ends before I'm ready, and panic jolts through me when the bluesy lead singer announces they're taking a ten minute break. Summer laces her fingers through mine as we walk to the edge of the dance floor.

"Don't hate me," she says, "but…I really have to pee."

I grip her hand. "Nope. You can't abandon me here with these people."

She giggles. "You say the word 'people' like it's a disease."

"People *are* a disease," I grumble.

"You can survive without me for five minutes." She kisses my cheek and then rubs her index finger over it, I suspect to wipe off the lipstick stain she left. "I'll be right back. Promise."

I watch in defeat as she saunters off. At the bar, I order a Sam Adams and a very efficient bartender in a white shirt and black tie hands me a bottle. "Thanks," I tell her.

I've barely taken a sip before Kamal appears. I'm surprised he didn't leech on to me the moment Summer and I stepped off the dance floor.

"That's some dress your girlfriend's wearing, Colin." He swishes the tumbler of bourbon he's holding. It's not the first one he's consumed tonight. I've seen him order at least three drinks since I got here, and who knows how many he ingested before that.

I make a noncommittal gesture, a cross between a shrug and a hand flutter, because accepting a compliment on Summer's behalf feels weird.

"Who are you?"

The question comes out of left field. I furrow my brow and search his expression, but I can't decipher it. "What do you mean?"

"What I mean is…" He throws back the rest of his drink and then slams the glass on the bar. "Another one," he barks at the bartender.

She flinches at his sharp tone. "Right away, sir."

"What I mean, Colin," he continues, as if the woman hadn't spoken, "is that I thought you were one of us." He gestures to the other three job candidates—two males, one female. All college-aged like me. "Neil, Ahmed, Robin. Me. You. The outcasts who turned to video games because of people like the girl you showed up with tonight."

My shoulders stiffen.

"All my life I've had to deal with those people. The pretty people." He accepts his fresh drink and takes several deep swigs. "The jocks and the cheerleaders and the popular assholes who think they're entitled to do whatever the fuck they want. They bully without consequences. They get everything handed to them on a silver platter. They float through life and expect everyone to step aside for them."

I set my untouched beer on the bar and speak in a measured tone. "I've never floated through anything. My mom's an ESL teacher, and my dad is a shift supervisor at a power plant. They work their asses of, and so do I. I spent all my free time in high school drawing and painting and playing video games. And playing hockey," I relent, even though I know it's a dirty word to him. "I play hockey because

I love it, and I'm good at it. Same way I'm good at game design," I finish with a shrug.

"You've got some real arrogance on you, kid." A flash of steel enters his eyes.

Summer chooses that unfortunate moment to return to the ballroom. She draws the attention of every person, male and female, as she struts across the shiny floor. She's stunning and nobody can look away. Everyone wants to be a part of that beauty, even if it's simply admiring her as she sashays past them.

It's her orbit.

That damn orbit.

Kamal slings back the rest of his drink. His disdain-heavy gaze never leaves Summer. "Look at her," he mutters. "You think she'd be with you if you weren't a jock? Bitches like her only want one thing, Colin." He laughs coldly. "I bet if I snapped my fingers and told her I was interested, she'd be on my dick faster than you can say *gold digger*. Why would she waste her time on some low-rent college athlete when she can have a billionaire, right?"

My lips thin. "You don't know her."

He chuckles.

Summer is halfway to us now. Her blonde hair catches the light of the huge crystal chandelier over our heads. Her diamond hairclip winks like a strobe with each step she takes.

"Trust me, I know her. Lordy, lordy, do I know her. All I do is date women like her. They don't give a shit about us, Colin. They're gone the moment a sweeter deal comes along."

I could argue, but what's the point? He's already made his assumptions about me and Summer, about what it means to be an athlete, a nerd, a pretty girl.

Summer reaches us, and she must glimpse something in my expression that worries her, because she takes my hand and gives it a comforting squeeze. "Everything okay?"

"Why wouldn't it be?" Kamal guffaws, before tapping the bar to signal the bartender. He smacks it again and again and again, like a bratty kid trying to get his mom's attention. "Bourbon," he snaps at the harried woman. He turns back to us. "So what's your major?" he asks Summer.

She blinks at the sudden change of topic. "Fashion—"

He interrupts before she's done speaking. "Of course it's fashion." Scorn drips from every word.

"You got a problem with fashion?" she asks lightly, but I can tell from her rigid posture that she's on guard. She manages a teasing laugh. "Because as far as I can tell, you sure do enjoy the company of models."

He doesn't laugh back. "I see. Someone like me can't date beautiful women? Is that what you're insinuating?"

"Not at all. And clearly you *can* date beautiful women, because you—"

"They're only with me for my money? Is that what you think?"

"Of course not. I just—"

"Of course you would think that," he snaps. His cheeks are slowly reddening. "And guess what, you're right. That *is* the only thing pretty bitches like you are after—money. You won't be signing any prenups, will you, Summer? No, no, no, bitches like you need to be taken care of. You need to spend all my hard-earned cash."

I move closer to Summer in a protective gesture. "That's enough," I say in a low voice. He keeps throwing the word *bitch* around, and loudly. I suspect he's talking about one specific woman—the girl from college who wouldn't sign his prenuptial agreement. But I don't give a shit if he had his heart broken by the Queen of fucking England. Nobody talks to or about Summer like that.

Kamal isn't intimidated by the menacing command. He laughs again. A high-pitched sound that grates on my nerves. "It's enough when I say it's enough." He tosses back the last of his bourbon and then tries to place the empty tumbler on the bar. Except he's about a foot away from it, because he's drunk as a skunk and lacking all coordination. So he sets the glass down—on nothing.

It crashes to the floor and shatters. Glass shards shoot in all directions, and I quickly pull Summer away from the mess. I look at the bartender. "Could you please call someone to come and—"

"Oh, they'll come!" Kamal hoots. "Someone always comes to clean up my messes. Wanna know why, Colin? Summer? Hazard a guess?" He starts cackling to himself. "Because I'm a billionaire! I'm a fucking god in the tech industry and I can buy and sell everyone in this fucking room! I—"

"You're drunk," I coldly interrupt.

"Oh, shut up, you dumb jock." He's so sloshed, he's rocking on his feet, but when I reach out to try and steady him, he slaps my hand away. "Fuck off. I don't need your help. And I don't need you working for my company. You got that? The position's been filled, Colin." He chortles again. "Thank you for your interest."

Summer takes a menacing step toward him. "What's the matter, Mr. Jain? You won't hire Colin because, what? He plays hockey and is better-looking than you?"

He takes a step back. Glass crunches beneath his expensive leather shoes. From the corner of my eye, I see several figures approaching. All around us, people are staring. Their curious gazes pierce into me. My spine won't stop prickling.

"Ms. Heyward, are you all right?" A tall, bulky man in a black suit and tie appears in front of us.

I have no idea who he is, but Summer does. She gratefully touches his arm. "I'm fine, Diego. But there's broken glass all over the floor. Could you ask maintenance to send someone ASAP?"

"Right away." He flicks a wary look at Kamal.

Kamal's busy staring at Summer. "Heyward?" he echoes. He furrows and unfurrows his brow, repeatedly. "Who the fuck are you?"

"Watch your language, Mr. Jain," barks Diego.

"Who the fuck are *you*?" is the retort.

"I'm the head of security at this hotel," the beefy man replies, baring his teeth in the scariest smile I've ever seen. "The hotel that Ms. Heyward's family happens to own. And I do believe it's time for you to retire for the evening, Mr. Jain. Why don't I have one of my associates escort you to your suite?"

"Fuck you. I'm giving a fucking speech in ten fucking minutes." He looks over at me and starts to laugh in loud, nasally snorts. "Well, good for you, Colin. Here I thought she was the gold digger, riding your big cock for your jock money, but you're the gold digger, eh? Digging for gold in her heiress pussy."

Summer flinches.

Diego steps forward.

Me, I sadly shake my head and meet Kamal's glazed eyes. "It's a really depressing world you live in, man. This world where everybody's a gold digger, where everybody's using each other, or competing against each other. This world where two people can't be together because they might love each other." I chuckle darkly. "Honestly? I'm glad you're not giving me the job. I'd rather be out on the street than work for someone like you. I don't even want to know what kind of toxic working environment you create for your employees."

I think Kamal tries to keep arguing, but I tune him out. Besides, Diego and his "associates" are prompt in escorting the drunk and belligerent billionaire out of the Heather Ballroom. I don't know what that means for the leukemia fundraising, but as much as I support the cause, I don't care to stay a second longer at this stuffy, shitty event.

In unspoken agreement, Summer and I leave the ballroom. I can tell she's upset because her teeth are digging into her bottom lip, but she doesn't say a word. Not a single word, at least not until we're riding the private elevator up to the penthouse.

The moment the doors ding open, Summer fixes me with a miserable look and says, "I'm breaking up with you."

# 29

# FITZ

I GAPE AT HER SLENDER BACK AS SHE STALKS OUT OF THE ELEVATOR and into the marble-laden foyer.

Did she just say she's *breaking up* with me?

"Like hell you are!" I roar.

Her stilettos echo loudly on the marble, and she stops to kick them off. I take advantage of the brief pause in her strides by charging forward to grab her arm. "Summer. What the hell."

She doesn't answer. Shrugging my hand off, she sets her small silver clutch on the mahogany credenza. Then she removes the clip from her hair. Somehow the hairstyle stays intact, and I realize it's being held up by a dozen tiny pins. She starts taking the pins out, one by one, as I watch in astonishment. She won't even look at me.

"What the hell is going on?" I demand.

Finally, she meets my confused eyes. "I cost you that job."

I blink. "What?"

"You didn't get the job because of me," she mutters. "Obviously that jackass had a bad experience with a pretty girl who turned him down."

"I'm sure he did, but I guarantee he also had a bad experience with some jock who beat him up. This had nothing to do with you."

"It had everything to do with me. You heard the way he was talking to me! The night would've gone smoothly if I hadn't come with you. But that's what happens when I go places, Fitz. I attract drama. I don't mean to, but it just frigging happens." She puffs out a bleak breath. "You hate drama and you hate attention and you just had an entire ballroom full of people staring at you because of me, because you were defending me. And the same thing happened at Malone's last month."

I rub the bridge of my nose. What the hell is she talking about? I defended her—and *myself*—because Kamal was out of line. I say as much, but she stubbornly shakes her head.

"I'm not doing this anymore, okay, Fitz? You prefer to remain invisible. Well, look what happened down there—the most visible thing ever!"

She's right. When Kamal had been screaming and cackling and acting like an overall jackass, I'd felt as if there were a bright spotlight shining on me. I'd sensed the nosy stares and heard the hushed whispers.

But when I told him off, I didn't care that the whole room was watching and listening. I only cared that Kamal was being rude to Summer, and that was unacceptable to me.

"Do you really want to talk about drama?" I ask her. "Because you're being a drama queen right now, babe."

"I am not."

"Yes, you are. You're overreacting. Going from zero to breakup without even talking about it."

"There's nothing to talk about. You don't want to be in the spotlight. I invite it. Sometimes intentionally, but most times not." She makes a frustrated noise. "That job was important to you."

"It was." *But you're more important.* I don't say it out loud. Not because keeping my emotions under lock and key is a habit of mine, but because Summer is marching off again, heading for the winding staircase that leads upstairs. The penthouse has three floors—don't get me started—and her bedroom is on the third.

I hurry after her. "Stop," I command.

"No." She keeps going.

"You're such a brat."

"You're such a bully," she retorts. "I want to be alone. We're broken up."

"We're not broken up!" I yell.

Jesus, I don't think I've raised my voice more than ten times my entire *life*, and now a couple of months with Summer and I'm on my way to yelling myself hoarse. She brings out a growly, primal side of me I hadn't known existed until she showed up and started driving me batshit crazy.

And...I frickin' love it.

I've spent years fighting so hard to avoid conflict. I let my folks spew their poison about each other because it's easier than the arguments and guilt trips that ensue if I try to make them see the light. I avoid social situations because I don't want any attention on me.

I date chicks who are as introverted as I am, because then they don't expect me to cut loose at parties or attend extravagant events like leukemia charity galas.

I didn't mind that existence. It's been nice and comfortable. Conflict-free.

But I never felt truly alive until Summer.

I don't want to be with a woman who hides in the shadows with me, because that enables *me* to keep hiding. And that's what I've done for years—hidden pieces of myself from my parents, my friends, chicks, the world. I want someone who encourages me to step out of my comfort zone, and Summer is that someone.

She drives me nuts. She does crazy shit like pull a girl's hair at a bar for calling her a slut. She feels up half-naked football players in our living room. She does cute little ballet jumps when she's making breakfast in our kitchen.

And yes, she makes me lose my temper sometimes, but I make her lose hers.

It's part of the fun.

"I'm going upstairs, Fitz. You can sleep on the couch or in Dean's room or any of the other rooms. But not mine, because we're broken up."

"Say that one more time. I fucking dare you."

She stops at the foot of the staircase and turns around. Her green eyes glitter with fortitude. "We're brok—"

I lunge forward.

She throws up her hands. "Don't you dare!"

Yeah, that's not gonna happen. I grab her by the waist and heave her wriggling body over my shoulder, clamping a hand over her ass. "We're going to sit down and talk about this," I growl, spinning toward the living room.

"There's nothing to talk about! Put me down!" She manages to wrench herself free, her bare feet slapping the marble floor when they make contact with it.

"Would you listen to me? We're not breaking up. It's not happening, Summer. I don't give a shit about the job at Orcus Games. I give a shit about *you*. That bastard was rude to you. He was rude to both of us, and I refuse to work for someone who treats people with disrespect or behaves that way in public. I put him in his place, and if I had the choice, I'd do it all over again, you hear me? Because he was a jackass to you, and I love you."

Summer's breath catches. "That's..." She gulps. "That's the first time you've ever said that."

"Well, it's true. I love you. You're my girlfriend—"

"Was your girlfriend."

"Are."

"Was."

I wrap my arms around her waist and tug her against me. When she gasps, I know she feels the erection pressing into her belly. "You can argue till you're blue in the face, but we both know we're not breaking up." My hand slides under her dress to caress her smooth thigh. "And we both know you love me too."

Her eyes narrow as she studies my face. "You're different."

She's right. I am. My patience is thin, and my nerves are shot. I'm still pissed at Kamal. Still pissed at Summer. Yet at the same time, I want to fuck her like I've never wanted to fuck her before.

Groaning softly, I cup the warm heaven between her legs. When I encounter her bare pussy, I shudder with desire. "You weren't wearing panties this entire time?" I croak.

"No. This dress can't handle panty lines. I'd never do that to Vera."

"Who's Ve—You know what, forget it."

"Fitz." She swallows again. "I'm sorry I cost you the job."

I shake my head at her. "You still don't get it, do you? You didn't cost me a job. Kamal Jain cost himself an employee. I'm a good designer. I'll find something else, I promise. But I'll never find another you."

Her lips part in wonder. "That's the sweetest thing you've ever said to me."

"I can be sweet when I want to." My knuckles graze her clit. "But right now, I'm feeling dirty." I slip a finger inside her. "Spread your legs so I can screw you against the wall."

Her jaw falls open at the wicked demand. "Oh my God. You're in a mood tonight."

"Yeah, I am. So for chrissake, stop trying to break up with me. Stop worrying about this job. Just stop and kiss me."

When my mouth covers hers, she finally quits arguing and kisses me back with a level of passion that steals my breath. I grind against her, but it's not enough. My aching cock is straining behind my zipper, and I'm too primed for foreplay.

"I just need to be inside you," I whisper in her ear. "I'll make you feel good later. Promise."

"You make me feel good always," she whispers back, and damned if my heart doesn't beat a little bit faster.

Thanks to Summer, I always keep a condom in my pocket these

days, no matter the occasion. I don't bother dropping my trousers. I unzip, pull out my cock, cover it up. Then I yank Summer's dress up, lift one of her long legs to my hip, and with one deep stroke I bury myself inside her.

"Oh my *God*," she moans.

The heat of her surrounds me, her inner muscles clamping around my dick as if to trap it in place. My skin is on fire. My heart beats in a sharp staccato against my ribcage. I'm hot and hard and in desperate need of release.

There's nothing graceful about the pounding I give her. The wall behind her shakes and the credenza rattles as I fuck her standing up. Her legs snake around my waist and she's so wet and tight I can't think straight. I can't stop the freight train of pleasure that slams into me without warning. I bury my face in the crook of her neck and tremble against her body, coming hard enough to see stars.

"Fuck yes," I grunt against her neck.

My hips keep rocking for several moments before going still. I know she didn't come, but I already promised I'd make it up to her. My knees start to wobble, but still I don't move.

"You feel so good," I mumble. "I never want to leave you—"

*Ding.*

We both jolt in surprise when the elevator doors slide open. The next thing I hear is, *"What the fuck!"*

It's Dean.

As in Summer's brother Dean.

As in my good friend Dean.

*How is this happening again?*

"How is this happening again!" Summer cries in embarrassment.

I honestly don't know. This is the second time someone's walked in on us while I've been lodged deep inside her. But this is a million times worse because it's her *brother*. I'm about to turn around when I realize that if I do, Dean will see my dick flapping in the wind and know where it was a second before.

"I'm gonna kick your ass, Fitzgerald!"

"Dean," Summer begs, burying her face against my chest. "Turn around. Please."

"Oh my fucking God. Are you having sex?" he thunders. "Right here?!"

"Dean! Turn around!"

He has the decency to obey her, but sounds utterly furious as he snarls, "Get your shit together and meet me in the living room. I'm walking past you guys right now, and I'm not looking, okay? Jesus fuck, I'm not looking."

My peripheral vision catches him stalking by, holding one hand to his face as a blinder. The moment he disappears, we snap into action. I pull out. Summer takes the condom and ducks into the nearby powder room. A toilet flushes, and then she returns and we reluctantly walk into the living room like two teenagers who just—

*Got caught having sex?*

Yup. Exactly like that.

When we're seated on the couch, Dean looms over us, arms crossed. "How long has this been going on?" he asks sternly.

I choke down a laugh. Hearing Dean (whose nickname in college was 'Dean the Sex Machine,' for chrissake) put on a Puritan tone and glare in disapproval is the ultimate irony. But I know this whole big-brother posturing is coming from a place of genuine concern. He adores his sister.

"A while," Summer admits.

"Uh-huh." He scowls at her. "Oh, and a heads-up? Next time you're trying to hide something from me, maybe don't post a pic on social media?"

She rolls her eyes. "I wasn't trying to hide it from you."

He's outraged. "So you *wanted* me to find out on social media?"

"No, you didn't even cross my mind. Fitzy and I went to a party. I took a picture of us together. I posted it on Insta. Nowhere in that chain of events did I think about you. Wanna know why? Because it had nothing to do with you."

"It has *everything* to do with me!" he fires back.

Ah. Now I know where she gets the drama-llama from.

Dean's murderous glare whips toward me. "This is my little sister, man!"

"I know," I answer calmly. "And I care about her a lot."

"Yeah, Dicky," Summer chimes in. "This isn't just sex between us, okay? I mean, we are having sex, lots of it, but—"

Dean drops his head in his hands. "Why, Boogers? Why do you have to say stuff like that?"

She huffs. "So you're allowed to talk about your sex life with me, but I can't talk about mine with you?"

"I never talk about my sex life with you! It's a taboo topic! Taboo!" He lets out a groan thick with aggravation. Then he inhales slowly. His gaze shifts between us. "That's it? You guys are together now?"

I look at Summer, who fifteen minutes ago was threatening to break up with me. No, not even threatening—she *did* break up with me. I just wouldn't allow it.

Her mouth hitches up in a rueful smile. "We're together," she confirms. "Colin is my boyfriend."

I bite the inside of my cheek to keep from laughing. The resignation in her tone is kinda adorable.

Dean gives a slow nod as he carefully studies my face. "So you're with my sister? You're my sister's boyfriend?" He sounds as resigned as Summer.

I swallow a sigh, because I know exactly where this is going. "Yes."

"Okay, then." He rakes one hand through his blond hair. "You ready?"

My sigh slips out. "Let's get it over with."

Summer's head swivels from me to Dean, confusion swimming in her expression. "What are you guys talking about?"

Dean gets to his feet. So do I.

"Sorry, Boogers. It needs to be done."

"Needs to be done," I echo guiltily.

When Dean cracks the knuckles of his right hand, understanding dawns in his sister's eyes. "You're going to hit him?" she exclaims, jumping to her feet. "What the hell! No way!"

"Fitz knows the code. He didn't follow it. Therefore…"

Dean's right. There is a code. Other teams might have rules about not dating a teammate's sister or ex or whoever else is off-limits, but our team never strictly adhered to anything like that. Our rule was much simpler—ask before you go there.

Even if the other guy says *hell no*, you could probably do what you want anyway, since there's no way for him to enforce anything. But that's not what the code is about. It's about respecting your teammate.

Dean cracks the knuckles of his left hand.

"You're insane. Don't you touch him, Dicky!"

She tries to throw herself between us, but I gently move her to the side. "Just let it happen," I tell her. "It's really not a big de—"

The fucker doesn't throw a punch.

He knees me in the balls.

I drop like a stone, stars flashing in my field of vision as the pain twists my gut. I curl over and grip my junk, trying to catch my breath. "Jackass," I croak, staring accusingly up at Dean.

"Dicky! Why would you go for his balls! We need them to make your future nieces and nephews!"

"Nieces and nephews plural? How many kids you planning on having?"

"A lot!"

"You're not allowed to get pregnant until you're at least thirty. I'm not ready to be an uncle."

"Oh my God. Life isn't always about you!"

They stand there bickering as if I'm not bent in half on the marble floor, gasping for air. "I'm not having kids with you," I wheeze at Summer. "I don't want to be part of your insane family."

"Oh hush, sweetie. It's too late. I've become attached."

You'd think it would be impossible to laugh while I'm writhing on the floor in agony.

But Summer Heyward-Di Laurentis makes everything possible.

# 30
# SUMMER

My last check-in with Erik Laurie takes place the Monday before the fashion show. I would've liked to talk to him after our History of Fashion lecture this morning, but he had a line of students waiting to speak to him. So I killed two hours on campus and then walked over to his office during his official hours.

I hate meeting in his office. I find he's always extra smarmy behind closed doors. He's already winked about four times, made one flirty comment about how I should walk in my own show, and now his hand grazes mine (intentionally, I suspect) as he passes me the schedule for Friday night. It's the equivalent of a band's set list, with the names of each student designer and the order in which they'll be debuting their lines.

A glance at the schedule reveals that Summer Lovin' is opening the show. Crap. I would've preferred to be somewhere in the middle of the pack. Opening a fashion show is a lot of pressure.

"I want us to start the night with a bang," he tells me, winking again. "Your swimsuits will do that, I suspect."

Ew. Why does he say things like that? Paired with the sleazy wink, his words make my skin crawl.

"Whatever you think is best." I paste on a cheerful smile. "So we're all set?" I want nothing more than to leave this man's office.

He smiles back. "All set."

Relief floods my belly. I hop to my feet and pick up my Prada tote. My head is down as I tuck the schedule into my bag, so I don't see Laurie round his desk. When I lift my head, he's standing about a foot away from me. Which is a foot too close.

I hastily take a step back. "Anyway, I'll see you Wednesday." We're having another lecture this week so he can return our midterms and discuss the final paper. "I'm excited to get my midterm—"

"How long are we going to keep fighting this?"

I blink, and he's no longer one foot away. It's a mere inch now. And his long fingers are caressing my cheek, unleashing a flurry of shivers—and not the good kind. I'm too stunned to push his hand away, and my brain is still stuck on the throaty question he'd voiced.

Keep fighting this? Is he for real? Does he think his pervy feelings are reciprocated? That we've been engaged in some forbidden love affair this entire semester?

"Summer," he says thickly, and I don't miss the flare of passion in his eyes.

I gulp. Hard. And then I lick my lips, because they're suddenly so dry that they're sticking together, and I need them to *un*stick if I'm going to get any words out.

Only, Laurie mistakes the lip-licking for a green light. To my horror, his head dips toward me, his mouth nearly landing on mine before I plant both hands on his chest and forcibly push him away.

"I'm sorry," I blurt out. "I don't know what you think is going on here, but…" My hands shake wildly as I shove my purse strap over my shoulder. "I have a boyfriend."

*And even if I didn't, I wouldn't kiss you if my life depended on it, you sleazy slime bag.*

*Hear, hear!* Selena agrees.

Laurie smooths out the lapel of his pinstriped blazer. "I see," he says tightly.

"Yeah, I'm sorry—" Why am I apologizing? I take a breath and remind myself that I have nothing to be sorry for. And that

I shouldn't have to use a boyfriend as an excuse. "But even if my boyfriend wasn't in the picture, I still wouldn't be interested. It would be inappropriate—" *Stop it, Summer! Again with the excuses?* Anger builds in my gut. Why do we do this as women? Why do we feel the need to justify why we don't like someone? "I'm also not interested in you that way," I finish firmly. There. No more excuses.

His jaw clamps tight. His eyes burn with something I can't decipher. It's not quite anger. Definitely not hurt or shame.

I think it might be betrayal.

"I'm sorry if I led you to believe otherwise," I add, even though I'm confident I didn't send him any signals to indicate I wanted him sexually.

One eyebrow arches slightly. "Are you done?" he asks in a tone cold enough to refreeze the snow that's recently begun to melt beyond his windows.

"I guess so," I mutter.

"Then I'll see you in class, Summer."

I leave the office, and the door shuts behind me. Not a slam, but he definitely closes it harder than necessary. I stand in the hallway for a moment, stunned by what just happened. I snap out of my trance when my phone vibrates with an incoming text.

> **FITZ:** At the computer lab working on code. Break time. Wanna meet for lunch?
> **ME:** Sorry, bb. About to walk into meeting with my advisor. See you at home xoxo

I'm not sure why I lie to him. I just don't think I can see him while my stomach continues to burn with humiliation. I'm suddenly questioning every discussion in class, when Laurie would nod in agreement at something I'd said, or praise me for a particular observation. Was it all bullshit? Just him pretending that he found me intelligent and insightful so he could get into my pants?

*Of course he was pretending, you idiot. On what planet does any professor think you're intelligent?*

I bite my lip to keep from crying. I want to tell my inner critic to fuck off, but I'm too distraught. And there's no way I'm telling Fitz what happened. He'll lose his shit if he finds out Laurie tried to kiss me. He'll probably hunt the professor down and try to throw down, and that won't help the situation in the slightest.

It's over now. Laurie made a move, I turned him down. I'll tell Fitz about it eventually.

Right now, I want to forget it ever happened.

But that's easier said than done, especially when it becomes apparent that Laurie doesn't want me to forget.

When he strides into the lecture hall on Wednesday, his gaze seeks out mine almost immediately, and the ice in his eyes sends a chill up my spine. Then he breaks the eye contact and greets the rest of the class with a broad smile.

"Guess what day it is, boys and girls!"

Titters ripple through the room, mostly from the females. In the row ahead of me, Nora whispers something to one of her friends, and they both giggle. She's actually backed off these past few weeks, her dirty looks and combative remarks slowly abating. I think she's accepted that I'm Laurie's "pet" and that no amount of Chanel-bashing is going to make him hate me.

I should give her a heads-up that all it takes to invite Erik Laurie's hatred is not allowing him to shove his tongue in your mouth.

"As you know, I'll be returning your midterms today."

There are excited whispers, intermingled with some groans and worried voices.

"Don't worry, for the most part you all turned in some excellent work. Many interesting papers in the bunch. Miss Ridgeway, yours in particular was a fascinating read."

Nora's head snaps up in shock. This is the first time he's singled her out to praise her. I can't see her face, but I imagine she's probably blushing happily.

"With that said," he continues, "I did notice that some of you had issues with the basic tenets of essay writing, such as how to correctly cite a source or organize a paragraph. I thought perhaps a tutorial is in order."

He snaps open his briefcase and removes a laptop that he sets up on the table near his lecture podium. "Now, I've found that sometimes in order to teach a student how to do something correctly, it's useful to show them what an *incorrect* version looks like. So we're going to dissect two papers, each of which earned a D-minus, and we're going to examine why that was." He winks. "Don't worry, these are midterms from a fashion history course I taught at UCLA a couple of years ago. I tend to reuse the same essay topics. I blame laziness."

That gets him more laughs.

He bends over his computer. "Let's start with this paper on the evolution of New York fashion."

I freeze.

That's got to be a coincidence, right? He *just* said he tends to assign the same topics. Anxiety roils in my stomach as I wait for the essay to appear on the projection screen.

And then it does, and the sick feeling shoots up to my throat, and I almost choke on bile.

A cover page fills the screen for about half a second before Laurie quickly scrolls to the first page.

But half a second is all it takes for me to make out my name on the cover sheet. The date underneath clearly indicates it was written and submitted this semester. UCLA, my ass.

And I'm not the only one who caught it. Ben, my bushy eyebrowed row-mate, shoots me a weird look. Nora twists around to frown at me before facing the front again.

"As you can see, the student had many issues with basic essay structure. Take a look at her thesis—she's very clearly told us what she plans to discuss in the essay and in what order. And yet the paragraph that follows doesn't follow this blueprint…"

And on and on he drones, picking apart the paper I'd spent the last two months slaving over. Crying over. My cheeks get hotter and hotter with each passing second. My stomach gets queasier and queasier. My classmates *saw* my name on that cover page. Or at least most of them did. They know I wrote it. Laurie did this on purpose, and he's winking and smirking and having a frigging ball down there as he dissects my work.

"As you can see, the student had all the bones, but none of the meat, if you will."

Nora snickers. Ben gives me a sympathetic look.

I desperately try not to cry. I glue my gaze to my hands, which are clasped in my lap. I don't want Laurie to know how close I am to tears. I refuse to let him see that his humiliation ploy worked.

The smug bastard is now pointing out a spelling error I'd missed when I was proofreading. Fitz missed it too.

"This isn't kindergarten. This is an Ivy League university. Spelling matters, children."

I shoot to my feet. I'm done. I've had enough. My hands shake like branches in a windstorm as I gather up my stuff and hurry to the aisle.

Laurie is still talking when I push open the doors and flee the lecture hall. I'm halfway down the hall when someone calls my name.

"Summer, wait." Ben rushes over to me, concern etched into his face. "Are you all right?"

"Not really." I gulp repeatedly, once again trying to suppress the tears.

"That's really fucking shady what Laurie's doing in there," Ben says flatly.

"Tell me about it."

"You need to report this to the department head."

"And say what?" I ask in a sardonic tone. "'Hey, I got a D-minus on my midterm. Fire the professor.'"

"No, but you can tell them that he humiliated you in front of your peers and implied that you're an incompetent writer and—"

"I'm sorry," I cut in, because I'm barely holding on by a thread here. "But I have to go."

"Summer."

"Ben, please. Just drop this." I gesture to the doors. "Go back inside and wait for your midterm. I bet you did great."

"Summer." He shakes his head angrily. "This isn't fair."

"Life isn't fair." My voice cracks. "But I appreciate you coming out here to check on me. I really do. You're a good guy, Ben. Thank you."

I squeeze his arm and then walk away.

---

At home, I find Fitz at his desk. He's wearing his headphones and tapping on the game controller that plugs into his computer. Or I think it plugs into it. I don't really understand his gaming system. He tried to explain it to me once, but I've already forgotten.

I pluck his earphones off, causing a startled Fitz to swivel in his padded chair. "Fuck, you scared me, babe." When he sees the look on my face, concern fills his eyes. "What's wrong?"

I inhale a slow, even breath. "I need to ask you something, and you have to promise to be honest with me."

"Okay…" His expression grows wary.

"Was my essay a piece of shit?"

"What?" He scrapes both hands over his face, clearly confused. "You mean the fashion essay? About New York and the first half of the twentieth century?"

I nod. "You told me I did a good job on it," I say shakily.

"You did a great job."

I search his expression and find nothing deceitful about it. And his voice is nothing but sincere. "Do you really believe that, or are you only saying it because we're dating?"

"Summer, if I thought your midterm sucked or that something about it was highly problematic, I would have told you," he says firmly. "And I would have offered to help you fix it. I don't see the point in lying about stuff like that."

I sink onto the edge of his bed. Once again, my eyes begin stinging, but this time I can't control a few teardrops from popping out and sliding down my cheeks.

Fitz is on his feet in a heartbeat. He kneels in front of me and places his big hands on my thighs. "Talk to me," he urges thickly. "What's going on?"

"I got a D-minus on the midterm."

That startles him. "For real?"

I nod slowly.

The surprise on his face slowly transforms into skepticism. "But that's practically a fail."

"I know," I moan, and as the tears continue to fall, I tell him everything that happened in class today. And then, since I'm already confessing humiliating things, I also reveal what happened in Laurie's office.

Fitz's eyes blaze. "That motherfucker. And now he's punishing you because you didn't want to sleep with him?"

I swipe at my wet eyes. "I don't know. Maybe I really did deserve a D."

"Bullshit. That was not a D paper, Summer. I'm sorry. I don't claim to be some essay-writing genius, but if I was a TA, I would've given you a B. *Maybe* a B-minus if I was being nitpicky about grammar, or a C if I was just in a bad mood that day. But a D-minus is total bull. He's absolutely punishing you." He angrily shakes his head. "You need to appeal the grade."

His confidence in my midterm dries my tears. "Can I do that?"

"I'm not sure how the Fashion department does it, but there's definitely an appeal process at this college and you need to take advantage of it." He cups my cheeks with both hands, sweeping his thumbs over my jawline. "You can't let him get away with this. You do *not* deserve that grade, babe."

*But what if you do?* my inner critic counters. *You're not exactly the brightest bulb in the—*

*Shut up,* I interrupt, mentally bitch-slapping the negative part of my brain that's been tormenting me for years. *Just. Shut. Up.*

I'm not going to listen to the critic. I'm going to listen to Fitz, who sounds so adamant that I did a good job on the paper.

And his faith in me steals the breath from my lungs. I throw my arms around him and hug him tightly. "I love you," I whisper. "You make me feel..." I pause to think it over. "Smart."

His husky laughter tickles the top of my head. "Smart, huh?" He runs his hands up and down my back before tightening his hold on me.

"Yes." I smile against the warm column of his neck, breathing in his familiar masculine scent. "I didn't appeal the plagiarism paper at Brown because I thought nobody would believe that I didn't intentionally cheat. But I should have done it. I didn't deserve to fail—I deserved extra help." I steel my jaw. "Because I have a learning disorder."

I tip my head to find Fitz gazing at me with pride in his eyes.

"I'm not stupid," I tell him, and for once, my inner critic remains silent. "I just learn differently. I worked my ass off on that midterm, and maybe there were a few run-on sentences and a paragraph or two that I could've rearranged. And fine, there was *one* spelling error—but come on, do you expect me to believe that not a single other person in the class had so much as a typo?" I jut my chin. "I'm appealing this shit."

"Damn right you are. Laurie can eat a dick."

"Damn right he can." I run my fingers over the stubble dotting his strong jaw. "Thank you for making me feel better about all this."

"Hey, it's my job as your boyfriend to make you feel better." Fitz's lips brush over mine in a reassuring kiss. "Don't worry, babe. You're going to appeal the grade, and the college will overturn it because it'll be clear that Laurie is a vengeful asshole. It's going to be fine." He kisses me again. "I promise."

# 31
# FITZ

Due to a scheduling conflict with the Arbor House, our venue in Hastings, tomorrow's junior fashion show will now be held at 7 p.m., rather than 9 p.m. We apologize to ticketholders for any inconvenience this may cause.

"CAN. YOU. FRIGGING. BELIEVE. THIS."

Rage twists Summer's beautiful features into something dark and primal. She looks as if she's prepared to drive to Erik Laurie's home and strangle him with her bare hands.

I don't blame her.

"A scheduling conflict?" she screeches. "The day before the event? He did this on purpose. He's trying to fuck me, literally *and* figuratively."

I don't laugh, because I'm furious on her behalf. When she'd emailed Laurie reminding him that half her models won't be available until this earlier show is well underway, she'd gotten a cold response stating that she'd simply have to redo the independent study next year.

Which is a slap in the face after she'd worked her ass off all semester.

"Are you sure he knew that Rex and the guys wouldn't be available until eight?"

"He knew," she says tightly. "I mentioned it several times during our check-ins. He wanted me to open the show, and I told him I'd prefer a later slot to give the football guys time to regroup after their retreat. Plus, it's a lot of pressure to go first."

"Can you go over his head?" I ask.

"To who? My academic advisor? Richmond can't stand me. And he's in love with Laurie."

"Maybe he'll see reason. It's not like you didn't do any of the work. You still have six models."

"I told all this to Laurie," she reminds me. She tosses me her phone.

I read over their email exchange again. After his rude reply, Summer pleaded her case, saying she has six models ready to walk in the show, and asking if she could simply not show the men's line. Laurie tells her that either all twelve models need to be there, or none of them. He once again reiterates that she will need to repeat the independent study.

Spiteful bastard.

"What am I going to do?" Her expression is dismayed, but she's not crying, which tells me she hasn't admitted defeat yet.

"There's gotta be a solution. You talked to Rex—there's no way they can make it back early?"

"Nope. Coach Deluca has them on lockdown. Apparently this hippie-dippie retreat is in the middle of the woods, miles from civilization. The bus doesn't collect them until five. They'll get back a couple hours after that."

I think it over. "Okay. So we've got six dude bathing suits."

"Eight. Rex and Lockett were going to walk twice."

"But you only need six bodies."

"Yes, but..." She shakes her head in frustration. "The suits are tailored for these bodies. That's why we had fittings."

"But," I counter, "we have their measurements, and I'm sure we could find guys who generally fit those measurements."

"Where are you going with this?"

*Yeah, where are you going with this?* a little voice squawks.

I exhale slowly. "We'll do it."

Her brows soar. "We?"

"Well, they," I amend. "I'm going to recruit my teammates." I'm already swiping my phone off my desk. "Hollis will definitely be on board, you know what a showoff he is. Hunter—" I stop. No, Hunter's out. He's barely spoken a word to us in weeks. "Nate, I can see saying yes." I scroll through my messages list. "We need someone a bit slimmer to replace Lockett."

"Jesse!" Summer suggests.

"If Katie lets him." I bypass Jesse's name and search for his girlfriend's. "Know what? I'll just text Katie directly. She wears the pants in that relationship."

"True." She purses her lips. "But who's going to fill in for Rex? Please don't get mad at me, but…he's got a huge package."

I close my eyes briefly. "Seriously? No guy wants to hear his girlfriend say that, Summer."

"I told you not to get mad," she protests. "Anyway, don't worry. He's not much bigger than you. You're almost the same—" Her eyes light up like it's Christmas morning.

"No way," I growl, reading her mind. "I'm recruiting for you, not volunteering as tribute." The thought of sashaying down a runway while a crowd of people stare at me makes me want to vomit.

"Fine. Then you'll need to poll your teammates about their penis sizes. Try to find me a big one."

I fight hard to contain my laughter. God. This girl.

"I'll see what I can do," I promise.

---

The good thing about not having a game the following night is that, in theory, most of my teammates should be available.

The bad thing about not having a game tonight is that nearly all of them already have plans. Half the guys went to a strip club in Boston. A few others don't pick up their phones. A couple of them consult their girlfriends, who say no fucking way.

Katie, luckily, is not one of them. She loosens the reins and gives Jesse permission to do it. Hollis, as always, is more than happy to help. It took some arm-twisting to get Nate and Matt on board, until Summer promised that the after-party would be teeming with hot sorority girls. The French-Canadian on our team, Pierre, is a huge, hairy fellow who's about the same size as the huge, hairy tight end, Bibby.

In twenty-four hours, I've scraped together five bodies.

I've yet to find a replacement for Rex, he of the big package.

In my desk chair, I glance down at my own crotch. I never thought I'd see the day where I'd be cursing the generous size of my cock. But I'm running out of both options and time. Summer left for the venue an hour ago to help with setup. She also signed up for cleanup, though apparently she agreed to this before Erik Laurie tried to stick his tongue in her mouth.

She emailed Laurie this morning telling him she's found replacements for her male models.

I desperately don't want to let her down, but I'm not sure who else to call. My gamer friends aren't exactly model material. Morris, Ray, Kenji…they're all short and scrawny, not to mention complete introverts.

I'm scanning my brain for other candidates when my phone rings. *Private caller.* I waste no time answering, because I'd told my friends that if they know anyone who'd be interested, to please pass my number along.

But when I answer the call, I'm hit with a sense of déjà vu. "Please hold for Kamal Jain."

Seriously? Why is he calling me? I haven't heard from him (nor wanted to) since our showdown at the Heyward Plaza last week.

"Colin!" he barks in my ear. "I hope I caught you at a good time! Would've called during business hours, but I was in meetings until six."

His rapid manner of speaking irritates me tonight. "What do you need, Mr. Jain?" I ask, unable to stop from being curt.

"We've been through this! Please call me KJ or—"

"No," I interrupt. "I'm not going through this song and dance again. Tell me what you want, otherwise I'm hanging up."

Silence crashes over the line.

I can't believe I just snapped at a billionaire.

I don't think he can believe it either. But when he speaks again, his tone is completely stripped of its usual confidence. "Colin. I'm sorry about the way I behaved at the fundraiser." He clears his throat. "I insulted your girl, and I was condescending to you. I regret my behavior."

I almost fall out of my chair. He's apologizing? Now *that*, I didn't expect.

"Sorry if I sound a bit rusty—I haven't issued an apology in… ever, maybe? People apologize to *me*, not the other way around. And to think I'm groveling to a jock! Who would've—"

"Really? We're back to the jock bullshit?" I sigh.

There's a pause. "Again, my apologies. I may be a bit biased when it comes to jocks."

"No shit."

"I didn't have the best experience with jocks in high school," he admits. "Though I'm sure you already suspected that. With that said, I truly am sorry, kid. I was an ass. And truth be told, you impressed me that night. The other candidates nodded and agreed with every word I said. They sucked up to me and raved about how amazing I am—don't get me wrong, I *am* amazing. But it gets old, having people follow you around, trying to suck your dick. You stood up to me, Colin. And more than that, you're immensely talented."

I'm glad he's not here to see my jaw drop.

"So." His tone grows sheepish. "If you're still interested in the position at Orcus Games, it's yours."

My jaw is on the floor now. Yeah, I absolutely didn't expect this. And I have to admit, I'm impressed that he was man enough to call me and apologize.

But at the same time, I can't forget the way he treated Summer with such blatant disrespect. I'm not sure if one apology makes up for that.

"I told you, I'm not interested in working for someone like you," I say brusquely.

"And I'm urging you to reconsider. I need someone like you on my team, kid. Someone who challenges me, stands up to me. Someone to remind me that before I was an arrogant prick, I was a nerdy kid who loved video games."

I hesitate for a moment. "If you want me to reconsider, then you need to give me time to think about it," I finally say.

"Understandable. Take a few days. Hell, a week, two weeks. But I require a firm answer by the end of the month."

"Fine. I'll get back to you. Anything else?" I'm being rude again, but the fashion show starts soon. And Summer is more important to me than this, as he aptly described himself, arrogant prick.

"Just think it over," he cajoles.

"I said I would." And I meant it. I'll take the time to decide if working for Kamal is worth it for me, but if he expects me to jump through hoops for him again, he'll be sorely disappointed. There's only one person whose hoops I'll happily jump through, and she's not even asking me to.

"I'll be in touch, Mr. Jain." And then I sign off with a series of words that never in a million years would I have imagined myself saying. "I've gotta go walk the runway at my girlfriend's fashion show now."

# 32
# SUMMER

"That man really loves you."

"I know," I answer Brenna, unable to fight a sappy grin.

We're standing backstage, watching as my boyfriend walks the lengthy runway bisecting the enormous ballroom of the Arbor House, a historic mansion in Hastings and our venue for tonight. Fitz's swim briefs hug his perfect ass, and his thigh muscles ripple with power as his long strides eat up the runway.

On the other side of the wings, Bianca and her Kappa sisters are also enjoying the show. Every time another half-naked hockey player steps onto the stage, they sigh dreamily. The girls already strutted their stuff to thunderous applause. My bikinis were a hit, but the plunging one-piece Bianca closed the girls' line with was the clear winner of the night.

Bianca catches me looking, and she gives an enthusiastic wave. I wave back with a smile. I didn't see Kaya in the audience tonight, which tells me she never ended up endorsing her sisters' side project. But who cares. The Kappas came through for me, and I owe them for that.

Beyond the curtains, Fitz reaches the end and does the turn like we'd practiced, albeit awkwardly. The people occupying the rows of seats on either side of the runway break out in applause, and my smile doubles in size.

As I suspected, the briefs are a wee bit loose in the front, since Rex's rocket is slightly bigger than Fitzy's. But that's not to say my man doesn't fill out a pair of briefs fantastically. And besides, I honestly wouldn't have cared if half the swimsuits hadn't fit. I'm just thrilled we managed to find replacements for all six players.

Someone else isn't as thrilled, though. Erik Laurie sits in the front row with the other members of the faculty, including Mallory Reyes, the department head. Laurie holds his program in his lap, fashionable as ever in a pinstriped suit and with his hair slicked away from his high forehead and clean-shaven face.

A face that's harder than stone as he stares at my model. Correction, at my *boyfriend*, who is so fucking hot it's almost… otherworldly. Yup. No other way to describe the oiled-up, muscled, tattooed man putting himself on display for me.

"I want to go out there and bang him on the runway," I growl. "In front of everybody. I don't even care."

"I don't blame you," Brenna answers. "Look at that body. He's magnificent."

He really is. And the relief on his face when he returns backstage is almost comical.

"I feel like I'm going to ralph," he groans.

I tamp down a laugh. "You were so good!" I assure him. "But, quick. We need to get Rex's trunks on you because you're walking again after Nate."

Each designer was given our own dressing space sectioned off by a curtain, and I shove Fitz toward mine. His second swimsuit is nowhere near as skimpy as the first one. I saved the trunks for last so he could be done with the awkward briefs right off the bat.

Fitz scratches his bare chest, then remembers that Brenna and I rubbed oil over all the guys before the show started. His big paw is glistening now, and he bites his tongue seductively before saying, "I'm all oily. Can you take these off for me?"

I roll my eyes. "Oily hands in no way prevent you from taking your own briefs off." But I still hook my fingers under his elastic waistband, because what woman would ever say no to sliding what's essentially underwear off this hottie's body?

I slip my hands under the briefs and squeeze his butt cheeks. His ass is so muscular, it's insane.

Fitz's eyes flare. "Don't do that," he warns. "You'll make me hard."

"You're the one who wanted me to undress you."

"You're right. What was I thinking?" He swats my hands away and drops trou on his own.

I have one brief, glorious moment to admire his sweet penis before he has the trunks on and is tightening the drawstring. "How do I look?" he asks.

"Fuckable." I reach around to smack his ass. "Now get back to work."

He chuckles as I usher him out of the dressing space and get him in position. Nate walks off the runway, and Fitz steps onto it, but before he walks, he winks at me and murmurs, "I wouldn't do this for just anybody, you know."

"I know. And I love you for it."

Brenna sighs as he disappears. "You two are so sappy."

"Yup. I own that." I grin at her. "You still seeing McCarthy?" She's being very mum about her love life lately.

She shrugs. "Not really. He's in Boston. I'm in Hastings. I'm not going to make that much of an effort for a Harvard boy."

"What if it was Connelly?" I counter. "Would you make the trek to see him?"

"What's with you and Connelly?" she demands in exasperation. "I swear, you're obsessed with the guy. He's an arrogant ass, Summer."

"But he's so hot."

"Arrogant asses tend to be hot. That's how they become arrogant asses."

Fitz returns with loud cheers in his wake, and I urge Hollis to get out there. He's closing my show, and he milks the finale for all he's worth. Flexing his biceps as he plants his hands on his hips. Showing off the hard ridges of his abs as he does his turn. And then my part is over and the Kappa sisters are hugging me, and a few of my classmates congratulate me on a job well done.

Ben is up next, so my friends and I clear the wings for him and his models. Brenna and the Kappas go to sit in the audience while Fitz and the others change into their clothes. I thank each of them profusely for their help, and a pang of sadness tugs at my heart at Hunter's noticeable absence. Fitz and I agreed it's best to give Hunter space, but it still sucks knowing I'd hurt him.

When it's just Fitz and me (and he's wearing clothes), I grab the back of his head to tug his mouth to mine. "Thank you," I whisper against his lips. "You literally saved my life."

"Well, not *literally*," he whispers back.

"Literally," I argue, and his lips twitch in humor before covering mine again.

Someone gasps from behind us, and we break apart to see Nora standing several feet away. At first she's pale with shock, but then her lips twist in a nasty grimace and she spits out, "I can't believe you, Fitz. That's who you were talking about? *Her?*"

And then she stomps off, her pink-streaked black hair whipping as she spins around.

I turn to him in confusion. "What did she mean, what you were talking about? When did you talk to her?"

"Right after we slept together for the first time," he says gruffly. "I told her I couldn't go out with her again because I started seeing somebody."

"Oh. You didn't mention that."

"To be honest, I forgot."

I'd forgotten about Nora too, at least in relation to Fitz. She's no longer a threat to me, although I do feel bad that she witnessed us kissing when I know she had a crush on him.

*Do you, though?* inner Selena Gomez asks. I can tell she's trying not to stick her tongue out at me.

Fine. Maybe I don't feel *that* bad.

"Should I go talk to her?" he says in concern.

"Absolutely not," I say cheerfully. "She's a big girl, and she'll get over it."

---

The fashion show ends around nine thirty, which was when it was scheduled to *start* before Laurie decided that tearing apart my essay and embarrassing me in front of the class wasn't enough. But his attempt to sabotage me tonight failed. And I don't miss the anger in his eyes when Mallory Reyes pulls me aside at the Briar-hosted after-party and raves about my designs. She can't get enough of the bohemian influence mingled with my modern glam style, and she says as much to Laurie as he stands there glowering at me over her head.

"Come talk to me before the semester ends so we can brain-storm your work placement for your senior year. I have some ideas." She glances at Laurie. "I adore this girl's style, Erik. It's a lot of fun."

"Very fun," he agrees, but the unchecked anger in his eyes betrays his airy tone.

I don't give a shit how much he hates me, though. The independent study is pass/fail, and there's no possible way he can fail me after Mallory spent the past ten minutes gushing about my work. Even better, she's the one who'll be reviewing my midterm appeal once I begin the process.

I have a feeling it's going to go in my favor.

I excuse myself and do some mingling. Fitz stays by my side, looking less miserable than usual at having to attend a social function. He's evolving, my sweet-penis man. I'm proud of him.

His teammates take up residence at one of the two bars. Since the party is being hosted by the university's Fine Arts department, the bartenders aren't serving anyone without ID. But most of us are of age, and I sip a wine spritzer while Fitz drinks a beer, and we stand there watching the crowd for a bit. Brenna is on the other side of the room chatting with Hollis. They're laughing about something, and every time she throws her head back, I notice a spark of hope in his eyes. Poor Mike. One of these days he's going to have to accept that she's not interested in him.

Fitz gets drawn into hockey talk with Nate and Matt, so I wander around and mingle some more. At one point I bump into Nora and nearly compliment her on her show. Her punk-rock inspired dresses had been pretty incredible. But her eyes blaze the moment we collide, so I simply murmur an apology and keep walking.

A bit later, I see her at the bar chatting with Laurie, and her expression is drastically brighter. She's sipping on a pink cocktail, and he's holding a glass of red wine. He touches her arm, and then he winks and tweaks a strand of her black-and-pink hair. She giggles.

Looks like Nora got her wish—she's finally the exclusive recipient of Laurie's attention. Well, she can have the slimy bastard. Good riddance.

The party is winding down when my phone vibrates in the back pocket of my skinny jeans. I pull it out to find a text from Rex.

**REX:** Saw on Snapchat da hockey boys rocked it. Pissed tho. We wanted to do it!!
**ME:** I know you did, sweetie
**REX:** Still on for the after party, tho? Got all these kegs here. Shame to waste em.

I walk back to the bar and address Fitz and the others. "Are you down for the after-after-party at Rex's?"

"Sure," Fitz says, although grudgingly. "If you want to go?"

"Absolutely," I answer without delay. "Daphne Kettleman will be there."

"Why do you care about this chick so much?" He gives a resigned head shake.

"Because she's Daphne Kettleman."

He scrubs his hands over his face. "Summer. I feel like I'm going to be saying this a lot, but… I don't understand you."

Nate snickers.

"It's okay, babe. Not a lot of people do." I smack a kiss on his cheek. "All right. Why don't you boys take off now? We're starting cleanup soon, so I need to stay for that, but I'll meet you at the Elmhurst house once I'm done."

"I can stay and help," Fitz offers.

"You already helped enough." My tone is firm. "Take Brenna and the Kappas, and go to Rex's. I'll be there in an hour, tops."

"I don't like the idea of leaving you alone here."

"Pussy whipped," Hollis coughs under his breath.

"I won't be alone," I tell Fitz. "Ben and Nora"—I make a face as I say her name—"volunteered to clean up too."

"Be nice," Fitz chides.

"Hey, I'm nothing but nice to her. She's the one who acts like a bitch to me." I send Rex a message that the party is still a go, then slide my phone in my pocket. "I'll text you when I'm on my way."

----

Forty-five minutes later, Ben and I have stacked the last of the chairs, boxed up all the hangers, and de-cluttered as best as we could. Someone from the university is supposed to collect all this stuff in the morning and return it to the Fashion department.

I gesture to the raised runway in the center of the massive room. "They don't expect us to take that apart, do they?"

"No, I think the crew's doing it when they come to pick up all the chairs and stuff."

"Okay. Good." I check the time on my phone. "You coming to the party?"

He rubs his fingers over his bushy eyebrows. "I don't know… A football party, huh?"

"You got something against football?" I tease.

"No, but I've received enough wedgies from football players that it's left me a bit scarred." His mouth widens in a cheeky smile. "I've also received enough BJs from football players to make up for that."

I gasp. "Ben, you bad boy! One, I didn't know you were gay. And, two, we have something in common—we both like athletes!"

"We had other things in common before," he answers dryly. "We're both fashion majors? We both love Chanel and Versace?"

"True. So are you coming to the party or not?"

"Sure, what the hell. Do you need a ride?"

"Thanks, but I drove here too." I'm about to slide my hand in my purse to fish out my keys, when I realize I'm not wearing my purse. I'd left it on the floor of the dressing area when Ben and I were folding up all the curtains. Nora had been helping at one point too, but I don't know where she ran off to. She probably took off to avoid having to spend time with me.

"I'll see you at Rex's," I tell Ben.

"Sexy Rexy," he murmurs.

"Oh God, please call him that to his face so I can see his reaction."

He snickers. "If I think it'll get me a BJ and not a wedgie, I will," he promises.

Ben leaves, and I hop onto the runway and walk toward the backstage area, where I quickly grab my purse. Before I can leave, I hear a female giggle.

I freeze, my gaze moving toward the corridor that leads to the Arbor House management offices. It also features a closet-sized bathroom that I used earlier tonight.

Another giggle echoes from the corridor. I'm pretty sure it's Nora, and my eyes narrow at the shadowy doorway. Who the heck is she with?

In a heartbeat, it dawns on me. Laurie? I suddenly realize I never saw him leave tonight, either. He just sort of disappeared from the party, same way Nora disappeared in the middle of cleanup.

I follow the giggles to the corridor and slant my head. Sure enough, a male voice. It's coming from the bathroom, and it's almost certainly Laurie. Then Nora's muffled voice, followed by Laurie again, as he says something that makes her laugh again.

Good for her, I guess. She's had a crush on the creep since the first day of classes. Now she gets to live the creepy dream.

I'm about to walk away when I hear her cry out.

It's not a scream of terror but an exclamation of surprise, as if he startled her. But it's enough to make me walk toward the bathroom to check if she's all right. I remember the look of betrayal on Laurie's face when I rejected his advances in his office. Granted, he released me the instant I said no. But he was also stone-cold sober that day, and on university property.

Tonight I saw him drink at least three glasses of red wine. Plus, he was already in a snit because I thwarted his evil agenda. I wouldn't feel right if I left without making sure Nora is—

"Stop it."

Okay, I heard *that* as clear as day.

I reach the door just as the sounds of a scuffle echo behind it. A thud, as if someone bumped into something. A soft clatter, as if an item fell off the counter and onto the tiled floor. The soap dish, maybe.

Nora's voice is firm. "Stop it. I said no."

And then I hear Laurie's smarmy voice mutter, "Cocktease."

There's another crash. Nora cries out again, and I almost keel over with relief when I turn the knob and find the door isn't locked. Thank God.

I throw it open and shout, "Let her go!"

# 33
# SUMMER

Laurie's hand is cupped between Nora's legs. Her hand is clamped over his as she forcibly tries to push it away. The sight turns my vision into a sea of red. I lunge at the professor, one arm slicing up and then down as I karate chop the back of his neck. He howls in pain and stumbles away from Nora.

"What the hell!" he roars, angrily rubbing the spot that the side of my hand connected with.

"Oh, I'm sorry," I snap back. "Am I interrupting something?" My stomach churns when I notice the bulge in his pants. That bastard. I turn to Nora, whose face is ashen, her fingers quivering wildly as she tries to smooth the hem of her rumpled dress.

"Are you okay?" I ask urgently.

"I'm fine."

She doesn't sound fine. Her voice is weak, and her legs are visibly wobbling as she comes toward me. I wrap a protective arm around her trembling shoulders. The fact that she lets me tells me how shaken up she actually is.

"Of course she's fine," Laurie says stiffly. "I don't know what you think is going on right now, Summer, but Nora was not in any danger from me. Your hysteria, not to mention your ludicrous assumptions about what was happening are not only insulting, but you also just left yourself open to an assault charge."

I can't stop an incredulous laugh. "You're going to have *me* arrested for assault? Are you kidding me? And I know *exactly* what was going on in here before I came in."

"Nothing untoward occurred between Nora and myself. Isn't that right, Nora?"

She doesn't respond. She simply shakes harder in my arms.

"You're disgusting," I hiss at our esteemed professor.

"You don't know what you're talking about," he spits out. "You interrupted a consensual intimate moment between me and—"

"A student!" I finish in disbelief. "Between you and a student! Even if it *was* consensual—and it didn't fucking look that way from where I was standing—how is it in any way appropriate?"

His lips flatten in an angry line. I wait for a denial, an apology, anything. What I get is, "I don't need to deal with this."

I gape. "Like hell you don't—"

But he's already storming off. Frantic footsteps reverberate backstage, then get softer and softer until a door finally slams. And then everything goes silent.

Nora's entire body is still shaking. "Thank you," she whispers.

"Hey, it's no problem." I tighten my hold on her. She needs it, otherwise I suspect she'll topple over. "But we need to go to the police now."

Her head snaps up, the top of it nearly clipping my chin. "What? Why?"

"He would've raped you if I hadn't come along, Nora. You know that, right?"

"Maybe not." But there's no conviction at all. She clears her throat, straightens her shoulders, and eases out of my embrace. "He didn't rape me, though. And I know how this will play out—my mom's a public defender. It'll be my word against his. All he did was stick his hand between my legs. There's no bruises, no evidence of assault."

"There's *me*. I'm the evidence. I saw him groping you. I heard you say no. Loud and clear."

"Summer, you know there's no point," she says bleakly. "The cops will give him a slap on the wrist. They probably wouldn't even charge him."

I have a sinking feeling she's right. I bite my lip as I work over our options in my head. There aren't many, but one rises to the forefront of my brain. "I think I know who won't give him a slap on the wrist," I say slowly.

"Who?"

I take her hand and say, "Come with me."

———

"We can't just show up at the dean's house," Nora hisses more than an hour later. She's in the passenger's seat of my Audi, and she's been protesting this course of action since the moment I told her.

"We're not just showing up," I remind her as I drive through the wrought-iron gates at the entrance of David Prescott's property. The dean lives in a gorgeous mansion in Brookline, a wealthy neighborhood outside of Boston. I'm pretty sure Tom Brady and Gisele live around here too. I suddenly have a vision of Gisele jogging past the dean's house, noticing my fabulous outfit, and inviting me over to her house for a drink. Oh my God. That would blow my frigging mind.

Unfortunately, we're not here to celebrity sightsee. We're here to report an attempted sexual assault.

"My father called ahead to tell him we were coming, remember?" Because my dad is awesome. Never mind terrifying when he needs to be.

And I guess Dean Prescott called in reinforcements as well, because he's not the only one waiting for us on the doorstep. Hal Richmond is with him, and he's the one who greets us.

"Ms. Ridgeway. Summer." As usual, his "accent" contains a patronizing note. "What's all this about?"

I let out a breath. "Something happened tonight, and, well, Nora doesn't want to go to the police, but I told her I couldn't in good conscience let it go unreported."

Prescott's eyes widen. "The police?" He opens the door wider and gestures for us to come inside.

Nora shoots me a panicky look.

I squeeze her arm. "It's fine. I promise."

As we follow the two men into a living room the size of my townhouse in Hastings, I dial my dad's number on my phone. He answers immediately. He's been waiting for my call.

"Hey, Dad, we just got here. I'm putting you on speakerphone." I glance at Prescott. "Dean, you know my father. I hope you don't mind if he listens in."

I see Richmond's lips tighten. I assume the word cloud in his snotty brain is now flashing "Preferential treatment!"

He can eat a dick.

"I know this is weird, but I'm from a family of lawyers," I explain to the men. "I'm not allowed to have any important conversations without legal counsel."

A chuckle floats out of my phone. "You got that right, Princess."

Nora seems to be fighting a smile. I'm surprised when it actually breaks free, and it's genuine. "Family of lawyers?" she murmurs to me. "Me too."

"Look at that," I murmur back. "And you thought we didn't have anything in common."

Maybe if she'd given me a chance instead of assuming I was an airhead, we could've been friends. But deep down I know that will never be the case. I'm a super-jealous person, and the fact that she went on one date with Fitz means I'll always want to claw her eyes out.

But I also watched her almost get raped tonight, and I wouldn't wish that on my worst enemy.

With Prescott and Richmond's rapt attention on me, I repeat the story of what happened tonight. Nora fills in her side of it, explaining how Laurie bought her two drinks and flirted with her all night until finally making his move after everyone had gone home. Both men wear murderous expressions when I mention where Laurie's hand had been when I opened the bathroom door.

"So I karate chopped him and—"

There's a choked laugh from my dad.

"Daddy," I scold.

"I'm sorry. I didn't mean to interrupt. It's just that you took karate for three months before you quit. And you were twelve. I can't believe you still remember any of the moves."

"I don't. Just that one," I admit.

"Well, it came in handy tonight," he says, and his pride practically pours out of the phone speaker.

"Anyway." I finish the story by admitting that this wasn't the first time Laurie made a move on a student. Nora stares at me in surprise as I reveal, "I had a meeting in his office and he tried to kiss me."

My father roars. "I'm going to *kill*—"

"Daddy, hush! You're a defense lawyer. You can't threaten to kill people. And he didn't push the issue when I told him I wasn't interested. Tonight he'd had a lot to drink, so maybe that contributed to his behavior." I level Prescott and Richmond with a stern glare. "But he can't get away with it. We can't have someone like that teaching at Briar."

"Absolutely not," Prescott agrees, while Richmond gives a grim nod. "Don't worry, ladies. Briar will be taking swift action. And, Nora, please remember you have access to counseling at the student health center. I encourage you to take advantage of that."

She nods weakly.

My dad speaks up. "As for contacting law enforcement, obviously nobody can force you to press charges, Nora—you need to do whatever you feel is right. However, should you change your mind, I will gladly serve as your counsel. Summer will give you my contact info. You can call me any time, day or night."

She bites her lip, her gaze slightly awed. "Thank you, sir."

Our late-night visit to the dean's house comes to an end. Nora and I thank them for listening, and as the men walk us out, I take my father off speakerphone and murmur, "Love you, Daddy. Thank you."

"Love you too, Princess. Oh, and by the way, I looked into that matter you'd asked about while I was waiting for your call. I didn't do it before, because...well, because your mom said it would be enabling your craziness."

"Dad!"

"Her words, not mine. Blame Mom."

"But you looked into what?" I prompt.

He answers with, "West Yorkshire."

I wrinkle my nose. "West Yorkshire?"

"That's where the fellow you're overly interested in hails from. Leeds, West Yorkshire. England."

My gaze flies to Richmond, who's walking ahead of us. He's actually British? I can't even.

"Thanks for telling me," I say glumly. "Love you."

When we reach the front door, Richmond stops me from exiting by saying, "Summer, a word?"

*Sum-ah.* Dammit. I hate being wrong.

"I'll wait in the car," Nora says.

I nod. "I'll only be a minute." I wait until she's out of earshot before crossing my arms. "What do you want?"

"To apologize." There's genuine remorse in his eyes. "I've been behaving like a bit of a wanker, haven't I?"

"Just a bit," I say flatly.

"I must confess—I went into our relationship with a hefty bias."

"You think?"

He gives me a look. "May I continue?"

"Sorry."

"I didn't grow up with money, Summer. I worked myself to the bone in order to attend university, as I wasn't offered a scholarship. Over the years, I suppose I developed resentment toward people like you, the ones who come from wealthy families that can pull strings for them. I didn't get into my first choice uni. Nobody called in a favor for me." He hangs his head. "I'm sorry for my behavior. And I'm especially sorry because you tried to warn me about Professor Laurie. You tried to tell me how uncomfortable he made you, and I dismissed those concerns."

"Yes. You did." I can feel the disapproval radiating from my pores.

"And you have no idea how deeply I regret that. It's ghastly enough, what Ms. Ridgeway endured tonight. But if something had happened to you because I'd ignored your claims?" He shudders. "I'm terribly sorry."

I exhale. "It's done now. And I hope that in the future, if a student comes to you with these kinds of concerns, you actually heed them."

"I will. I promise. And I also promise to be a little friendlier during our meetings." He chuckles dryly. "But please, don't expect me to transform into a warm and fuzzy creature overnight. I am British, after all."

# 34
# FITZ

I've been reduced to a basket case by the time I hear the key turn in the lock. It's nearly midnight. I left the party the moment Summer called to tell me what happened to Nora and that they were on their way to see the dean. I would've hopped in my car and met her there, but she insisted I stay home. Something about too many cooks in the kitchen.

Apparently, her father attended the meeting via speakerphone, which is a relief. I feel better knowing someone close to Summer was there to support her.

Now I dive off the couch and take her in my arms before she can even shut the front door. "I'm so glad you're back," I groan. "Are you okay?"

"I'm fine," she assures me.

"How's Nora?" I ask as Summer unbuttons her coat.

"She's fine too. I karate chopped the bastard before he could do any real harm."

I take the coat from her cold hands and hang it up for her. "And the dean?"

"He said he'd take care of it."

"He freaking better. There's still no chance of Nora going to the cops, though?"

"Even my dad said there's no point." Summer runs both hands

through her blonde hair. "I hate this world we live in, Fitzy, where shitty people can get away with shitty things."

"I know," I say soberly. Shitty things do happen, but I'm confident Erik Laurie will face real consequences.

Only last week I was reading online about three professors from major institutions who had been fired in the last month alone. One of them had even had tenure. Sexual harassment is a huge topic in the news these days—no way will Briar let something as serious as this slide.

I press my face to Summer's neck and breathe in my favorite scent on earth. Chanel No. 5. The only scent a lady should ever own, someone told me once. "I was worried when you told me what happened."

"I was worried when I *saw* it happen." She takes my hand and leads me toward the stairs. "Let's not talk about it anymore. I just want to take a hot shower, and then get in bed and catch up on *The Bachelor*."

My mouth tips up in a wry grin. I never dreamed I'd fall for a girl who's into cheesy reality shows. Ever.

But luckily, that's just one facet to Summer Heyward-Di Laurentis.

There is a plethora of other sides to her. The side that teases her older brothers. The side that adores her parents. The side that instantly becomes best friends with people, because she goes into every relationship with a full plate of trust. Other people remain guarded when they meet new people, but not Summer. Summer is trusting and open.

And she's smart, in spite of her writing difficulties. Her vocabulary rivals mine. She listens to longwinded fantasy tomes on audiobook and actually discusses them with me. I've never had a girlfriend who could sit there and dissect Sir Nornan's journey to the Glass Forest and recite all the reasons he was stupid to use the angel's sword, prematurely revealing its existence to the cave dwellers that protect the Great Beyond.

So yes, Summer is everything.

She's my muse. My sketches of her are already being transferred onto my computer to create the assets for the new video game I'm designing.

She's my laughter, because everything she says makes me laugh.

She's my trigger, because holy shit do we scream at each other sometimes. I never knew I was capable of expressing raw emotion, didn't think I even had it in me.

She's my desire, because I can't take a step without wanting to be inside her.

But most of all, she's my heart.

"I love you," I tell her as we walk down the hall to my room.

"Love you too," she whispers.

Her gaze flickers briefly to Hunter's door.

"He's not home," I murmur, and I know we're both thinking about how much we hate that our roommate is still pissed at us.

But Hunter will get over it. And if he doesn't, then I'll take that L. With a heavy heart, of course, but I've gained something I know can heal the pain of the loss. I've gained Summer.

For the first time ever, I truly feel like I'm living life instead of hiding in the shadows. My folks can keep hating each other, but the next time one of them calls to spew their hatred, I'll make it clear that I don't want that negativity poisoning my life anymore. Even if it means hanging up the phone. Hell, I had no qualms hanging up on a billionaire earlier.

When I was waiting for Summer to come home from the dean's house, I did take the time to think about Kamal's job offer. And I've concluded that maybe he does need someone like me at Orcus Games. Someone who won't kiss his ass. Someone who'll tell him when he's being a jackass. So I'm toying with the offer, but I'll decide later.

Right now, I want to take a shower with the woman I love and then climb under the covers and watch a silly reality show with her.

"You have the worst taste in television shows," I inform her as we enter my room.

Her green eyes dance mischievously. "But you love me anyway, right?"

I tug her toward me, my lips seeking hers. "Yup." I give her a slow, teasing kiss. "I love you anyway."

# The End

**Read on for a sneak peek into *The Risk*, the next book in the bestselling Briar U series**

# 1

# BRENNA

My date is late.

Now, I'm not a total bitch. Usually I'll give guys a five-minute window. I can forgive five minutes of tardiness.

At seven minutes, I might still be somewhat receptive, especially if the lateness is accompanied by a heads-up call or text informing me he's going to be late. Traffic is an evil mistress. Sometimes she screws you.

At ten minutes, my patience would be running thin. And if the inconsiderate ass is both ten minutes late *and* didn't call? Thank you, next. I'm walking right out the door.

At fifteen minutes, shame on me. Why the hell am I still at the restaurant?

Or, in this particular case, the diner.

I'm sitting in a booth at Della's, the '50s-themed diner in Hastings. Hastings is the small town I'm calling home for the next couple of years, but luckily, I don't need to call my father's house "home." Dad and I might live in the same town, but before I transferred to Briar University, I made it clear I wouldn't be moving in with him. I already left that nest. No way am I flying back to it and subjecting myself to his overprotectiveness and terrible cooking again.

"Can I get you another coffee, hon?" The waitress, a curly-haired

woman in a white-and-blue polyester uniform, eyes me sympatheti-
cally. She looks to be in her late twenties. Her nametag reads "Stacy,"
and I'm pretty sure she knows I've been ditched.

"No, thanks. Just the bill, please."

As she walks off, I pick up my phone and shoot a quick text to
my friend Summer. This is all her fault. Therefore she must face my
wrath.

**ME:** He stood me up.

Summer answers instantly, as if she's been sitting by her phone
waiting for a report. Actually, forget "as if." She totally has. My new
friend is unapologetically nosy.

**SUMMER:** OMG! NO!!
**ME:** Yes.
**SUMMER:** What. a. dick. I am so so so so sorry, Bee.
**ME:** Meh. Part of me's not surprised. He's a football player.
They're notorious douchecanoes.
**SUMMER:** I thought Jules was different.
**ME:** You thought wrong.

Three dots appear, indicating she's typing a response, but I
already know what it will be. Another long-winded apology, which
I'm not in the mood to read at the moment. I'm not in the mood for
anything but paying for my coffee, walking back to my tiny apartment, and taking off my bra.

Stupid football player. I actually put makeup on for this jerk. Yes,
it was just supposed to be an evening coffee date, but I still made an
effort.

I bend my head as I rummage around in my wallet for small bills.
When a shadow falls over the tabletop, I assume it's Stacy returning
with my check.

I assume wrong.

"Jensen," drawls an insolent male voice. "Got stood up, eh?"

Ugh. Of all the people who could've shown up right now, this is the last one I want to see.

As Jake Connelly slides into the other side of the booth, I greet him with a suspicious scowl rather than a smile. "What are you doing here?" I ask.

Connelly is the captain of the Harvard hockey team, AKA, THE ENEMY. Harvard and Briar are rivals, and my father happens to be the head coach of the latter. He's coached at Briar for ten years, winning three championships during that reign. *The Age of Jensen*—that was the headline of a recent article I read in one of the New England papers. It was a full-page write-up about how Briar is killing it this season. Unfortunately, so is Harvard, all thanks to the superstar across the booth from me.

"I was in the neighborhood." There's an amused gleam in his forest-green eyes.

The last time I saw him, he and a teammate were lurking in the stands of Briar's arena, scoping us out. Not long after, we kicked their asses when our teams played each other. Which was tremendously satisfying and made up for our loss against them earlier in the season.

"Mmm-hmmm, I'm sure you just *happened* to be in Hastings. Don't you live in Cambridge?"

"So?"

"So that's an hour away." I give him a smirk. "I didn't know I had a stalker."

"You got me. I'm stalking you."

"I'm flattered, Jakey. It's been a while since someone was so besotted with me that they drove to a whole other town to track me down."

His lips slowly curve into a smile. "Look, as hot as you are—"

"Aw, you think I'm a hottie?"

"—I wouldn't spend the gas money to come here just to get my balls put through the wringer. Sorry to disappoint." He runs a hand through his dark hair. It's a bit shorter now, and he's rocking some scruff that shadows his jaw.

"You say that as if I have any interest in your balls," I answer sweetly.

"My metaphorical balls. You wouldn't be able to handle the real ones," he drawls. "*Hottie.*"

I roll my eyes so hard I almost pull a muscle. "Seriously, Connelly. Why are you here?"

"I was visiting a friend. This looked like a good place to grab some coffee before I drive back to the city."

"You have a friend? Well, that's a relief. I've seen you hanging out with your teammates, but I assumed they have to pretend to like you because you're their captain."

"They like me because I'm fucking terrific." He flashes another grin.

*Panty-melting.* That's how Summer described his smile once. I swear, the chick has an unhealthy obsession with Connelly's chiseled good looks. Phrases she's thrown around to describe him include: hotness overload, ovary explosion, babelicious, and mackable.

Summer and I have known each other only a couple of months. We pretty much went from strangers to best friends in about, oh, thirty seconds. I mean, she transferred from another college after accidentally setting part of her sorority house on fire—how could I not fall hard for that crazy girl? She's a fashion major, a ton of fun, and is convinced I have a thing for Jake Connelly.

She's wrong. The guy is gorgeous, and he's a phenomenal hockey player, but he's also a notorious player off the ice. This doesn't make him an anomaly, of course. A lot of athletes maintain an active roster of chicks who are perfectly content with 1) hooking up, 2) not being exclusive, and 3) always coming second to whatever sport the dude plays.

But I'm not one of those chicks. I'm not averse to hookups, but numbers 2 and 3 are non-negotiable.

Not to mention that my father would skin me alive if I ever dated THE ENEMY. Dad and Jake's coach, Daryl Pedersen, have been feuding for years. According to my father, Coach Pedersen sacrifices babies to Satan and performs blood magic in his spare time.

"I have lots of friends," Connelly adds. He shrugs. "Including a very close one who goes to Briar."

"I feel like when somebody brags about all their friends, it usually means they don't have any. Overcompensating, you know?" I smile innocently.

"At least I didn't get stood up."

The smile fades. "I wasn't stood up," I lie, except the waitress chooses that moment to approach the booth and blow my cover.

"You made it!" Relief fills her eyes at the sight of Jake. Followed by a gleam of appreciation once she gets a good look at him. "We were starting to get worried."

We? I hadn't realized we were partners in this humiliation venture.

"The roads were slick," Jake tells her, nodding toward the diner's front windows. Rivulets of moisture streak the fogged-up panes. Beyond the glass a thin stripe of lightning momentarily illuminates the dark sky. "Gotta be extra careful when driving in the rain, you know?"

She nods fervently. "The roads get really wet when it's raining."

No shit, Captain Obvious. *Rain makes things wet.* Somebody call the Nobel Prize judging committee.

Jake's lips twitch.

"Could I get you anything to drink?" she asks.

I shoot him a warning glare.

He responds with a smirk before turning to wink at her. "I would *love* a cup of coffee—" He squints at her nametag, "—Stacy. And a refill for my sulking date."

"I don't want a refill, and I'm not his date," I growl.

Stacy blinks in confusion. "Oh? But…"

"He's a Harvard spy sent here to get the goods on Briar's hockey team. Don't humor him, Stacy. He's the enemy."

"So dramatic." Jake chuckles. "Ignore her, Stace. She's just mad that I was late. Two coffees, and some pie, if you don't mind. A slice of…" His gaze travels to the glass cases at the main counter. "Oh damn, I can't decide. Everything looks so tasty."

"Yes you are," I hear Stacy mumble under her breath.

"What was that?" he asks, but his slight smile tells me he heard her loud and clear.

She blushes. "Oh, um, I was saying we only have peach and pecan left."

"Hmmm." He licks his bottom lip. It's a ridiculously sexy move. Everything about him is sexy. Which is why I hate him. "You know what? One of each, please. My date and I will share 'em."

"We most certainly will not," I say cheerfully, but Stacy is already hurrying off to procure some stupid pie for King Connelly.

Fuck.

"Listen, as much as I enjoy discussing how your team is trash, I'm too tired to insult you tonight." I try to tamp down my weariness, but it creeps into my voice. "I want to go home."

"Not yet." The lighthearted, somewhat mocking vibe he's been giving off hardens into something more serious. "I didn't come to Hastings for you, but now that we're having coffee together—"

"Against my will," I cut in.

"—there's something we need to discuss."

"Oh, is there?" Despite myself, curiosity pricks at my gut. I cover it up with sarcasm. "I can't *wait* to hear it."

Jake clasps his hands on the tabletop. He has great hands. Like, really, really great hands. I've got a bit of an obsession with men's hands. If they're too small, I'm instantly turned off. Too big and meaty, and I'm a bit apprehensive. But Connelly has been blessed with a winning pair. His fingers are long but not bony. Palms large and powerful but not beefy. His nails are clean, but two of his knuckles are red and cracked, probably from a skirmish on the ice. I can't see his fingertips, but I'd bet they're callused.

I love the way calluses feel trailing over my bare skin, grazing a nipple…

Ugh. Nope. I'm not allowed to be thinking racy thoughts in the vicinity of this man.

"I want you to stay the hell away from my guy." Although he punctuates that by baring his teeth, it can't be classified as a smile. It's too feral.

"What guy?" But we both know I know who he means. I can count on one finger of one hand how many Harvard players I've fooled around with.

I met Josh McCarthy at a Harvard party that Summer dragged me to a while back. He initially threw a tantrum when he found out I was Chad Jensen's daughter, but then recognized the error of his ways, apologized via social media, and we got together a few times after that. McCarthy's cute, goofy, and a solid candidate in terms of FWBs. With him living in Boston, there's no chance of him smothering me with affection or showing up at my door unannounced.

Obviously, he isn't a long-term option. And that goes beyond the whole my-father-would-murder-me matter. Truth is, McCarthy doesn't stimulate me. His sarcasm skills are severely lacking, and he's a bit boring when his tongue isn't in my mouth.

"I mean it, Jensen. I don't want you messing with McCarthy."

"Jeez, Mama Bear, retract those claws. It's just a casual thing."

"Casual," he echoes. It's not a question, but a mocking I-don't-believe-you.

"Yes, casual. Would you like me to ask Siri to define the word for you? Casual means it isn't serious. At all."

"It is for him."

I roll my eyes. "Well, that's him, not me."

Yet, inside, I'm troubled by Jake's frank assessment. *It is for him.* Oh boy. I hope that isn't true. Yes, McCarthy texts me a lot, but I've been trying not to engage unless it's something sexy. I don't even respond with "LOL" when he sends me a funny video link, because I don't want to lead him on.

But…maybe I didn't make our fling status as clear as I thought I did?

"I'm tired of watching him walk around like a lovesick puppy." Jake shakes his head in aggravation. "He has it bad, and this bullshit is distracting him at practice."

"Again, how is that my problem?"

"We're smack in the middle of the conference tournament. I know what you're doing, Jensen, and you need to stop."

"Stop what?"

"Stop fucking around with McCarthy. Tell him you're not interested and don't see him again. The end."

I mock-pout. "Oh, Daddy. You're so strict."

"I'm not your daddy." His lips curve again. "Though I could be if you want."

"Oh gross. I'm not calling you 'Daddy' in bed."

Proving she's the master of bad timing, Stacy returns as those words exit my mouth.

Her step stutters. The loaded tray she's carrying shakes precariously. Silverware clinks together. I brace myself, expecting a waterfall of hot coffee to scald my face as Stacy lunges forward. But she recovers quickly, righting herself before disaster strikes.

"Coffee and pie!" Her tone is high and bright, as if she hadn't overheard a thing.

"Thanks, Stacy," Jake says graciously. "I'm sorry for my date's potty mouth. You can see why I don't take her out in public much."

Stacy's cheeks are flushed with embarrassment as she scurries off.

"You traumatized her for life with your filthy sex fantasies," he informs me before digging into his pie.

"Sorry, Daddy."

He snickers mid-bite, a few crumbs flying out of his mouth. He picks up his napkin. "You're not allowed to call me that in public." Mischief dances in his green eyes. "Save it for later."

The other slice—pecan, from the looks of it—sits untouched in front of me. I reach for the coffee instead. I need another hit of caffeine to sharpen my senses. I don't like being here with Connelly. What if someone sees us?

"Or maybe I'll save it for McCarthy," I counter.

"Nah. You won't do that." He gulps down another bite of his pie. "You're breaking it off with him, remember?"

Okay, he really needs to stop issuing orders about my sex life as if he actually has a say in it. "You don't get to make decisions for me. If I want to date McCarthy, I'll date him. If I don't want to date McCarthy, I won't date him."

"Okay." He chews slowly, then swallows. "Do you want to date McCarthy?"

"Date, no."

"Good, so we're on the same page."

I purse my lips before taking a slow sip. "Hmmm. I don't think I like being on the same page as you. I might be changing my mind about the dating scenario... I should ask him to be my boyfriend. Do you know where I can buy a promise ring?"

Jake breaks off a flaky piece of crust with his fork. "You haven't changed your mind. You were over him five minutes after you had him. There're only two reasons why you're still screwing him—either you're bored, or you're trying to sabotage us."

"Is that so?"

"Yup. Nothing holds your attention for long. And I know McCarthy—he's a good kid. Funny, sweet, but that's his downfall right there. 'Sweet' won't cut it with a woman like you."

"There you go again, thinking you know me so well."

"I know you're Chad Jensen's daughter. I know you would take

any opportunity to mess with my players' heads. I know we're probably going to be facing off with Briar in the conference finals in a few
weeks, and the winner of that game gets an automatic bid to the
national tournament—"

"That auto-bid will be ours," I chirp.

"I want my boys sharp and focused on the game. Everyone says
your dad's a straight shooter. I was hoping the same thing could be
said for his daughter." He tsks in disapproval. "And here you are,
playing games with poor, sweet McCarthy."

"I'm not playing games," I say irritably. "We hook up sometimes.
It's fun. Contrary to what you believe, the decisions I make have
nothing to do with my father or his team."

"Well, the decisions I make are for my team," he retorts. "And
I've decided I want you to stay the hell away from my boys." He
swallows another mouthful of pie. "Fuck, this is excellent. You want
some?" He holds his fork out.

"I'd rather die than put my lips on that fork."

He just laughs. "I want to try the pecan. You mind?"

I stare at him. "You're the one who ordered the damn thing."

"Wow, you're cranky tonight, Hottie. I guess I would be too if I
got stood up."

"I didn't get stood up."

"What's his name and address? Want me to go rough him up a
bit?"

I grit my teeth.

He takes a bite of the untouched dessert in front of me. "Ah
fuck, this one is even better. Mmmm. Ohhh, that's good."

And suddenly the captain of the Harvard hockey team is
groaning and grunting in pleasure as if he's acting out a scene from
*American Pie.* I try to remain unaffected, but that traitorous spot
between my legs has other ideas, tingling wildly at Jake Connelly's
sex noises.

"May I go now?" I growl. Except, wait a sec. Why am I asking for *permission*? Nobody is holding me hostage here. I can't deny I'm mildly entertained, but this guy also just accused me of sleeping with his guys to ruin Harvard's chances of beating Briar.

I love my team, but not *that* much.

"Sure. Go if you want. But first text McCarthy to tell him it's over."

"Sorry, Jakey. I don't take orders from you."

"You do now. I need McCarthy's head in the game. End it."

I jut my chin in a stubborn pose. Yes, I need to define things with Josh. I thought I'd stressed the casual nature of our involvement, but evidently he's reading a lot more into it if his team captain is referring to him as "lovesick."

However, I also don't want to give Connelly the satisfaction of siding with him. I'm petty like that.

"I don't take orders from you," I repeat, tucking a five-dollar bill under my half-empty cup. That should cover my coffee, Stacy's tip, and any emotional distress she may have suffered tonight. "I'll do whatever I want with McCarthy. Maybe I'll give him a call right now."

Jake narrows his eyes. "Are you always this difficult?"

"Yes." Smiling, I slide out of the booth and slip into my leather jacket. "Safe drive back to Boston, Connelly. I've been told that the roads get really wet when it's raining."

He chuckles softly.

I zip up my jacket, then lean forward and bring my mouth inches from his ear. "Oh, and Jakey?" I swear I hear his breath hitch. "I'll be sure to save you a seat behind the Briar bench at the Frozen Four."

# ACKNOWLEDGMENTS

You guys have no idea how much fun it was to dive back into the college hockey world with *The Chase*. Plus, I got to get reacquainted with my hockey-playing hotties and some very cool chicks who I've been dying to introduce everyone to! As always, putting this book in your hands was not a solo effort. It would not have been possible without the help of some very amazing people:

Edie Danford, for whipping this manuscript into shape (and forever branding the phrase frightened turtle/genital simile into my brain).

Sarina, Nikki, and Gwen, beta readers, friends, and just overall sexy ladies.

Aquila Editing, for proofing this book (I'm so sorry for all the typos!!).

Connor McCarthy—my personal college hockey player who endured so many questions (most of them random and a little insane) and answered them like the champ he is. Thank you so, so much for all your help, dude. It meant the world to me. I hope your girlfriend likes the book!

Viv, just because.

Nicole—assistant extraordinaire. Holy moly, you continue to amaze me with your support, efficiency, work ethic, general awesomeness, and how you never blink at even my craziest requests.

Tash—assistant, bestie, beastie, breastie, lifeline, therapist, shopping enabler, eye-roll soulmate. You are everything.

Nina—my angel from heaven. I'm sorry for all the candles you have to light for me. We both know I wouldn't survive without you.

Natasha and Vilma, for your continued support. It means everything.

Damonza.com for the absolutely stunning cover!

My author friends (you know who you are! Pssst, Vi!) for sharing this release and offering love and support for the series. Love you guys!

And of course, the bloggers, reviewers and readers who continue to spread the word about my books. I am so thankful for each and every one of you. Thank you for taking the time and doing all that you do.

# ABOUT THE AUTHOR

A *New York Times*, *USA Today* and *Wall Street Journal* bestselling author, Elle Kennedy grew up in the suburbs of Toronto, Ontario, and holds a BA in English from York University. From an early age, she knew she wanted to be a writer and actively began pursuing that dream when she was a teenager. She loves strong heroines and sexy alpha heroes, and just enough heat and danger to keep things interesting!

Elle loves to hear from her readers. Visit her website www .ellekennedy.com or sign up for her newsletter to receive updates about upcoming books and exclusive excerpts. You can also find her on Facebook (ElleKennedyAuthor), Twitter (@ElleKennedy), Instagram (@ElleKennedy33), or TikTok (@ElleKennedyAuthor).

Don't miss the rest of the *New York Times* bestselling OFF-CAMPUS series from ELLE KENNEDY

# THE DEAL

## She's about to make a deal with the college bad boy...

Hannah Wells has finally found someone who turns her on. But while she might be confident in every other area of her life, she's carting around a full set of baggage when it comes to sex and seduction. If she wants to get her crush's attention, she'll have to step out of her comfort zone and make him take notice...even if it means tutoring the annoying, childish, cocky captain of the hockey team in exchange for a pretend date.

## ...and it's going to be oh so good

All Garrett Graham has ever wanted is to play professional hockey after graduation, but his plummeting GPA is threatening everything he's worked so hard for. If helping a sarcastic brunette make another guy jealous will help him secure his position on the team, he's all for it. But when one unexpected kiss leads to the wildest sex of both their lives, it doesn't take long for Garrett to realize that pretend isn't going to cut it. Now he just has to convince Hannah that the man she wants looks a lot like him.

# THE MISTAKE

## He's a player in more ways than one...

College junior John Logan can get any girl he wants. For this hockey star, life is a parade of parties and hook-ups, but behind his killer grins and easygoing charm, he hides growing despair about the dead-end road he'll be forced to walk after graduation. A sexy encounter with freshman Grace Ivers is just the distraction he needs, but when a thoughtless mistake pushes her away, Logan plans to spend his final year proving to her that he's worth a second chance.

## Now he's going to need to up his game...

After a less-than-stellar freshman year, Grace is back at Briar University, older, wiser, and so over the arrogant hockey player she nearly handed her V card to. She's not a charity case, and she's not the quiet butterfly she was when they first hooked up. If Logan expects her to roll over and beg like all his other puck bunnies, he can think again. He wants her back? He'll have to work for it. This time around, she'll be the one in the driver's seat...and she plans on driving him wild.

# THE SCORE

## He knows how to score, on and off the ice

Allie Hayes is in crisis mode. With graduation looming, she still doesn't have the first clue about what she's going to do after college. To make matters worse, she's nursing a broken heart thanks to the end of her longtime relationship. Wild rebound sex is definitely not the solution to her problems, but gorgeous hockey star Dean Di Laurentis is impossible to resist. Just once, though, because even if her future is uncertain, it sure as heck won't include the king of one-night stands.

## It'll take more than flashy moves to win her over

Dean always gets what he wants. Girls, grades, girls, recognition, girls...he's a ladies man, all right, and he's yet to meet a woman who's immune to his charms. Until Allie. For one night, the feisty blond rocked his entire world—and now she wants to be friends? Nope. It's not over until he says it's over. Dean is in full-on pursuit, but when life-rocking changes strike, he starts to wonder if maybe it's time to stop focusing on scoring...and shoot for love.

# THE GOAL

## She's good at achieving her goals...

College senior Sabrina James has her whole future planned out: graduate from college, kick butt in law school, and land a high-paying job at a cutthroat firm. Her path to escaping her shameful past certainly doesn't include a gorgeous hockey player who believes in love at first sight. One night of sizzling heat and surprising tenderness is all she's willing to give John Tucker, but sometimes, one night is all it takes for your entire life to change.

## But the game just got a whole lot more complicated

Tucker believes being a team player is as important as being the star. On the ice, he's fine staying out of the spotlight, but when it comes to becoming a daddy at the age of twenty-two, he refuses to be a benchwarmer. It doesn't hurt that the soon-to-be mother of his child is beautiful, whip-smart, and keeps him on his toes. The problem is, Sabrina's heart is locked up tight, and the fiery brunette is too stubborn to accept his help. If he wants a life with the woman of his dreams, he'll have to convince her that some goals can only be made with an assist.